Search Me

Search Me

Greg Levers

As stated in the beginning narrative, the law enforcement anecdotes presented in this writing are 98% factual. I have tried to recreate events, locales and conversations from my memories of them. In order to maintain anonymity, I have changed the names of individuals and places. I may have changed some identifying characteristics and details such as physical properties, occupations and places of residence. Some details have been altered to prevent injury or death to sources.

Barry Truman is a fictional character and this is a work of fiction. Names, characters, businesses, places, events, locales, and incidents are either the products of the author's imagination or used in a fictitious manner. Any resemblance to actual persons, living or dead, or actual events is purely coincidental.

Scrutiny Analysis
1440 Beaumont Avenue A2-153
Beaumont, CA 92223

Printed in the United States of America
First Printing, 2019
ISBN: 9781686436468

In Appreciation

The author experienced many "close calls" as to his personal safety over a long career. He was subjected not only to danger, but to excitement and, frankly, to fun. Probably because of those opposing influences and a lot of luck, he managed to survive the years with minimal physical and mental damage.

He was fortunate that he never had to engage with terrorists in a struggle for life as many of his good friends did during the terrorist attacks which resulted in multiple deaths and injuries in San Bernardino, California in 2015. Surviving victims will see those images and experience that feeling of terror for years to come. Many officers from several agencies risked their lives that day. Even officers not involved in the firefight were traumatized by the visions of bodies and carnage unnecessarily caused by malevolent and cowardly assassins. This is not as much a dedication as an expression of appreciation for these heroes.

Author's Note

The author's intent is to present the stories generated from the thirty-five-year career of a California probation officer. Some of these accounts are happy or humorous while others are tragic or sad. Some stories have components of various conflicting emotions. Barry Truman had a great time in his profession but it also took its toll. Law enforcement work can be fun and exciting but also depressing and demoralizing. Barry was immersed in it all. Ultimately, he had to deal with the ongoing emotional impact the best way he knew.

Intertwined in Barry's exploits, the author applauds and also indicts the operations and practices that take place in modern corrections and law enforcement, making this work a reference piece for discussion. Barry Truman is a fictional character but the law enforcement anecdotes presented are 98% factual. He develops many skills and makes many mistakes during the course of his career and it is hoped the reader will benefit in some small way while at the same time be entertained.

In some instances, specific techniques, entities and resources used by law enforcement are not described in detail so as not to provide the criminal element with information that could assist them in their aberrant endeavors and hamper the ability of police agencies to protect the general public.

The Beginnings

Barry never intended to make it a career. After all, he was a music major trying to pay his way through night school. Little did he know that his temporary employment would span thirty-five years.

At age twenty-one Barry Truman had not resided long in Southern California. Born and bred in a small town in Ohio, he was constantly struggling with multi-ethnic surnames, street names and such. Muscupiabe and Yucaipa were fictitious names used for television productions - not actual destinations - and Jesus had but one pronunciation.

It could be said that he was commencing a life experience with emphasis in two primary areas. He was enjoying the sun, fun and diversity as only California could provide, along with the added bonus of mountain skiing thirty minutes away from the beautiful San Bernardino Valley.

In contrast, he would be introduced to and immersed in the sick, criminal underbelly of that same region and to individuals that could only be described as demonic. One such individual, in particular, committed heinous acts against children that would torment him throughout his career.

Understanding the reality of trying to change things for the better, Barry endeavored to do at least one impactful thing to protect society.

The Nightstand from Hell

Steve Mortsoob was Barry's best friend. After working together for several years at Juvenile Hall, they were both promoted to probation officers and assigned to the main office in the city of San Bernardino. It was a friendship born out of mutual trust and support.

Steve and Barry both supervised high-risk felons. On this particular Tuesday morning, Steve hit up Barry right at 8:00, wanting to know if they were going to search the residence of a specific probationer who resided in the city of Fontana.

Barry had examined the case the day before and noted that the subject, Thomas Catalina, had an extensive history of drug sales and manufacturing. It was amazing that he wasn't in a state or federal prison somewhere. His case was what was termed an "Interstate Compact" case from the state of Oregon. No specific information had been received about any recent illegal behavior in California but Mr. Catalina had not reported to the Probation Department as directed by officials in Oregon. Barry didn't need much reason to search the guy's house anyway. Besides, Barry felt that criminal histories carried a lot of weight - and like Steve always said, "if it walks like a duck and talks like a duck, it is probably a duck."

In an explanatory tone, Barry had to disappoint Steve, "I have to go to court this afternoon and I don't want to get stuck on a search and upset the Judge. Catalina has a large property."

Mortsoob had looked at the case file as well and had a feeling this would be a fun search. "Oh, come on Barry, ya know this guy is doing bad stuff!"

"He probably is but it will have to wait until tomorrow. Besides, I can get extra people to help us tomorrow and today we're a little short."

Tomorrow ended up being too late. Independently, the Fontana Sheriff's office received specific information regarding Mr. Catalina and his residence and searched his place that night after going through the process of obtaining a search warrant. There are entities in place to prevent different law enforcement agencies from stepping on each other's toes but they were not utilized in this case. That is not that uncommon. It's just one more thing to do.

Barry was initially very upset. Here was an agency that jumped on his case without even consulting him. The truth was since Catalina just moved from Oregon, his probation status was unknown by agencies other than the probation department.

In this instance, the Fontana Sheriff's office saved Barry or Steve or some other officer from death or, at the very least, from real physical harm. The case agent from the sheriff's office and Barry conversed the next day. The crime report was not yet prepared but the bomb squad's supplemental report was available.

Barry sat back in his chair and reviewed the bomb squad report, expressively commenting, "Jesus." The methamphetamine operation was sophisticated enough that there was a nightstand present designed to explode when its drawer was opened. The report included a diagram of the device. The nightstand apparatus was battery-powered and all self-contained. A mercury switch was present so that any movement of the nightstand would close the contact and initiate the explosion. The only way one could safely open the drawer was by using a magnet to disable an electrical contact.

Officers routinely open drawers during searches. The only way an officer would be aware of such a device would be if specific information was received from an informant. That's why the bomb squad went along at the onset. They knew about the device, generally how it was constructed and how to disable it.

The explosive charge was installed in such a way that any person opening the drawer without interrupting the circuit, would, at the very least, be blinded. The purpose of this type of device is two-fold - to destroy evidence which could be drugs, documentation and/or money and to cause injury to investigating officers.

Barry knew with certainty that, had he not been subpoenaed to court, someone on their team would have been seriously injured. This was a close call early in his career but he always carried that information in his head. For that matter, even years later he would show the bomb squad analysis of the nightstand to officers he supervised so that they might at least be aware of this type of threat.

Barry never met Mr. Catalina. He was not at home when officers searched his residence and it was believed he left California. There was unsubstantiated information that he turned up dead in a motel room in Las Vegas.

A Word About San Bernardino County

The County of San Bernardino is the largest county in the contiguous United States. Its vast borders stretch from the greater Los Angeles area to the Nevada border and the Colorado River, encompassing a total area of 20,160 square miles. It is larger than Switzerland. You could drive across Barry's Ohio home county in about twelve minutes so when he first entered San Bernardino County, just a few miles from Las Vegas, he thought his cross-country journey was over, until he saw a sign that read, "San Bernardino 180 miles."

Talk about a rich history. Mormons, prostitutes, miners, cowboys, Indians, desperadoes and farmers coexisted in the San Bernardino Valley at one time or another. This truly was the wild west and violence was a part of its dusty past. Despite its rowdiness and lack of refinement, people from the East flocked to California with the railroad. People fell in love with the San Bernardino Valley's climate and access to the Pacific Ocean and the San Bernardino Mountains. Grapes for wine were planted, densely in Redlands and Ontario, later to largely be replaced with orange groves and then housing developments.

Barry always remembered a story told by a boss and local historian about land being sold in the middle of the desert to easterners who were anxious to reap the rewards from owning orange grove property in California. They would ride the train across the desert near towns like Danby, Fenner and Goffs, west of the Colorado River, and be shown what appeared to be orange grove property. Purchasing deeds to these acres was a limited time offer, as it wouldn't take very long for the oranges to fall off of the needle-like leaves of the Joshua Trees.

Barry always wondered about the advance party that must have spent hours sticking oranges on the trees.

People don't think about Southern California being a desert land but, in fact, most of it is. The San Bernardino Valley is really on the edge of the desert with a semi-arid climate. Irrigation diminished the dryness to a certain degree at least in developed areas but, in its population infancy, it would have been very dry and dusty. To this day, decomposed granite swirls around wherever there is no vegetation.

Most people are familiar with the stories of Wyatt Earp and his brothers in Dodge City and the gunfight at the O.K. Corral in 1881. What is less known is that Wyatt, his brothers, father and other family members spent the majority of their lives in San Bernardino County. They originally camped right next to what is now the probation department and government center and they also resided in Redlands and Colton - For that matter, the family first came to the valley when Wyatt was a teenager.

San Bernardino County today certainly offers modern living but there is still a western feel when compared to coastal counties or metropolitan areas. The Sheriff still has an annual rodeo and the desert still has many places where the only reason people reside there is because they "don't play well with others." Homestead shacks are ever present in certain areas and the region is perfect for making methamphetamine or conducting other illicit operations. Barry liked the desolation of the desert, ripe for exploration. He embraced it. It made a person feel alive but it was unforgiving and it garnered a great deal of respect. Even in a modern vehicle, a person could still parish in the desert.

The CITY of San Bernardino is a different animal with different risks. It looks beautiful in the early morning hours near the main government buildings. The sun coming up over the mountains against the foreground of palm trees is special. But a few hundred yards away, heroin addicts are wandering around, looking for something to exchange for drugs to make them feel better. Later in the day and evening, the crime baton is handed to the methamphetamine users. They scurry about, doing all sorts of scandalous stuff until they crash, usually before dawn. This is why theft and violence are so prominent in the city. More than once the city has received recognition for sporting the most murders in comparison with other like-sized cities.

Barry always enjoyed the classic story told by his neighbor, the Time Warner cable installer. It was entertaining in a distorted sort of way. Barry was commenting on the fact that anything that wasn't tied down in San Bernardino was very likely to be stolen.

This neighbor said he was working close to the city center, up on a pole on 10th street. He knew the neighborhood was a little dicey so he made sure, even more than usual, that his truck was all locked up before he climbed the thirty-foot aluminum ladder and secured himself, standing on the utility pole steps. His work was completed in about five minutes at which time he commenced his trip downward. Except that there was no ladder to step on. It was nowhere to be seen. He went on to explain that he was fortunate to have a radio so he only had to wait at the top of the pole for twenty minutes for another worker to come with another ladder to get him down. Barry just couldn't help but laugh, "You got to be kidding me!" Such are the stories from the city of San Bernardino.

Small Town Ohio Roots

Barry's childhood was spent in a small town in Ohio by the name of Norwalk. Nowhere is perfect but Norwalk was pretty close. This is the type of environment that many parents can only dream about. It's so much easier to raise children in a community where many people know one another and there are no fences between properties like in California. If little Barry would do something inappropriate, chances are a neighbor would report the infraction to his parents. So, Barry was cared for and loved and never really worried about criminals or violence.

Halloween was Barry's favorite holiday. You could be whoever you wanted to be, dress like Spiderman, Frankenstein or the more traditional ghost, and collect candy and just have a great time. Afterwards, cider or hot chocolate awaited Barry and his friends. When he got a little older, his mother would even take a break herself from giving out candy, put on a costume and go out the back door and trick or treat at the neighbors, harassing them until finally revealing her identity. Barry did remember everyone checking their candy after trick or treating because someone found a razor blade in an apple in Cleveland. But this was really an anomaly and hundreds of kids in costumes still roam the streets on Halloween in Norwalk, seeking treats. Halloween would always symbolize joy and innocence for Barry.

The City has not grown much in the last several decades and is still relatively safe but the influx of opiates has impacted life to a degree. Violence is still not commonplace but property theft has increased. Addicts steal stuff. Barry learned over the course of his career that there were different ways to combat drugs in the community but he sensed that local law enforcement never transitioned from issuing speeding tickets to developing a true, aggressive program for putting heroin dealers on notice and dealing with the trafficking of diverted pharmaceutical narcotics. He guessed that, in the short term, that revenue from tickets was the driving force. Nevertheless, comparatively speaking, Norwalk is still a safe place to live.

Everyone Has to Start Somewhere

In order to fund his schooling, Barry worked in construction, at a car dealership, at a cotton mill, in a fast food restaurant, a YMCA and then as a campus supervisor at Yucaipa High School. Yucaipa is a moderate sized community to the east of San Bernardino. A Campus Supervisor was really more like a security job with no tools but, fortunately, most rule infractions amounted to smoking cigarettes and there was a small group who enjoyed marijuana. Barry would occasionally hear someone yell, “narc!" The irony would be that a few years later, he truly would be a “narc."

The job consisted mostly of boredom and walking, but mostly boredom. There were a few times where Barry would have to deal physically with some sort of a student disruption or threat, but as a former high school wrestler, this was never a problem. In fact, as Barry’s career advanced, he always relied somewhat on modified wrestling moves to deal with people when physical force was necessary.

Becoming a Probation Officer was really a natural progression from working at the San Bernardino County Juvenile Hall. It paid more and Barry wasn’t behind locked doors. It was really similar to transitioning from working the jail to going on patrol. It didn’t take long for Barry to embrace most of the various posts he served at the Probation Department. They were all different but the concept was, despite the message being lost at times, to protect the community. Barry preferred dealing with adults and conducting investigations and he was fortunate to be assigned to some very special units. He had to negotiate the bureaucracy like everyone else but he really believed in the accountability side of supervision and he gave it his all. He decided early on that at the very least, he wanted to do something impactful for the public good. It sounded cheesy but that was Barry.

Capable but Shy

Barry was athletic - six feet tall and solid. He always felt his physical strength had helped him in many ways, particularly with dealing with thugs throughout his career. He always wondered how much harder it might be for cops or probation officers that were weaklings to do their job - because despite all the weaponry and support systems, males always physically size up other male opponents.

Barry was less capable when it came to meeting girls. When in the company of the opposite sex he had a shy way about him. When he first came to California a girlfriend from Ohio by the name of Julie Joseph lived with him for a while. It didn't work out but she left him a special gift that would serve him well. More on that to come.

Barry was tentative around Ohio girls let alone these fast moving, fast talking Southern California models. Steve and Barry would spend a good amount of time in the evening visiting various watering holes around the Inland Empire, the nickname for an area primarily comprised of communities in San Bernardino and Riverside counties. There were quite a few businesses that provided loud music and alcohol and fun for all. Steve and Barry were too young to realize that there were better places to find women but there was quantity if not quality and plenty to drink.

Steve also tended to be shy but he was technically more sound in his attempted acquisition of young ladies. He talked Barry into going night skiing in Big Bear. Well, more accurately, he convinced Barry that the ski slope and bar were excellent places to pick up women. He led Barry through the process of renting all the necessary ski equipment.

"Okay, secure your skis and poles over there," pointing to a ski rack near the building. "Bring everything else with you."

Barry followed Mortsoob inside and into the bar area. "We are having a drink first?" Barry inquired.

"This is where you pick up the chicks," said Steve.

"But after a while, we go skiing, right?"

"Well, that all depends on what happens here," Steve said in a Swedish accent.

Steve's heritage was Swedish but his accent was totally contrived, although it sounded authentic. He would periodically reflect on spending time with his old friend, Jean Claude Killy, a French Olympic skier. He made sure he was speaking loud enough for the brunette in the tight red ski pants at the next table to hear.

Even with these efforts, no headway was being made. At some point Barry decided to actually try his hand on the slopes. He immediately enjoyed skiing as it was a totally different experience from traversing the gentle hills around Mansfield, Ohio. Night skiing in particular was so much more inviting at Southern California temperatures. Barry later discovered that during the day, it was sometimes too warm just wearing a sweater.

A couple hours later, Barry picked up Steve in the bar and they proceeded to drive down the mountain. No young ladies were reeled in on the slopes or in the tavern.

But Steve and Barry would keep at it, occasionally connecting with a girl or two. A young hippie-like girl invited Barry home one evening after a couple drinks at the Brass Key in Highland. Barry had a major cat allergy and this girl had at least fifteen of the critters. He tried to hang in there but was a respiratory mess within ten minutes. After that happened on one more occasion with another hospitable cat owner, Barry made it a practice to first ask the question, "Do you have cats?" before he took anything past the introduction. Sometimes in a dance/meat market environment with a loud band playing, he would have to yell the question across the cocktail table. It seemed cold but it was just a matter of survival and the efficient use of time and resources.

Steve eventually met a woman at one of these dance places and he fell in love. They ultimately married, leaving Barry to fend for himself. He went through several very brief relationships. Most of them ended amicably. They just weren't the right fit. The term soulmate is often used as the label for a perfect match but Barry would have been happy with "okay" or comfortable.

There was the one pretty blonde who had an extreme high-pitch cartoon character voice and she used it a lot. Barry was waiting for Daffy Duck to walk in the room. Then there was Wanda who was all output and no input - you know the person that thinks of what they want to say next instead of listening to you? The last time Barry left her apartment, he said, "You're sweet Wanda but I'm out of here." She just continued to disperse whatever thoughts she was waiting to share and said, "See you tomorrow."

A pretty nurse by the name of Rosie spent time talking to Barry at some sort of work party at a Highland tavern. She was of interest. She seemed somewhat cynical but Barry guessed her attitude was hardened in the emergency room. She was older than Barry and, at some point she asked him, "Do you know how old I am? How old are you?"

"I'm twenty-six."

Rosie quickly added as if to make it clear and set the record straight, "Well I'm thirty - four."

Barry assured her that she looked much younger and she did - at least in a dark tavern. They sat close and talked about lots of superficial things for an hour or so. She eventually gave Barry her number. He agreed to call her the next day and they would figure out the details for meeting. When he did so, she made sure he knew that she had children. Barry didn't think much one way or another about that. The nurse felt that it might be nice if he just came over to her house in Fontana the first time rather than to go on a formal date. Plus, she used up her baby sitter the night before for the party.

Barry followed her directions and arrived at a modest residence situated on a mostly dirt lot. Kids were running all over the "yard" and neighborhood. Rosie sat on the stairway to her porch and greeted Barry.

"I wanted to bring everything in the open at the start because most men have no real interest in an older woman with children. Those four are mine," pointing to two boys spinning in circles and two more wrestling in the dirt. They looked to be aged between six and twelve.

Rosie was not fixed up as far as clothing, hair or makeup. Sitting in the sunlight, she looked much older than Barry and one could tell that she had spent a lot of time worshipping the sun. It was almost as if she wanted Barry to see her at her absolute worst. They briefly spoke and sat on the stoop and at some point, Barry told her, "I see what you're doing here and I appreciate your honesty. I have to be honest as well and, as much as I enjoyed our talk last night, I'm not sure I'm ready for four kids all at once. I have none."

"Yes, this is my baggage and I wanted you to see it right away. I don't want to fall in love and you decide later that this is too problematic."

Rosie and Barry amicably parted, agreeing that it was fun socializing together. They could have a great time for a while but life was just too short to have to push reset any more than necessary. Barry drove off thinking that her technique was similar to his up front "cut to the chase" cat interrogation. Find out from the start if there is a deal breaker to save time, resources and distress. Invest your capital in someone without cats or four children.

Barry was set up on a blind date with Carla, later to be known as "the machine." She was a pretty young brunette with a softness about her that concealed and contrasted with her business-like way of making love. She had two cats so Barry and Carla spent most of the time at Barry's apartment. The problem with Carla was that she was a true nymphomaniac. Now male readers may ask, "And you're complaining?" To that, Barry would say, "Yes, and I can tell you have never spent any time with a true nymphomaniac."

Carla's torso moved forcibly up and down in rhythm similar to a jackhammer. Sex was all that Carla thought about. Either she was thinking of having sex, having it or she had just gotten through with it. A partner like this is great for about one night. Barry would try to watch a football game or eat a sandwich and she would be cuddling and rubbing on him - all the time. He would try to scoot away and she would stay with him like a magnet, moving her hands all over him and putting her fingers in his mouth. He would be reading a book, working on a car or talking to his mother who was in the next room and Carla would be grabbing him between his legs while making moaning sounds. He would be talking to his boss on the phone and she would yank down his zipper and take him in her mouth. It was just too much.

And, of course, you couldn't trust her. She had already shared with Barry her many exploits in all sorts of untypical locations and situations so her capabilities were well known. Just to name a few sites, she spoke of elevators and meat lockers and storage sheds and inside her neighbor's tree house. She had lots of electronic toys but when she tired of those Barry was sure her desires would initially overflow to neighborhood victims and then to the greater San Bernardino area. Look out LA Basin.

Barry did the only honorable thing he could do. Barry didn't love Carla anyway and Carla wasn't really interested in Barry once he was clothed, so she was passed off to Barry's oldest brother, Ed. Whether this was done with finesse is unclear but Carla and Ed were together for a few months and they would socialize with Barry so there were no hard feelings. As a matter of fact, Barry's older brother, Earl, felt left out and told Carla so. She laughed in such a way as to say, "Wait until I'm done with Ed." Barry and Earl and Ed would reminisce and laugh about the girl nicknamed "the machine" for years to come.

Isabella Lopez was one of the few co-workers Barry dated. Well, he went out with her one time. She was a generation or two from Spain and, perhaps, that's why her complexion was very light in contrast to her dark hair. She was pretty and very nice but, after they kissed, the first date became the last date. Much to their surprise, Barry broke out in a major rash around his mouth. The two of them sat there and tried to assess the situation. At first, they were guessing makeup was the culprit but eventually they came to the same conclusion - Barry was allergic to Isabella's saliva. It was a unique problem but it was real. They both decided that they would just have to remain friends.

They continued their friendship but their assignments split them up over the years. Isabella was working on a graveyard shift and, according to Mortsoob, who remained more closely in touch with her, she was experiencing mental health problems. She would call him up and report that people were stalking her when there was no indication that this was really happening. A few years later, she jumped off a boat somewhere around where Natalie Wood drowned off of Catalina. Unlike Natalie, there was no question about foul play with Isabella's drowning as she was observed by several people jumping into the water. Barry always thought that would be a hard way to take your own life. He always wondered what was disturbing her to the point of killing herself and wondered if it could have been prevented.

And speaking of kissing problems, Barry dated a young lady for only a brief period of time because he just couldn't get over her mustache. Many women have soft facial hair above their upper lip and that's a nonissue. But the mustache on this woman was like iron, like she had been panning gold for a few days and didn't have time to shave. Barry had never kissed his brother but, after kissing her, that's what he guessed it would feel like.

It would be a while until Barry had a love interest for more than a few moments.

Just What Is a Probation Officer - Or A Parole Agent?

To put it simply, probation officers and parole agents both monitor the activity of persons who have been convicted of crimes and ordered on probation or parole. There are many assignments in probation and some positions in parole that support the basic idea of supervision in other ways or they carry out assignments for the court or the parole authority.

For instance, probation departments prepare reports for the court on convicted felons and other people who have violated the law. Parole agents prepare reports for the Department of Corrections. Juveniles get in trouble as well but Barry was fortunate in that he spent the bulk of his career working with adults. With adults, there are no schools to deal with or parents to counsel. Juvenile or adult, probation or parole, everyone being supervised is given a list of terms and conditions to follow. If they are not followed, the probation or parole agent may submit information to violate the grant. More than likely, the individual will be arrested pending a hearing.

While it always mildly irked Barry that very few people outside of the criminal justice system understood the difference between probation and parole officers, he also had to acknowledge that the differences were slight. Traditionally, probation officers supervised individuals before state level incarceration and parole officers supervised them subsequent to state level incarceration but even that was changing somewhat as Barry's career winded down. Lawmakers in California trying to save a buck were sending more and more of the individuals that would have been supervised by parole officers to the local probation departments.

In some other states the supervision duties are sometimes intermingled and there really is no difference between parole and probation. And then there are federal probation officers who have more differences than similarities.

Traveling around the country for various training classes, Barry discovered that the role of the probation officer was varied. Some jurisdictions see the probation officer as some sort of counselor with authority while others view him or her as being more law enforcement oriented - like a cop with a list. Some probation officers in Europe are merely regulatory officers and do not have the power of arrest. Federal probation officers report aberrant behavior to the United States Attorney and, later if appropriate, a warrant is issued, usually served by the United States Marshal's Service. This is a source of frustration for those federal probation officers that previously worked for state or local governments as they no longer have the power to immediately arrest someone for violating their probation grant.

Barry thought himself fortunate to work in one of the jurisdictions where law enforcement was emphasized. While he was expected to assist probationers in their rehabilitation, he was primarily tasked with enforcing the terms and conditions of probation and to incarcerate those individuals that violated those terms and conditions.

Over the course of Barry's career, he saw the role of the probation officer evolve from assisting in the rehabilitation of the individual to one of protecting the community by ensuring that rules were being followed. If not, incarceration would take place. Not that all methods to help an individual were eliminated, but the priority was with protecting the community. Barry had no problem with the change as he was always more interested in solutions that had a tangible result. If a sex offender is violating his (usually his but sometimes her) terms, counseling may or may not be helpful. But if he is locked up, he isn't going to be victimizing anyone in the community during the time he is in custody.

In law enforcement oriented counties, probation officers are subjected to many of the same dangers as are street cops. But on a daily basis the job of patrol officer is more hazardous. Officers are dispatched to an assortment of calls each and every shift with lots of surprises, some of them very dangerous. Some probation officers in certain assignments may be working in a similar role and, as such, they are exposed to the same dangers. But many other probation officers do not work in these types of assignments and, as such, often are subject to a lower level of threat. Also, as a rule, probation officers are not dispatched to calls. Rather, they self-dispatch. In other words, they select a destination and advise the dispatcher rather than the other way around. That doesn't guarantee their safety but it does lessen the surprises.

That being said, on the street, the average felon does not distinguish between a patrol officer or a detective or a probation officer or a parole agent or a welfare fraud investigator. Any one of these officers can take them to jail and so none of them are very popular.

Barry carried a Glock 17, a brand of a nine-millimeter pistol, along with an asp, pepper spray and a TASER. For trivia mongers, TASER is an acronym that stands for the inventor, Thomas A. Swift (electronic rifle). When in plain clothes positions such as in narcotics or monitoring sex offenders, Barry would carry a concealed Glock and pepper spray.

The Search Term - A Powerful Tool

The fourth amendment in the United States Constitution protects American citizens from unreasonable search and seizure. This was a main provision in the Bill of Rights of 1791, put in place due to the experience of the American colonials with the English authorities. In short, the concept of "every man's house is his castle" required a certain process to be followed before the government could knock down the door of that castle.

In modern times, generally there are two ways for law enforcement officers to be allowed to tread on private property. One is to obtain a search warrant from a judge. Officers have to present documentation to convince the judge that there is probable cause to believe illegal activity is taking place on a specified property or by a person. For instance, a confidential reliable informant might purchase heroin at a house for an officer. The officer then attempts to corroborate that drugs are likely being sold there by surveillance, research, other information, etc. When the officer sells his or her case to a judge in writing, the judge may issue a search warrant for the premises. Everything being searched for must be specified and an inventory is generated after the service of the warrant.

A search warrant may be issued for evidence in other crimes and there are a number of different types of search warrants. All of them take time and effort to prepare, get signed and to serve them. They are only good for a specific period of time, perhaps ten days.

The second way to legally be able to search a house or property is to enforce a term of probation or parole. When a person is placed on probation or parole there are legal differences but all of these individuals have a list of things they must do and not do. A sex offender might have to stay away from schools or a burglar with a drug problem may be required to go to drug counseling. One of the most important terms generally ordered is that the person has to submit to search and seizure without the necessity for law enforcement to obtain a warrant. So, the felon is, in effect, waiving his or her fourth amendment protection.

Any law enforcement officer knows it is so much easier enforcing this term rather than putting together a search warrant. Also, search terms are much more flexible. For instance, if in attempting to search a residence it is discovered that the subject has relocated and a new address is secured and corroborated, that new address is now subject to search. This applies to vehicles, outbuildings, storage units and the like. It is not necessary to modify or amend a search warrant and have the judge approve the change.

Since many of the officers that worked with and for Barry were probation officers, they had to be reminded that search warrants are not the same as arrest warrants. Searching and arresting become blurred in probation and parole work because either one can happen upon the authority of the officer. A person not on probation or parole however, has not given up his or her rights and so cannot be searched except in specific situations but generally not without a search warrant.

An arrest warrant is another order by the court but, unlike a search warrant, it does not include the search of property. It is a warrant for a person's arrest. A search warrant is not an arrest warrant although, if the results of the search show that a crime was committed, people will probably be arrested based on the evidence.

Barry was blessed with many specialized assignments over the course of his career. Not only did this give him a breadth of knowledge but it kept things somewhat fresh. His skills increased over the years from minimal to exceptional. He became a very accomplished investigator. While he dabbled in gangs, electronic monitoring and property theft, his true expertise was with sex offenders, drugs and eventually computer forensics.

The common thread to all of Barry's assignments was the task of searching - searching homes, businesses, storage units, boats, vehicles, outbuildings, vast properties and computer storage devices, just to name a few. Barry estimated that just in considering private residences, he participated in searching over 2500 of them. Most probation and parole officers search a disproportionate number of places just due to the nature of the job and the usual order of a "search term." And most of them get really good at it.

More on Mortsoob

Steve Mortsoob was a great coworker and a better friend. He was smart and loyal. While very conservative, he was very creative. An excellent cartoonist, he also acted in local thespian productions. He appreciated music but when he was personally singing a rendition and had a few too many beers, he seemed to lock in on Amazing Grace.

When they initially met, Steve had recently been discharged from the US Army, having served as an airborne sergeant in Vietnam. The Vietnam stories he shared were all funny and entertaining and no one ever got hurt or killed. But as the years passed by, it became clear that he was tormented by demons from events he experienced during his service.

As mentioned earlier, Mortsoob was a giant physical specimen, towering above most. He was gentle and considerate, however, and proper in many respects. He always opened the passenger car door for his wife and he was attentive and considerate with all the women in his life. Conversely, Barry had never seen anyone who could drink beer faster and in such quantity as Steve Mortsoob.

It's Always Nice to Have a Good Boss

Barry was fortunate in that for much of his career, he was a subordinate to a competent supervisor and later administrator by the name of Frank Botman. Mr. Botman was a legal beagle who also had an interest in the investigation and apprehension side of working cases. He would actually get out from behind his desk and join his officers for high profile searches or to investigate unique cases.

If he didn't have an answer to a question, he would find out. Barry admired this approach. He would later say that, as a supervisor, he never really had to know anything. He just had to know who to call. Simplistic perhaps but it was a statement with a lot of truth.

Frank made his own job simpler by insuring the people who worked for him were competent. If you surround yourself with good people, unnecessary heartache and stress are avoided. It's amazing the number of administrators that do just the opposite as they feel threatened by knowledgeable subordinates. Mr. Botman would not micromanage and he wholeheartedly supported his officers. He would give his officers a great deal of latitude in exchange for only one thing - if there was a large seizure of contraband or if an important arrest took place or if a spaceship landed on a county car, he wanted to be advised immediately. He did not want to hear it from someone else or listen to it on the radio. Barry always felt keeping Frank abreast of significant developments was a small price to pay in order to work for a great guy.

Unfortunately, officers, just like any other employees, don't work their entire career for the same person let alone for a bunch of wonderful people. Barry felt lucky to have worked for several excellent bosses but one very glaring example of the opposite was one Carl Becker.

Carl Becker - Rat-Bodied Man

Physically, Carl Becker, aka, "Pecker Becker" looked like a rat. His gait was one of arrogance but he was skinny, unkept and it looked as if he might be carrying some disease. He was best known for boogers. Everyone in the agency observed him at one time or another leaving them everywhere he traveled - on chairs, car steering wheels, file folders - everywhere. Unfortunately, although gross, his boogers were by far not the worst thing he left behind. Instead, during his entire career he left personnel casualties - people that were not promoted because of him, people who couldn't sleep nights because of him, people who were on high blood pressure medicine because of him and so on and so on.

When Barry thought of Carl Becker, he was reminded of that quote, "Everyone lights up a room - some when they enter and some when they leave." Becker was definitely in the "leaving" group. Many people thought Becker was evil. After all, he ruined many a career and would not hesitate to throw another employee or subordinate "under the bus" if it suited his purposes.

Barry knew better. Becker was not evil. He was amoral and callous and uncaring but not an operative of Satan. At least Barry didn't THINK he was.

Early in his career, Becker was somewhat of a "screw-up" and then when he became a supervisor of probation officers he was just an annoyance. Experienced employees didn't mind working for him because he was rarely at work. He liked seasoned, knowledgeable officers working for him as they would take care of the workload without needing guidance. Becker always had a competent secretary that could direct the workflow and field questions regarding his whereabouts. His efforts to secure employees of high caliber was the one thing he had in common with Frank Botman. They just set it up that way for different reasons. Botman wanted to make his job easier but also wanted officers that would do their jobs and protect the community.

Becker wanted people that didn't need supervision so that he could abandon his post to work outside of the department with politicians and sometimes to work on his own campaigns. In his own mind, he was a local big shot and he constantly attempted, sometimes successfully, to parlay his perceived importance and connections to gain favor with the department's upper management. The fact he never did his "job" was ignored.

The two times a year he dropped by his work unit and stabbed an officer or two in the back for something that HE didn't take care of was tolerated because it was so wonderful when he was gone the vast majority of the time. Plus, everyone from the top to the bottom in the organization knew he was worthless, so the occasional "stabbings" of his employees were relatively harmless, so to speak.

The way he did business, or more accurately, did NOT do business, provided plenty of humorous stories for the troops. When Becker took over a new work unit, one officer that worked for him for several weeks noted that he had not met Becker. He wondered how long he could work without seeing his boss. For entertainment purposes, this officer made a game of it. And in so doing, he never actually met Becker for eight months. Barry recalled that it was by accident that they finally met and, on that monumental occasion, Becker had just exited the bathroom stall without even getting close to the running water, just like always. Carl Becker acted irritated that this officer almost ran into him.

Becker queried his secretary, "Who was that?" She was on the phone so did not answer but later told him that the ship that had passed him in the night was someone he was supposed to supervise. Becker and his officer of eight months proceeded on their paths with no further interaction.

Where Becker became a true menace was when he was promoted into management. The only reason people could surmise why he was promoted was because of powerful friends. Barry didn't doubt some of his connections but he knew for a fact that many of them didn't like Carl either. Be that as it may, Becker was now in charge of several work areas and was actually getting involved in decisions that affected people on a daily basis. The rumor was that when he was promoted it was made clear by top management that one of the conditions was that he actually had to be at work. Now confined to the premises, he messed with everything, particularly things that were working seamlessly.

Often officers and particularly supervisors would become angry with Becker and become engaged in verbal altercations. This did not really affect Becker as one would have to have feelings to have them hurt. So, he would generally display an incredulous look on his face when a subordinate would verbally confront him.

Now this is not to say that Becker was fearless in confrontations that had a possibility of causing him physical harm. He had been beaten up as a youngster and was occasionally trounced on as an adult but outside the workplace. He was a slumlord and everyone was entertained when one of his tenants decked him, breaking his glasses and giving him a black eye.

Once, Barry's short tempered good friend was working for Becker and he took exception to an insulting comment directed at him. This resulted in him coming very, very close to placing another fist in Carl's face. Becker always brought out the best in everyone. It's probably just as well composure prevailed as this sort of thing in the workplace would probably have created more Becker fallout. Still, Becker being decked would have been fun to see. If not for the probable fate of his friend, Barry would have paid big time to watch the show.

Barry had minor verbal confrontations with Carl over many decisions or directives that made no sense. Sometimes they worked contrary to protecting the community and sometimes they were just mean-spirited. On one occasion, Becker denied a request for one day of vacation so that Barry could move on his home's escrow closing date. Becker insisted that Barry and another supervisor did not reduce the number of felons on caseloads as directed. As such, Barry could not have the vacation day off. Barry soon learned that Becker was the one given the directive to reduce caseloads by his superiors and he didn't complete the task, so he chose to dump his failure on Barry and his co-supervisor.

Barry was a long-term employee in good standing with lots of vacation time and an advance notice for this day off. He HAD to move on that day. As such, he did what he rarely thought proper and went over Becker's head. Becker's boss also did what he rarely did and approved Barry's time off, circumventing Carl.

Shortly thereafter, Becker set up a meeting with the deputy chief and directed Barry and his co-supervisor, Tom Baquette to attend. The two administrators sat at the end of a long oak conference table and the two invitees sat at the other end. When Barry heard the first questions from Becker starting with, "Isn't it true that on... I directed you to..." he knew this was a meeting related to disciplining the two supervisors or, at the very least, to improve Becker's image in the eyes of his boss.

That was the final straw. Barry made sure what Becker was saying, "Carl - let me get this right - you are saying that you told Mr. Baquette and me to reduce the numbers in those caseloads?"

Becker confirmed, "Yes, that is exactly what I am saying."

Barry abruptly stood up and leaned towards Becker and exclaimed, "Then you Carl are a fucking liar!"

At this point Becker slid slowly down in his chair. He didn't know how to do his job correctly but he was experienced at getting beaten up. He had the look of fear in his eyes. Later on, there was a disagreement between the supervisors as to whether Becker peed his pants. Even in this civilized society and work place violence dialogue, when men deal with men it always gets down to physical dominance - and Barry could crush Becker's neck with one hand if that's what he desired. But the deputy chief ended the session quickly. As they exited the meeting, he was trying to settle down Barry, an individual known for rarely losing his cool. He told Barry, "Don't worry Barry, we all know Carl's a liar."

Carl kept his distance from Barry for the rest of his career. He became the poster child for a legacy of meanness. At Becker's retirement celebration, many members of the community and political world attended but the only people present out of the 1200 employee strong probation department were the two administrators the agency ordered to attend.

Judicial Review Board

Barry and Steve began spending time together away from work. Their friendship began following grave yard shifts and was sort of a debriefing at a couple local taverns. There were a lot of physical altercations between staff and prisoners in those days and graphic and lively discussions just naturally followed these events. Joseph Wambaugh called it "choir practice."[1] Barry and Steve called it debriefing and eventually it was renamed Judicial Review Board or JRB for short. That was because participants over the years were from various law enforcement and justice agencies and more decisions were made in that atmosphere than one might think.

The meeting initially commenced routinely on most mornings at 0600 hours, the earliest a California bar is permitted to open. In later years, it took place on Tuesdays, in the evening as that would follow the shifts of the majority of participants. But the roots were planted in those days of early mornings. There might be six to ten co-workers in attendance or it could just be Barry and Steve. Barry thought that most people had no idea what goes on in taverns at 6:00 a.m. One would have to work graveyards and then adjourn for cocktails to find out.

The patrons at dawn were varied in purpose and presentation. Some of them, Barry thought, had very interesting, perhaps tragic stories. Jimmy Burns Cocktail Lounge on "D" Street hosted them all. There were alcoholics who might be customers at any time of the day or night. There were several men that would come in for a quick shot on the way to work, which rather surprised Barry. He surmised that they were probably alcoholics as well. And, of course there were the regular

---

[1] "The Choirboys by Joseph Wambaugh (A Delta Book) 1975

folk like Steve and Barry that enjoyed a beer after work and it just happened that work ended at sunup. By the way, you don't want to forget your sunglasses as departing from a dark tavern in California into the sunshine is brutal on the eyes.

Getting back to the patrons, the biggest surprises came around the holidays. When the boys first witnessed the graveyard shift at the main post office having their Thanksgiving dinner at Jimmy Burns, it was surreal. Here is was - 6:15 a.m. and about fifty people, men and women, were shuffling through a serving line, helping themselves to all the expected culinary delights of the holiday. The crew would witness these activities from time to time. It's part of the routine of people who are employed by companies or agencies that work while most people are sleeping. Barry could sense that the bartenders, particularly if they were also the owners, liked the presence of "regular" workers to counter the impact of the inner-city customers.

Barry guessed that at one time, perhaps in the 1950s or 60s, Jimmy Burns was a location frequented by a different demographic, middle class couples stopping by for dinner and a drink. Not anymore. Just like the Shanty, this was not safe late-night entertainment.

Much of the time it was Mortsoob and Truman sitting side by side with maybe three or four other patrons present. Their relationship was one of trust, loyalty, honesty and a common interest in Coors Light. They were not reluctant to tell each other anything. They didn't judge each other. I guess you would call it a "true blue" friendship. Barry was pretty sure that if he sat down at the bar with Steve and admitted to committing a homicide, there would only be words of support. He might say something like, "Well, he (or she) had it coming." That was Steve.

Christmas Spirit

Buck Rogan made a good impression when he met Barry for the first time. He was punctual, clean and polite. It was hard to believe this fifty-year-old man stabbed someone in the Dirty Bird, a historic tavern in downtown Redlands. He explained that, "I am a real asshole when I drink."

Buck was obviously sober and he showed Barry his ninety-day pin from Alcoholics Anonymous. This was his first offense but he still was fortunate that the Court granted him probation.

"What happens when you drink again?" Barry probed.

"I'm through with that. I've come to realize that I can't handle it," he said clearly with a focused tone.

Mr. Rogan submitted a urine test although Barry could tell that he didn't have alcohol in his system. It was one of those skills that law enforcement officers, particularly probation and parole officers, develop over a period of time, probably due to conducting hundreds of drug and alcohol screening tests and then seeing the results.

Barry scheduled a follow-up appointment for after the first of the year and Mr. Rogan departed.

About two hours later, Barry was going over several cases with Mr. Botman. He brought up Buck Rogan's case details and his recent office appointment and commented, "I wish everyone I supervised was that cooperative."

Within minutes of announcing his wish out loud, Barry received a call from a confidential informant that Buck Rogan was consuming alcohol at his residence, a house he shared with his wife, Shirley. After Mr. Botman finished laughing, Barry just shook his head and stopped by Mortsoob's office.

"Do you have time to help me check out this alcoholic in Redlands?"

"Not really but just let me submit this recording to word processing and I'll get my gear."

Mortsoob was always good to have along not just because he was Barry's best friend and was very competent but also because he was the biggest guy in the department. His presence routinely caused uncooperative people to reconsider being belligerent.

Barry and Steve headed for the city of Redlands, where Rogan resided. While en route, they heard the Redlands Police Department dispatch center broadcast about a disturbance at a home on Fern Street, the address of Buck Rogan. Barry transmitted that they were on the way and requested a patrol unit be dispatched to meet them at the home. Barry and Steve and two patrol units arrived at the residence at the same time. It was dusk but it was evident that there was some activity in the front lawn.

This was just a few days before Christmas and in keeping with the holiday spirit, the Rogan's had a Christmas tree on the front lawn. It was all decorated and illuminated with colored lights. Except that it was supposed to be in the living room. Instead, it was on its side in the front yard and Mr. Rogan was yanking it away from the house. Because the long power cord was still attached to an inside outlet, he was having trouble pulling it, especially since he kept falling down on the grass.

Buck Rogan could be heard yelling before officers exited their vehicles. He was shouting loudly at his wife who was standing in the front doorway.

"Merry Christmas, bitch!" he slurred at the top of his lungs.

Then he noticed Barry getting out of his car and greeted him with, "And you go fuck yourself!"

"Oh Jesus," Barry murmured to Mortsoob. "Guess who's going to jail for Christmas."

Steve commented, "Well it IS a nice tree."

One of the Redlands officers remarked, "I have to agree with you. Except for the fact that it is being dragged across the lawn, it is a handsome symbol of Christmas."

Rogan, who was either lying on the ground or oblique to it, still tugging on the tree but not yet electrocuted, seemed to pick up on the fact that officers were making light of the whole situation. He became enraged and charged directly towards Barry, shouting, "I'm going to kick your fucking ass!"

Barry prepared to take him to the ground when Mortsoob's giant arm came crashing across Rogan's upper chest, essentially "clotheslining" him. He went to the ground and Barry flipped him over and cuffed him behind the back while he was still stunned. They loaded him in the back of a patrol unit and he went to county jail for the holidays. Subsequently, he was committed to State Prison.

Bob the Speed Dealer and A Lesson Learned

Bob Rudolph was on probation for selling a quarter pound of methamphetamine. He was reporting that he lived at a residence in the community of Arrowbear, a quaint mountain village near Running Springs. The word was that he was the biggest meth dealer in the vicinity. He also owned a legitimate business in the same town. It involved a towing/wrecker service and salvage property although word was that the family was actually being supported by methamphetamine sales. He had a wife and a young boy.

Barry chose a Friday morning near the end of the month to search Bob's house and business property. There is quite a bit of guesswork involved in trying to anticipate when someone is holding a significant quantity of illicit drugs but, if possible, an effort is made. Sometimes an informant can zero in on exactly when the "mother lode" is in the primary subject's possession but, in this instance, that was not the case. Barry picked a date that would take in consideration "mother's day," the slang term for the first of the month when people on public assistance receive their government check. Bob was not a quarter gram dealer so, being further up in the hierarchy, he should be holding his drugs a few days before the end of the month.

As there was a lot of real estate to search, Barry recruited four other probation officers, his supervisor and two deputy sheriffs. The business property was particularly large with cars and tools and machinery in various outbuildings. The business was searched first and two officers secured the residence so that evidence could not be destroyed before the entire team arrived. Bob was allowed to sit on the couch without being handcuffed as long as he behaved. He was a speed dealer but he didn't use the drug himself so he was calm and actually very personable.

After two hours of searching the business property, nothing substantially illegal was located. People that have never conducted searches don't realize how exhausting the activity can be. Items have to be moved and opened and there is usually climbing or crawling involved. People that hide illicit items try to put them in places where they are difficult to locate. Items could be low or high or buried or concealed in everyday containers.

Barry remembered arresting a methamphetamine dealer in Yucaipa, California a year earlier after stumbling on the guy's stash. He had been searching through the individual's truck when he bumped into a loose twelve-volt car battery. Visually, it fit right in with items often present in a truck bed but it just didn't seem heavy enough. Further investigation revealed that the entire top to the battery snapped off and that inside was methamphetamine packaged for sale, electronic scales, notes and paraphernalia. It was an entire criminal case in a battery - and enough product to keep fifty people awake for a couple nights in a row.

The point is that searching can be difficult and everything needs to be examined. Officers in Arrowbear then turned their attention to Bob's residence and commenced searching. Bob was detained in the living room but his wife was given some latitude as she was getting her first grader ready for school. She was not happy the team was there. One officer tried to stay with her as she packed a lunch and dressed the boy. He was primarily making sure she didn't pick up a sawed-off shotgun or something similar that would harm officers. Keep in mind that all these things are judgement calls and Barry's team had every right to have her sit down with Bob and if the kid missed school, that was just too bad. But these kinds of decisions can cause an officer a lot of grief especially if nothing illegal is located - and, at that point, nothing of that nature had been located. Barry and his supervisor did not want to deal with Carl Becker's unreasonable wrath and the sheriff's deputies didn't want the watch commander up their shorts.

The little kid finally got picked up by the bus in front of the house and, right after, Bob's work pants were located in the master bedroom. Methamphetamine packaged for sale in fourteen different bindles was located in his right front pocket. Now the game changed. Mrs. Rudolph was directed to sit by her husband. She was still complaining but not like before as she realized that something had been located. Thank goodness bad guys can be sloppy. With all the places available to hide stuff, it sure helps if they have it readily available and in an incriminating location, like in a pants pocket.

Further searching revealed a bag of manure in a wet bar sink in the master bedroom. Most people don't keep bags of manure in their sinks or, for that matter, in their bedrooms. Barry noticed that the side had been cut out of the bag and some of the manure was actually in the sink. It appeared as if something had been removed out the side of the manure bag. Sandwich size zip-lock type baggies were nearby. Trying to disguise odors is a common method to keep drug-sniffing dogs from locating drugs that are being transported.

Officers now started focusing on locations where larger amounts of methamphetamine could be located. Unfortunately, nothing more could be found. Bob Rudolph went to jail and was later sent to State Prison as he had a terrible habit of selling methamphetamine and this was not the first time.

But there is an epilogue to this story. Immediately after the search and arrest, Barry's informant contacted him with further information. Apparently, the little first grader went down to the bus stop with one pound of methamphetamine in his cute little backpack. Mommy retrieved it at school after Barry took Bob to jail. She did her job in making all the officers feel guilty so that they wouldn't even consider looking in the tyke's backpack before he caught the bus. This was an early lesson that Barry would always remember and share with other officers.

Nielsen Rating

After being outsmarted by a six-year-old, Barry and Steve met Vince, a Highland Deputy, for cocktails at the Shanty in the tenderloin district of San Bernardino. The Shanty was an old-time bar that probably had undesirable patrons at midnight but as long as the sun was still up, it was quiet and relatively safe.

JRB (Judicial Review Board) after hours sessions were not without rules. One important rule was that participation was by invitation only. This was a relaxing time and undesirable co-workers were not included. Another rule was that work stories would cease at agreed-upon times. The entertaining stories were not the problem. A lot of laughter about how a physical altercation ended or how someone accidentally handcuffed another officer would bring the house down. But complaints about stupid management decisions or disciplinary problems or negative aspects of the work environment just seemed to extend the work day rather than provide an outlet.

It would get to the point in these sessions where someone would announce there would be no more work stories. Inevitably someone else would exclaim, "Just one more!" This might even be parlayed into two or three more business stories but Vince eventually called it on this day and started talking about females, specifically good-looking females at work and who was hot and who was not wherever they may be. Even though he started the topic of discussion, he eventually excused himself as he had dinner waiting at home.

Barry and Steve remained, staring at the back bar, "zoning out." At some point, Barry then asked Steve who he thought was hot. As the conversation also included non-coworkers, Steve quickly responded,

"Kathy Ireland!" She was a very attractive model at the time and Barry agreed that she was, indeed, good-looking.

"So, who do you think is hot?" Steve anxiously questioned.

Barry thought for a second and responded, "Leslie Nielsen."

Steve looked towards Barry and asked "Leslie Nielsen?" He had a surprised tone to his voice.

"Oh yeah, Leslie Nielsen is real hot," Barry said with emphasis.

Now to understand the upcoming bar scene, a little knowledge of the Star Wars saga is helpful. There was a scene in Stars Wars Episode VI - Return of the Jedi [2], where Darth Vader was watching the Emperor torture Luke Skywalker with some sort of electrical energy emanating from his hands. Skywalker is an enemy of Vader but he is also his son. Vader can't exhibit facial expressions because part of his dress is his big scary black mask. As such, the effect and/or emotions of Darth Vader pondering the killing of his son by his boss is conveyed to the audience by Vader slowly moving his head towards Luke and then towards the emperor and back and forth. He eventually saved his son and killed the emperor.

Mortsoob said nothing but turned his head towards Barry just like Darth Vader. He then turned back, looking straight at the back bar. Expressionless and silent he again slowly looked at Barry then looked forward.

After a few more seconds of silence, Mortsoob took a drag off his cigarette and calmly said, "Leslie Nielsen is a guy."

"What?"

Steve repeated very deliberately, "Leslie Nielsen is a guy!"

Their conversation eventually sorted out the matter. Barry had seen a promotional advertisement for a movie called the "Poseidon Adventure." The actors' names were flashed on the screen as they climbed up a ladder. Barry thought Leslie Nielsen was the name for an actress named Carol Lynley. She was a beautiful blonde woman who paraded around in little red shorts throughout the movie.

Barry always thought that had he really expressed interest in another male, that Mortsoob would have to digest that but, ultimately, he would be okay with it. At least Barry thought so.

---

[2] Screenplay by Lawrence Kasdan and George Lucas.

Barry then could only wonder if he had expressed his attraction to Leslie Nielsen to anyone else. This exchange certainly provided an entertaining story for years to come.

Working Interstate Compact and Courtesy Cases

As Barry became more experienced, he recognized an advantage to scrutinizing interstate compact cases - ones being sent to other states and, particularly ones accepted from other states. Always devoted, Barry, nevertheless, saw no harm in getting a free trip to another state, especially if it was one he had never visited.

An example of an outgoing case/probationer would be someone convicted in California that has a reason to move to another state or, in the case of a courtesy case, an individual convicted in or residing in San Bernardino County with reason to move to another county. For instance, Probationer Joe gets convicted of selling methamphetamine in San Bernardino County. He is sent to jail but he gets released at some point and wants to move to Kern County because he has a job offer there. If it appears legitimate, he is allowed to move there provided the Kern County Probation Department agrees to supervise him. Once there, the Kern County Probation Department checks on Joe and reports back to San Bernardino County if he screws up. In these cases, the supervising agency is pretty much like a "tattle tale." That agency reports the violation but it is up to the sending jurisdiction to do something about it. If Joe decides that he prefers spending his time with the methamphetamine community in Fresno instead of working, a warrant from San Bernardino County would bring him back home to answer to the violation.

Interstate compacts are very similar except that the process is guided by the "Interstate Compact" agreement that each state has endorsed. So, occasionally, it becomes necessary for the Probation Officer in the originating jurisdiction to travel to the jurisdiction of supervision to testify as to, in this case, Joe's probation conditions and the authorization to conduct searches. This usually only occurs when a new serious crime has been uncovered in the course of supervising the person on probation.

Travel occurs more often for the officer regarding incoming cases. Since the court with jurisdiction is somewhere else, the Probation Officer supervising the case might have to travel to testify to secure a conviction. Barry worked these cases hard. Probationers from small jurisdictions with relatively serious cases were good material.

Over the years, Barry helped prosecute offenders in New Mexico, Oklahoma, Virginia, Colorado and Michigan and in many California counties. He was always entertained by his experience in a jurisdiction in New Mexico that had a slightly different procedure unfamiliar to Barry.

"Mr. Truman. Did your agency provide you with per diem funds for your travel?" asked the District Attorney. This was not a deputy district attorney. This was "The" District Attorney.

"Yes, they did sir. I was thinking about eating dinner downtown at the tavern with all the beer taps if that's a good place."

"That's a very good place. Did your agency give you drinking money?

"No sir, they don't pay for alcohol."

He motioned towards his secretary telling Barry, "Stop by Marlene's office and she'll give you a check to cash at the bank across the street for drinking money."

"Oh - a - okay. Thank you."

"No - Thank you sir for coming all this way to keep this guy locked up!"

Marlene had the check ready by the time Barry got to her desk. He evaluated the whole thing in his mind and couldn't really come up with any reason why it would be improper to accept the money. Apparently, that was the way they did it there.

He cashed the thirty-five-dollar check and augmented his San Bernardino County meal with several New Mexico draft beers. Good state.

Arthur Drisco

Interstate Compact paperwork arrived for Arthur Drisco, a sex offender/murderer who last resided in Arizona. As stated before, Interstate compact represents an agreement between the states having to do with extradition and supervision.

Barry had met some pretty serious criminals and he would meet more, including interstate serial murderers. Drisco was by far the worst. His crimes were very similar, regardless of the jurisdiction. He would sodomize young boys, usually between the ages of six and twelve and then he would murder some of them, presumably to avoid successful prosecution. His criminal history showed this happening in at least six different states but, for various reasons, some technical, the arrests did not result in convictions consistent with the crimes and he would usually be released after minimal custody time. In some instances, he was housed in mental health facilities for a few years and in other cases, the fact that a body was never recovered was problematic. He would then move on to another state and find another little boy to victimize. Jurisdictions had a way of dropping their serious charges assuming he would be prosecuted in another state. Other times, witnesses would be unavailable. There were a variety of reasons for this extremely dangerous person to be on the loose. Sometimes he would abduct boys and sometimes he would groom[3] them and later molest them.

---

[3] A term used to describe the process that a sex offender utilizes to earn the trust of a youth prior to sexually victimizing him or her.

Drisco "skated" last in Arizona and was sent to California with almost no conditions. It was obvious that this was what was negotiated in court in order to get some sort of conviction for a reduced charge rather than no conviction at all. The state of Arizona was not thought of very fondly at that time but, in retrospect, Drisco was such an evil person, no one in law enforcement or the courts would have done this on purpose. Barry just hoped it didn't transpire because of incompetence.

Barry was allowed to verify his residence and to meet with Drisco upon arrival pursuant to the interstate compact agreement. After that, no one was allowed to go to Drisco's house and he wasn't required to report to the Probation Officer or any other authority. He did have to report his address changes to the sheriff's office.

Technically, in those days, Barry could have denied compact supervision due to the lack of appropriate terms and conditions. In reality however, Drisco would just be allowed to stay in California by way of Arizona with no connection whatsoever to local authorities.

A review of Drisco's file showed a history of violence beginning at the age of sixteen when he threw a meat cleaver at his step-father. His known aberrant sexual behavior began when he was seventeen and in the Army. He molested two little boys. He served four years out of a ten-year sentence. A psychiatrist reported that he was a man "who is impulsively violent with an uncontrollable fondness for little boys." Little boys in Michigan and Wisconsin were molested and killed. One boy was strangled with the child's own belt. Investigations unsuccessfully dragged on having to do with murdered little boys in Costa Mesa and Anaheim Hills, California. And now, he was in Barry's office in Big Bear.

The meeting with Drisco was brief. Most of it amounted to him registering his address pursuant to law and the lone requirement of his probation. He was forty, dark-haired, trim with a soft manner but with cold, almost glazed looking eyes.

"I have your entire criminal history here and I am quite surprised you aren't in custody somewhere."

Drisco's speech was deliberate and he was cautious when he spoke. "There are a lot of mistakes on that record."

Barry continued, "I'm curious. The crime you committed in Arizona was just as gruesome as your other ones from across the country. How did you get on probation?"

"It was just a matter of me being innocent; I only pled guilty to the reduced charge so I could get it over with. You know you can't come by my house."

"I read your paperwork."

This was unlike any indoctrination interview Barry had conducted. All he could really do was make sure the guy thoroughly understood that he had to report any address change to the jurisdiction he was in and the jurisdiction to which he relocated prior to moving. There was no sense lecturing this guy as he was a demon who knew the score. Talking to Drisco made Barry's skin crawl and his blood pressure rise.

This Arthur Drisco case was a major departure from the ordinary and a tremendous source of frustration for Barry. Barry knew sex offenders with an appetite for young boys or girls and knew that they just don't change. He knew Drisco was already working on his next victim in the small mountain community of Big Bear Lake and there was nothing he could do about it. This case would haunt Barry for years.

Drisco moved to a rental property north of a community called Fawnskin. It is a quaint and quiet Big Bear suburb on the edge of the San Bernardino National Forest. Drisco's place was nestled in the pines, far enough out to avoid detection but close enough to do what he did best, that is to victimize little boys. He was like a mountain lion near a campsite ready to find a dog or small child all alone and drag it back in the wilderness.

Generally, A Recipe for Success

When Barry wanted to relax or sleep or lower his blood pressure, he would always relive a simple moment in time when he was sixteen years old in Norwalk. It was high school football practice in August and it was what was referred to at the time as "two-a-days." Everyone on the team would practice in the morning, shower, take a break for lunch and then resume in the afternoon. While practice in the afternoon commenced with reinstalling all the still-wet-from-perspiration gear, including one very cold jockstrap, the break in between the sessions was to be savored.

One particular day was perfect. It was cooler than normal for August, about 78 degrees. Barry sat alone on a grassy hill leading up to the municipal swimming pool. The grass was both cool and soft. Children's excited voices could be heard along with the sounds of splashing. There was a slight smell of chlorine in the air.

Barry ate his peanut butter and jelly sandwich and pieces of fresh celery and then pulled out one of the most beautiful red tomatoes one could imagine. Never would Barry ever taste a tomato out west that came close to this home-grown Ohio variety. Some people still think they are superior due to the combination of the almost black soil and rain water instead of irrigation. Barry opened up a very small piece of aluminum foil to access the salt that his mother had wrapped up. He ate the entire tomato, lightly salting it along the way. One would never eat a hydroponic tomato in that fashion.

Barry laid back into the soft grass and fell asleep. When he awoke, a light breeze could be felt. While minutes later he would again be tortured on the practice field, this moment of pure relaxation was embedded in his memory, something to be drawn upon during his lifetime whenever needed.

The only exception for its success was upon hearing more heinous news about Arthur Drisco. It was the helplessness that was maddening - being unable to prevent him from harming another little boy.

The Duck Inn

Barry, his two brothers and Mortsoob decided to patronize a local watering hole in San Bernardino, one that they had never visited. This was an inner-city bar with a reputation for police service calls, a place that the British would refer to as "a bit dodgy." As it was the middle of the afternoon, this was not so much a concern. Regardless, Barry wanted to do anything that did not remind him of Arthur Drisco.

Steve, familiar with the case, commented, "You know there have been many idiots executed in this country that did not do one quarter of what that guy did."

"Yep, well let's forget that demon for a while." Barry was becoming exhausted thinking about Drisco.

"Copy. Let's drink some beer then."

Barry used to laugh at all the Hollywood movies that would include scenes where the characters arrive in a bar, usually somewhere rural in the United States where they would be subjected to harassment, scorn or physical assault based on the fact they were "strangers." In truth, Barry and Mortsoob had been in drinking establishments across the United States and beyond with virtually no one harassing them. People, even bar people, are generally pretty decent as long as you are not the source of the friction. Behaving like a guest and not being annoying or condescending is a good start.

But this was the "Duck Inn" and if problems were going to occur, they might materialize in a place such as this. Perhaps this is what the screenwriters had in mind. Only a few patrons were present so Barry, Steve, Earl and Ed all took stools at the bar.

Another man came in sporting a fancy fishing rod and this drew the interest of everyone but Mortsoob. He remained at the bar, smoking Marlboro reds and drinking Coors.

Beers were consumed and, at some point, a bookish-looking man with jet black hair, perhaps standing five-foot eight, walked in the front door and took up a vacant seat beside Steve. He was an intense fellow with a weasel-like face and Barry, who was standing in the vicinity, could hear him conversing with Mortsoob. Conversing is probably not the right word as he really was just telling Mortsoob things. Steve would shake his head as in agreement while drawing heavily on his cigarette and inhaling one twelve ounce Coors after another. To the weasel's credit, he purchased one or two of these beers for Mortsoob. It was later determined that he was a regular patron and he thought Mortsoob was visiting the tavern for the first time by himself.

Time passed and laughter and frivolity prevailed until the weasel abruptly got up from his stool and faced Barry with a determined look on his face.

"Fuck you all!" he shouted. He raised his fists as if to challenge the interlopers.

The group took up defensive positions but didn't immediately respond as all of them were taken by surprise having no idea what the issue could be. Also, it was ludicrous for this guy to pick a fight with so many big people.

Attempts to ignore this crazy person were unsuccessful as he continued to shout obscenities towards the group.

All this noise got the attention of Mortsoob who had been enjoying his alcohol-induced stare of disengagement through his own cigarette smoke. He turned towards the weasel and sarcastically inquired, "What the hell are you doing?"

"We're about to kick these arrogant sons of bitches' asses, that's what we're doing!"

It was at this time that everyone surmised that this guy thought six-foot, five-inch, Steve Mortsoob was in his corner. After all, as was later determined, he had been complaining to Mortsoob about this bunch of arrogant newcomers that he just didn't like. Steve just kept saying, "Uh-huh" between beer and smokes, which, apparently was interpreted by the weasel as agreement.

When Steve figured out that the weasel thought that he was an ally instead of a good friend of the group being threatened, he just started laughing. This made the weasel pause in reflection. Within a few more seconds, his eyes became wide as he reevaluated the situation. Not only had he threatened three large men, each physically capable in their own right, but the very large man he had set up to be his ally, was actually his adversary. He sprinted past the bathrooms and out the back door. Everyone in the Duck Inn laughed loudly and the owner, who never liked the guy, announced, "This round is on the house!"

Probation Investigations

Barry's first assignment as a probation officer was as an investigator, not to be confused with a criminal investigator. Barry would be lucky enough to do both during his career but he got his feet wet writing investigative reports for the Superior Court.

As a rule, a probation investigator intervenes in the criminal process after an individual pleads guilty or is found guilty by jury. Let's say Tom Smith commits a burglary and is convicted one way or another. Most plea bargains or negotiations specify a range of penalties. Tom is now ordered to contact the probation department where an officer will be assigned to investigate and recommend a sentence. The latitude concerning the recommended sentence is dictated by law but also by the practices of the particular jurisdiction.

In a felony matter, the recommendation will generally be between probation (usually with jail time) or commitment to the State Prison. The investigator will want to talk with Tom as well as the victim(s) and review all of the police reports and associated information. Any criminal history will be assessed. After considering all the information including the circumstances of the offense, a recommendation is submitted to the court. In California, if a commitment to State Prison is recommended and there are several crimes and/or victims and the crimes are under certain categories like sex crimes or violent crimes, decisions will have to be made as to terms of confinement pursuant to criminal code.

The position of probation investigator is high pressure and stress-loaded. The cases and court deadlines just keep coming. Barry remembered working several twelve-hour days just trying to prepare for vacation. And he could never get sick enough to take time off.

Even years later when this assignment was way behind him, if he would experience nightmares, they would be about investigations being late.

Criminal Investigations

The role that Barry excelled with and that he loved the most was that of a criminal investigator. This really amounts to collecting information to build a case that can be proven in court or can be used in locating a felon. There were good investigators and there were bad investigators and Barry felt that investigation skills were important in occupations outside of law enforcement as well.

For instance, a patient goes into a doctor's office complaining of respiratory problems. A good doctor will ask him or her questions and, perhaps follow-up questions before he or she makes a decision. Maybe the patient works removing asbestos from condemned buildings or his or her family has twenty-six cats inside the house. The bad doctor will never discover that crucial information and will act and/or prescribe based on this limited faulted information. The flowchart says to prescribe an antihistamine so that is what the bad doctor does.

An automobile mechanic that doesn't listen to a customer's description of sounds or circumstances where the problem presents itself is making the same mistake. The information received from the customer must also be parsed in order to make the correct diagnosis.

The list of occupations goes on and on. Diagnosis and action has a much higher chance of being correct with competent investigation. In law enforcement, documentation and evidence collection are crucial as well as the knowledge of the law but, the primary talents involve interviewing people and processing many different pieces of information and then putting everything together.

LuAnne Landers

Barry understood the domestic violence syndrome better than most as it seeped into his personal life in his early twenties. LuAnne Landers was his girlfriend for about a year. Steve Mortsoob and his girlfriend had introduced her to Barry and they quickly hit it off. She was attractive and fun and her somewhat sad looking eyes were adorable. At age twenty, she was separated from her husband. Barry later learned that this was at least partially due to him pushing her around. Barry didn't think to connect the dots early on when she said her father had routinely hit her when she a child.

LuAnne had a year-old baby named Trish that was always being dropped off with someone so that Barry and LuAnne could go party with friends. As far as Barry could tell the two of them were getting along quite well although he was beginning to question LuAnne's quality as a mother. When they first started dating, Barry was happy that LuAnne was able to drop off the child but, ultimately, it was more like, "You're going to leave Trish with a babysitter again?"

Problems started to arise. LuAnne would continually be late for important events and once did not pick up Barry from the airport. This would bother and irritate Barry but he would always understand and forgive her. Barry thought LuAnne may be seeing someone else as she continued doing things to upset him. Finally, the situation came to a head. One would think that Barry would be the one confronting his girlfriend but, in fact, it was just the opposite. LuAnne was upset because Barry was so amiable and reasonable and thoughtful. She had done everything she could think of to get a rise out of him including not picking him up at the airport. They discussed it further. She actually equated physical and emotional abuse to love. Her motives were suddenly crystal clear. She wanted Barry to yell at her and push her around and maybe even use his fist to punish her. Then she would know that she was truly loved.

"You're just too nice," she would say.

Barry was stunned. He gathered his thoughts and told her that he wouldn't be able to express his love that way. If she wanted someone to beat her up, she would have to go back to her husband or find someone else. LuAnne kissed Barry gently on the lips and left his apartment.

Other than a chance meeting at a wedding six months later, Barry didn't ever see LuAnne again. Maybe he should have been more upset about her leaving him but, considering the circumstances, he really thought it best. Ironically, with training and experience, he would later become somewhat of a domestic violence expert.

Domestic Violence

Barry thought it curious that crimes of domestic violence were novel in 2014 in the National Football League. Throughout his career, he worked with victims and dealt with the defendants that were responsible. While there certainly are cases of women being the perpetrators, the vast majority of the Domestic Violence (DV) criminals are men.

The Burning Bed was a movie in the 1980s starring Farrah Fawcett. She portrayed a woman being physically and emotionally assaulted by her husband and her efforts to extricate herself from that environment. Barry always thought she did a good job acting in the movie and that the domestic violence syndrome and predicament for some women were accurately represented.

The perpetrator in that movie was a law-abiding citizen in every other respect. Such is often not the case. Individuals being supervised on probation or parole for a domestic violence crime or that have come under the jurisdiction of the court, more likely than not have other offenses in their criminal history. In these caseloads lurk drug dealers, carjackers, robbers, burglars or worse. It's rather like domestic violence is just one aspect of their criminality. Barry would learn that sometimes a woman would get beaten up for "taking a little off the top" referring to using some of the drug she was supposed to be safekeeping or selling for her drug dealer husband. Domestic abuse really is a part of the criminal culture. Things aren't going well trying to get that Colt pistol from your connection? Let's beat up the girlfriend to relieve some tension. Dinner is late or non-existent? Push the old lady into the stove, and step on the baby at the same time.

Barry had no use for abusers of women or kids. Only insecure, demented cowards committed those crimes. They were almost as bad as sex offenders.

Working with the victims was challenging as well. Once in the domestic violence merry-go-round it is very difficult for victims to jump off. The vast majority of these crimes occur with no other witnesses so the victim's cooperation is usually necessary to convict the perpetrator. The victims "flip flop" on whether they will cooperate with the prosecutor so many cases get thrown out.

Victims often get used to the syndrome but the lucky ones are gathered up by caring friends or associates that get them away from the perpetrator. They really need time to get their "mind right," that is to understand that they don't deserve to be pounded on for any reason. The behavior is very similar to that demonstrated by people who are swayed and ultimately transformed by cults.

After a DV offense is committed, there are two things that the perpetrator tries to accomplish. He tries to get back in the good graces of the victim by apologizing and/or promising never to do it again and he does everything to keep the victim from cooperating with prosecutors. Sometimes being nice is all that is needed but, if that doesn't work, he will not hesitate to threaten the victim with further bodily harm. And often the victim is worried about finances should the guy be locked up leaving her with no additional income.

Many states including California now have laws that essentially command the responding officer to arrest first and answer questions later. These laws were designed to remedy a situation in the past where the cops show up and observe a "she said, he said" situation that did not meet the criteria for a case that would stand up in Court. While a few poor souls do now get arrested that shouldn't be arrested, it really is a good law as it provides some protection for women at least in the short term.

Barry was trying to help a twenty-three-old girl understand that she didn't have to tolerate getting regularly hit in the mouth. Adding to her situation was that she relied on the perpetrator's income and had nowhere else to stay.

Celeste was one of the lucky ones. An organization, which will be referred to as Sanctuary House, that helps domestic violence victims in the San Bernardino Valley, took her in. This home was expressly operated to shield these women from the offender while straightening out their way of thinking, empowering them to move forward without the spouse.

Barry needed to contact Celeste at least one more time and was eventually able to locate the facility. Driving through acres and acres of orange groves, he eventually spotted a large Victorian style home which looked like it belonged on a southern plantation. Driving up to a giant iron front gate, he was immediately met by two women that could only be called guards.

They accosted Barry verbally saying, "You are in the wrong place!"

It took a while to convince them that just because Barry was a male at their front door, he wasn't a threat and just might be a good guy. Once they realized Barry was the probation officer for the offender that beat up Celeste and was trying to help her, they calmed down and cooperated. Barry fully understood their position. They try to keep the location secret but in the event a perpetrator is able to find it, he would be a definite threat.

To give the NFL a pass, Barry guessed the level of expertise in that enterprise was devoid of understanding domestic violence. His suspicion was that they had too many attorneys and not enough investigators in the organization. He was happy that whatever their motivation was, it was good that they were finally treating domestic violence seriously.

Technology Summary

Over the course of his career, Barry would see many changes related to available technology augment and sometimes curtail his work. In the beginning, everything was on paper and computers were not of the desktop variety. Booking cards at the jail and juvenile hall were just that - cards.

Barry was introduced to his first "powerful" computer at the College of Wooster in Ohio. At the end of his career he would be using a smart phone with way more computing power than that room of wire and metal cases but, at the time, it was pretty amazing. It consumed the entire room and one would think it would house all of the knowledge of the solar system, but apparently not; it had to be connected by modem to a massive computer somewhere else on the planet. The connection was "dialup" so once the number was dialed, a phone receiver was placed in a cradle until the end of the session. The data transferred over that connection would be minuscule by today's standards.

Officers dictated reports to machines with magnetic belts when Barry was hired. He never really understood those. Then came cassette tapes and at some point, word processors replaced those bulky typewriters with some sort of correction tape on them.

Radios of different types were always part of the business but cell phones did not come into use until the 90s. They were a blessing. In the old days, an officer might return to the office after extensively searching a residence, happy he or she confiscated a quarter gram of methamphetamine. Then the officer would listen to the answering machine, that was hooked to the old black or beige office phone, and learn that a quarter pound of the stuff was in the back of the dryer.

Before long everyone had a computer with software to network and search databases for subjects and augment investigations. Tracking devices were utilized as well as plate readers. Social media investigations were helpful particularly for sex offenders and gang members.

Vehicles were equipped with MDCs (Mobile Data Computers) so that all databases such as criminal history, jail systems, firearms systems and the like could be accessed from the field.

To attempt to keep track of offenders, electronic monitoring was used so it could be confirmed they were at home. The Global Position System technology was utilized to be able to locate particular categories of felons such as sex offenders, gang members and domestic violence perpetrators. Technology was finally getting to the point where it was assisting law enforcement in some ways. But there is always a "but."

Electronic Monitoring

What's great about being a probation officer is, if you're lucky, you are assigned to many different areas where you develop all sorts of distinct skills and add to your knowledge base. At one point, Barry was in charge of the Electronic Monitoring Unit, an assignment that he felt was insignificant in the whole scheme of things. He would eventually gather very valuable information from becoming familiar with this technology and a sister technology, the Global Positioning System or GPS.

Electronic monitoring is meant to ensure that a particular individual is home during certain hours. Offenders are generally allowed to go to work and counseling and maybe church but the rest of the time they are expected to be at home. Participants wear a device that is secured around their ankle. This ankle bracelet communicates with a receiver that is plugged in to an electrical outlet and a phone line. If the individual gets too far away from the receiver, an alert will be sent over the phone line to the company that monitors the devices and that information is, in turn, provided to the probation officer. There are false alarms but, in most instances, they work fairly well. Of course, as with any type of technology, it can be defeated.

Barry's initial lack of interest in the program was partially due to the fact that it was used as a substitute for jail for low-level offenders while their court hearings were pending, such as drunk drivers or white-collar criminals. Not that a drunk driver cannot be a significant threat to the community but, compared to many criminals, they just weren't that exciting to keep an eye on. If they did violate their release terms, they would just sit in jail until they were sentenced. They weren't even on probation.

Barry became real interested when a participant, Philip Barnes, was accused of killing a man in Corona. Barnes lived about forty minutes away in Rialto and this is where he was required to stay while on the electronic monitoring program. He was enrolled in the program because of a drunk driving offense and documentation showed that he was at home when the murder was committed.

Since Mr. Barnes was positively identified by three eye witnesses as the person who shot the victim, his case eventually went to trial. He was known by the witnesses and the victim. Barry was perplexed by how Barnes could be in two different places at the same time so he began by interviewing the actual technology people at the electronic monitoring company instead of the sales people he normally contacted.

He learned that there were vulnerabilities that were not previously shared. Without getting too specific, there was a clever way one could defeat the electronics. Barry decided to test the equipment himself so he had the device attached to his ankle and he installed the unit at his home to communicate with the device and the central computer. At the risk of being stigmatized in social settings, he tried various techniques to fool the equipment over an entire weekend. He documented his whereabouts and compared this information with the generated reports back at work. Sure enough, he was able to leave his residence for long periods of time and the equipment was none the wiser. Now he knew how Mr. Barnes could have left his home, committed the murder and returned without anyone being alerted.

Barry contacted the Riverside County prosecutor regarding his findings. Barry offered to testify. The prosecutor agreed that the defendant undoubtedly used his electronic monitoring status as an alibi. The prosecutor went on to explain that since, technically, Mr. Barnes was detained at home in a government electronic monitoring program in another county at the same time as the murder, there was no way a jury would return with a guilty verdict. The case was ultimately dismissed and Mr. Barnes was free to go.

Clean Urine Will Set You Free

Despite the prevalence of various technological modalities, an integral part of the supervision of probationers or parolees is the urine test. Administering these tests is the least glamorous part of the job, but necessary. Drugs and alcohol are a part of the majority of crimes committed so the court or parole authority often prohibit their use while these people are under supervision. It is one of the terms of probation or parole.

This begs the question, "Who cares?" There are really two answers here. These people are not your law-abiding neighbors. They have committed crimes, often under the influence of some sort of substance. Using drugs or alcohol interferes with their treatment program in that they are not allowed to use any chemical legal or illegal.

But more importantly, substance abuse may be incorporated tightly with the crimes they commit. For instance, a sex offender may have consumed alcohol before he violated that little girl or boy. So, for him or her, alcohol use could make it much more likely he or she would commit a similar offense again. Prohibiting this person from consuming alcohol would be very important. A burglar who drinks and steals things might be given a chance to get "back on the wagon." The risk is too high for the sex offender who rapes a child under the influence. If his urine sample comes back positive for even alcohol, he needs to go to jail.

But usually one positive test result will not result in incarceration for your run of the mill felon. Felons can become desperate, however, if they have submitted multiple positive tests and their probation or parole officer is likely to arrest them. This is where the phony/diluted/tainted samples are submitted. Diluted samples, which are usually diluted with water to reduce their concentration, are detected by the laboratory but the results are often inconclusive. They are considered "dirty" but are not as convincing as a bona fide positive test result.

Tainted samples may include substances that are designed to impact the test methods or equipment in some manner or alter the urine and, as far as Barry knew, they didn't really do much of anything other than register as an "adulterated sample."

Then there is the phony sample which is just a matter of filling the bottle with someone else's urine, someone who is hopefully "clean." In this effort, siblings and spouses are recruited to supply the urine. It's just a matter of getting their urine into the official bottle without the officer noticing.

Most of these schemes can be quelled if the officer does as trained, that is to watch the urine go from the body into the bottle. The reality is that watching fluids emerging from private parts over a period of years does not appeal to most people so every officer deals with this in their own way. Barry was no different. He always felt you could tell by the subject's movements whether something was up and if the donor moved in a suspicious manner, he would be required to strip down for inspection. Barry found approximately ten devices during the course of his career using this method. Without revealing the most successful device for submitting someone else's urine - and it isn't the rubber penis - the most complex arrangement was really a urine delivery system. It started at a bladder taped on the felon's back and finished with a plastic tube with a valve that was operated close to the bottle. This guy deserved some sort of recognition as an engineer.

Barry felt that, over the years, he may have missed an exchanged sample, particularly when he was very busy or distracted but that was far better than staring at hundreds of penises.

Once he received a call from a very upset wife of a burglar. She had agreed to let him submit her urine sample in place of his. She was okay with it at the time but after the guy left Barry's office, a free man in a great mood, he picked up his girlfriend and proceeded directly to San Manuel, a local Indian casino.

"And go ahead and tell him where the information came from! That son of a bitch can rot in jail."

The following week, Barry called the unfaithful and apparently ungrateful individual in to the office.

"What's up Mr. Truman? I just saw you."

"I got your urine test result."

"But I KNOW it was clean!"

Barry elaborated, "Well there is good news and there is bad news. Which do you want to hear first?"

Mr. Unfaithful wanted to hear the good news first and Barry continued, "Your urine test results came back from the lab and the sample was absolutely clean."

"Great - well then what is the bad news?"

Barry explained, "It seems you are pregnant."

Of course, that was a little white lie but further interrogation revealed the truth and since the last three tests were positive as to the presence of methamphetamine, "Mr. Faithful" was taken into custody.

A Short Baseball Story

Despite the fact that very few officers had any desire to pay too much attention to bodily fluids leaving the body in a stream to the collection bottle, there were exceptions. A female probationer showed up at the office to submit a urine sample and Barry told her he would have to locate a female officer to "do a test."

The probationer said, "Fine, as long as it's not Johnny Bench."

The only Johnny Bench Barry knew was a former catcher for the Cincinnati Reds. "What do you mean?"

"That lady, you know - Johnny Bench." The woman crouched very low, separating her feet at the same time, mimicking the actions of a major league catcher waiting for the ball from the pitcher. At the same time, she jetted her neck forward and looked straight ahead with a focused look on her eyes. What she was describing was an officer crouching way down and intently watching her on the toilet supplying the sample.

From the description provided, Barry suspected "Johnny Bench" was in fact officer Nadine Williams. Later that day he ran across Officer Williams and he was quick to greet her. "Johnny! How ya doing?"

Nadine was of course perplexed and after some laughter now involving everyone else in the unit, Barry explained about the probationer not wanting to be tested by Johnny Bench.

"That's the only way to be sure when I'm doing a test. I have to be able to see!"

She was right of course but no one in the agency was as thorough and who followed the letter of the law like Johnny - er - a - Nadine.

Comments About Private Testing

Some police, probation and parole agents are not very attentive when it comes to supervising urine testing. Clearly, the worst law enforcement officer has a better chance of getting the subject's actual urine specimen than private medical labs do. There are really two reasons for this. Nurses and medical personnel definitely do not envision their job description as including watching people pee. You can't blame them. Also, they don't understand the population. Many are used to getting specimens from law abiding citizens. They are not looking for sneaky, scheming or scandalous activity.

Medical personnel will send a subject all alone into a bathroom with running water (which can be used to dilute the sample) or, more likely, where a sample can be substituted. At the best, personnel will be in bathroom but they won't truly know what to look for (or care).

Another thing to consider. In order to properly monitor these situations, it may be necessary to conduct a personal search. Who is going to do this and on what authority?

Barry was actually subject to an interesting testing method by a medical testing organization as part of the recruitment process for a special federal law enforcement position. He didn't get the position but it wasn't due to his test results. And of interest to urine collectors is his test result was not "diluted." Diluted samples are often blamed on drinking too much water before testing.

Not used to submitting to tests himself, and having somewhat of a "bashful kidney," Barry drank tremendous amounts of water prior to the test. He even took a gallon canteen of water to drink on the way to the physical and he finished it off before his arrival. He was extremely happy when it was time to provide a sample.

This medical facility's strategy of avoiding false samples was to have each candidate go into an empty room and then hand out their clothes. Through the crack in the door, Barry was handed a small Styrofoam cup to use for his sample.

There was no running water which was a good idea but a false sample could easily be hidden from the worker even with her taking all his clothes. It wasn't as if she (and for Barry it was a she) was going to examine his naked body. But at least the medical organization tried to prevent cheating.

Aside from that, the whole thing was quite comical. Imagine Barry standing totally nude in a room that was really an office with no furniture but with very plush and clean wall to wall light blue carpet. It felt really odd. He glanced at himself and scanned the empty room. The only thing to keep him company was that white cup. He chuckled to himself. He was actually happy no one was watching him submit his sample but soon a problem arose.

Barry was so relieved when he began urinating, he let out an audible breath. *But now, how will I stop?* The little cup was rapidly getting filled and Barry looked around at all the carpet and he was unsure he could stop the twelve gallons of liquid from leaving his body. With maximum effort, he was able to avert a very embarrassing accident. He knocked on the door, unloaded his sample to the nurse and quickly located a bathroom.

Internet Intervention and A Diet of Carrots

Search the Internet for products that can be ingested to clean or flush the system. The idea is to obtain a favorable test result which would reveal no sign of drug or alcohol usage. There are a multitude of products that claim to accomplish this. It's a racket. These concoctions are not just marketed for felons. They are aimed at individuals attempting to get hired or remain employed.

The reality is that each drug including alcohol has a detection time frame for clearing from the system and that is not really going to be altered. Everyone has their opinions but in the world of the felon, rumors abound and individuals will try everything to beat the test anyway they can.

Probably in poor taste but out of the necessity for humor and as a rescue from tedium, Barry and his colleagues added to the rumor mill. It was common practice to ask subjects submitting samples if they were taking any prescribed medications. The laboratory needs this information to rule out legitimate reasons for positive test results. Some prescribed medications can look like illicit drugs or interfere with their detection.

This being said, it was not part of the procedure to ask individuals if they had consumed large quantities of carrots in the last twenty-four hours. But that's just what they did, straight faces and all. Knowing how tight-knit the supervised criminal element was, they could only imagine the uptick in carrot sales around San Bernardino and the surrounding areas.

Here's Your Red Phosphorus

A search early on would prove to be a great learning experience. While Barry would eventually excel when it came to investigations, that time was yet to come and he was still relatively inexperienced.

James Bland was a twenty-six-year old probationer who resided in Muscoy, an unincorporated community adjacent to the city of San Bernardino. He was a new probationer who failed to appear for his first appointment. Barry's supervisor, Frank Botman, was smart and seasoned and he saw something in Bland's case file that screamed "search me!"

Along with three other probation officers, Barry approached the residence and knocked on the door. While waiting for a response, it was noted that cameras were mounted on the eaves of the house in three locations. Barry thought, "This guy must have an interest in video equipment." Mr. Bland eventually answered the door and cooperated as the threesome searched through his home.

Since Mr. Botman gave instructions to be thorough in the search, Barry was checking every nook and cranny. No one found much of anything that would represent a violation of probation or the law but Barry did find a big bag of reddish powder underneath a wet bar. He had no idea what this was but decided to confiscate it just in case it was some kind of drug. One of the other officers was sure it was Indian makeup, whatever that was. James Bland maintained that he did not know anything about the powder. The powder was seized and he was thanked for his cooperation.

Back in the office, all the officers continued to discuss the bag of powder. Barry thought it odd someone would package up this Indian makeup in black garbage bags, place the bags inside a suitcase and put it in a concealed location. Barry's coworker again said she knew what Indian makeup looked like and "that's what that is!" Humoring Barry, she called someone at the Sheriff's office for advice. From her description, whomever she spoke with said that whatever the substance was, it wasn't illegal. With no apparent reason to keep the bag of powder, Barry returned it to Mr. Bland.

About three months later, Barry was searching a mountain residence with Sheriff's deputies. He came upon about a quarter pound of a red powder substance that looked just like the powder at Mr. Bland's house. One of the deputies that had been assigned to Narcotics Division was ecstatic. He recognized the powder right away as red phosphorus, a precursor chemical for the manufacture of methamphetamine. Barry said, "You sure that's not Indian makeup?"

It was then that he realized that he had released ten pounds of red phosphorus back to a probationer who was directly involved in the manufacture of a hell of a lot of methamphetamine. Mr. Bland undoubtedly thought it was some sort of setup and was probably looking over his shoulder for some time. At some point, he must have figured out that his probation officer was just stupid.

In retrospect, what this taught Barry was to trust his instincts and to develop sources to fill in his gaps of ignorance. Most law-abiding citizens do not have cameras mounted all over their eaves and not every officer of the law is an expert in drugs. In other words, they may not know more than you when they give advice. For what it's worth, Barry did save his agency about $10,000 in Department of Justice disposal fees. You can't just throw that stuff in the trash.

Understanding the Demographic

A funny thing happened to Barry over the years dealing with felons and searching hundreds of houses. Moving through the community undetected as a law enforcement officer gave him a unique view of the low socio-economic and/or criminal culture. Keep in mind that this is just a perspective and not an excuse or cause to sob.

He really was exposed to two separate aspects of the culture that caused him to be both cautious and sympathetic. Quite simply, the first invaluable conclusion was that there are very dangerous people in the community and officers need to be extremely careful. This is, of course, something officers are always told but seeing it from the inside out made Barry always be prepared for violence coming his way. Drugs and money are always accompanied by guns. It is merely a way of life for some individuals and/or families.

The second observation that may seem incongruous to the first aspect, but is not - is that the average day to day burden on a community felon and his family can be overwhelming. Doing basic things can be difficult. It's hard enough for the average law-abiding citizen to make sure all the mundane but necessary tasks that society requires are accomplished. Drivers licensing, paying insurance premiums, keeping up with bills, maintaining vehicles, maybe even handling a budget are but a few of these tasks.

But your average felon needs to get money to fix his car and for gas to get to the Department of Motor Vehicles to get his driver's license and vehicle tags. Hopefully, he makes it without getting pulled over by law enforcement. Of course, the DMV will send him to court to get some sort of paperwork and so he needs to get money to pay off his numerous traffic warrants so that he isn't taken back in custody when he goes to court. In the meantime, a traffic officer writes a fix-it ticket for his cracked windshield because he had just enough money for a tire and gas but not for cosmetic upgrades.

Needing money for everything, he can try to borrow it but frankly no one will lend it to him. He is a crook among crooks. He can also get a pay day loan at one of those little shops of horror that essentially keep all their patrons broke forever. And finally, he can sell a few grams of methamphetamine to raise the funds. And unless he's a true professional dealer, he and his significant other are probably going to use some of the product so hopefully there is net profit that will cover his obligations.

Probably before he can accomplish all his tasks, he will get arrested on the warrants. The good news is that the custody time will count towards some of those fines. But while he is in custody, he will lose the job he got at the Goodwill store, a job he obtained to get his parole agent off his back.

Once released, he will return to his woman in her apartment if she has not been evicted. Pondering his next move, he will light up a GPC cigarette, a generic brand popular in the community because it is the absolute cheapest smoke on the market. Unfortunately, a pack of GPCs is still ridiculously high for our felon because some politician wants to extract more tax money to fund any and everything. Perhaps the politician is well-intentioned, looking out for the health of the public. But the person really hurt is our felon. If you're thinking about protecting his health, remember that he spends a lot of time in methamphetamine labs and smoking cigarettes is the least of his problems. It's really one of the few legal things where he derives pleasure.

Barry once had a conversation with a local criminal attorney about "helping these people." Keep in mind that this attorney was in court to make a motion to withdraw because of "professional considerations." This was really due to his client not paying his bill and is referred to informally and off the record as a "green motion." Since he was appointed by the court, he was requesting to be relieved by the court. Everyone nods and the criminal gets another attorney, perhaps a Deputy Public Defender.

The attorney was criticizing Barry for not offering his client more treatment options and that if he had helped his client in the past he may have avoided another arrest.

Barry told the attorney, "Well you could have given him your car!"

"What are you talking about? Why would I give him my Mercedes?" he asked.

Barry explained, "When you leave your buddies tonight after cocktails, you drive away knowing how very careful you should proceed. Perhaps you choose certain ways to go home based on your knowledge of traffic enforcement. As long as you drive carefully, there is no reason for you to be stopped by a police officer as all your vehicle's equipment is working fine. After all, your car is only eight months old."

Barry continued, "Your engine runs smoothly and those properly aimed xenon high discharge headlights illuminate a football field in front of you. If you encounter an obstacle, your anti-lock brakes work as designed and allow you to stop or steer to avoid the problem. If, for some reason, a lighting feature fails or a tire starts losing air, there are myriad warning lights to give notice."

"Yeah, yeah," said the attorney probably knowing where Barry was going with this.

"On the night of your client's recent arrest," Barry interrupted, "he had been drinking and using methamphetamine and was piloting a 1987 Ford Taurus with bald tires. To make matters worse, it was raining and his wiper blades should have been changed ten years before Obama was elected. The weather-beaten plastic lenses covering the headlights barely allowed any light through. He had a slim chance of being able to stop before running into that construction barricade. Fortunately, the crew was not on site at the time. Now you couldn't do anything about your client's intellectual deficiencies or judgement, but you surely could have at least given him the necessary equipment to avoid the accident and subsequent arrest."

The attorney had nothing really to say beyond mumbling. Barry left feeling somewhat vindicated. Of course, the Court relieved the attorney of his sacred duty to defend the impoverished felon.

Further Information About This Population

Barry sometimes felt that, by and large, the "good guys" or the law-abiding citizens, including himself, were spoiled. Not that they didn't have financial problems but they generally were able to buy basic cleaning supplies and at least wash their clothes. Often, when Barry would arrest a woman in her residence, she would ask if she could put a different shirt on or change her shorts or pants. If she was cooperative and if what she was doing would not threaten officers, Barry would allow her to make a "smell check" of her clothes that generally were lying on the floor of one particular room of the house or apartment. She would then determine which garment smelled the best and select it for her trip to jail. Men rarely did smell checks, perhaps being less discriminating.

And for whatever reason, many of the living quarters for felons and their families suffer from abject sanitary neglect. Barry was particularly annoyed when kids were forced to live in deplorable conditions including dog feces all over the floor. Babies would negotiate these "land mines" while crawling on the floor. Barry would get irritated with representatives from Children's Services when they claimed there was nothing they could do. Finding a toddler in diapers in the back yard of a residence when the temperature was 47 degrees, Barry was appalled that, according to Children's Services, it had been determined in court that children could adapt to these temperatures. As long as there was running water, practically any conditions were permissible. It was incredible.

Tommy the Maid

On occasion, Barry would push the envelope when he had authority in the case of a probationer or parolee. Barry visited a probationer by the name of Tommy in the city of Highland in a home with his wife and three children. Dog feces was all over the carpet in all the rooms. It made matters worse when Barry stepped on a dog turd. He confronted the twenty-six-year old probationer regarding the disgusting conditions at which time Tommy proceeded to blame his wife because she was a "shitty" housekeeper.

Barry interrupted his dialogue, "Excuse me but your wife is not on probation. YOU are the one on probation and from now on YOU are the maid."

Barry continued, "If I return here and discover that your house is not cleaned up and a safe environment for your kids, then YOU are going to jail."

Barry made it clear that this was a directive in accordance with his probation terms, specifically one that read, " .... obey all reasonable directives of your probation officer." Some of Barry's co-workers questioned whether that was a reasonable directive. Barry responded, "Well if a directive to protect kids is unreasonable, I just don't get it."

Barry made a point to return unannounced to Tommy's house two weeks later. The place looked the same. Barry stepped in poop again and the probationer went to jail. It wasn't the crime of the century but the judge backed up Barry's decision and the guy spent ninety days in jail. Barry returned again six months later and the carpet was free of animal feces. He arrested the guy for having methamphetamine in the cookie jar but there was no longer dog feces on the carpet. Barry wasn't sure of the moral to that story but, at least, the kids didn't have to play in feces. Tommy went to state prison.

Mortsoob Bachelor Party

Steve Mortsoob was getting married to Glenda in the late 70s and Barry and other men were planning a bachelor party. Barry was the best man. Steve was emphatic that he didn't want any "dancers" or strippers. Barry, knowing Steve well, honored his request. Instead, everyone thought it would be fun to purchase a rubber blowup doll to come to the party. Barry was purchasing it at the Fun Corner on Baseline when one of the owners, a woman that was probably 75, informed him that the doll had no underwear. "Oh" Barry said, "She needs those?"

"Yes, that would be appropriate," she pointed out. "They have some very nice ones at JC Penney, but we also have some pretty ones here if you would like to look at them."

She seemed to be an authority on this so Barry spent the next five minutes or so with this very nice and attentive woman, browsing through large piles of panties. The woman would hold a pair up and say, "These would be very nice" or "these are definitely sexy and only $2.99."

At some point Barry cut this dialogue off and quickly made his selection, not the most expensive panties but, also, not the least expensive so as not to be considered cheap. Barry and the others had fun at the party kidding Steve in various ways with the doll. The rubber doll was the group's guest. Everyone was drinking of course and the night wound down with Steve, Gerry Hunts, and Barry drinking Jack Daniels until about 4:00 in the morning.

Barry rarely consumed booze but, that night, the whiskey tasted like water. He and Gerry decided to go visit their old night shift friends working at the local Juvenile Hall. Steve said that he would wait for their return but he probably passed out shortly after their departure.

Now the actual visit with friends was unremarkable or perhaps faint in memory, but the trip to the "hall" was a joy. It was a beautiful night and the top was down in Barry's bright red Karmann Ghia. Gerry was riding in the back so that Barry's date, the blowup doll, could ride "shotgun." It would be easy to criticize her for going along with only her panties, but she actually showed the boys a great deal of respect by not complaining about her hair getting blown or the fact that Barry was driving intoxicated. While driving intoxicated was not viewed at that time as the serious crime it is now, Barry was still later embarrassed about it.

What's amazing is that Barry didn't get pulled over by the San Bernardino Police or the California Highway Patrol. He was driving right down Baseline Avenue, a main thoroughfare. Hardly another car could be seen. Chances are some officer spotted the moving spectacle but did not want any part of it, especially at the end of a graveyard shift.

Taking the Plunge

It never really occurred to Barry that after Steve was married, he would be less available to belly up to the bar and to bond with the guys. Also, other male friends were being knocked off one by one. It seemed to Barry that there was a wedding every few months. Marriage had been something to avoid for as long as possible. But now, there was no one to play with. His mindset gradually morphed from dredging up someone that liked to party to seeking a possible mate.

Enter Michelle Suchar. She was a probation officer that supervised juveniles. When she spoke, she always seemed to do so in a caring tone. It was obvious that she was bright and just as obvious that she was very "cute." Large brown eyes peered through straight light brown hair. She had a reputation as a productive employee. Barry was attracted to her and, in the back of his mind, he thought she would make a good mother.

Barry, always awkward when it came to asking for a date, made a concerted effort to cross paths with Michelle. She did not work in the same office so some harmless deceit was necessary. Barry looked at the unit rosters, found a listing for a guy he knew fairly well and then came up with an excuse to visit him. In the course of his visit he came upon Michelle and asked her some legal question about juvenile confinement time which he really could care less about. She explained the general concept as she knew it.

"Oh, I think I remember that. Isn't it similar to custody credits like we calculate in adult division?"

Barry was known for having all the answers but this day he feigned confusion and he continued, "Could you show me that on paper?" He wondered if she was suspicious of his ignorance.

Michelle quickly went to her desk and Barry followed. She sat down and began scribbling some numbers on a yellow pad while Barry stood close to her pretending to observe the calculations. A bouquet of vanilla with a sliver of citrus emanated gently from her hair or skin or whatever. He felt flushed and a little short of breath. Even though he was a bundle of nerves, the feeling was intoxicating.

She concluded the lesson and Barry thanked her and began to leave, not yet developing the courage to cross the line and make his intentions known. Suddenly, as he was leaving Michelle's office, he stopped abruptly and turned towards her. "Would you ever be interested in meeting me for coffee at the "Taj" which was short for Taj Mahal, which was slang for the ornate government center that sat right next to the old encampment of the Earp family.

Michelle had a surprised look on her face and she hesitated as if processing things in her mind. Then she responded, "That would be great."

Barry arrived for coffee five minutes early. Michelle was already seated in a circular booth. She looked far more beautiful than he had ever realized. They exchanged pleasantries and Barry asked her what she would like. "Oh, just black coffee. Thanks." This was a simple but important sign that Michelle may not be "high maintenance."

Barry returned with their coffees and scooted around the table so as to be close to Michelle but not too close for a first meeting. She spoke about her assignment and the people she worked with. Barry was more focused on how she spoke rather than the content. She apologized for talking so much and put Barry on the spot. "I've been rambling. Please tell me about your job. I know it's much more exciting than mine."

Barry was content listening to Michelle but he gave her the basics as to his assignment and they laughed about their jobs and funny employees in their respective work units. Conversation became more comfortable. As Barry became more animated, he inadvertently bumped her knee with his. He made a concerted effort not to hyperventilate. She was just so enthralling and even touching her with his knee was pleasurable. An hour went by in a flash for both of them and they simultaneously and abruptly got up to return to work. On the way outside, Michelle softly asked, "Don't you think we ought to do drinks or dinner?"

"Let's do both," an upbeat Barry responded.

"Excellent idea! Friday or Saturday?"

"I'm part of some sort of sweep Friday but Saturday works." They exchanged contact information and agreed to firm up the "date" later that day.

They later decided to meet for drinks at the Castaways, a restaurant with a view over the entire valley, and that she would pay for drinks and he would pay for dinner. Barry agreed, making sure that, "you like McDonalds." They both laughed.

Even at this early stage it seemed like they were both in charge and both following along. As strange as it sounded, it was like a relationship consensus.

They went out to dinner again and to a movie. Barry learned that Michelle liked Brussels sprouts and also liked her hand held. Michelle listened intently while Barry talked fondly of his home town in Ohio. They seemed to be a perfect match. Michelle was very sexy and confident with a little bit of an edge at times. She was clever and insightful and Barry very much liked to talk with her.

Before long, he very much liked to do other things with her, again and again. She was like the ultimate partner in bed, submissive at times and forceful at others. She wanted to examine every nerve on Barry's body and also her own.

They continued to spend time together but neither of them smothered the other. Barry still saw Steve whenever he could and he would find other things to do when Michelle wanted to be with girlfriends, particular her old college roommate, Tricia.

Just a few months passed and Barry came to the conclusion that Michelle was his soulmate. She would be his friend, his lover and the mother to their children. He asked her to marry him when they were sharing a bowl of popcorn on her comfortable old corduroy couch. Michelle's eyes teared up a little. She cleared her throat and softly responded, "I would love to be your wife."

After the large wedding day sendoff by family and friends, many from work, the couple spent the next few years enjoying each other and life. Michelle was having difficulty getting pregnant but Barry always thought one could adapt to having children and also to not having children. There were advantages to each situation. The important thing was that they were together.

Use of Force Training

There are many different types of training classes that law enforcement officers attend. Some have to do with the application of the law or the study of interviewing techniques. The most important training sessions teach or remind an officer how to do his or her job and not get hurt.

From an agency perspective, Barry realized that standardized training was necessary. Every employee was schooled in the same fashion and it really helped in the area of civil liability should someone commence litigation making claims of a lack of training. Again, civil liability becomes more of an issue the bigger an agency gets.

Barry had been schooled for years in different techniques to handcuff subjects and to defend himself. The idea is for an agency to teach the same techniques to all officers in a standardized manner in order to more easily defend the government against litigation should a citizen get shot or injured. There are a couple realities here. First, different administrations decide on different techniques so a way of installing handcuffs or striking a suspect may change with different leaders. Second, most officers use the techniques taught in conjunction with what has already been learned or what actually "works."

Despite being schooled in eleven different types of hand to hand combat and defensive tactics, Barry always went back to high-school wrestling techniques. He paid more attention to training on strikes and blows that would immediately impact people and combined techniques that worked. Wrestling is more limited to restraint but also allows for slamming someone against a block wall or immobilizing a subject until restraints can be installed. This hybrid model would not officially be approved for civil liability reasons but the reality is that an officer will always default to muscle memory created by hundreds of hours of practice - not a two-hour session every quarter or so.

Officers are constantly being coached about the tools they have at their disposal. In dealing with aggression and defense, along with their semi-automatic handguns, officers carry collapsible asps, Tasers, radios and pepper spray. Verbal skills are also considered to be a tool - and in many ways, they are perhaps the most persuasive. Barry was hoping that more devices were not added as he was concerned of one too many choices. There are too many things that an officer has to think about in a split second without adding on more options. Ideally, the correct tool for the level of threat should be deployed. Of course, everybody knows that when things go south quickly, it would be wise to just pull out the gun. Barry knew that he could always put it back in his holster. No one needs to get killed because of a weapons confusion delay.

Having too many tools is also a problem for some women. Slim female officers don't have a whole lot of room on their belts for more tools. Barry had a close friend whose waist couldn't be over eighteen inches around and she had to really cram stuff in. Depending on the agency, some equipment can be secured on the upper body but consider that other items can include a police radio, multiple handcuffs, a flashlight or two, keys, gloves, digital recorder, extra magazines, perhaps a video camera and other items as required. As for a lack of places to attach things around the waist, full-framed men and women aren't affected so much.

Each one of these "tools" has its pros and cons and Barry was quite familiar with them. In examining just one of them, pepper spray is propelled from a container compressed with air. The liquid contains the chemical capsicum, pretty much the same substance made from peppers that it is in hot sauce. The idea is to get the irritant in the suspect's or a dog's eyes so that any threat will be diminished. Training deals with pointing and spraying from a proper distance and also experiencing getting sprayed from the trainer. Properly deployed, pepper spray can be very effective. And, of course, everyone that has used it has, at times, missed their target, sometimes hitting the good guys.

It doesn't work on everyone or on all dogs. Sometimes all the officer has accomplished with dogs is to make them really angry. Then there are the times a dog, particularly a furry one, that has been sprayed and become docile, later walks through a house being searched and spreads the chemical through the air, contaminating everyone.

Of course, the ultimate tool is the gun. Barry could complain about many training sessions in his agency that had little to do with the job but he was always impressed with the training having to do with discharging your weapon. The range staff were always excellent and officers were exposed to various scenarios. Barry was fortunate that he also received training with various different systems involving lasers, wax bullets and video interaction. There are numerous systems out there that try to help officers make correct decisions under stress and in a split second.

Attorneys that are experts on officer involved shootings teach officers on what to consider and when to shoot. Believe it or not, most officers in training situations do not discharge their weapons as soon as they should.

Barry wasn't a dead eye at the range but he always felt he could fire under stress and be pretty darn accurate at close range. It was his feeling that most gun fights would take place close and fast, so whenever he had the opportunity to do additional shooting after qualification at the range, he would simulate shooting fast and close. As a result, he could draw his weapon and hit "center mass"[4] and headshots all day long.

There is always training to teach officers when they should remove their firearm from the holster. Anyone that works on the streets where crimes are often committed or goes to houses where criminals live or does anything that could prevent them from returning to their family intact, pulls their firearm out a lot. That is the responsible thing to do. Successful quick drawing is mostly done in cowboy movies. A felon can point a weapon and fire before an officer can draw. Once the threat appears to be gone, the weapon can always be returned to the holster.

---

[4] An area on the upper human body below the throat and above the navel where vital organs are present.

Barry always thought there should be training sessions for "putting away" firearms. Obviously, the firearm is being put away as often as it is drawn. It might be put away to chase someone or go over a fence, to deploy another tool, to handcuff a subject, to engage in a physical altercation or just by routine. Depending on the situation, it is not as easy as it may sound. It needs to be in the officer's hand or secured in the holster, but not lying on the ground.

More on Handcuffing (Because It's Done All the Time)

Like everything else, methods for installing handcuffs change every so many years. This is not because bad guys have different wrists from decade to decade, but because personnel in charge of agencies change. They bring in different providers for training and they all have their own ideas on how someone should be handcuffed. This is an area where Barry and the other former wrestlers used to chuckle off to the side as they all knew that what you did at crucial times was going to be what you did over and over and over. Again, it's called muscle memory.

Certainly, new employees need something to guide them and so it was necessary. But it was entirely ludicrous to change this training every few years. Barry just went through the motions in handcuff training. He had been taught about ten different ways to install handcuffs over the years.

Barry remembered one trainer who was an Orange County deputy that knew the score. He offered prudent options for cuffing but made it clear that you need to get them on anyway that you can. It's always nice to receive training from someone with a lot of experience. The trainers that stressed making sure that the keyholes were always facing the right way probably did a lot of transporting and transferring of prisoners in controlled and calm environments. In the real world of arrests, people often resist and fight and generally make it difficult to rely on one regimented way to install cuffs.

Anybody that has been fighting with a suspect where several officers are involved and arms and legs are flailing around knows this to be a fact. Sometimes you just ratchet them on regardless of where the key hole is or what technique was used to manipulate an arm or hand or whatever. Barry always remembered on one occasion being in a pile of bodies and almost handcuffing one of his fellow officers. In another pile of humanity where handcuff installation was the goal, Barry screeched with pain. "That's my ankle!" causing his partner to stop twisting it.

There are a few basic techniques/tips regarding handcuffing that Barry personally attempted to adhere to:

Never install just one cuff without having control of the other. Talk about a major weapon to swing around at officers.

If a subject is cuffed, never use your fingers or hands to grab the chain between the two cuffs. The subject will either intentionally or inadvertently pinch the hell out of your fingers.

With rare exception, do not install cuffs in the front like you see many times in the movies unless you want to get hurt or you want the subject to escape.

Save yourself a lot of aggravation later and try to use handcuffs with bigger openings on very large subjects. Barry knew that quite a few big guys being arrested lie about having bad shoulders but many actually do have shoulder problems and more than a few of them have been dislocated during handcuffing. Many big men are rigid and/or muscular which makes it difficult to hook their big wrists up behind their backs. Double-cuffing, or using two sets of cuffs, is frowned on by many officers primarily because being decent is often confused with being weak, but, Barry never had any problem with double-cuffing as long as it was done in the back. He was probably a little more sympathetic than most as he was muscular, rigid and had very large wrists. As such, in hand-cuff training he COULD be cuffed in the conventional way but it was damn uncomfortable and he often finished class bleeding with a cut or two on his wrists.

Finally, never totally trust cuffs. They are not meant to be a permanent way of securing someone. They can be defeated if someone knows what they are doing. Some gangs practice defeating handcuffs as part of their in-house training.

You're Getting Sleepy

Barry always felt there was a lot to learn from the hypnotist case. Robert Hearthstone was placed on probation in Kings County for practicing as a medical doctor without a license. If he would have made his money helping people quit smoking with hypnosis, his practice would have gone unnoticed. Instead, he claimed to cure everything including brain cancer. Having been turned into authorities by numerous victims, he was convicted of several misdemeanors and sent to jail for a brief period of time. Not being very popular in a small community, he relocated to San Bernardino County where he hoped to live "under the radar."

That may have been possible had he stopped treating people with hypnosis, a requirement of his probation grant. Once Barry took over the case and received word Robert was back in business, he worked with deputies in the Twin Peaks Sheriff's station to develop a plan to prove Hearthstone was again fraudulently treating people.

It was decided that Deputy Trudy Nelson would answer an advertisement that Hearthstone had taken out in the local paper. She telephoned him and told him she read his ad and wondered if he could help her. The call was, of course, recorded. Trudy was bright and it was a wondrous thing to hear her use her innocent and cheery voice to really determine what Hearthstone was up to. "I really need to quit smoking," Trudy began.

Hearthstone responded, "That's not a problem. You will be smoke free and you won't even miss cigarettes."

Trudy continued, "And I have a high school reunion coming up and I would like to lose about twenty pounds. Can you help me with that?"

"Absolutely," Robert remarked.

While Hearthstone was not supposed to treat anyone for anything, Barry really wanted to see the scope of his promised treatments. In that spirit, Trudy continued, "I should have mentioned this right off but it depresses me so much I put it to the back of my mind."

"What is bothering you?"

Trudy began sobbing. She pretty much convinced Barry. "My regular doctor says I have breast cancer but I have been reluctant to do anything about it. I just hate the idea of possibly losing my breasts."

"Please don't let that get you down. I have procedures that will rid your cells of that invader. You are a good candidate for hypnotherapy."

"You can get rid of the cancer?" Trudy questioned with an excited tone.

"Yes, we just need to set you up with an appointment."

Trudy made the appointment for the following day and thanked Hearthstone.

Trudy was accompanied by Barry and two other deputies to the appointment and Robert Hearthstone was taken into custody without incident.

Now the second part of this story has to do with the prosecution. As a courtesy case from another county, Kings County, the probation matter needed to be heard in that jurisdiction. Both Trudy and Barry would be required to attend.

Trudy was the star witness. Her employer was the San Bernardino Sheriff's Department. Since the County of San Bernardino is the largest county in the contiguous United States, the Sheriff's office responsible for covering that vast territory has the largest air force of any law enforcement agency in the country. The twosome was flown to and from Hanford, California in a Sheriff's Department Cessna. As most counties do not have this capability and in-state witnesses would normally drive when subpoenaed, it took Kings County personnel by surprise and a period of time passed before Barry and Trudy were picked up at the airport.

Before court, Barry and Trudy visited the Kings County Probation Department. It was quite refreshing and an illustration of why small is often better than large. They were told the Chief Probation Officer was waiting for them.

"The Chief PO wants to see us?" a concerned Barry questioned. He looked towards Trudy and said, "That's not good news."

In his home county, that probably meant someone was in trouble or something had gone wrong.

The chief, a fit-looking male, probably forty years of age, greeted Barry and Trudy. Low and behold, he knew everything about the case and he thanked the two for coming to testify. The chief was actually involved in the search of Hearthstone's residence in Kings County. The case had garnered the attention of the local media and he clearly wanted to see Mr. Hearthstone go to jail.

Now the reason Barry was so astonished about the chief being so involved and knowledgeable, was that in San Bernardino County, at the Probation Department, that was generally not the case. Partly due to the culture of the social scientists that commanded a department changed by the times into an armed law enforcement agency, cases and case details were rarely day to day topics in the administration building. Also, a small agency is a lot better at being organized and informed than a massive agency. The San Bernardino County Probation Department was ten times larger than the Kings County Probation Department. With that size, you get detached command and control, dysfunction, hordes of procedures and morale problems. These are systemic problems that are just inherent with the girth of the beast.

The smaller agency relies more on common sense than procedures (that can never cover everything). People know one another and spend more time informally networking together rather than dealing with attorneys, unions, ergonomic specialists, human resource consultants, work performance plans and the like.

Barry was always entertained by the San Bernardino County parking procedure for employees. Keep in mind that there are approximately 22,000 people employed by San Bernardino County. The procedure is six pages long. Yes, SIX pages long. In Barry's home town in Ohio, he would probably be told to park over by the tree.

The case was discussed and the court hearing commenced after lunch. Barry testified followed by Trudy. It was really pretty uneventful. It was clear that Hearthstone was in violation of his probation grant. Defense counsel argued for a continuance purportedly so that he could locate a witness but the judge was inclined to deny it.

"These officers have come all the way from San Bernardino County. They have testified and they need to get back to their jobs."

Hearthstone's attorney continued to argue for a continuance. "My client cannot be deprived of his liberty because a continuance is inconvenient for witnesses." He looked at Barry and Trudy with disdain.

"Due to the burden on these officers and the additional costs associated with their return appearance, I am inclined to move on to the sentencing phase."

Hearthstone's counselor quickly offered, "We will stipulate that regardless of the sentence, that the defendant will pay for all transportation costs for both trips to and from Kings County for these officers.

The judge then directed Barry to prepare a memo citing all travel costs to be presented at sentencing. Barry and Trudy again flew to Hanford two weeks later. There were no new witnesses or testimony of any kind. Barry submitted the memo immediately before sentencing.

Hearthstone certainly was locked up. But the most entertaining feature of the sentencing was the matter of the transportation expenses. The defense attorney made the assumption that his client would have to come up with money for mileage and wear and tear on a government vehicle used for two trips to Kings County, a trip of about 200 miles each way.

Instead, he was presented with a copy of a detailed invoice for two trips, calculating aviation fuel, wear and tear, pilot layover and a bunch of other stuff. The total amounted to $2215.00. The attorney whined and argued about the figure until the judge told him to sit down.

"I can certainly sympathize with you counselor. I had no idea that the witnesses flew up from San Bernardino. But the fact of the matter is that you agreed to pay their costs - and that is so ordered." Barry and Trudy presented stoic expressions but they were chuckling inside.

Testifying

Barry started out his career being squeamish and all stressed out about testifying but as the years went by, he thought it was fun. He even looked forward to taking the stand.

Despite the fact that officers would joke about going to "testi-lie," most experienced officers followed the perhaps corny admonishment, "Always tell the truth." Aside from being the right thing to do, the most valuable asset you possess is your credibility. And as Steve Mortsoob would often say, "Credibility is the only thing that they can't take away."

There are other basic tips when testifying including taking your time and thinking about your answers. This is also helpful in allowing time for the District Attorney to object if need be.

There is always a concern that a specific question will be asked because the answer may reveal the weakest part of the case. Barry learned that ALL cases have a weak spot but rarely does an interrogator discover it. There's no sense worrying about. If it does come up, just tell the truth and let the chips fall where they may.

That doesn't mean an officer has to volunteer information on the stand. He or she just needs to truthfully answer the questions as posed by either camp. Barry would often just wait for one particular question that might expose a weakness or a technical problem. He knew if it was asked and answered that the case was dead in the water. But not offering unsolicited information doesn't fall under deceit; that is just playing by the rules just like everyone else in the courtroom. You are a witness. Only answer what is asked.

Dropping the Ball

On one occasion, Barry was asked about a single urine sample. The positive test result from that sample would undoubtedly cause this person to be incarcerated; it was the last positive result of many.

The attorney led Barry through the handling of that bottle and specimen.

"…So, then you handed the bottle to my client."

"Yessir," said Barry.

"And then you supervised the collection of that sample."

"Yes."

"And then you had my client seal the sample with tape with his UPC code. Did he put his initial on the tape?"

"Yessir."

Barry knew the answer to the next question would sink the entire violation. The attorney was going to ask what happened to this particular sample next. Barry had no idea. He had the offender place it on a file cabinet where all the samples were kept until there were enough to fill an eight-cavity box to be delivered to the laboratory. There was a 99.9% chance that the officer that collected the last sample to make up the cardboard box of eight, deposited it in the USPS box for delivery. After all, the UPC code for that offender and his initial were on his sample. But, technically, the chain of evidence was lost between Barry and the officer that packaged all the samples up.

The attorney continued. "What is the routine delivery method to get urine samples from your office to the laboratory in Menlo Park?" Barry thought, *He dropped the ball!*

The entire line of questioning had to do with the steps taken on this particular sample - Now he was being asked for the routine method for delivery of any sample.

Barry even gave him a break and repeated his question back to him. "Your question is what is the routine delivery method to get samples from our office to the laboratory in Menlo Park?"

"Yes!" he said in a rather smart, impatient tone.

"The routine procedure is to deposit the samples in the United States Postal Service box at the front of the building. From there it's up to the mail service to make delivery to the lab."

"No more questions."

Really?

Barry would relish the times when an attorney would ask a question not knowing the answer, something discouraged in law school.

"So, Mr. Truman, how long did it take to examine my client's hard drive?"

"Oh - I guess with examination and documentation, I have about seven hours in it."

"So, after all that time, am I to conclude that these ten pictures, that you say are child pornography, are all you could come up with?"

Barry calmly responded, "Well I can't speak to what you conclude, but these ten images of child pornography were each the best representatives of those particular series as delineated by the National Center for Missing and Exploited Children. In total, there were 1853 illegal images that I located."

"Objection!" defense counsel exclaimed.

"You asked the question," the judge dryly responded.

Stranger in the Night

A similar situation came up in a parole hearing. Barry was never asked the question, "Have you ever seen this parolee before?"

When he was subpoenaed, he struggled to remember the case. There were so many cases. Barry figured when he appeared it would all come back to him. He started getting concerned when he ran into the parolee's wife in the waiting room. She certainly knew Barry and was asking questions about the possible dispositions. Barry asked innocent questions about where they lived and such and he was able to ascertain that it was a methamphetamine case of some type that happened in a trailer in Yucaipa. Unfortunately, that didn't narrow it down much.

The hearing began. Barry saw the parolee and still didn't recognize him. The parolee recognized Barry as the one who arrested him so that was good. Barry was handed his report and it was clearly of his making. But still, if they asked him to identify this guy, he couldn't do it.

Sometimes a little soap and water can make miraculous changes in one's appearance.

The hearing officer never asked him to identify the guy.

"Officer Truman, is that your report you are holding?"

"Yes, your honor, it is."

"Is that your signature on the report?"

Barry examined it. "Yes, your honor."

The Court made a finding and the guy was given another six months in prison. Barry never did remember him.

Newberry Springs Event

Billy Platt was released on parole following a term in State Prison for committing an armed robbery. Choosing to remain in the same line of work, he paid close attention to the rumor that an old guy and his blind son kept $20,000 in a safe on their property in Newberry Springs.

Newberry Springs is a small unincorporated community about thirty miles east of Barstow in the California desert. To truly appreciate the isolation, just imagine yourself on a wagon train like you see in an old western movie where the travelers either die of thirst or eat each other. The people who live in this area are tough, resilient individuals.

Anyway, Platt lived in Barstow but figured it would be easy to steal the safe from an old guy and a blind guy. Just in case someone unexpected was on the property, Billy coerced his buddy, Tommy Trujillo, to go with him. Besides, Tommy had a car.

Little did Edgar Thomas and his son, Larry, know that they would be visited on late Saturday afternoon by the twosome. But like so many properties in the desert, the Thomas property was large, flat and sparse. And as anyone in law enforcement knows, a bad guy or good guy can be seen coming from miles away.

Edgar could see Platt and his accomplice exiting their car by a prominent mesquite tree at the front perimeter of the property, about a quarter mile away from their trailers. He alerted his son to the fact that strangers were approaching and noted that one of them had a long trench coat on. This was curious as the outside temperature had only cooled to about 105 degrees. As Billy and Tommy approached, Edgar was able to more accurately assess that these two visitors meant trouble. He called 911 fully realizing that the nearest deputy was probably in Barstow.

In the next few minutes, Platt would learn that the rumor regarding the old man and his blind son was accurate. One can never tell about stories such as this as they are often shared among felons networking while using methamphetamine. Even without the methamphetamine, common criminals are generally not very truthful, reliable or for that matter, smart.

Tommy was not armed and his role was to overpower the blind guy in the trailer where the safe was located. Billy had a sawed-off shotgun under his trench coat and he would not allow the father to intervene, murdering him if he must.

While the information regarding the Thomas family was generally accurate, the total story did not unfold until Tommy tried to manhandle the son. Larry was in fact blind but the reason he was sightless was because of a wound suffered in Vietnam. He was a martial-arts instructor during his tour. When Tommy first yelled at him and pushed him, Larry quickly determined Tommy's location and the beating commenced. Tommy was beat up so thoroughly, he initially could only crawl out of the trailer and plop down onto the desert floor, moaning as he landed on a small cactus.

Billy realized something was wrong and pulled out his sawed-off shotgun. Then the father came out of another trailer with two .357 magnum revolvers, one in each hand. Edgar commenced firing both revolvers in the direction of Platt, who was far enough away to make his two shotgun blasts ineffective. Both perpetrators were utterly surprised and scared. Edgar never hit the perpetrators but the sound alternating between the blasts of each handgun was deafening, even in the middle of the desert. Billy and Tommy both ran off the property falling more than once and colliding with cactus along the way. They eventually jumped into a culvert, unable to get to their car. When the sheriff's deputies from Barstow arrived a mere twenty minutes later, both subjects were still in the culvert, trying to cover themselves up with dirt.

Barry did the investigation for the Probation Department and recommended commitments to State Prison for both subjects. Both of them were, in fact, sentenced to State Prison for several years.

Within a few weeks, the City of Barstow presented awards to the father and son for courage and bravery. Barry was pleased that the good guys won and that their efforts were recognized. And he couldn't help chuckle when he thought of those hardened criminals cowering in the ditch.

Kathleen Brown, Music Teacher

Investigators for the Probation Department periodically are assigned cases that have received significant media attention. These would generally be cases that were not typical or were particularly heinous. The vast quantity of referrals for probation reports are for drugs, theft or domestic violence. These types of cases might make the papers in Barry's Ohio hometown but in big, bad San Bernardino the circumstances would have to be more noteworthy, e.g., massive quantities of drugs, terrorist act, government embezzlement, a baby murdered by being thrown against a wall during a domestic dispute, etc.

The case that fell into Barry's lap was one he had already read about in the local newspaper. Thirty-six-year old Kathleen Brown walked into the lobby having been released on bail and Barry knew right away she was the high school music teacher that had been sexually victimizing a seventeen-year old student since he was fifteen. Of course, the male student didn't complain about being victimized until someone blew the whistle on the whole thing and his parents became involved. While they expressed shock and distress, it was believed that they knew the entire time.

Anyway, Kathleen was an attractive brunette who admitted her culpability. This was smart as she was recorded in numerous phone conversations delineating a great deal of sexual activity with the victim in several locations around the high school, especially in the music room.

Barry knew that it was always good to work closely with his supervisor on cases such as this as the narrative and recommendation were bound to end up plastered all over the newspaper. Mr. Botman was Barry's supervisor and he was often consulted about this case. Barry ultimately put together a very comprehensive report with a recommendation for five years of probation, registration as a sex offender, custody time on weekends and a term that Ms. Brown couldn't provide instruction for minors. No one, it seems, is ever happy with recommendations for these types of crimes. The victims are minors but some states don't even prosecute sex cases involving older juveniles, especially if the ages between the victim and offender are close. Ms. Brown was quite a bit older than the victim but she benefited in this instance due to the fact that she was a woman. In these types of crimes, many people seem to view convicted women differently than convicted men. It's just the way it is. Opinions vary a great deal as to punishment. Some individuals ultimately will feel that the sentence is too punitive and some will believe the person should be locked up in State Prison.

The Court agreed with Barry's recommendation and Kathleen did her weekends and reported to the officer who supervised her in the community. The media attention eventually diminished. Barry did not see her again until he got a surprise visit at his office, about six months after sentencing. She was happy and looked healthy, sporting elegant business attire. "May I speak with you?" she said to Barry. Barry brought her into his office and asked her what he could do for her.

"My attorney and my therapist tell me that I need to form relationships with age appropriate males. I'll tell you the truth - I just think younger males are like Greek gods, with their smooth-toned bodies. But, alas - I must change my ways."

Kathleen scooted up closer to Barry's desk and added in a soft tone, "Would you be interested in getting together?"

Keep in mind that all the time Kathleen was talking, Barry was remembering everything she did to and with that young man - the escapades that were so specifically described in the five-inch thick District Attorney's file. My Lord, there were few musical instruments not involved. John Phillip Sousa would have rolled over in his grave if he witnessed the way that his beloved sousaphone was used. And Kathleen had a fondness for the clarinet. As such, Barry was notably flustered and there were things happening out of view on his side of the desk. And he knew his face must be red.

Barry, who was thirty-one years old at the time, admitted that he was flattered but that he was prohibited from associating with probationers. Barry then noticed his own wedding band and added, "And, besides I'm married."

The image of pretty Michelle flashed in his mind and he felt guilty for something he hadn't done.

Kathleen then asked, "I can see your ring and I understand your rules but what if I had my case transferred to Los Angeles County?"

Barry was cordial in explaining that, unfortunately, he couldn't associate with her regardless of the county of jurisdiction and he was able to tactfully escort her from the office. She said that she would stay in touch.

Barry felt a little uneasy as he wasn't sure if he was such an ethical high character individual or if it was just a matter of knowing how indiscreet this lady really was. After all, the prosecutor had an easy time of securing a conviction as the detectives had her on tape for hours, detailing the sex acts that were committed to/with the victim.

Barry then hustled into Botman's office to disclose all to ensure that he not weaken and that he remain employed and married. Better to confer than confess, Barry thought.

Kathleen did not stay in touch. Word was that she obtained employment at a private school for young girls in Los Angeles County. This was apparently allowed. Barry always hoped she recovered and had a good life.

At first Barry didn't think he should tell Michelle about this very unique proposal but then he thought, he hadn't done anything wrong and, besides, it's an entertaining story.

By the time he got home, Michelle was already there and was drinking a beer with Tricia. They looked sheepish which led Barry to believe they were gossiping about someone.

"Who are you guys talking trash about?" Barry inquired. Whoever or whatever they were conversing about had nothing on his story. He shared the content of the meeting with Kathleen Brown. Tricia, who rarely minced words, exclaimed, "That slut!" and they all laughed and opened another beer.

There's Something About Barry

Actually, there is not. It is the nature of his job. Aside from Kathleen Brown's interests, which were pragmatic, ones of convenience and lust, there is something about the relationship between some probationers and their probation officers. Barry always thought it was similar to the effect that sometimes develops in the patient/therapist relationship.

Probationers or parolees sometimes become attached to their officers. They fall in love. After all, the probation officer may know quite a bit about their lives even down to intimate details. The PO has searched their homes, property and person and collected urine samples from them. They discussed dysfunctional relationships and possible abuse, sexual or otherwise. The PO listened to them. And there is one more dynamic which is not present in a traditional therapy scenario; the probation officer is undeniably in charge. Despite not consciously approving of this, some persons on probation or parole actually find this situation alluring. The probationer has to do whatever the PO says. *The PO is in charge of me.*

Barry came across this from time to time. The situation is very delicate and prone to cause problems. Being heterosexual, his interested parties were female probationers and informants. Barry would acknowledge the dynamics but set boundaries and take steps to protect himself and to prevent anything from getting out of hand.

But of course, some individuals would be obsessed or crazy or manipulative and Barry would utilize other methods. One twenty-two-year-old brunette that looked like Salma Hayek, moved to Big Bear from some northern county and was assigned to Barry. She may have been in love or just manipulative and trying to garner favor but her flirtatiousness spelled trouble, enough so that Barry wouldn't go to her residence without witnesses. Barry knew that becoming involved with felons in this manner was stupid for a lot of reasons including the fact you would lose your job. There were enough women to get involved with who were not on probation.

Any law enforcement officer working with informants has to navigate these same minefields of temptation. The officer has a tremendous amount of control over the informant as information is often being exchanged for the subject's freedom. The officer emphasizes that he or she will take precautions to protect the person's identity and often tells them to "be careful," which can be perceived as "caring." Add to this the fact the officer and informant are meeting, by necessity, alone and in secret. Perhaps they smoke a cigarette together in close quarters. An officer could be tempted particularly if an informant is infatuated with them or just very willing to engage in a sexual relationship. Similar to the situation with the parolee or probationer, the informant could try to garner favor and/or blackmail the officer.

Barry knew more than one male officer to succumb to pretty female informants. Some were demoted, suspended and others terminated. The whole mess would result in divorce for some. Barry wasn't sure if it was his good judgment that prevented him from getting caught up in "snitch sex" or the fact that, at least initially, all his female informants were another officer's discards and therefore, not very appealing. One officer in particular had all the attractive young ladies and Barry's certainly improved as time went by but he never crossed that all important line. He did wonder from time to time, how he would handle these situations if he were in his early twenties rather than in his thirties or forties.

But There Was Something About Les

Barry fully understood how an officer could succumb to the charms of an attractive probationer or informant. A friend of his, Les Brown, became sexually involved with a lovely creature who was on probation for check forgery. Following a search of her residence, her husband was taken into custody for possessing assault weapons. It was determined that she was aware of guns being in the house but her behavior was more stupid than it was criminal. As such, she was not arrested.

After her husband's arrest, she called Les back and asked him to come back to her house, on the pretense of making sure another firearm that was in their storage shed was not illegal. He stopped by and determined that the cap and ball firearm did not fall within the meaning of the Federal Firearms Act. Les suspected she wanted him to examine more than the firearm and they feverishly initiated a relationship that lasted almost until her husband was freed a year later.

Everything was fine until a warrant was issued by mistake for her arrest. These things happen in the humungous operation known as the criminal justice system. Anyway, in order to gain her freedom, she ratted on Les. After a brief investigation, he was fired. Wife, mortgage, three kids, a real mess.

Barry could understand the temptation. The woman was beautiful, athletic, sensual, really kind of misplaced in the world of street felons. Les later told Barry that he was totally consumed and obsessed by her and he absolutely could not help himself. But how could Les not have monitored her case to ensure no mistakes were made? Barry always felt bad for Les as he was one hell of a guy and, with giant exception, one hell of a PO.

Alfred Succumbed as Well

Alfred Melendez was an older probation officer that was in charge of what is called from time to time as a "banked" caseload. Thousands of cases sit neglected in file cabinets, cases representing probationers that have been determined to not really need supervision by anybody. The determination as to what cases get sent there changes every few years depending on politics and whatever lame rating system is being used. As much as the powers that be would like to convince the public or their bosses that there is some science involved in making these determinations, the fact is that it doesn't really matter. The decisions are usually made by some career bureaucrat attempting to show how he or she has created a system that will protect the community.

The officers that work with cases such as this respond to requests from all areas of the criminal justice system including various different law enforcement agencies, the court, probationers, victims, personnel from State Prison, the jail, from Interstate Compact authorities and every other possible entity. The fact that someone in charge has determined that these cases will not be serviced, really only prevents the officers from initiating an action. It doesn't stop the myriad outside requests or prevent these people from being arrested.

As such, it is a really bad assignment to work. There is no possible way to keep up with the work so the stress is overwhelming. Morale is about as low as anywhere in the system and Alfred Melendez had an additional stressor. He worked for Carl Becker.

Whether that had anything to do with what happened at the end of his career is up for speculation. Alfred was very much in love with a man from Rialto. Unfortunately, this individual was a felon on parole. Barry never knew how or why Alfred crossed the clear-cut line where fraternizing with criminals is not only unethical but will likely result in termination. The relationship did not come to the attention of the agency until Alfred and his lover were contacted by patrol units. They were in a parked vehicle right in front of a Bank of America ATM during the late-night hours. This suspicious activity will always draw attention.

Officers questioned the twosome and realized quickly that the driver was on parole. The officer conducted a search and found a small amount of cocaine concealed in a flashlight. On behalf of his lover, Alfred objected to this and, at some point identified himself as a probation officer, showing his badge. He tried to convince the patrol officers that he was working and supervising the driver. In light of the presence of drugs and other questionable circumstances, his explanation was discarded, but he wasn't arrested. His parolee partner, however, went directly to jail.

Alfred's problems commenced upon the word of the incident getting to agency authorities. As he was clearly of retirement age, he was given the option to retire. Had he been younger, he would have been fired. Barry always liked Alfred but, again, it was hard to figure why he would make such a poor decision.

Just Call Me Jay

Jay Fredericks was a Parole Agent assigned to a unit in the San Bernardino desert area. He had a good reputation and actually lived in the same area where he worked, something not that common in the industry today. When on his own time, Jay enjoyed associating with young ladies and he used to laugh that, in the desert communities, a fellow needed two women to get a full set of teeth. There were apparently exceptions.

Jay met a young lady at Pappy and Harriet's, a tavern and restaurant in the rural community of Pioneertown, on the outskirts of Yucca Valley. This establishment is not into frills but the beer is cold and the food is good. Just ask Paul McCartney, who made a surprise appearance in 2016.

Jay and Heidi each had burgers and Jay sprung for the check. They hit it off and ended up at Heidi's house in Yucca Valley. Jay later said that she smelled so nice and had an alluring softness as long as she was quiet. Sex with her was incredible but he panicked afterwards when she asked him for his last name. He had just ended a long-term relationship and really wasn't ready to commence another one. Besides, she had an annoying cartoon character voice that could only be tolerated for a short period of time and with a lot of alcohol. It was her only known derogatory characteristic but it was a deal breaker for Jay.

"Jay Wilson," came out of Jay's mouth. After all, it was still his first name. He just borrowed his Parole Administrator's last name. It was a harmless little white lie. He told her he had to get up early for work and he would contact her. Except that they never exchanged numbers. Her failure to do so was unintentional. They kissed and parted.

As the next day unfolded, Heidi was daydreaming about the night before but realizing that Jay would not be able to call her without her digits. He had been to her house but it was dark and they had been drinking and *What if he can't remember where I live?*

Not knowing how resourceful Jay would be in locating her, she called the nearby state parole office asking for Jay Wilson. It took another number and a couple call transfers to connect her with Jay Wilson.

"This is Jay Wilson. May I help you?"

"Hi there. Remember me? Heidi?"

Barry always thought it was funny how some people can distinguish voices quite well and others don't have that ear. Heidi was of the latter group. She believed she was talking to the Jay that had rocked her world.

"Refresh my memory," Wilson asked so as not to be embarrassed by not recognizing someone he ought to know.

"Okay, I know you haven't forgotten that quickly, especially considering the things you did to me," Heidi responded in a sultry voice. "You left me like a rag doll."

Wilson was at a loss for words.

She continued, "I don't ever remember going four times and then having a man finish me off with-"

Wilson interrupted her. "Excuse me ma'am but I think you have made a mistake."

Once Heidi realized that her missing lover had given her a phony name, she was upset and more than happy to help identify him.

Jay Wilson, a very religious man, was upset that some underling would use his name in such a way and felt that a crime had been committed. Heidi went on with her life, licking her wounds.

Administrator Wilson used his status to prod the sheriff's department to investigate the incident. The inquiry didn't get very far but the entire matter was a great source of comedy in the Yucca Valley station. Barry was working closely with the detectives that investigated the "crime" and was able to get all the information firsthand.

The Parole Administrator had telephoned the investigator and insisted that Jay Fredericks be arrested for impersonating a peace officer. The investigator told Mr. Wilson "he IS a peace officer." Wilson argued unsuccessfully for an arrest to be made for something.

The investigator later told Barry that the only thing Frederick's boss should be upset about is the fact "he didn't get any."

Jay was suspended for thirty days. Barry always felt that the whole event was worth a good chewing out and nothing more.

These things end up in the rumor mill and this story was so compelling that a song was actually written about it. Barry didn't recall the tune but the lyrics went as follows:

She called just to tell me she loved me,
But I knew that was probably a lie,
And I'm sorry to say, that I'm the wrong Jay,
Can't get her out of my mind,
Can't get her out of my mind.

One More Temptation

When Steve Mortsoob was a probation investigator, he was interviewing a known associate of the Hell's Angel Motorcycle gang. There is really little difference between "members," "affilliates" or "associates" of a gang as they all will respond the same way in protecting the gangs' interests.

Mike Barro was both a mechanic and an attorney and he was at the beck and call of the Angels with both of these skills. Barry would later become very familiar with this individual.

As often is the case, Steve's task was to check into the crime, the defendant's criminal history and other factors and recommend to the Court what penalty should be imposed. Penalties for felonies range from being released on probation with up to a year in jail to a longer stint in State Prison.

Mr. Barro was out on bail so he was interviewed in Mortsoob's office. Noting that Steve had a coffee table type of book featuring classic mustangs, he inquired, "I notice your book. Are you a Mustang fan?"

"Why yes I am. I like classic cars in general but I really like old, fast Mustangs."

"Oh wow, yeah, after my Harley's, Mustangs are my favorite," Barro commented.

Steve brought the discussion back to the crime and, about fifteen minutes later he asked Barro the standard closing question, "So what do you think the Court should order at sentencing?"

"Mr. Mortsoob, quite frankly I'm hoping that you will give me a favorable recommendation. I've learned my lesson. As a matter of fact, if I don't spend too much time in custody, I can see a 69 GT350 or perhaps a 428 Super Cobra Jet in your future."

Steve Mortsoob, an experienced and knowledgeable investigator, was not tempted. Not only was it just wrong, but he knew that gesture would just be the start. That's how the Hells Angels do business. They have people in many different law enforcement agencies at many different levels that are beholden to them. Sometimes it merely takes a love connection or relationship to buy a dispatcher or records clerk and sometimes a little blackmail works wonders.

"Thanks for coming in Mr. Barro. Don't forget to appear in Court for sentencing.

This Bud's for You

Barry and several other probation officers were standing around laughing about things. After all, despite the danger and pressures that officers face, there are a lot of funny stories to share. They were congregating on the fourth floor right by a large exterior window with a view to the street.

Barry noticed a Nissan pickup come to a stop followed by its driver exiting the vehicle. The skinny young driver then threw what appeared to be an empty can of Budweiser Light in the bed of the truck. Barry didn't think a whole lot about it until he saw the same guy in the probation department waiting room. Since Barry was "officer of the day" or "OD" he approached the individual and asked if he could be helped.

The guy said the judge had sent him over from Court to get approval to leave the state. Through follow-up questions, Barry was able to ascertain that this person was only on probation to the court and the probation department had no authority to do much of anything with him. The probation department does attempt to assist the court whenever possible and in this particular case, intervention was prudent in that this guy had what is professionally referred to as a "piss poor" attitude. He was not intoxicated but he had the audacity to have at least one beer between the court and the probation department, a distance of one-tenth of a mile.

This individual had been ordered by the Court to seek anger management counseling when he arrived in Illinois. Barry instructed him to follow through with that and to enroll and complete alcohol counseling. He was to send proof to the Court within six months or a warrant of arrest would be requested.

He was livid and demanded an explanation for having to attend alcohol counseling. Barry explained, "because you sir, have alcohol in your system at this very moment." The kid denied having consumed any alcohol. Barry continued as he moved closer, "Yes, you have been drinking beer - Budweiser beer!"

Anger turned to amazement for this young lad. His objections diminished. Then Barry finished him off, making motions with his nose as if he was smelling limburger cheese. "In fact," said Barry, "I'm positive it is Bud Light!"

The stunned probationer then asked for the address to send his proof of completion, thanked Barry and went down the elevator. These were the things that were not cataloged in the procedure manual but they just seemed like the right thing to do. And, of course, they are always entertaining to share.

Ashes to Ashes

By and large, Barry was a careful officer but, of course, boredom sometimes sets in and mistakes are made. Prior to searching a residence in the Verdugo Flats gang area of San Bernardino, Barry and his fellow officers conducted a protective sweep of the premises. This is a routine maneuver that involves officers going room to room to determine if any subjects are present, particularly for subjects that could threaten officers. Once it is determined that the property is "clear" then everyone can relax a little while they continue their mission which is often searching for contraband.

After beginning to search a bedroom in this house, Barry could hear a woman in the living room exclaim, "Watch out for Rubio!" Hearing this, everyone escalated to high alert, thinking someone had been missed during the protective sweep. Guns were drawn and everyone focused on finding a hiding subject. Everyone calmed down after no one was located and officers watching the woman and others in the living room said that it was a misunderstanding.

Probably since Barry was so happy that he didn't get shot in the back, he got lax. He had rubber gloves on which is a very good idea but was breaking a cardinal rule, that being, "don't reach where you can't see." Following this rule is important for your safety, particularly to avoid injury from sharp objects such as syringes/needles.

Barry reached up on top of this tall dresser, opened the lid to a wooden box and felt around with his gloved hand. He retrieved his hand and found it to be covered with thick dust. He was perplexed but then realized to what the woman was referring. The side of the box was inscribed, "Rubio" and the dust wasn't dust. It was ash. Whoops.

Barry later realized that he was actually very familiar with that felon prior to him becoming ash. Rubio never seemed like the type of guy that would have minded if a little of his ash was lost.

Jeep Trips and A Ghost from the Past

Barry released some of his frustration with work by participating and organizing four-wheel drive trips in the California desert and mountains. Most of the informal members owned jeeps, including Barry, and they would take trips just for the challenge of the terrain or to try to locate long lost artifacts from George Patton's Desert Training Center. There were always rumors about bunkers full of tanks and weapons. There was even a story about a row of tanks that could occasionally be seen from the air but then the tanks would disappear in the shifting sands.

Several of the individuals who went on these trips worked with Barry so it provided an outlet even at work to sometimes talk about equipment or trip planning. Officer and four-wheeler Matt Drake actually visited the army archives in Washington, D.C. in order to more thoroughly investigate the deployment of military equipment in the California desert.

About half the time Barry was in Frank Botman's office there were serious discussions about current cases and capers. The other half of the time, the conversations were about suspension systems, traction devices and tires.

Barry, who drove a 1983 Jeep CJ-7, would sometimes be distracted when he would glance inside the rear of his rig and spot his winch line safety accessory, an item that reminded him of his first true love. She was Julie Joseph, a girl that followed him to Southern California from the state of Ohio. Julie may have grown up in Ohio but she looked more like she grew up in Orange County, California. Her light brown/blonde hair was long and straight with a soft luster. Her body was toned and ultra-feminine supported by long tanned legs. Her eyes were sensuous while at the same time, probing. She was smart and funny and, Lord knows why she followed Barry to the West Coast.

It was probably his fault, although he can't remember the details, that they split up after living together for a brief period of time. He was barely twenty and she was much more mature them him. He took this intelligent, beautiful woman for granted and lost her. She eventually married a fellow California schoolteacher and stayed out west.

Barry always remembered how cute she looked when she gave him an afghan for a present. Although Barry wasn't one to get cold, she wanted to make sure he had something to keep him warm. She cried as she presented it to him, explaining that it was the first time she had ever crocheted and she used the wrong yarn for the project. She used rug yarn, the kind of yarn that you use to make, well, rugs. Barry, who was puzzled, feigned excitement and thanked her and said it was a fine-looking gift. Then when Julie put it over his legs, he barely suppressed laughing out loud as the afghan was so heavy he could hardly get out from underneath it. It was as if two giant dogs were situated across his lap.

Barry lost Julie but he always had her gift, and it became very valuable on Jeep trips. Experts recommend that when using a winch, you throw a hefty tarp or heavy rubber mat or something of substance over the winch cable to protect you from getting cut in half in the event the line breaks. Julie's "afghan" was so heavy that it protected Barry and all his friends for years to come, and it was always a reminder of what could have been and therefore would cause Barry momentary regret.

There were lessons to be learned after losing Julie but Barry was always better about fine-tuning his craft than refining his relationships. Thank goodness for Michelle.

Assignment - Mountains

One of Barry's favorite assignments was working as the probation officer for adult division in the San Bernardino Mountains. This mountain range comprises over two thousand square miles of rugged terrain and includes San Gorgonio Mountain, the highest point in Southern California at 11,489 feet. Most of the population resides somewhere between 4500 and 7500 feet in elevation so snow is commonplace in the winter months. Barry was comfortable with the weather due to growing up by Lake Erie.

Barry supervised up to 100 adult probationers that lived primarily in the Big Bear and Lake Arrowhead areas. He worked closely with sheriff's personnel in both the Big Bear and Twin Peaks stations.

There are distinct advantages to working in these relatively small communities. Unlike many metropolitan areas "down the hill" in the valley, everyone in law enforcement and other government offices is "on the same page." Barry formed working relationships with deputies, detectives, code enforcement officers, constable's employees, court staff and so on. This is not only enjoyable but it makes everyone's job much more efficient and safe.

Big Bear on the "back-side" and Twin Peaks on the "front-side" of the San Bernardino National Forest reminded Barry of his small town in Ohio. There were seasons to enjoy or contend with and really friendly people. Many people who resided in the mountains worked down in the valley so they missed the sunny beautiful weather during the day and arrived home just in time to be cold. The locals told Barry his job was perfect - he lived in the valley but spent his days in the mountains. While the inversion layer over the San Bernardino valley blocked the sun light and trapped in all the smog and allergens, breaking through it to see the blue sky above and smell the fresh air was a wonderful thing.

Most of Barry's coworkers in the valley, where his agency was based, really didn't understand much about the mountains. When it was a cool, overcast, miserable day in the valley, it was assumed that the weather in the mountains was even worse. Barry would not dispel this notion and he would chuckle as his four-wheel drive GMC broke through the layer of crud to a beautiful day. After all, as long as no one wanted Barry's job, he most likely would not be moved to a new assignment. He was able to work in the mountains for ten years.

Setting Precedent

Early on in Barry's assignment in the mountains, a twenty-seven-year-old sex offender by the first name of Danny came into the Twin Peaks Sheriff's Office for an initial probation appointment prior to a stint in jail. After reviewing his file, Barry was surprised that this guy wasn't in State Prison. He had committed sex acts against not one, but three twelve-year-old girls. One was a niece and the other two were friends. The incidents happened at two different times and places. There were obviously problems in getting appropriate convictions in court so Danny pled guilty to a lesser felony and was granted probation with one year in local custody.

After being oriented as to his probation grant and the requirements to be met, Danny left the office, never to return. Barry did a little checking around and determined there was a good chance he was at a trailer park down in the valley in Highland. Barry assembled a team and attempted to locate him at the park but it took too long to figure out which trailer to search. It was learned after the fact that Danny had seen the team from the far end of the trailer park and had plenty of time to make his escape. Danny now knew for sure that Truman was actively looking for him.

Barry attempted to find him in other locations in the community but was unsuccessful. He did, however, speak to an informant who advised that Danny left the state of California to live near family in some town in Tennessee.

In these early years, accessing the Internet was not accomplished by interacting with a graphical user interface, the way most of us navigate online today. Fortunately, Barry was an early adopter of computer hardware and software and knew the appropriate arcane commands to search the country for concentrations of residences occupied by families with the same surname as Danny. This would not work if his surname was a very common one. Fortunately, it was not. Barry determined that residents with his unique surname were amassed around a very small community in Tennessee.

Taking "a stab in the dark," Barry made a couple calls to determine agency jurisdiction for the community in question. He then crossed his fingers and called the sheriff for the area in question. Now a couple things can go wrong here. First, the information could just be bad and Danny would be somewhere else or these people, surnames and all, were not his people. Second, in small communities, many people know one another so this could help you or hurt you. Perhaps the sheriff is a good friend of Danny or his family and not realizing the scope of his conduct, might alert him.

In this instance, Barry lucked out. Sheriff Wakeman knew who Danny was and that he had recently arrived from California and moved in with a cousin. After Barry explained that Danny was a sex offender with multiple victims and that he was a fugitive who, if brought back to California, would be sentenced to State Prison, the sheriff became very interested. Contacting unfamiliar persons on the phone, regardless of the fact they are peace officers is always a "crap shoot." But it was obvious that Sheriff Wakeman knew what he was doing and was bright and motivated.

"We have no use for that sort of person around here!" Wakeman pronounced.

Barry said that he would fax all the necessary information including all the terms and conditions of probation as well as a request to act as the Probation Officer's agent and search any property under Danny's control. He assisted the sheriff in locating the multi-state warrant "on the system."

"Good luck and please let me know how it goes and if you get him in custody."

Barry got a call early the next morning from Sheriff Wakeman. "We got him!" he said proudly.

"All right! Did he run?"

The picture was clearly drawn for Barry by Sheriff Wakeman. It was obvious some things work a little differently in small jurisdictions. In

San Bernardino County, officers would organize an arrest team but nothing as elaborate as in making preparation for arresting murderers or terrorists or rapists or other even more dangerous people. But this was a very big deal in this small Tennessee town.

"Nah - we had the house surrounded with officers from my agency, the police department and the FBI. We put the helicopter up just in case, but he put his hands over his head and walked out the front door after the situation was explained to him over the bullhorn."

Barry couldn't help but be thoroughly entertained by this.

Danny was extradited back to California and sentenced to State Prison. Barry could never have imagined how that one case would save him a lot of grief with the other felons he supervised in the mountains. A burglar from Blue Jay, a small community close to Lake Arrowhead, told him that word got around about Danny and everyone now knew not to run on PO Truman. That was an unintended consequence of the entire escapade but Barry would take it.

Big Bear Cavern Case

Probationers have to be employed or be seriously looking for a job. Tom Banks was on probation for a drug offense. In a routine interview, he stated that he working "under the table" for an eccentric guy that owned a property in a desolate area near Baldwin Lake outside of Big Bear. He stated that his employer, a strange fellow by the name of Peter Campbell had him doing all sorts of manual labor related to a series of commercial gas tanks he was using underground. These were gas tanks such as used at a BP or Shell station but they were not used for petroleum storage. Rather, they were interconnected in an underground labyrinth for unknown reasons, perhaps survivalist purposes, at least that is what Tom thought.

Tom said that one area underground had horse stables and another had a shooting range and armory. There was an abundant supply of automatic and military type weapons. One of the entrances went through an old western town facade. It was all quite incredible. Barry mentioned this to a couple detectives in the station and they indicated that, in fact, they had heard rumors that were consistent with the probationer's information. They knew the person that owned the property and said that he had plenty of money and would sometimes fly to Washington to lobby or testify on certain issues. Local deputies wanted to get inside and look for themselves but they did not have a legal right to poke around the property.

Conversely, Barry had an absolute legal right to attempt to visit his probationer at his place of employment to verify said employment. He had no contact information for the employer and it was his understanding that the employer did not know his employee Banks was on probation. Generally speaking, if someone is doing something illegal, they will not knowingly hire someone being supervised on probation due to the waiver of the "search and seizure" clause for that individual. For a criminal, that's like stabbing yourself in the stomach.

At some point, Barry drove onto Campbell's property with a station deputy by the name of Charlie in an effort to confirm Tom Bank's employment. The property consisted of several acres of pine forests on rocky uneven terrain. Fire roads crisscrossed the area. Barry went ahead and engaged the four-wheel drive in his rig as there were some pretty steep dirt roads and the ground was wet from recently melted snow. After driving for five minutes or so, there was a sharp curve at the top of a hill. The two officers noted a group of about ten metal tubes attached parallel to one another on a makeshift stand. There were wires leading down towards the ground from the back of each tube. The front cluster of the tubes was directly pointed toward the lower front of Barry's GMC. Barry and the deputy were startled, not knowing for sure what the hell was pointed at them. Barry accelerated over the crest of the hill and made the sharp right turn.

While this device looked threatening, nothing happened and they continued on. They saw the western town facade and stopped. At this point Barry and Charlie yelled loudly for anyone to respond as the intent was to contact the owner or the probationer. No one responded and the door to the general store was locked. They joked that Wyatt Earp was probably close by. The twosome wandered around the wooded property calling out for some kind of acknowledgement. They came across an opening leading into the side of a hill. It was not a natural cave; rather the eight- foot opening was all metal and its appearance was that of the opening to a mine shaft. Charlie and Barry walked into the "cave" still calling out for anyone to respond. Nothing could be heard and now their vocal efforts were bouncing off the hard acoustics of the shaft. Natural light had completely disappeared but there were occasional light bulbs illuminated and hanging from the top of the shaft. They checked to make sure their own flashlights worked. It seems like you need your light when you least expect it and often during daytime hours.

There are times when things do not feel right. It's like the subconscious picks up a threat that the conscious mind can't process. Maybe it's a magnetic thing or another dimension thing. Who knows.

The fact is that the feeling that something isn't right exists for every peace officer at certain times. In this case, both Charlie and Barry drew their guns but continued to walk in.

Maybe two hundred feet into the shaft, Barry and Charlie came upon two closed eight-foot high stout metal doors leading in opposite directions. Another illuminated bulb hung between the two. There was too much to go wrong here. Barry and Charlie looked at each other as if to say, "Let's get the hell out of here."

They drove off the property after never contacting anyone with the idea that a return visit was needed with far more firepower than what their two Glock handguns provided.

Debriefing with the station detectives, it was recommended that Barry contact the bomb squad concerning the tube device. He quickly learned from the bomb experts that what they had seen guarding the property was what the California Penal Code called a "launching device." An explosive charge with a projectile would be placed in each of the tubes and ignited by the electrical arc caused by spark plugs. The spark plugs were energized by an electric current sent through the wires that were hanging at the base of all the tubes. What was clear was that Barry definitely had enough information to secure a search warrant for the premises. He had a lawful right to visit the property and both he and the deputy saw the device which represented the commission of a felony. And, of course, this type of device was consistent with the information about assault rifles and an underground armory. Lastly, one of the two individuals providing the information was Barry's felon probationer that was employed there. A few details such as property description and other standard information for an affidavit were all that was needed to secure a search warrant within a few hours.

But Barry didn't know how to write a search warrant. He spent his time searching probationers that had already waived their fourth amendment rights. Just a few years later, as a narcotics officer, he would be writing and serving many of them. But that was then and this was now. He approached the two station detectives who acted excited after they heard the information from the bomb squad. It would only be a matter of time until they secured a warrant to search the entire property. Barry imagined that Alcohol, Tobacco and Firearms (ATF),

SWAT, the Sheriff's Bomb Squad and a host of other agencies would be needed for the serving of the warrant.

Except, nothing ever happened. The station detectives were not giddy anymore. Someone from above had obviously shut it down. Barry could never get an explanation from anyone in the station. In discussing the case with Frank Botman, the only thing they could surmise was that no one wanted another Waco.[5] It did not end well. Or, more likely, there were intelligence agencies involved in one way or another. Either way, Barry didn't dwell on it. He had experienced similar things before and discovered that sometimes it is wise to stop asking questions. But it sure would have been fun.

---

[5] The Waco, Texas siege took place at a compound belonging to the Branch Davidian's carried out by state and federal officers in early 1993.

Catch Me If You Can [6]

When Barry's area of supervision was in the San Bernardino Mountains, he often went to court to represent his own cases and others for the agency. It was a small mountain court in Big Bear and Barry worked closely in front of the judge in the company of the deputy district attorney and defense attorney. Being so intimate, the somewhat informal proceedings were efficient and often fun. One of the more personable local attorneys who would often be appointed by the court to represent the multitude of law violators was Dan Lambert. He was skilled in plea negotiations, getting the least amount of time in custody for his clients. He was well-liked in the community and he socialized with other members of the criminal justice system in Big Bear.

As such, it was a big surprise when one Tuesday morning, Barry was assigned a new felony case under the name of Dan Lambert. Despite the fact Mr. Lambert was still appearing in court, representing local criminals, he did not possess a law degree. He had been convicted accordingly, receiving jail time on weekends. He was released on probation at which time he continued working as an attorney in the mountain court during the week. Sometimes the bureaucracy is a little slow on the uptake.

From the moment Barry received the case, calls came in regarding Mr. Lambert's involvement in various types of fraud, a pyramid scheme and a multi-million-dollar investment scam. Dan Lambert was a conman.

---

[6] 2002 American crime film based on the life of conman Frank Abagnale.

Dan was still conning the citizens of Big Bear during his first few weeks of probation supervision. He had everyone convinced that he was a bona fide attorney but there was a mix up about him not paying his bar dues. Keep in mind that he was also handling local non-criminal cases like wills and civil suits so, like any good conman, he needed to keep the game going for as long as possible.

Barry decided that it would be prudent to search Lambert's home and office. While that was being planned, an FBI agent by the name of Anne Phillips telephoned. She had worked a case on Mr. Lambert, alleging that he bilked over ten million dollars from investors in several states. The case commenced in federal court but the FBI was looking for additional information. Also, she held a federal warrant for Mr. Lambert. Upon hearing of our upcoming search, she made the determination to not intervene but to arrest Mr. Lambert after the fact. Ms. Phillips would, of course, be interested in anything that was located by officers related to their federal case.

FBI agents stayed on the perimeter while sheriff's deputies and probation officers contacted Mr. Lambert at his business in downtown Big Bear. Rather than escaping at all costs, he attempted to "slip away" around the building to his vehicle just like a conman. Barry quickly caught him before he was able to drive away.

"Barry! What are you doing here?"

"Mr. Lambert, I believe you know why I'm here."

"If it's about that my bar fees, that is just a bureaucratic snafu. That should be straightened out by tomorrow."

"Nice try Dan. We are going to search your business and these officers," motioning to the FBI agents, "have business with you as well."

"Oh," was all that Lambert could muster.

Mr. Lambert was arrested and carted away by FBI agents. As a side note, Anne Phillips was very nice, capable and also very attractive. When Barry would later testify in Los Angeles at a bail hearing, she installed her handgun under her dress when they left the building on an errand. It was the first time and last time Barry saw a thigh holster on the stockinged leg of a woman. She didn't reveal it as an exhibitionist act. It was accomplished in a very routine manner. Barry later commented that it was funny the things that you remember from your career.

During the search, full color brochures used to coerce investors in the multi-million-dollar scheme were discovered. Pictures of stars and well-known professional football players were on these handouts to give the impression they were investors as well.

Other documents including business cards and checks were found in Mr. Lambert's name making it clear that he wasn't just impersonating an attorney but also a Tax Law Consultant and a Certified Public Accountant and other types of investment positions. And it goes without saying that he was the president of the financial securities company that stole millions from people in various states.

It was not realized until later that a seized box of files included materials that the federal judge had earlier ordered Lambert to produce. Since he represented to the court that he didn't have any such materials, the federal judge was livid when he heard of the seizure. It's never wise to upset a federal judge.

The box was turned over to the feds without anyone noting that a small baggie containing cocaine was sandwiched between a couple documents. It was embarrassing to Barry and his team but really a small part of this very large-scale case. Anne mentioned it more from a humor standpoint than as a criticism. The find did suggest that the conman and/or his friends enjoyed cocaine at least in a recreational manner.

Other items seized included evidence of smaller scale fraud and misrepresentation. Sometimes an investigator needs to concentrate on the big picture to not get bogged down in minutia. Dan was in violation of his probation grant but his federal exposure (maximum years in custody) took precedent. Other than testifying in federal court to ensure Mr. Lambert wasn't released on bail, Barry never saw him again. He was sentenced to federal prison for a number of years. His local time ran concurrent to that commitment.

Finally, due to the fact that Lambert, a non-attorney, represented hundreds of criminals in state court, each defendant had to be given the option of returning to court with a real attorney. Keep in mind that some of these individuals had received sentences to jail and prison while being represented by a conman. Very few defendants requested new proceedings. The vast majority accepted their guilty pleas and sentences negotiated by Dan Lambert, phony attorney at law. He might not have been official, but Barry and other court officers were impressed by his skill.

Catch Me If You Can Two

It's not often that a prisoner escapes twice in the same day but that's exactly what happened. A simple transport to jail of one Martin Brown turned into an all-day affair. Martin was a giant of a man. He was six-foot four and 245 pounds of muscle. He looked like he was just released from prison displaying the results of pumping iron as opposed to a subject out for six months with enough time to let their muscles atrophy. His criminal history consisted mostly of violent acts.

A mistake started the entire incident as the transport driver didn't activate the rear door lock. The vehicle did not have a cage and Barry was sitting by him in the rear seat. Martin merely unlocked his belt, opened the door and he was in the wind. Actually, more accurately, he disappeared into a housing project in the tenderloin district of San Bernardino, known as Waterman Gardens.

Numerous probation and police officers joined in the door to door search in the projects. Clothing remnants were found suggesting that he had changed his look. As everyone was about to give up, he was located in a giant dumpster. He refused to come out of the container so one officer deployed his pepper spray. It ricocheted off of Martin's forehead and sprayed directly in Barry's face.

Barry yelled, "That was me!" He disengaged and somebody found a hose and proceeded to decontaminate him.

At the same time, Martin was hosed down with subsequent sprays causing the dumpster to fill up with a mist that partially contaminated everyone nearby.

Martin was taken into custody but this time he was secured in the rear of a cage car. Barry drove an escort vehicle just in case. The prisoner was decontaminated using a garden hose at a Taco Tia and everyone proceeded to the West Valley Detention Center.

Following the two officers and Martin westbound on Interstate 10, Barry noticed the transport vehicle appeared to be moving back and forth in the lane, more severe than when a driver is texting or intoxicated. Barry inquired on the radio but he couldn't understand the return transmission. He would later learn that Martin was kicking the inside of the left rear door, causing the vehicle to swerve. The vehicle slowed as they exited at Etiwanda, the off ramp for the jail. Just then, the left rear door flew open and Martin exited. His legs were just so powerful he was able to defeat the lock on the car door by bending the door out.

Barry parked on the dirt and observed Martin run across the freeway between speeding cars. Barry only briefly entertained the idea of running across five lanes of 80 mile per hour dense traffic. It's one thing to see this in a movie but something totally different to consider in real life. That being said, escapees are desperate enough to undertake such things.

Barry found another way across the freeway that didn't kill him but slowed him down. Heading southbound, he could see Martin about a tenth of a mile ahead of him. Martin and Barry were running over chaparral towards an industrial area. Barry never realized there was such desolate territory right off the freeway. Both Barry and Martin were exhausted and at some point, they stopped to rest, eye-balling each other from afar. They continued on over a railroad track and Martin disappeared in an industrial supply area. Barry radioed that he had lost visual contact of the subject. Officers were converging from several agencies and Barry heard "Forty King" was in the air and en route. Just then, he saw Martin jump on a slow-moving train, heading east. For some inexplicable reason, he jumped back off and again disappeared between piles of supplies and trucks and forklifts. In retrospect, Martin would have been better off continuing to ride the rails.

Barry advised that he had again lost visual. He could hear the helicopter up above. He reevaluated the situation and scanned the entire area while he caught his breath. It was at this time, he thought, just for a split second, that he noticed a shadow near an eighteen -

wheeler trailer in the adjacent supply yard. This was at least one hundred yards away. He disregarded it and advised that he had lost the subject. By that time, a perimeter was in place around the search area, perhaps a square mile.

There were no employees on any of these properties so there was no one to question. Having no other leads, Barry figured he might as well check out the truck trailer in the adjacent property, the trailer where he may have seen a shadow.

The rear was open and was illuminated enough so that Barry could see. He pulled his Glock.

"Martin! I know you're in here!" Barry lied. The trailer was filled with metal pipes and gear, just the kind of stuff to use on a probation officer's head.

"Martin! Come out of there! There are more cops outside than you have ever seen!" Barry hoped that was the case. He knew they were close but they may not have known what property or exactly which truck Barry was checking out.

All of a sudden, Martin stood up at the far front of the trailer. He was holding a three-foot-long steel pipe in his left hand. Barry was about ten feet from him, pointing his Glock directly at his chest.

"Put it down Martin!" Barry shouted. He continued, "Drop that fucking pipe!" Barry was fully prepared to shoot but he hoped that Martin would drop the pipe. Despite common perceptions, law enforcement officers have no interest in shooting people unless they have no choice.

The pipe made a loud reverberating sound when Martin dropped it to the floor of the trailer. Officers began appearing at the rear trailer entrance. Several more pulled weapons allowing Barry to re-holster and safely handcuff the guy.

"Code Four, one in custody," Barry radioed. With that, he could hear "Forty King" accelerate away to the next call.

Police cars were all over the place. Martin was hogtied and secured lengthwise with a "hobble"[7] in a CHP vehicle. This time, a sheriff's

---

[7] A hobble is a strap often made of nylon used to reduce the mobility of a prisoner.

patrol unit, a sheriff's captain and Barry escorted the man to the West Valley Detention Center. There would be no third escape.

There are lessons to be learned here, the most impactful being to trust your instincts. Barry wasn't positive about the shadow but fortunately he had enough time to check it out.

Cynicism is Fun

There is no way that an officer can deal with criminals for years without it affecting one's perceptions. Barry knew this and tried to keep it in perspective but recognized there would always be some negative impact. The most one could really do was to minimize the effect. He was fortunate that he had many interests outside of work, interests totally unrelated to law enforcement. He would use these interests to cleanse his mind and reflect. It helped that he kept in close contact with friends and relatives in small town Ohio, a world far away from the sorted, dark environment of the criminal communities of Southern California.

There were certain concepts/facts that tended to be part of an experienced officer's mindset. An example of this would be the concept that people tend to lie. Some would say you know when a criminal is lying when you see their lips move.

Officers are very suspicious when the same elements arise that have pointed to a particular crime or activity in the past. This isn't always correct, of course, but it is part of an officer's experience and difficult to dismiss offhand.

Barry was accused of being cynical by a good friend from Ohio that was visiting when Mortsoob and he offered their opinions on an entertainer at a pizza parlor. After all, here was a thirty-two-year old white male making balloon figures for children at a pizza joint. In conversing with the man, who was dressed as a clown, it was apparent that he was of average intelligence or above. He was a neatly dressed clown and he was very organized in his approach to making wiener dogs, elephants and other animals.

While Barry's Ohio friend probably thought it noble that this young man was volunteering or, at the best, getting paid a few bucks to entertain the pizza patrons, Barry and Mortsoob saw something entirely different and talked about it, somewhat in jest but with an underlying belief that they may be right in their assessment.

Steve commented, "I always like to see a young man thrive in the role he has chosen for himself."

"I'm just happy someone is working with the kids," added Barry.

Barry's friend noted the chuckles and remarked, "So you seriously think this guy is something other than a nice guy that makes balloons?"

"Oh, probably not," Mortsoob said. "But it is real hard for us not to put two and two together."

The known information about this balloon man coincided with sex offender profiles. He was white, educated, organized and putting himself in a position to interact with children. He seemed very employable so one might ask the question, "Why is he working for nothing or next to nothing when other jobs are available that don't require a clown suit?"

Barry and Steve had arrested subjects over the years that were dressed in various costumes including clown suits and Santa Claus outfits. Sex offenders use these props to get close to kids, to earn their trust prior to sexually victimizing them. This is part of "grooming."

While Mortsoob and Barry were very suspicious, they truly hoped they were wrong. They kidded about it as that's what people in the industry do. That's how they keep sane. Steve and Barry had seen so many victims affected for the rest of their lives by sex offenders. Their acts are devastating to little boys and little girls and to their families, both in existence and yet to come.

One week later Barry read an article in the newspaper about a young white male being arrested in Riverside for molesting a seven-year-old boy. His job was to dress as a clown and make balloons at a restaurant. It was not the same guy but the circumstances were eerily similar. Barry almost sent the article to his friend but then realized that no one that is outside the business would truly appreciate the law enforcement mindset.

Good for Mortsoob

Steve had always talked about changing agencies. The sheriff's department paid more money than the probation department and the retirement was vastly superior. Plus, by being a deputy, his role would be more straightforward. As a probation officer, he might be assigned to the juvenile division or one of many other jobs, some of them not very appealing. With the sheriff's department, after he put in his time at the jail, he would work on the streets as a deputy doing what he liked best, that being investigating crime and arresting criminals. So, he followed through.

He was at the stage of the process where he needed to successfully complete the academy. He knew this was coming so he began running and working out. He even ceased smoking at least for the near future.

Barry mostly spoke with him on the phone for a few months as Mortsoob decided to forego Judicial Review Board. Weekday mornings he "flew dawn patrol" as he liked to say, so he needed to get to sleep. He rationed his beers to just a few at home while in the academy.

"I'm going to graduate!" said Steve on the phone.

"That's great! Jail?"

"Yep - starting in eight days." The jail is where every deputy begins.

"Well then we have time for a little celebration my friend." Barry was really happy as Steve would get so frustrated with the department. He would get irritated when they were more concerned with window dressing than doing something tangible to protect the community. He was always incensed about special programs that wasted resources that could be used in the community augmenting public safety.

Steve agreed to a send-off at the current site for JRB, Morgan's in Redlands. Morgan's is an old family tavern owned and operated for many years by Jimmy Kelly. He had taverns in his blood as his father ran an Irish pub in New York City.

Morgan's used to be a cowboy bar with granular borax soap in the men's room but, over the years, it transformed to a somewhat trendy environment. Sometimes Barry felt there was too much trendy and too little borax. One thing that never changed was the offering of outstanding one dollar tacos on Tuesdays. Also, the two bartenders that served the JRB attendees were excellent, friendly and could make a substantial drink. Barry gave them a heads up that there may be a few more guests than usual for Steve's send-off.

Steve, Earl and Barry got there early, sitting beside Big John, a stalwart supporter of JRB. He had just retired from the probation department. Earl was the first to toast Mortsoob. "I think we need to sing a hymn," and in unison they chanted, "hymn, hymn, fuck him!" Everyone laughed and prepared to be appropriate for the additional well-wishers that were about to walk in.

Barry took Steve aside and commented, "It's not going to be the same out there, big guy. But you know I wish you well."

Steve nodded and ordered another round of drinks. The evening went well. It was emotional at times but thoroughly fun.

Victim Impact

Barry came in contact with many victims of crimes over the years as a probation investigator and an investigator of new crimes. Their stories are often sad but sometimes inspiring. Here are a few memorable ones.

Sorrow Beyond Description

There's nothing worse than hearing a parent express their feelings over the loss of a child. Barry could never get this particular experience at a family residence in Fontana out of his head. It was a mom and dad showing Barry their deceased daughter's bedroom, recently altered somewhat to convert it into a memorial.

The seventeen-year old girl was posing in her cheerleader outfit in a sixteen by twenty matted and framed photograph on the wall, the way she looked before being mowed down by a drunk driver. There were other smaller pictures of her as well and many things displayed as she left them - a hairbrush, things girls put in their hair, a blouse hanging on one of those standup mirrors.

Her parents spoke in soft, weeping tones and, other than those sounds, the residence was void of noise. Barry didn't say much and was cautious when he did speak, trying to make benign comments of sympathy.

When he left the house, he was exhausted, feeling bad and fortunate and distressed, all at once.

A Strike for Justice

Normally, the attempted rape of a senior citizen would make anyone upset or angry. This one was a little different. Edith Montgomery was eighty-four years old and anxious to tell Barry the story. While he was verbally walking on eggshells, Edith was very animated and talking about the crime in a matter of fact tone.

James Flynn was a Canadian citizen who decided to crawl through Edith's San Bernardino bedroom window at around dusk. It is not clear if he saw Edith or if he just wanted to rape someone or if he was a thief taking advantage of the situation. Doesn't matter. He got on top of Edith and ripped her nightgown down the front.

Edith explained that he was moving about over her with his pants down and he maneuvered such that his penis was close to her face, "and I saw his tail hanging down so I craned my neck and latched on to it with my teeth and bit it as hard as I could!" Then she laughed. She told Barry, "He didn't know who he was messing with!"

The original call for service to the San Bernardino Police Department came in as a man in a front yard on Lugo Avenue bleeding profusely. Barry always thought they should have given this lady a medal.

Measures

Pamela Doe was thirty-two, pretty and a victim of a brutal rape. The perpetrator was waiting for her in her Loma Linda home when she came back from a dinner with friends. Barry met her at that same house to get her statement for the rapist's sentencing hearing.

Some of the things that are considered by the court in sentencing are the measures taken by victims subsequent to the commission of the crimes. How has their life been changed? These measures tend to emphasize the impact of the crime. These could be something like the installation of security alarms or something simple like a person never goes out alone at night. Many times, the specifics are generally only shared "off the record" as it would be irresponsible to give any information of this type to the perpetrator.

In this instance, Barry was parked when the victim arrived. She got out of her car and told Barry to wait a second. Two large Dobermans exited her jeep and she let them in her front door. She then introduced herself to Barry and said, "It will just be a minute or so until they check inside."

Sure enough, these well-trained dogs walked out the front door together, their job of checking the entire interior of the house for intruders completed. Barry remembered thinking how tragic, but how smart. Talk about impact.

Tragic but Could Have Been Worse

One of those close calls that elicit nightmares took place in the High Desert in Adelanto, California. Barry and Roberto were checking on a sex offender by the name of Ralph who had sexually assaulted a twelve–year-old girl. The visit was initially low key and Barry was mostly interested in the computers this individual was using. He suspected that they contained child pornography.

With the exception of rapists, sex offenders tend not to be violent and so Barry and Roberto had not yet done a "protective sweep" of the premises for their own safety. They were more concerned with him executing a rapid command to lock his hard drive or erase a folder.

In speaking with this subject, Barry noted him to be sweating on this cool evening. His voice was quivering. "Why are you so nervous?" Barry asked.

"I'm not nervous," he said, nervously.

"Berto, there's something going on there," Barry said intensely.

Barry and Roberto had conducted many searches together so they picked up on each other's state of alert. They quickly put the sex offender face down on the floor and handcuffed him.

"You can't do this!" Ralph complained.

Roberto told him in a very focused tone, "Shut the fuck up and don't move until I tell you to." Roberto was attempting to get quick compliance so that he and Barry could see what Ralph was worried about and see if it was something jeopardizing their safety. Obscenities and voice tone are so important in times like these.

Guns drawn, Barry led the way and they slowly and methodically went from room to room occasionally peering around doorways to make sure Ralph had stayed put. This was not a huge residence but there were many small rooms.

Barry pointed his Glock around the bathroom and then with his left hand pulled back the shower curtain that was over the bathtub. *A person!* Barry knew from his experience and training that the most dangerous people are those running or hiding and also that these decisions are split second ones. If he wasn't still holding his trigger finger out straight, a safety procedure called, "master grip," he may have shot an unarmed thirteen-year old girl. Barry also knew that if someone is truly a threat and you hesitate, you may very well end up dead.

"Jesus, who are you?" Barry asked in an exasperated and impatient tone. Roberto confirmed that it was the original victim that Ralph had assaulted. The girl was developmentally disabled and Ralph was apparently able to coax her back in his house and continue to sexually victimize her. When officers made a surprise visit, he put her in the bathtub and told her to be quiet.

Barry and Roberto then dialed it down and tried to comfort the girl as she was obviously scared and upset from the entire episode.

Needless to say, Ralph's cuffs were not removed and he was transported to jail, a precursor to a stay at State Prison.

Multiple Victims

One assignment Barry had for a couple years was interviewing convicted desert perpetrators that were in custody and preparing court reports with recommendations as to sentence. Talking with serious offenders every day at the jail was wearing on him. Listening to copious lies from murderers and rapists while smelling their jailhouse breath was getting old.

Barry would usually be methodical and organized in his questioning starting with getting general information for a document called a "face sheet." Doing things in a consistent order is always a good idea in that this serves an officer well if testimony is being given at a later time regarding a specific interview.

On this day Barry was bored and wanted to divert from his normal order. So, when Vernon Blott, a convicted murderer, sat down on the other side of the jail grill, Barry made sure he was speaking with the correct person, introduced himself and then asked, "So why did you kill him?"

Despite the fact Vernon was found guilty, Barry fully expected him to deny the crime or, at the very least, come up with a convincing reason why he accidentally carried it out.

Instead, Vernon said in a steady voice, "He ate my dog."

This surprised Barry but, after a pause, he questioned Vernon more about this and also consulted the sheriff's reports for more detailed information.

Sure enough, there was a high likelihood that the "victim" DID eat Vernon's dog. Many dogs were disappearing in a desert area called the Wonder Valley near Twentynine Palms. Many of the local residents had suspected Vernon's neighbor as the one who would kill loose dogs and eat them. He admitted as much to one of the neighbors who made an earlier report to the sheriff.

One could say that the "official victim" ate the wrong person's dog. Not that he deserved to be murdered but one could surmise that there were really three "victims" in this case.

Angry Beyond Words

The downtown streets of San Bernardino in the 1930s were adorned with cute little houses rather than the government buildings and blight of the twenty-first century. A few of these little residences remained in the high crime areas still occupied by their original owners.

Harriet Kennedy, age 90, was one of these residents along with her like-aged neighbor, Nyda Thomas. The houses were similar to duplexes in that the outside wall on one side was shared or joined to the other. It was August and the temperature inside Harriet's place was way too high for comfort, even in the evening. As such, she opened her door, leaving the screen as the only barrier between her and the San Bernardino ghetto.

A twenty-two-year old male from a notorious family of crime in the city, noted the vulnerability while walking southbound on "D" Street. He pushed in the screen and, by the time he finished dispensing his evil for the night, Harriett had been raped and tied up, locked in a closet probably so the criminal could escape unscathed. It's amazing he left her alive. His criminal history was extensive and included numerous violent acts.

Barry interviewed Mrs. Kennedy in that same residence. It was still terribly hot and now humid and Barry asked if would be okay if the door was opened just while he was there. He felt a little sheepish asking considering that she now routinely was suffering all the time in that sealed up non-air-conditioned house.

"By all means. As long as you are here, we can get a little breeze."

The whole interview was depressing and Barry was glad when it was concluded. Mrs. Kennedy then asked in a sweet, pleading voice, "Could you possibly stay here for just a little bit?"

"I suppose so. What did you need?"

Harriet then explained that she had not been able to visit her long-time friend and neighbor, Nyda Thomas, for the longest time, since her son had visited from Duluth. If Barry was there, her neighbor could walk the twenty feet between their front doors and visit for a while. Ever since the rape, Nyda had been locked up tight in her house as well.

Barry had other obligations but he couldn't abandon this lady. "Sure, have her come over."

After a quick phone call, Nyda was in Harriet's living room in about three minutes. They talked and gossiped and laughed about the little things in their life for about one hour and fifteen minutes. Barry did as much paperwork as he could until he was honorably able to extricate himself from the role of bodyguard.

The whole episode was so heart wrenching and something Barry would never forget. He knew the legal limitations in the case but, personally, he wished the bad guy would fry.

Everyone Is Guilty

Barry learned early on that, as a probation investigator, his job was to recommend a sentence, not retry the case. Adult felons referred for reports are just that - felons. They have either pled guilty or been found guilty. Often, despite conviction, the felon will claim innocence to the investigator and explain that he just took the deal upon the advice of counsel. This is a trap for an inexperienced investigator. Barry was fortunate in that he had good supervisors like Botman to keep him on task. Occasionally there were individuals whose behavior probably didn't warrant a certain conviction but, throughout his entire career, Barry only received one case where he truly didn't believe the guy "did it." This was the matter of thirty-one-year old Julio Garcia. Mr. Garcia was out on bail when he kept his appointment with Barry at the probation department in San Bernardino. His wife and two children came as well. When it became apparent that Mr. Garcia did not speak a lick of English, his wife was allowed in the interview room to interpret. No one else was available. He was in the United States not as an immigrant or an illegal alien but as a competing boxer.

What initially stood out was the appearance of the whole family. Everyone was clean and groomed and dressed like it was Easter Sunday. The little boy who was probably six, was dressed in a suit and the girl, probably eight years old, wore a white fluffy dress with lace. Mr. Garcia's wife was about twenty-eight years old. She was very pretty with the coloring and frame of Natalie Wood.

Now these superficial things should not make an impact but the reality is, they present an inconsistency with the average person appearing for an interview. It's like they didn't read the felon's handbook for preparing for an interview. This book dictates that you don't shower, you wear the cleanest dirty shirt on the floor and you certainly don't come as a family.

Sometimes, when a man or particularly a woman, is in fear of being arrested at the probation office, he or she will show up with their kids, hoping that this will be a roadblock to their incarceration. Finding people to take care of kids or calling Children Services is a pain and felons know this. But that wasn't the case here. Mr. Garcia was out on bail. The most he could accomplish was to put his best foot forward.

Mr. Garcia was charged with Assault with a Deadly Weapon, an offense that allowed for incarceration in the State Prison. He had stabbed a person on the street for unknown reasons. He had no known prior offenses so the plea that was negotiated required supervised probation and a stay in the county jail of one year. Early in the interview Mr. Garcia claimed that he didn't fully understand the interpreter in court and that he did stab the individual but that it was in self-defense.

Mr. Garcia said he was walking with his wife and two kids between the boxing arena and their car when they were confronted by three Hispanic males. One of these men, the largest one with a mustache, held a knife in a threatening manner for unknown reasons. He was later identified as Jose Luna. He came towards Mr. Garcia. Mr. Garcia routinely carried a knife which he pulled out to protect his family. He stabbed Luna in the chest before he could do them any harm. While the wounded man laid in the street, the two other subjects fled on foot.

Mr. Garcia, legally in the country but not a US citizen, then became worried as he heard sirens and he shuffled his family back to their relative's home. The police were able to locate Mr. Garcia easily after the stabbed man claimed he was attacked without warning or provocation. Garcia was arrested and his knife was located and confiscated.

Using Mr. Garcia's wife to interpret, Barry informed them of the possible outcomes, one being incarceration in the State Prison. They were both adamant that Mr. Garcia's actions were in self-defense and that his guilty plea was not fully understood.

Mr. Garcia tried to calm his wife as she sobbed. The little girl was trying to console Mrs. Garcia as well. Even in light of the tension in the room, both children were remarkably well-mannered. Barry thanked them for coming and made sure they knew the correct time and date to attend court. They thanked Barry and left the building.

Barry knew that innocence was not something for him to be concerned with but he couldn't help but think that something was wrong with this case and a terrible injustice was about to be leveled. Barry discussed the matter with Mr. Botman and they agreed that Barry needed to dig for more facts.

First, Barry made sure he had all the information about the "victim's" criminal history as well as the perpetrator, Mr. Garcia. Inexplicably, no one had ever checked on Jose Luna or at least the information wasn't included in the District Attorney's file or the police reports. Barry discovered that he was a gang member from Pomona, California, visiting a couple thug relatives in San Bernardino. His criminal history included Robbery, drug offenses and, guess what -

Assault with a Deadly Weapon. He wasn't currently on parole but he was in prison three years earlier on that ADW.

Mr. Garcia's criminal record was checked with negative results and further checked through Interpol for any criminal activity in Mexico. Nothing was revealed but Barry knew that criminal record reports from other countries, particularly Mexico, were not always accurate.

Barry then read the police report with a fine-tooth comb. The items taken into evidence were listed at the end of the report and the knife taken from Mr. Garcia was Item #101. Other items included paperwork that had been dropped by Mr. Garcia on the street and a picture of the victim's stab wound. Then Barry noticed Item #108. It was another knife, a retractable type with a blade of about five inches. Entered by the item on the list was, "located by curb in street."

Barry was amazed. There was no mention of this in the narrative of the police report. This prompted a phone call to the arresting officer. He was on vacation and no one else knew anything of any importance about the case.

Barry and Mr. Botman spent several minutes discussing everything having to do with Mr. Garcia's court case. Here was a professional fighter taking his wife and two kids to find three adult males, all gang-bangers, so that he could stab one. It just didn't make any sense. The knife that was confiscated but not dealt with in the narrative of the police report seemed consistent with Mr. Garcia's claim that Mr. Luna had a knife. At the very least, someone had a knife other than Mr. Garcia and it probably wasn't his wife or two children.

It certainly is plausible that a non-English-speaking defendant could be nudged through the various processes in the courthouse without truly understanding the situation. It doesn't happen as often as criminals would lead one to believe, but it does happen. Mr. Garcia pled guilty and now he was stuck with it - or not.

Barry was required to submit a written recommendation based on the convicted offense but he chose another path. He called the deputy district attorney and presented all the information he had uncovered with the idea that, at the very least, Mr. Garcia might be able to withdraw his plea to ensure his constitutional rights weren't trampled on. Then Barry called the deputy public defender and provided the same information. Both agreed something was amiss and they communicated with each other, agreeing to deal with it on the court date. Barry did not write a report.

Barry's thoughts on the matter carried a lot of weight as he was not known as being a lightweight (or a "tree-hugger" as they call them in the industry) when it came to crime and punishment. So, it was as the district attorney commented, "If Truman thinks this guy is innocent, he's got to be innocent!"

Mr. Garcia appeared in court but he wasn't allowed to withdraw his plea. Rather, upon the recommendation of the District Attorney, his case was dismissed in its entirety. Barry was pleased.

Anderson's Inspiration

Barry often complained about a lack of resources when it came to operating incognito in the community. So much could be accomplished when officers didn't look like they were ready to invade Poland. There is definitely a place for full uniforms and gear and government looking vehicles but not when trying to be covert. Depending on the era, undercover vehicles were not always available in the probation department.

Bob Anderson was Barry's boss for a period of time and he agreed with Barry about the dearth of covert resources. Bob was also an inventive "out of the box" thinker. This came into play in trying to secure the arrest of Wanda Fredericks. Fredericks had an arrest warrant for possession of automatic weapons and she was believed to live in San Bernardino close to the government center. It was highly likely that she lived in a specific residence but there were not enough collaborative factors to justify forcible entry. Also, there was a substantial security screen in place over the front door. Wanda was not a big woman but she had a reputation for being violent, and, of course, she usually had guns.

This would have to be a finesse type entry, the kind Barry and his boss liked.

But how to do it? Barry's vehicle said government loud and clear. It was a plain white full-size, four-wheel drive Blazer with government license plates.

Anderson spoke up, "You have to use the resources you have to your advantage."

Barry responded in a smart-ass manner, "You mean we pretend to be cops?"

"No," Anderson explained, "our equipment really only says we are government - and everyone in government has different goals." He went on, "Maybe some government officials could be viewed in a positive light."

Barry was anxious for Anderson to get to the point.

Anderson said, "We can be earthquake inspectors."

Earthquakes were definitely on everyone's mind as a major one had shocked the southland a few days before and caused damage. But "earthquake inspectors?" Barry questioned.

The next day Barry and Anderson parked the big government Blazer right in front of Wanda's house. Another team was nearby just in case but it was just Barry and Anderson in sight and approaching the front door. Bob had a clipboard and Barry had a camera hanging from his neck.

Wanda actually responded to the knock and opened the inner door. She talked to Barry and Bob through the heavy security screen. The two imposters explained that they were state earthquake inspectors and they were going to various neighborhoods checking for damage.

"No, I don't got no damage" she explained. Barry quickly said, "We are authorized to write checks on site in the event of damage. We just have to take a picture."

Wanda responded, "Did you say damage? Yes, I do have some damage!" and she slid the deadbolt and opened the security screen for the fraudulent inspectors.

Barry wasted no time as he handcuffed Wanda while at the same time revealing their true identities. She was, of course, upset, but mostly at herself for falling for the scheme. Barry thought to himself, money works every time.

The other two officers entered the residence as well and a brief search was conducted. A fully automatic assault rifle was loaded and resting on Wanda's bed. The rifle went to evidence and Wanda eventually went to State Prison.

The California Bar

Mike Barro, the same Mike Barro that tried to buy Steve Mortsoob's allegiance with a fancy Mustang, the same Mike Barro that was an attorney for the Hells Angels, was now on probation and, according to a source, was selling methamphetamine from his San Bernardino home.

Barry collected a team and conducted a search at which time about a quarter pound of methamphetamine with scales and packaging materials were located in his home office. Of course, he denied it was his.

Hells Angels speed is a sight to behold. Other than the required precursors, there are an assortment of ingredients involved in the manufacture of methamphetamine and these vary from cook to cook. Some are entirely unnecessary. Various things are used to wash the product at the end of the process such as acetone or denatured alcohol. As such, the results are varied. Dirty looking meth often comes out of "Beavis & Butt-Head" [8] household labs. But Hells Angels meth is white and dry with a nice fragrance. Once, when Barry was assisting a special drug task force on a Hells Angels member shipping meth to Europe, a GIANT bag of what was thought to be "cut" [9] was discovered during a search. It wasn't known until later that the cut was actually meth. It was just so pure. To give credit where credit is due, Mexican National methamphetamine can be very nice as well.

Anyway, Barry arrested Mr. Barro and he was not happy.

---

[8] An American teen animated sitcom created and designed by Mike Judge.

[9] A non-drug substance added to a drug in the act of cutting. Example: sugar, flour, etc.

"Truman, you cannot do this! This is chicken shit!"

"Chicken shit? This is your second drug charge and, let's see, you have a charge for possessing an automatic weapon and then there's the underage client you slept with. What is it you want me to do?"

"Just let me out for a day and then I'll surrender to you. I have my bar review hearing tomorrow to see if they will lift the suspension on my license."

"No, you're going to jail." Barry did not waiver.

"Please - just one day!"

"Mr. Barro. If I let you out to attend your hearing with the bar, I would be disrespecting every person I have ever arrested that had important things to do the following day. I arrested a guy a couple weeks ago that missed his job interview at the Chevron station."

"Truman, you are as good as dead!"

Barry did not think that was a good way to sway the discourse. "Stand up. Time to go to jail."

Barro struggled around in his handcuffs, fighting and kicking officers. As he was inserted in the Crown Victoria, he threatened again, "Truman, you are a dead man!"

What's amazing is that Mike Barro eventually only got about six months in jail and his license to practice law was returned. Anyone else would have gone to State Prison. One could guess that he may have given up some information in return for leniency but that was highly unlikely as the Hell Angels do not take kindly to snitches. It was probably more a case of attorneys looking out for attorneys. Remember the judge is an attorney as well. Judges just can't seem to visualize sending one of their brethren to prison regardless of how much of a blight they are on the community. By the way, Mike Barro continued to practice law, still "associating" with the HA.

If there's a silver lining here it's that Barry wasn't murdered. Apparently, even the Hells Angels thought Barro was stupid.

Narcotics

Barry wondered if there were any other government jobs where you went to work wearing your favorite worn out T-shirt to match your unshaven face. He reported to a secret location to work on street level narcotics cases. Actually, both "street level" and "narcotics" were misleading as in the metropolitan areas of San Bernardino County, even Barry's "street level" teams confiscated up to 400 pounds of methamphetamine. Between 300 and 400 methamphetamine laboratories were busted each year as well.

Barry learned when testifying in federal court not to use the word "narcotics" unless speaking of opiates. The general term of "drugs" described all drugs including methamphetamine, the drug of choice in San Bernardino County. In state court, this was just an insignificant matter of semantics.

Barry was a member of one of five teams, each located in a different geographical area within the county. This was necessary due to the size of San Bernardino County. The east/west borders alone reach from Los Angeles County to the Colorado River.

Each team had eight to ten officers, mostly sheriff's employees but also officers from city police and probation officers from the county. Each member would develop his or her own cases and then the group would come together to serve search warrants, conduct surveillances and participate in special assignments. This was Barry's favorite assignment of all time. And that was not just his opinion. Regardless of agency, it was everyone's favorite assignment.

Barry had unknowingly prepared for narcotics work all his life. He worked for a Cadillac agency in his teens, delivering cars all over the country, often picking up and escaping from the inner-city Cadillac plant in Detroit. He drove fast and relatively safe, grasping the concepts of following and being followed.

He learned how to type due to his best friend in high school being in love with a pretty blonde in typing class. He would have never taken typing without the need to support his friend. Who would have figured the advent of computer driven word processing and the value of keyboard skills for preparing search warrants on the fly.

And Barry was one who could spin a story or two which is something of great value when pretending to be someone else.

Barry's early adoption of computers was of great assistance as well for research, working with databases and locating fugitives.

Finally, as a natural analytical thinker, Barry loved piecing together the bits of information that formulate investigations.

Barry's biggest weakness was in the area of observation skills. He knew this and worked on it but never achieved the same proficiency that some street cops attain. Even if a patrol officer had difficulty transitioning to the totally different demeanor preferable for a narcotics officer, just the average street cop had incredible observation skills.

"What is he holding Barry?" Mandarin asked looking down an alley.

"What is who holding?" answered Barry.

Experienced patrol officers see things in a flash in small windows, probably because they spent so much time patrolling and looking. Barry did neither. He figured everyone had their limitations.

Surveillance was a big part of working on a drug team and the skills learned would serve Barry well, particularly when he later supervised a sex offender unit. On the street level teams the term "undercover" wasn't used in the sense that an officer would live for months at a time in the drug community. There were people who would do this but they were working in higher level teams or in special programs or they would be "special" deputies, individuals who were not bona fide peace officers. This designation would prevent the tainting of a full-fledged peace officer in compromising situations. So, the role Barry's team members would generally fill was more of a cameo undercover appearance, pretending to be someone else for short periods of time. This would allow movement through communities without causing a stir. This is often how information is collected. An officer has to look and act like someone else when on surveillance, which might amount to sitting in a car or following another vehicle. Perhaps one of the guys would pretend to be someone's uncle from out of town trying to sell a chemical used as a precursor to the manufacture of methamphetamine.

Barry may have had some skills but he learned early on that he did not have a "gun butt." He had to come up with various concealed holsters to securely hold his Glock. Most everybody else on the team would put their gun under their shirts and inside their belts to the back. When Barry did this, his gun would fall past his small behind and down his jeans leg to the ground. Very embarrassing.

Officers were always meeting with informants and part of protecting these people was looking and acting the part. It took Barry a while to transition into acting like many of the people to whom he was mingling. Without knowing it, when you work in the business, you take on certain mannerisms and patterns of speech and even a gait that marks you as a cop. Just like a cop is suspect of certain individuals that display characteristics consistent with criminals, the same criminals can often identify law enforcement officers.

Particular types of vehicles can be problematic if they suggest that the driver is a cop. Narcotics officers are their own worst enemies when it comes to picking a ride that blends in. Probably due to the freedom of the position and the impact television shows have on everyone, including cops, it is desirable to drive the fanciest, fastest, coolest machine available. Corvettes, supercharged Mustangs, Dodge Chargers and similar vehicles are the norm but stick out like sore thumbs when anonymity is desired. Barry teamed up with an officer that was the exception and whose black, tattered Honda Accord was totally unnoticed.

But when surveillance became difficult without getting up close or there was a need to hang out in a truly ghetto area, everybody wanted to ride in or borrow Barry's car, known affectionately as "Special K." Barry would have liked to take the credit for selecting such a wonderful undercover ride but the fact was, it was the only vehicle available from the motor pool.

It was a late 80s Chrysler 'K" car, an ugly sedan that at one time was part of a fleet used widely in government. The paint was faded blue and the headliner was torn. In the spirit of John Anderson, Barry wanted to take advantage of the available equipment so he converted the old "K" car into a special ride that blended in driving or parked in the impoverished neighborhoods of San Bernardino. There wasn't really much to do. He took all but one hubcap off and threw a bunch of empty beer cans on the floor boards. Naturally, he never washed it. Oh, and he selected a Delaware license plate for the rear. There was a big box of license plates in the narcotics offices and the sergeant's rule was, "you can use any one you like as long as the number doesn't come back as stolen." Special K would display a different plate from time to time depending on need or just for a change.

Barry would have to contend with his junker when parked at his house. He did not live in the ghetto. To prevent upsetting the neighbors and to avoid the slim chance that a bad guy might pass by and see it parked in his driveway, he covered it up with a nice car cover, as if it were a Maserati.

Special K was so convincing that it would be routinely stopped by various officers of the law figuring it surely contained someone that could be arrested for having warrants or drugs or guns or dead bodies or whatever. On one surveillance assignment in a desert community by the name of Adelanto, it fit in so well that one of the lookouts for the house Bruno and Barry were watching was relaxing on the fender. The lookout was looking for cops, talking to Bruno and Barry, who were collecting information on the house and, of course, the lookouts.

Once a friend with the sheriff's office stopped Barry and Sparky in the East Valley. He rolled his eyes when he recognized the twosome. "You guys know your taillights aren't working, right?"

Since the taillights were wired through a switch so they could be turned off, Barry responded, "er - a - yeah."

This was not a problem with city and county officers but California Highway Patrol officers seemed to lack of sense of humor. Barry and another officer were pulled over in the Redlands area probably due to the fact it was difficult to believe that such a vehicle could make it all the way from Delaware. The twosome identified themselves to the CHP officer.

He commented, "Your plates come back "not on file."

"Yeah, that's the same thing we got back before we put them on - but they aren't stolen."

"Please, get that piece of shit out of here!"

"Right away sir."

Special K's humble condition was as the officer had described. One of the first times Barry gassed it up at the county motor pool, the director of the fuel division refused to believe that it was actually a government vehicle. A heated discussion ensued but dissipated after the vehicle identification number (VIN) was verified. The director just shook his head. "That's ours?" From there on out, Special K was a source of comedy whenever Barry pulled in.

More On Surveillance

Surveillance is utilized in investigating crimes other than narcotics. It is extremely valuable in assembling a criminal case for a variety of crimes. There is just no substitution for watching and listening to people involved in a criminal endeavor.

One aspect of surveillance that is not conveyed in movies and television is how difficult it is to watch someone without being detected. On the "big screen" you can see everything that is going on and nobody can see you. In reality, you just can't pull up across the street with your daylight running lights glowing and start gazing through binoculars.

Setting up at just one static location requires some finesse. Where do I park? Does my car look like a cop car? Can I be seen and, if so, do I fit in and does it make sense for me to park there? Am I one of two adults sitting in a vehicle? And of course, it doesn't help if you look like a cop. And then there are the neighbors. Understandably, they will get nosy if you are parked in front of their house. In very rare instances, you might correctly identify yourself but this is usually not a good idea. Whomever you confide in may very well tell another neighbor, admonishing them to keep silent. That next neighbor will do the same and before you know it, someone is unwittingly informing the subject under investigation.

If you are in a dedicated surveillance vehicle or if you are monitoring a camera from another location, that makes some of these points moot - but you still always have to be thinking. A business name on the side of the vehicle doesn't have to be real but does it identify the type of business often utilized in that particular neighborhood? Will people notice if the phone number does not look right for that area? What happens when that phone number is called? Like everything else in law enforcement, each case and setup is unique. But as Barry would say, "it ain't as easy as it looks."

Another aspect of surveillance not mentioned much is how boring and tiring it can be, especially on cases that go on for a period of days and nights, especially nights. Frankly, you run out of fresh officers. And, naturally, officers have husbands and wives and soccer games and birthday parties, etc. Barry was working on one property for several nights trying to establish if the felon was actually staying there. It wasn't a difficult setup as he was watching primarily for vehicles but he needed to stay in position until about 4:00 each morning. He later admitted to Mortsoob how he dosed off on the front seat of his car at three in the morning for a half an hour.

Barry had many more stories of officers falling asleep due to being exhausted. The most amazing one involved all the narcotics teams being used on twelve hour shifts to locate four subjects that had escaped from the central jail. Barry was taking a cap nap in the passenger seat while his partner, Bruno, was driving them to investigate a lead in Los Angeles. Barry awoke and glanced at the Honda Accord speedometer. The fact they were traveling 105 mph westbound on Interstate 10 at 300 hours did not surprise him but he was amazed when he glanced at Bruno and realized that he was sleeping too.

"Bruno!," Barry exclaimed.

Bruno opened his eyes with a startled look. "Damn!" he mumbled. Both Barry and Bruno were really quite relieved, and amazed at how straight the vehicle had been traveling. Bruno couldn't have been sleeping for too long.

Drisco Reprise

It had been years since Barry went to the Oktoberfest celebration in Big Bear. When he was assigned there, he really did not want to go back to the same place on his time off. Now that he was assigned to narcotics, he would only occasionally travel to Big Bear on duty. So, it was time to drink beer at the Octoberfest. Barry was just settling down with a pint of Ritter Brau with Michelle, Tricia, Earl and his sister, Kimberly, when his afternoon was transformed from frivolity to helplessness.

There, on the other side of one of those long banquet tables was sexual serial predator Arthur Drisco with an attractive brunette and her son, who looked to be seven to nine years old. From the way they were interacting, Barry could tell it was a new relationship. Drisco had met Barry that one time but that was when Barry was clean shaven with short hair. He now looked more like a homeless person. Plus, the place was chaotic and plenty of beer cups stacked on tables and dancers were cluttering up the field of view.

What to do? Due to the insane order from the Arizona State Court, no law enforcement officer was even allowed to contact Drisco when Barry was assigned to Big Bear station and he assumed such was still the case. Barry started contacting sheriff's deputies working in security capacities at the Octoberfest to let them know what was going on. The few deputies that were vaguely familiar with the case were only mildly interested. They were not assigned to the Big Bear Station when Drisco arrived.

Barry finally found a familiar face in uniform, a sergeant who fully appreciated the evilness of this predator and the situation at the festival. But all Barry really did was ruin Sergeant Jacob's night as well.

Jacob said that they were still not allowed to contact or visit Drisco but that he was always a major concern for the few deputies who were aware - and there weren't many. Jacob wasn't sure what Drisco looked like so Barry pointed him out.

"Can we separate the woman and reveal all the facts on Drisco?"

Jacob said "no."

Apparently, that had come up in the past and the agency was threatened with a lawsuit. To make sure, Jacob contacted his lieutenant. It was made clear to Jacob that there was nothing anybody official could do to intervene or make notification to the woman.

While Barry's companions were enjoying themselves, he had ceased drinking beer, trying to sort out what could only be described as a tragedy. He knew that Drisco had met this woman and was "grooming" her in order to get to her son. He watched them drinking and dancing and enjoying themselves until he couldn't take it anymore. He convinced Earl and the girls to leave and that he could drive them down the mountain since he only had one beer.

On the way down the hill, Michelle offered her opinion. "I don't know why you can't walk up to that woman and tell her the facts!"

"She wouldn't believe you," interjected Earl.

"I agree with Michelle," exclaimed Kimberly.

Tricia added, "Me too!"

"Look it. The sheriff's office was already slammed with a lawsuit for doing something similar. If you would covertly try to do it through a non-law enforcement third party, the lady wouldn't believe the information. He has totally brainwashed her!"

Michelle continued with her opinions on the matter until Barry finally couldn't take it. The fact that he was helpless was driving him crazy. "Please, can we not discuss this anymore?"

The car went silent. This event would keep Barry up all night and torment him from that day forward.

Surveillance Shorts

The Forest

Barry was alone in "Special K", parked on a residential street somewhere in the city of Loma Linda. It was a good location as he was not directly in front of any residence and he just had to pay attention to see if a particular vehicle arrived. It was a one-way street so the driver's side was up against the curb. It was one small part of a multiple vehicle operation to locate an escapee from the central jail. This would be an all-nighter so Barry had snacks, water, soft drinks and a cigar.

A couple hours passed and it was obvious that 97.3% of the neighborhood residents were in bed. Maybe one car passed every half hour. It was warm and Barry had his windows down so the air could pass through. Let's see. I guess it's time for a cigar.

Barry had just gone to the tobacconist and selected a mild Connecticut wrapper corona with tobacco from the Dominican Republic. Barry did not smoke many cigars but when he did, he wanted a good one. Firing it up with a wood match so as not to taint its bouquet, he pulled the smoke into his mouth and released it, appreciating the mellow and slightly nutty flavor.

All of a sudden, Barry heard a noise that startled him. It sounded like something moving about in the tree lawn right by his door, perhaps a snake. He turned to locate his gun on the seat when it seemed like gallons of water heavily sprayed through the driver's window. The automatic sprinklers for the tree lawn had activated and, within a few seconds, Barry and his one and only cigar for the evening were drenched. He cranked up his window and looked in the mirror at his face and cigar both dripping at the same time.

There were no witnesses. He recalled the expression, "If a tree falls in a forest and no one is around to hear it, does it make a sound?" No one was around to see or hear this comedy but Barry didn't need an audience. He sat alone laughing out loud.

The Pigeon of Peace

On another occasion, Barry was alone in an unmarked Toyota pickup following a suspected drug dealer through the city of Colton. There were no other vehicles involved in the surveillance as Barry had just happened to come across the suspect. He had already decided to keep his distance and not get "made." Just getting a general idea where the subject was going was enough and would be helpful in the future to set up a multiple vehicle surveillance to pinpoint his destination.

Following three cars behind on a busy main street, Valley Boulevard, Barry was surprised when a large white pigeon landed on his windshield. It somehow got lodged under the driver's side wiper blade and was flapping its wings trying to escape. All of a sudden Barry's vehicle did not blend in. He activated his wipers thinking that would release the animal but that only caused it to move with the wiper while flapping. Barry noted kids in a car moving slowly in cross traffic pointing at the spectacle with wide eyes. Looking past the bird, Barry could see that the two occupants in the suspect vehicle were amazed as well. Barry wasn't "made." After all, officers trying to go unnoticed don't let pigeons hitch a ride. At this point, Barry pulled over to the side of the road and picked up the wiper, releasing the bird. No harm, no foul but the surveillance was over.

Happy Birthday to You

The next tale resulted in the seizure of four hundred pounds of methamphetamine, quite a bit for a street level narcotics team. It all started with that first surveillance in the city of Fontana. The house was modern and large and situated in a fairly nice neighborhood. The principals who were linked to large quantities of precursors for the manufacture of methamphetamine were at this residence for unknown reasons. That's how a lot of these things start, not knowing much.

Barry and Bruno were in a vehicle to the far rear of the property and four more vehicles were set up in the front and on adjacent streets preparing for different scenarios. It was dark. There was activity in the backyard and the twosome strained to see what was up. With optics, Barry could see a figure moving back and forth high and to the inside of the rear fence. Every movement was radioed to the other vehicles over a period of about twenty minutes. Something was happening in the trees as well. It was nothing consistent with criminal activity seen before.

Wait. The male subject moving back and forth was manipulating a piñata by pulling a rope through the trees. The piñata is manipulated up and down while the blind-folded kids try to hit it with a bat. They are all hoping to break it apart to release a plethora of candy on the ground. Barry laughed in that they had all these cars out here, doing a surveillance on a kid's birthday party!

With everyone disappointed and somewhat entertained, the surveillance was abandoned. Was the information wrong? Was there a mistake?

No is the answer to both questions. Keep in mind that over a period of another two weeks a very large methamphetamine case was put together and these were the correct suspects. But there are two important key pieces of information here that apply to this type of work. First, criminals do some of the normal things that everyone else does like go to birthday parties. Second, even if it appears nothing has been yielded from a surveillance, such is not the case. In this instance, most of the occupants of this house were law-abiding relatives and not involved in the manufacture of methamphetamine. As one of Barry's esteemed university consultants coined it, "The absence of data IS data." Something is always gleaned from surveillance work even if it is learning that nothing is going on at the place being watched.

Who's on First?

Acting on a lead, Barry identified a cocaine dealer in the Del Rosa area of San Bernardino. Lamont Johnson had a lengthy criminal history including many drug and weapons charges. This was a bad guy. Barry decided to follow Lamont to collect information possibly about his supplier or to identify associates. Barry was in "Special K" and Bruno was assisting in his faded black Honda Accord. This was a moving surveillance at night which can create headaches. Dealers are paranoid anyway and seeing headlights in the rearview mirror makes them more nervous.

The twosome followed Lamont's relatively late model BMW about ten miles to an economically distressed area near Mount Vernon Avenue. Lamont drove around the various neighborhoods as if to see if he was being followed. Bruno held back to keep his vehicle undetected and so all three cars wouldn't be bunched up in some dead end.

This was a good idea because Barry got suckered into a cul-de-sac. Not having much choice, he turned past Lamont at the end around the cul-de-sac and all of a sudden Lamont was following Barry. Dismayed, Barry tried to drive away but "Special K" was no match for the BMW. They proceeded to race around the Mount Vernon neighborhoods for several minutes while Bruno lagged behind just in case.

With the situation not looking good, Barry thought he lucked out when he spotted a San Bernardino Police Officer standing by his patrol car, smoking a cigarette at Mount Vernon and 6th Street. He turned at that intersection as fast as he could, squealing his tires, driving almost out of control hoping the officer would jump in his unit and light them up. The BMW followed and then came Bruno.

Unfortunately, the officer seeing the out of control chase, decided to turn his back to it all and finish his cigarette. Perhaps he was off at eleven and he just didn't want any part of whatever he just observed.

This reverse, high speed surveillance continued until both Barry's and Lamont's vehicles came to a dead stop on some obscure dark street. Lamont opened his door and stood up and Barry did the same. Barry was concerned knowing that Lamont was undoubtedly carrying a gun so he stayed behind his vehicle.

Lamont shouted, "What the fuck are you doing following me?"

Keep in mind most the time criminals fear they are being followed, they think another bad guy is trying to rip them off of product and/or money. The police are only suspected next.

Time for bluffing. Barry exclaimed, "Following you? You're the dickhead following me!"

That seemed to do it. Each driver exchanged one more "fuck you" and they drove their separate ways. See Lamont was never sure. Barry and Bruno would save Lamont for another day. Another day never happened as Lamont was killed by a shotgun blast to his stomach somewhere in that same geographical area a couple weeks later. Case closed.

Sun Spots

There are all sorts of different surveillance vehicles from bare bones vans to ultra-high tech. In most of the ones Barry was familiar with, even if there was some provision for cooling, it never worked right. If it was summer in Southern California, straws were drawn to see which poor soldier was to be left inside. If a vehicle is parked, it can't be left running to power the air conditioner as that is a dead giveaway. The most comfortable ones do not need anyone inside. They are equipped with fancy cameras that can be accessed from afar.

Patrick McGee was a very competent senior probation officer that worked for Barry. He suspected that a sex offender who had reported an address in Highland, actually lived in Victorville. He had received anonymous information to that effect. The informant also advised that the felon was living with a woman and her seven-year-old daughter. A surveillance team followed him to a particular residence in the city of Victorville but more information was needed to establish residency. He could merely be visiting a friend and no child could be seen by officers. Patrick wanted enough corroborating information so that, if necessary, forcible entry could be accomplished.

Barry drew the short straw and earned the lone spot in the back of the surveillance van. This particular vehicle fell into the realm of "bare bones." It had a radio and headphones and one could look directly at anything outside, day or night with no one being able to look in. The business signs on the outside were for a plumbing service with an appropriate phone number for the area. It was all that was needed but there was one problem. It was August in the Southern California desert and there was no provision for cooling the interior.

The way it worked with this particular van was that once parked, the driver would get out with a bag of tools and disappear in the neighborhood to be picked up by another officer. The person in the back, in this case Barry, would stay put and do the actual observations.

But there was a small miscalculation at the start. Patrick was driving and, rather than parking under the shade of a tree, he left Barry right in the line of sight of the glaring sun.

Barry was prepared for a hot day at work but not this hot. He wore shorts and had an ice cooler filled with water and soda. The empties could be used for personal relief but there was no need. Barry was so dehydrated, all his body wanted to do was drink.

He watched and documented and drank and watched and drank some more. The subject drove up, got out of his car and then used a key to get in the front door. This was pretty compelling but Barry wanted more. He didn't even need his binoculars to clearly see that the subject was putting out the various trash cans for pickup, the kind of thing a resident would do. He photographed some of this. When he went back in the house, Barry could see a young girl standing near the front door.

There was now enough information to show that the subject was in control of the residence and the presence of the young girl made quickly acting on the information a prudent decision. Barry called the team members who were dispersed in the area to contact the guy and force entry if necessary. He was in violation of his probation and a direct threat to the young girl.

The two officers who could not be involved in the actual entry were Barry and Patrick. Patrick returned with his bag and drove the van away. Surveillance vehicles can never be compromised by being part of the "take down." Barry guessed by this time it had to be between 130 and 140 degrees in the back. He missed all the excitement at the house but he was so glad to get an ice-cold soda at McDonalds. He was soaking wet and, despite it still being very hot outside, he was experiencing chills.

"Patrick! What were you thinking? In the sun? Really?"

"Sorry boss. I was just trying to set you up so you had a great vantage point."

The offender was clearly residing at the unreported location with the girl and her mother. It appeared they all slept together in bed. He was arrested and within three weeks he was transferred from county jail to state prison.

Even after returning home and crawling in bed, Barry was shivering as if he had the flu. He assumed his temperature control system was somewhat over taxed. Despite the discomfort, Barry felt it was worth it. It always felt good to do something tangible, something that would protect little kids now and in the future.

The following day Barry hydrated a bit more as he met Steve to celebrate his departure from his jail assignment. He would now be working in a patrol unit in the desert. They didn't get too crazy as Steve again was flying "dawn patrol" in his new assignment. At least now that Mortsoob was "out" he would be more available for both work and off hours activities.

Informants

One of most powerful tools in an investigator's bag is the informant. Getting information from persons who have knowledge of criminal activity or who are able to circulate near the criminal activity is invaluable. Barry's experience in using informants was primarily in the area of drug sales and manufacture but that is not to say that an informant only provides the information being sought. In other words, an informant seeking specifics about the location of a drug laboratory might, as a matter of course, find out something about a murder or an identity theft operation. Barry would also attempt to get information from individuals regarding the location or activity of sex offenders but those informants are not of the same ilk as your average drug informer.

The most commonly used informants are criminals themselves. Their motive is generally to work off an arrest of their own or for profit. Many of these subjects get arrested for a relatively minor offense such as possessing a small amount of methamphetamine. They help officers in an effort to stay out of or not be sentenced to jail. These people often get the closest to the criminal operation but they are the least reliable. Their information in a search warrant is only given so much weight. A confidential "reliable" informant has a track record, even if it is not extensive, of proving in the past that he or she's information was accurate.

Some confidential reliable informants are lured by the excitement. They feel like they are in a police television show. Sometimes they take unnecessary risks. Some are motivated by money. If they can provide information that results in the seizure of a large amount of product, they can do well financially. Barry worked at the street level so information on very large operations was generally shared with the upper level teams. He did come into contact, however, with some of these high-level informants. One of them made a very good living giving up information on truckloads of narcotics all over the country.

Then there are citizen informants. The best of these have a criminal past but have cleaned up their act. They know the criminals in the community and can piece together what is going on just by seeing particular cars parked at the same house. And they aren't directly involved and lured by drug use. Even better, some of these people feel like they are on a crusade to rid the community of drugs - drugs that almost ruined their lives.

Of course, all informants don't fit so neatly in a classification. Barry had one female informant for years that was involved with methamphetamine laboratories by marriage and just liked socializing. She started giving up information after getting caught for cashing a bad check. As such, she started out as a criminal informant but provided information for fun or convenience later on.

Once she got tired of her husband and turned him in to give herself a break. Her information was golden. An officer is lucky if he or she has a "golden goose" as an informant. This woman would walk around Fontana and just pay attention to what was going on. She even gave Barry the name of a white supremacist who "capped" a suspected informant. The only thing she ever asked for in return was a pack of Marlboro "Reds."

Keep in mind that people running criminal operations do not think highly of snitches. Particularly in the world of methamphetamine, participants tend to be paranoid. Practically everyone will be accused of informing. Sometimes the suspects will be bluffed using different techniques such as, "Your name was read in a search warrant," which just doesn't happen.

Sometimes criminal participants who could be someone's informant are tested by being given specific information. For instance, your informant is shown a location where methamphetamine chemicals are being stored. But they aren't really stored there and your informant is the only one that was shown that location. So, during the execution of a search warrant, an officer, anxious to be successful, goes directly to that location. This is not good news for the informant and, of course, it is not a prudent way to conduct a search. As such, Barry always prepared his informants for these ploys to hopefully keep them above ground. And it doesn't hurt to remind the good guys to avoid searching right away where the contraband is thought to be located. The possibility always exists for them to unwittingly burn your informant. And, of course there are some officers that are oblivious to the welfare of informants and care much more about their own career aspirations.

"Snitches get stitches" is an old phrase that suggests that one who informs on another's illicit activities to the authorities will suffer harm. Barry knew that the reality was that one who informed on criminal activity and only received stitches would be lucky in deed. It is difficult to separate drugs and money and violence. One who informs on a person making money in the drug community often pays with their life. Barry and most officers understood this and efforts were made to protect these people.

When Barry first started working routinely with informants, wise officers explained that, once that person was signed up or formally working as an informant, he or she was essentially owned by that officer. It was that officer's responsibility to do everything possible to protect his or her identity. Barry always took extreme care in this regard. Not only was this the right thing to do but it was a matter of credibility. The word would get out as to which officers try to protect you and which officers will get you killed.

Protection of informants was something broached in narcotics school but Barry always felt it was something that should be stressed even more. Also, sometimes new narcotics officers didn't get scheduled for school until months after they began working in their narcotics assignment.

Barry had a close friend in another Southern California police agency that shared a story about two brand new narcotics agents. The agents visited a trailer park to contact a Mexican national to see if he would provide information on a methamphetamine laboratory in exchange for not being prosecuted and deported for possessing a small amount of the substance. Rather than contacting the individual in another setting or some other discreet manner, the two officers flashed their badges to the trailer park manager, essentially notifying

EVERYONE that they had business with this individual. They left the park, seemingly unaware that this prospective informant would, at the very least, have a lot of explaining to do to the Mexican Mafia.

Barry's friend went on to say that, a few days after this meeting, the same subject was found floating in Lake Elsinore. When his body was examined, it was determined that, prior to death, both his eyes were burned out, probably with some sort of poker or steel rod. It was unclear if there was an investigation into the crime or if anyone in law enforcement would get in trouble.

Barry ran into his friend a couple months later and asked him right away, "What happened to those brand-new narcs in that Lake Elsinore thing?"

"Oh, you mean the fishing accident?" his friend responded.

Apparently, the Mexican national was not technically signed up as an informant so no investigation took place when he had his "accident."

Barry would repeat this "story" to any officer working with informants so that it was clear that bad things truly can happen.

Narcotics High Finance

Each officer was given an amount of money to use to pay informants for their activity and/or information. Each officer in Barry's unit was given $200 a month. Keep in mind that informants that provide information on large scale cases can make thousands of dollars but those are special allocations. Barry discovered that some informants would provide valuable information for nothing or maybe for the gold standard in the tenderloin district, a pack of Marlboro Red Cigarettes.

The monthly audit was not on a designated day or date so officers never knew when it would occur until the sergeant announced it was time. It would catch Barry and the others invariably by surprise. It was suggested that everybody keep their personal money in one pocket and their "buy money" in the other but nobody did that. They just spent what they had knowing that they were responsible to produce $200 in cash or in informant receipts or a combination of both each month. As soon as the audit was announced, officers would scramble with last minute emergencies perhaps at the same time stopping by the ATM. But, ultimately, there was never enough money for everybody so Barry and the others would take turns and pass the cash. Specifically, officer A would give the sergeant let's say $100 worth of receipts and $100 in cash. The sergeant would enter that information in his audit book and give officer A a fresh $200 for the next month. Officer A would, in turn, walk out of the office and loan officer B whatever amount of money he was lacking for his own accounting. It was like the passing of a baton or, more topically, like a drug deal "going down." It continued with pretty much the entire unit. The guys always suspected that the sergeant knew. After all, he was very smart and, at one time, he was a regular narcotics officer. And while technically not proper, all the money had to be produced by each officer at some point in time. So there really was no impropriety.

Other Related Tasks

Bar Duty

Every once in a while, Barry would be assigned to bar duty. This was a real treat. Sometimes it had to do with drug sales or manufacture or it might have to do with collecting information for another agency or investigation. If it was in support of the officers of another agency like the Alcoholic Beverage Commission, Barry and his fellow officers had a good chance of being bored to tears sitting on the perimeter around an establishment mainly for security in case something went wrong while the ABC people drank beer.

When the opportunity was there to actually sit at a bar and drink on the government dime, it was truly an uplifting feeling regardless of the specific assignment. Barry would think to himself, how does it get any better than this?

There was usually one officer that carried the government funds for everyone. Barry would often coax this person to start buying more beers so they didn't look like cops drinking on the taxpayers' money. Any experienced bartender is going to get wise when two or three men are sitting at the bar sipping their beers like they are tea.

Admittedly, drinking alcohol on duty can be a problem and it is a fine line between fitting in and being too intoxicated to conduct a proper investigation. What if for some reason, someone has to pull their weapon or worse? Maybe they actually have to discharge their weapon. No one wanted to really think of such things. Barry's team never experienced any of these problematic situations while drinking but it is certain that some officers somewhere had.

Barry accompanied two other officers, Brad and Dean, to a nightclub and sat down at the bar. It was mid-afternoon so the place

was not crowded. The threesome drank beer for about forty-five minutes and, at some point, Barry asked Brad what were they supposed to be doing there. Barry suspected that the bartender might be dealing speed or there were under-aged girls being victimized. Brad responded, "I'm not sure" and he posed the same question to Dean, who was controlling the money.
"I have no idea."

They all looked at each other, chuckled and shrugged their shoulders. They were just so happy about drinking beer for free, no one bothered to check.

Barry drew the short straw and called the Sarge. "Danny, what is it we're supposed to be watching at the bar?"

Danny was amazed. "How long have you knuckleheads been sitting there drinking beer?"

"Not long Sarge. We just need our assignment."

Somewhat irked and entertained all at once, Danny, revealed, "You are supposed to watch the operation of the business to see who is really giving the orders and running things. We think the guy actually in charge is a felon who cannot have a liquor license or run that type of business. We believe the person named on the liquor license is just presented for the authorities and does not really have anything to do with operations."

"Oh, okay. Thanks, Sarge!"

"And you guys stay sober!"

"Yessir."

Barry returned to the bar and enlightened the group. No one was really sure who was at fault for the snafu but the group consumed a few more beers and collected the necessary information. It was clear that it WAS the felon who in charge of the place. He checked the till, gave directions to bartenders and servers and was actively involved in ordering supplies. He even was heard speaking on the telephone, saying, "Yes, I'm the owner." Assignment completed.

A Little Vice

There are several different kinds of vice investigations. The team would be assigned these cases due to flexibility, availability and being at the disposal of two different law enforcement agencies. Barry didn't participate in many of these but, when he did, they were a refreshing change from narcotics. Assignments to check out "massage" parlors would often be initiated following complaints from community members.

For example, a woman might suspect her husband to be visiting a massage parlor and getting special services. She tells another member of her church congregation who happens to know a ranking member of the sheriff's office. The sergeant of one of the drug teams eventually gets the call that takes the team off of narcotics and temporarily makes them vice officers.

Such was the case with Barry's first massage parlor. He was there only in a support role but the event would always be memorable. A special deputy was sent into the business in the city of Highland for a "massage." The idea is for the arrest to take place before the deputy is actually involved in sexual activity. This makes the case so much easier to prosecute.

The deputy was directed by the case agent to call out a "bust signal" when the worker brought out a condom. He would look at the condom and say, "That's not big enough." Everything was recorded and was being listened to by Barry and three other officers in a vehicle outside the business. Ideally, when the bust signal was heard, everyone would go inside, detain everyone, make arrest(s), and secure the business for the purposes of conducting a search by warrant or by consent.

One can never anticipate every contingency and in this particular case, how would anyone have known that the worker would have the condom in her mouth and possess the oral skill to unroll it around the special deputy's equipment? Knowing that the bust signal made absolutely no sense, he stammered and hesitated until it was just too late.

Barry and the others didn't know exactly what was going on until talking with the special deputy but they could hear on the "wire" the sounds of someone who had received his "happy ending." The laughter could not be contained in the vehicle.

Even with the sexual conduct that wasn't going to be filed with the District Attorney, the team entered the business. The girls, all of Asian descent from Los Angeles, were interviewed and a consent search was conducted. The place was clean like a hospital with no clutter or drugs. Barry was so used to looking for various drugs and manufacturing necessities that half way through the search, he asked, "What is it we are looking for?"

"Rubbers!" one of the other guys said.

Barry learned that condoms are the evidence needed to prove any cases related to this type of activity. And hundreds of them were located in a hidden cavity.

The operator was cited for some pandering charge. The business was closed. It opened back up the following day. It was really more of a political visit.

Nice House, Nice Yard and A Nice, Fast Dodge Ram

Barry always liked the cases that required more investigation than usual and enjoyed when everything just came together. The fluidity of the way cases transpire was exciting and rewarding. A good example was the case of Guy Farrar. Barry had heard of Mr. Farrar for years. According to Barry's sources, he was the biggest methamphetamine dealer in the Highland area. Nothing could be corroborated but one of Barry's sources had an excellent track record so his information about Mr. Farrar's activities was believed.

Nothing more came of the information until Barry, now working in narcotics, overheard a conversation in his sergeant's office about a Guy Farrar.

"What's this?" inquired Barry of his sergeant. Barry's eyes were wide open.

"One of our patrol officers has a citizen informant that says that Mr. Farrar is manufacturing methamphetamine in his house in Highland."

"I have old information on that same guy. I've never been able to obtain additional information on him. But I can still contact my informant related to that case."

Sergeant Nady had the patrol officer come in to the narcotic's office and they discussed the case. It was decided that Barry would work the investigation and also handle the new source. Barry was elated. He had always been trying to find out more information on this guy. One of the difficulties had been that Mr. Farrar did not have a criminal history beyond traffic infractions. Also, his exact location was unknown. Barry found out soon enough that this new source could pinpoint his residence and provide other valuable information.

With information to work with, Barry was then able to watch the house and collect information about visitors and activity at the residence. It was a typical single-level dwelling situated in a middle-class neighborhood. Mr. Farrar could be linked to his home through the license plates on his vehicle, which was parked there frequently and all-night long. He took care to keep his name off of property records for the house but Barry was able to nail down his residency through other means.

It is commonplace for lots of activity to take place where methamphetamine is being sold, particularly in small amounts. That type of activity was not going on at this house but periodic visitors could be identified through license plates and criminal history inquiries. Some of these people did, in fact, have criminal histories involving drug sales. The puzzle was coming together. A lack of small transactions was indicative of larger quantities and/or manufacture. All that was left was for Barry to write a narrative to convince a judge that felony activity was taking place at that location in order to secure a search warrant.

The judge was convinced. The dated information, the very new information with specifics and the surveillance results fit the criteria of a three-prong probable cause argument. He signed the warrant.

Everyone met at the Highland sheriff's station on a Friday morning. Twelve officers in total were in the parking lot preparing their gear to execute a residential search warrant.

The residence was only two miles away and Barry made the customary final pass by the house for any last-minute updates prior to search warrant service. He returned, pointing out that Farrar's truck, a late model full-size Dodge Ram was parked in the driveway. This was good as it's always nice to have your primary subject at home. It aids in proving the case.

Three patrol vehicles and five narcotics cars headed towards the house at 7:15 a.m. The warrant was not approved for night service so it could not legally be served before 7:00 a.m. When they arrived, Barry immediately noticed that the Dodge Ram was now gone. This was unfortunate but just one of the unexpected changes that occur during these types of operations. The team was there and the warrant would be served.

Forcing entry can be dangerous but is also exhilarating. As a consolation prize for finding this new informant and turning the informant over to Barry, it was agreed that Officer Keans would be at the front door and, if necessary, force entry.

Barry yelled what is referred to as "knock and announce" or "knock and notice." Essentially this is legal notice that a search warrant is being executed. Entry must be demanded or requested and the serving agency called out. A loud knock at the door would possibly allow the owner to open it before it is forcibly compromised. In this case, while knocking, Barry announced, "Sheriff's Narcotics, Demand Entry, Search Warrant!" This was repeated again.

No one answered the door. Barry repeated the announcement. No response was heard. After about thirty seconds passed, Officer Keans kicked the front door in by the dead bolt, making it unnecessary to use any special equipment. While one of reasons for these announcements is to allow the occupant the opportunity to open the door, the length of time required between notice and forcibly entering differs depending on the circumstances of the case.

No persons were located during a protective sweep of the home but it was clear right away that the equipment and chemicals were present to prove large quantities of methamphetamine were being manufactured at that location. It was a good lab. "High fives" followed and everyone went out and moved their vehicles to spread them out in the neighborhood. The marked cars had to be driven away. This is common practice so as not to alienate associates from stopping by during a search. Also, in this case, the primary subject had left and there was a good possibility that he would return.

Low and behold, not more than ten minutes had passed when the Dodge Ram slowed in front of the house and then sped off with squealing tires. Realizing that was the primary subject, two narcotic units and a captain gave chase. Through an interview with Farrar days later, Barry would learn that he was about to pull in his driveway when he saw the glint of a belt badge from one of sheriff's "brass" that had come by to view the seizure.

While officers followed the subject at high speeds through the orange groves, Barry and three other officers continued searching through items in the residence. The lab team was already en route.

Listening to the chase on the radio, Barry could tell that the subject was driving at speeds approaching 125 miles per hour. The dispatcher kept asking if this was a pursuit. "Confirming you are in pursuit?"

No one wanted to call in a pursuit because all the cars involved in the chase, including the captain's, were unmarked narcotics vehicles. A lack of adequate lights and sirens technically prevented these vehicles from engaging in a pursuit.

The officers giving chase put the dispatcher off for a minute or so explaining they were keeping a visual on the subject but eventually they had to come clean with someone answering, "Negative. We are not in pursuit."

Paperwork in residences provides all sorts of information to support an investigation and is often times forgotten by investigators. Even one utility bill can establish who belongs to a house. There could be a receipt for a storage locker or a list of chemicals for manufacturing. Financial documents might be located. Barry was sorting through bills when he remembered that the informant had also told him Farrar had a girlfriend in Huntington Beach. He quickly located the phone bill. Sure enough, there was one number with a Huntington Beach area code that was called probably thirty times.

Barry placed a call to the Orange County Sheriff's office and after a couple more calls to zero in on the jurisdiction, lucked out and spoke with a drug unit sergeant that not only covered the right area but was smart and motivated.

Just like in any other business, you have talented, cerebral players and then you have some lazy and/or dull employees. This latter group in the law enforcement business is referred to as a "bunch" of "lops."

Barry explained the entire case to the sergeant. This guy had undercover cars around the girlfriend's condominium within thirty minutes. Guy Farrar's Dodge Ram was there. Two narcotics officers, one of them nicknamed "Beachcomber", due to his very low-key approach, volunteered to drive to Huntington Beach to continue the investigation. Off they went for a drive that should have taken one hour. They arrived in thirty-seven minutes.

Barry got the call from Beachcomber. They arrested Farrar easily as he was completely surprised. In addition to the laboratory in his home, a search of his truck revealed two pounds of methamphetamine and a loaded .357 revolver.

Despite the fact that Mr. Farrar did not have a criminal history, the scope of his offense and activity resulted in his incarceration in state prison. Barry always liked these adrenalin-filled and fluid investigations and he was especially proud of this one.

Speaking of Cash

In Southern California, where illegal substances are just a stone's throw across the border to Mexico and where methamphetamine is still manufactured in mass by Mexican organizations, thousands of dollars are generated from sales. Much of this money needs to be transported back to Mexico and/or laundered in the US or in Mexico to prevent scrutiny from law enforcement agencies.

Sometimes it is advantageous to rent a home, usually in a nice neighborhood, where cash can be stored away from the drug operation pending dispersal or transportation. Barry came upon one of these homes in Corona, California. He was along for the ride on another team member's case. There were four officers total. Barry was not familiar with the case but he was ultimately intrigued by the experience.

Used to forcibly entering homes all over Southern California and beyond, Barry was familiar with bad neighborhoods, cat urine and filth and always clutter with the exception of the homes of white collar criminals or sex offenders. This home was in a nice neighborhood and the interior was clean and tidy. It was tidy partly because there was no furniture, just wall to wall carpet that smelled like it was ready to show to a prospective buyer.

There was one piece of furniture in the form of a kitchen table with no chairs. On top of that table in the midst of a modern granite counter and stainless-adorned kitchen was a stack of $100 bills over two feet high. That was the only personal property in the entire two-story house. There wasn't a stitch of clothes or even a shaving kit, and no illegal substances. There also was no paperwork except for a rental agreement with what turned out to be a phony name.

This made the job easy for the four. Sparky Lewis, the case agent, documented the find while the money was counted, once by each of the three remaining officers. The pile turned out to be exactly $525,000.

Now, Barry never saw an officer steal a dime in his career but he guessed since this was such a large sum, much care was taken to ensure no one would be tempted or even accused with no basis. This seemed prudent.

Before the money was packaged up, all four officers stood back and looked at the pile. There was a moment of silence broken by Officer Lewis commenting, "Pretty amazing - I've never seen $125,000 in cash in one place like that."

It would later be a great story for retirement parties and such.

Search Warrant Stories and Screw-ups

Oh - That Door!

Barry received information from a criminal informant who had given him good information in the past. A residence in San Bernardino was being used for the manufacture of methamphetamine. Barry was able to corroborate the information with a citizen informant and from running plates from vehicles coming and going from the property. Also, the primary resident had a criminal history of - guess what? - manufacturing methamphetamine.

The only problem arose due to changes that were made to the residence prior to the service of the search warrant. It's always good to get an idea as to the layout of the property to be entered for safety and efficiency. Unfortunately, the criminal informant hadn't been there in about two weeks and wasn't aware of a slight structural modification. When Barry knocked and announced and kicked in the front door, a tremendous crash could be heard, more accurately the sound of glass and wood breaking. As Lisa and Barry continued to scream "Sheriff's Narcotics" they walked in on top of the back of a china hutch that had been covering the former doorway. Had correct or more recent information been obtained from the criminal informant, officers would have known that ten feet to the right of the door that Barry kicked in was an unlocked screen door, the new entryway to the residence.

Barry was an antique clock enthusiast and he cringed when he saw the circa 1886 E.N. Welsh Patti vintage pendulum clock in pieces on the floor along with broken dishes and the little fragile things people put in china hutches.

Fortunately, there was a methamphetamine laboratory in the back. It was not a large-scale lab but a meth lab just the same. When things don't go according to plan it's always better if the criminal activity that was thought to be at that location, actually is. A married couple in their early thirties was arrested.

Barry thought it odd that neither one of them cared much about the damage including to the clock. Maybe it wasn't grandma's clock and it was stolen property. Or maybe it was that the lifestyle of a criminal conflicts with forming attachments whether personal or inanimate.

Excuse Me Reverend

One of the biggest mistakes in serving search warrants is kicking down the door of the wrong house. Many technical errors in a warrant can be overcome such as the wrong street number on the paperwork - as long as the warrant is served at the house that was intended.

This is what sometimes happens. There is an expiration date for the serving of search warrants. In California, this is ten days. An officer is scheduled for vacation and there isn't enough time to serve his or her warrant or warrants before relaxing at "The River."[10] Another officer is assigned to be "case agent" for that investigation and is responsible for serving that warrant(s) within the legal time frame.

Unless this new officer helped the original officer investigate the case, he has never seen the house. By law, there is a physical description of the property in the warrant but the new case agent just looks at the address, not knowing there is a typographical error in the number.

He or she serves the warrant at the wrong house creating a civil liability nightmare.

Barry was present three times this happened and, fortunately, the occupants opened the door and, after some shouting and eventual discourse, the error was discovered. By the way, cops don't like to be wrong.

The classic story turned out okay only by the graciousness of the occupants. Barry and four other officers forced entry into this quaint

---

[10] The Colorado River.

house from the 30s in San Bernardino. The door was not answered following the somewhat brief "knock and announce." Apparently, the reverend, his wife and three children were not able to get up from the dining room table in time. The scene looked like a Norman Rockwell painting with the entire family sitting around the table. Having not yet taken a dinner break, the food smelled wonderful.

The reverend was quick to point out that the drug manufacturing was taking place across the street. A neatly bearded man of about forty-five years old, he accepted the many apologies that followed. He was promised and received a first-class replacement for the front door and frame and never filed a complaint or a lawsuit. Sloppy work by the police but a classy minister. Barry was embarrassed like everyone on the team but, in a way, his faith in mankind was restored.

Up, Up and Away!

One of the upper echelon drug teams needed assistance in serving a search warrant for a several-acre property nestled up against the foothills in north San Bernardino. One of their people wrote the warrant. Barry was just part of the team that was assigned to help. The briefing revealed that the long storage building to the rear of the property was the suspected location of a massive marijuana grow, perhaps based on utilities or infrared readings. Barry wasn't really sure. They were eight of the twenty-five officers that converged on this property.

There was a little house, later determined to be a chapel, that SWAT members surrounded, having to negotiate the rugged terrain in that area of the property.

Barry was part of a contingent that had to run about a tenth of a mile up a driveway, slowly graded to the top. They were assigned to secure the long building and did so, totally exhausted.

One of the garage doors was open and the area was quickly searched for persons with negative results. Much to everyone's surprise, instead of massive cultivation, there was internal combustion, as ten or more exquisite exotic and classic cars were parked.

The entry team was not pleased when they heard of this as they had just forced entry in the chapel only to find an elderly lady that was living there and taking care of the facilities. There was nothing illegal and certainly not a "major grow" anywhere on the property. Somebody screwed up and didn't do their homework but Barry and the other officers were just glad it wasn't them.

Barry never did get the background on that operation. It was kept real 'hush, hush" but he did know that, aside from a new entryway, this elderly woman got a free tour around the valley in "Forty King," the name for one of the sheriff's department helicopters.

Aptitude

With the helicopter case in mind, Barry was always reminded that law enforcement officers are no different competence-wise than mechanics or waiters or doctors. There are excellent ones, mediocre ones and crummy ones. Also, most officers do not have incredible skills in every area. This is no different from a family practice physician not knowing much about brain surgery. Then factor in emotions and ego and honesty and the combinations can be very interesting.

What really is preferable is a bright, honest, well-adjusted officer that has expertise in a particular assignment. Oh - and one very important additional characteristic. In most law enforcement assignments, you want someone that has investigative abilities. Some of this is learned and some of it just comes natural.

Barry always figured that if an officer was at least of average intelligence and was honest with no major character flaws, he or she could be quite capable. Even new to assignments, a well-adjusted officer will not be worried about ego and will consult with more skilled personnel, especially initially. But a dishonest officer with a screw loose here or there was another matter. These are usually the people who generate law suits.

Barry was quite capable himself although it took a while to get up to speed as to some skills, including writing search warrants. He eventually became an expert for the purposes of drug sales and manufacture. This being said, he would not be able to properly put together a murder investigation and fortunately did not have to. In that regard, he knew the basics of his role, which was not to contaminate any murder scene.

Some officers are not suited for the clandestine way narcotics investigations are conducted, having come from riding a patrol sled. One of the experienced "narcs" used to say, "You can take the officer out of patrol, but sometimes you can't take the patrol out of the officer." Some would adapt and eventually be able to covertly gather information and conduct business while others would walk, talk and carry themselves like they were responding to SWAT calls.

Barry was fortunate in that his narcotics team pretty much consisted of high-character bright guys. Several of them were excellent investigators. Interviewing is an important part of the investigation and Barry just loved hearing an expert interrogator work his or her magic. Beachcomer would talk to a victim or witness or perpetrator like they were all going together to a beach party. He was so non-threatening that practically everybody would tell him everything. He would even read the required Miranda rights in such a way that they were technically correct but not intimidating. Most suspects agreed to talk.

Beachcomber would open the conversation with something like, "Are these fine-looking ladies always around here?"

"Yeah, pretty much all the time," the perpetrator might respond.

"Okay - cool!" in a tone more appropriate for someone accepting a courtesy beer.

"So, you didn't smack her in the face until after she "took a little bit off the top?" referring to taking a little of the speed for herself.

"No, not until my brother told me what she was doing."

"Oh okay," Beachcomber would say in a light-hearted manner.

By the time he was through with the interview he had collected important information to successfully prosecute the person. And he had not made an enemy.

At the other end of the spectrum was one bad apple, really not too bad for an eight-person unit. This guy was relatively bright but he scored at the bottom on all of the other attributes Barry valued. Officer Mandarin had character flaws that involved ego and often lead to heavy-handedness and he didn't tell the truth when there was no need to lie. He would fabricate information and do stupid stuff that was often dangerous. He was the sergeant's worse nightmare.

Mandarin's Yucaipa Search Warrant

Each officer would generate cases and use the rest of the team to join in as needed. The team would convene for a lot of arrests, parole and probation searches, "knock and talks"[11] and the service of search warrants. Generally, the only person that knew the case well was the officer that carried out the investigation and put the pieces together. Everyone else was there to assist for safety and efficiency.

Officer Mandarin needed assistance with the service of a search warrant in the city of Yucaipa. Since the information provided to the team by Mandarin, the case agent, included the possibility of an underground methamphetamine laboratory, eight narcotics officers and a couple of local deputies assisted with the entry.

Every officer has a reputation generated in part by the quality of their investigations. That track record could consist of good investigations or bad investigations and Officer Mandarin would definitely be in that later group. For a long time, he managed to avoid any repercussions for crummy capers or was just plain lucky.

Barry had been present during some of Mandarin's search warrants that were just plain wrong. They usually amounted to bad information, totally fabricated information or errors that lead to quite a few kicked in doors at the wrong place. He would argue with the sergeant about legalities all the time. The Sarge would have to scream at him at times.

"Mandarin!" yelled the Sergeant. "You have to get consent BEFORE you go in the house!"

While these things were always on the mind of Barry and the other team members, they were participating in a support capacity and had nothing to do with securing the search warrant that was composed by Mandarin and signed by a Superior Court Judge.

The house was rather nondescript and similar to surrounding structures which all may have been built in the early 60s. No activity could be seen on the property. Entry was forcibly accomplished at the front door after no one responded to Mandarin's "knock and announce." Officers entered and made sure the premises was "clear" of bodies. Since there was no one present and entry had been

---

[11] Contacting residents where there is information about criminal activity but no legal right to enter, devoid of further incriminating information.

accomplished, most of the officers went on to other things. That left Mandarin, Barry, Bruno and a deputy.

A quick cursory search revealed nothing illegal so everyone looked to Mandarin for guidance. He said there was definitely something underground so he had Barry and Bruno use shovels in the back yard to dig holes in suspicious spots. After about half an hour of digging in likely locations and where dirt had been disturbed or grass was dead, the only thing the twosome managed to accomplish was to make the yard look like giant gophers were at work.

"Mandarin, are you sure there is something underground?" Bruno asked.

"Absolutely," he said, "but help me inside the house because my source specifically identified an area under the floor. Oh, and Barry, I will need your pick."

"Okay, be right back," as Barry went to retrieve the "pick" from the trunk of Special "K." The "pick" was a six-foot long hardened steel rod with a pry end and a pointed end. It was invaluable on occasions where obstacles needed to be pried or coaxed. Barry brought the tool for Mandarin having no idea what he needed it for inside the residence.

For the next few minutes, Barry and Bruno watched Mandarin take the giant rod and thrust it up and down on the kitchen tile floor. He would lift the rod up as high as he could and smash the beige and white patterned ceramic tile with the pointed tip. After most of the tiles were shattered, nothing seemed to be below them other than dried grout and shattered wood. Barry irritated Mandarin when he asked if he was sure about his information. Maybe Mandarin was thinking about a recent article in the CNOA (California Narcotics Officers Association) magazine showing pictures of a drug tunnel under a Mexican national's kitchen tile floor. Perhaps, Mandarin had visions of this case being the "investigation of the month" in the next issue.

"Yeah, my information is good and the search warrant authorizes searching under floors and behind walls and such."

Barry and Bruno looked at each other and proceeded to follow Mandarin's further instructions. Again, they weren't privy to Mandarin's informants or information and he had a signed search warrant. Over the next two hours, they managed to pull out kitchen cabinets, make exploratory holes in walls, rip up the wall to wall carpeting and pry up the subfloor. At some point a sheriff's captain, who had been listening on the radio, stopped by. He was not in Mandarin's chain of command and was assigned to a different division. This would happen from time to time as the "brass" would get curious as many of them were nostalgic about their days "on the streets." Plus, it was an opportunity to get out from behind the desk. The Captain took one look at the massive destruction and turned around abruptly saying, "carry on" before he walked quickly back out the front door. He wanted no part of it.

Bruno finally convinced Mandarin to conclude the search just as he was about to slice these nice leather chairs with his knife. Nothing illegal was ever located and no owner or renter or other occupant ever returned to the residence while the search was on-going. Barry's guess was there might have been something to Mandarin's information and that this house was somehow related to the criminals. If there was contraband or if there were tunnels, they were somewhere else. No one ever filed a lawsuit or even inquired probably because the owners were illegals, making methamphetamine somewhere else or both. The damage had to be at least $50,000.

Eventually, Mandarin would have all his cases thrown out by the DA and he would be transferred back to patrol.

Legal Vs Prudent or Lawful but Awful

Barry would always school his officers on the difference between legality and prudence. Pretty much, all prudent actions are legal but all legal actions are not necessarily prudent. Sometimes, you can do things differently in order to escape these situations and sometimes you are just stuck.

Mom

Barry would often cite a case where he was assisting in the search and arrest of a pedophile in the unincorporated community of Bloomington. The perpetrator was forty-five years old and still living with his mother, who had to be around eighty. She was frail looking and she walked with a cane. The guy was annoying and resistive but his elderly mother was "completely off the hook."

Assigned to watch after her in the living room while officers searched and talked to her son in a bedroom, Barry was subjected to continual verbal abuse.

"What are they doing back there?" she exclaimed. "They have no right to be here!" she continued. "I'm going to see for myself!"

"Ma'am! You need to stay right here and sit down."

"I will not sit down!"

Barry gave in a little and allowed her to stand up as she was not trying to leave the living room. If she left the room she would be deemed a threat and he would act. The living room had a wooden floor and was sparsely furnished. She was standing with the help of her cane behind a small, lightweight wicker chair.

She continued to strongly object to everything the officers were doing. Rather than turn the television off, Barry tried to distract her with it. "Did the weather come on yet?"

"What? oh no, not yet." He used this tact a couple more times and was partially successful in interrupting her train of thought while trying to engage her in conversation. This technique worked better in manipulating methamphetamine users whose train could be derailed pretty easily.

Unfortunately, her son loudly complained when he knew he was going to jail. Officers had found a pair of little girl's panties in his dresser along with child pornography.

She was now yelling her complaints towards the bedroom and in the direction of Barry. "I am going to sue everyone here. No one will have a job when I am through with you!"

At this point, the lady looked at Barry and said, "You will pay!" She then grabbed the chair with her available hand and threw it across the room. The lady demonstrated a little power as it slid on the wood floor coming to rest just short of where Barry was standing.

Barry rolled his eyes and yelled to the arresting officers, "Hey, are you guys back there about ready to roll?"

Sensing what Barry was dealing with, they brought the pedophile out in cuffs and the bagged evidence and everyone left with mom slamming the door behind them.

Barry knew from the start that he had the absolute legal right to control any occupants for the safety of officers present. After escalated verbal commands and perhaps some healthy obscenities, he would have physically engaged a younger occupant for merely not sitting down. People who do not obey the commands of officers are a danger. But while legal and often necessary, the use of physical restraint and/or force on the elderly is something best avoided if at all possible. Even if the person isn't injured, it never looks good to anyone not present. An officer has to judge how much "crap" he or she will take in order to avoid critical analysis from pencil-pushing administrators such as Carl Becker and/or the media.

Barry remembered many occasions where there were no good options. You do the best you can do based on the circumstances and your training and experience. For Barry, he would never cross a line that would threaten anyone's safety. But his actions would always be judged by "Pecker Becker" playing Monday morning quarterback and criticizing every move made.

In this instance, the old lady was a clearly annoying but she couldn't overpower anyone and one could visually see that she had no weapons beyond her cane and, of course, the chair. She was following instructions well enough where she wasn't leaving the room, retrieving a weapon, interfering with the search or creating any other kind of hazard. Barry didn't like the situation at all but, ultimately, no one had to fight with the lady and their mission of searching and arresting the perpetrator was accomplished.

Grandma

Officers are often criticized for being heavy-handed or just plain stupid in dealing with law-abiding citizens and criminals. The reality is that most of them do an incredible job of sorting through great deals of information and reacting while at the same time not subjecting themselves to undue danger.

Barry would always school his officers that in many situations where elderly people are present and, at least somewhat cooperative, you can be both safe and respectful. It has to be remembered that just because someone is in their golden years, it doesn't mean that their pre-retirement occupation was at the Methodist Church. Unfortunately, some of these people were crooks and their morals do not all of a sudden reverse field in old age. In other words, they can still be dangerous.

Often, they interfere or distract or cover up or hide. Barry had been lied to by many old women that sounded like "Aunt Bea."[12] One must be careful and suspicious.

Barry liked to share the story of the sweet old woman at the home of a gang banger in Victorville. A couple gang members were present and they were handcuffed and secured so that a search of the residence could be conducted. Grandma sat on the couch with a shawl covering her lower body. She was very polite and seemingly helpful. Barry was

---

[12] The Andy Griffith Show.

very polite but assertive in his instruction, "Ma'am, I need you to show me your hands and we're going to move you over to another part of the couch."

The woman was taken aback but did not object as Barry peeled back her shawl, revealing what turned out to be a loaded sawed-off 12-gauge shotgun resting right against her right thigh. The weapon was retrieved and grandma was allowed to scoot over to a section of the couch that had already been searched.

The two gang members hung their heads as it was their hope that officers, not wanting to bother a nice old woman, would not check her area. Sometimes they don't. Even though grandma was the one concealing the weapon, the two gang members were the ones arrested and charged. The point Barry would make when sharing that story was that many times officers can be both tactful and safe. But, of course, if it is a choice, safety is always the paramount concern.

Twin Peaks Toiletry

Ken Michaels was a deputy out of the Twin Peaks Sheriff's Station. Twin Peaks is a small community near Lake Arrowhead in the San Bernardino Mountains. Michaels was known as a "hard charger." In other words, he worked hard at putting cases together and wanted to use his performance to advance his career. He was young, intelligent, diligent and a nice guy. For some reason, the combination of Ken and Barry produced some remarkable cases. They seemed to have the "golden touch" in that they had worked together on several cases that almost always netted new crimes or information. Usually they were drug cases.

The most unique case accomplished by the golden team was an investigation involving Christopher Thomas and his wife, Crystal. Ken received information from an informant in the mountain community of Crestline that the Thomas family was routinely selling "eight balls" of speed. An "eight ball" amounts to about 3.5 grams of methamphetamine. Barry noted "Crystal" was an appropriate name for a methamphetamine dealer. Mr. Thomas was a relatively new probationer and Barry had not met him but a review of his case file showed prior offenses for dealing methamphetamine. This new information caused Barry to ask Ken if he would assist in a search of the Thomas' residence in nearby Crestline. Both Ken and Barry confirmed the correct residence using records and good old surveillance as it's never a good idea to raid the wrong house.

On a cold winter evening, Ken, Barry and four other deputies made their way through the snow to the front door of the house. There was a slow response in answering the door but forcible entry was not necessary. Mr. Thomas eventually greeted officers and invited everyone in. He was a sturdy looking mountain man sort of guy, stocky with blond hair. The house was really not much more than a cabin but it was clean and warm.

As is standard procedure, officers ask questions to establish who else is in the residence and control is maintained of anyone located for officer safety. A protective sweep is conducted to visually inspect all areas to ensure there are no uncontrolled subjects that would threaten officers. Once all occupants are located, they are generally seated in one area, often the living room, where one officer can watch them. This allows the other officers to search their assigned areas without fear of being shot in the back.

In this instance, Mr. Thomas said from the start that his wife had been very ill and was in the bathroom. Barry said they would have to check that room as well for everyone's safety and he and Ken went to the bathroom door.

Knocking while at the same time slowly opening the door, Barry immediately saw a woman sitting on the toilet about ten feet away facing him from the back wall. "Ma'am, for our own protection, I need to make sure no one else is in here."

"No, you can't be in here. I'm using the bathroom!"

Even though the woman was sitting on the toilet, her private parts were covered up by her nightgown. Barry looked behind the door and in the tub and was able to establish that this girl was the only person in the bathroom. Barry was taken aback somewhat not only by the situation but by the fact that, except for looking ill, this woman was very pretty, with long brown hair. People who immerse themselves in the methamphetamine community usually look pretty bad in a short amount of time.

"The name's Crystal, correct?"

"Yes."

"Crystal, we need you to come out in the living room so we can safely go about our business."

Crystal, looking pathetic, glanced up at Barry groaning, "I have a nagging medical problem and I've been ill all day. I have diarrhea and can't get off the toilet without making a mess."

Barry explained to her that they couldn't leave her on the toilet and she would have to join her husband on the couch. Mr. Thomas interjected, "She really is telling the truth."

Barry looked at the woman and told her "you need to finish up and come out here."

While one of the deputies took Barry's place, looking through the partially opened door, Barry and Ken conferred out of earshot.

"I think she's full of shit but let's get a female deputy out here," Ken said in a low tone.

Barry thought that was a good idea and they proceeded to search the residence while keeping an eye on Crystal. It was taking a while for the female deputy to arrive and one of the deputies was talking about pulling her off of the toilet. In the meantime, another deputy found a prescription bottle on the coffee table that was in Crystal's name for some sort of medicine. It was current. Additionally, during the search the telephone rang and Ken took the call. It was a doctor's office checking on Crystal Thomas. Apparently, she had called them and they were returning the call. So now two pieces of information tended to support some sort of illness for poor Crystal and Barry and the boys had just about yanked her off the toilet.

These are the kinds of events where the balance between decency and safety is tackled. Officers use skills and instinct to negotiate these situations and they are rarely given credit for the required intellect and finesse. Anyone can kick a door down and make an arrest but it takes an astute cop to intelligently evaluate and act on every odd ball situation that arises.

The female deputy finally arrived and she was able to supervise the bathroom activity much more closely without fear of complaint or accusations of insensitivity or perversion.

Another few minutes went by and Crystal still insisted she could not get up from the toilet. Ken decided to call his sergeant at the station and ask for his opinion as to pulling her off the seat. Ken gave him all the information that they had received including the appearance that she was sick, the prescription and the call from the doctor. The Sarge initially said to go ahead and grab her but then said, "Wait a minute. That's Truman's case, right?"

"Yes, it's his probationer," Ken responded as if a light went on.

"Then, have HIM pull her off the toilet." That was entertaining for everyone except Barry. Everyone suspected she was up to something but, just in case, no one wanted to make the decision to drag her out of the bathroom.

But then the situation quickly changed. The female deputy had someone take her place at the bathroom door for a moment, allowing her to approach and whisper to Ken and Barry, "It looks like she is tearing up toilet paper and dropping it in the bowl."

This suspicious behavior shifted how officers perceived her from sick to sneaky. As such, with the female deputy leading the way back into the bathroom, Ken and Barry each grabbed and pulled her arms and told her that she was going to have to get up. She objected but did not offer physical resistance. She was searched by the female deputy and taken to the living room where she could be watched along with her husband.

Ken, who returned to the toilet area, called to Barry, "Check this out." Barry went back in the bathroom and noticed a look of excitement in Ken's eyes. Ken gestured to the toilet and Barry could see large bags in the water covered by some feces but mostly by torn up pieces of toilet paper.

Crystal had been sitting on and trying to conceal two one pound bags of methamphetamine. It was an easy case for Ken to put together and prove. Mr. and Mrs. Thomas went to jail and ultimately to State Prison.

Barry knew that Michelle and Tricia would love a rundown on this case. They always enjoyed hearing about females in interesting and/or scandalous roles. He gave them the summary when he got home.

"And her name is Crystal? That is classic!" remarked Tricia.

All three of them laughed while relaxing with beers in hand.

The Demeanor Scale

Ideally, in order to be effective, skilled and safe, a law enforcement officer needs to have the ability to operate with a low-key demeanor but also to be able to "dial it up."

For instance, a relaxed cordial officer can be much more effective in investigating matters than an officer being overly aggressive for no particular reason. All sorts of information can be extracted by engaging in a friendly dialogue. Barry became particularly accomplished in interviewing sex offenders in part by presenting a nonjudgmental persona and discussing the crime and asking questions in such a way as to convince the perpetrator that he or she is not that different from many other people.

The upper end of the spectrum is where officers need to be when people fail to cooperate, things just don't seem right or, of course, when individuals fight or run or threaten anyone. These types of behavior can easily lead to officers or others getting injured and an aggressive response is absolutely necessary.

Early on, Barry was one of six officers who were securing subjects in the living room in preparation for a residential search. All of a sudden one of the officers that was also on SWAT charged across the room and threw this kid against the wall with substantial force. Barry thought to himself he didn't need to do that.

Except the kid wasn't the only thing that bounced off of the wall. A chrome .22 caliber Raven pistol spitted out of his hand, eventually landing on the floor.

Barry didn't see the glint of chrome in the kid's hand and if he had, he probably would not have acted as aggressively. Many of these examples revealed themselves.

So, while in the beginning, Barry was low key all the time, after a few close calls, he learned to "dial it up" in a major way. Sometimes that's absolutely necessary to ensure your safety and the safety of those around you.

Barry and Chief Probation Officer Hancock had a conversation about this entire subject on a couple occasions. The reality is that many officers always operated at only one part of the spectrum. To be complete and skillful they need to learn to operate all across the spectrum. The Chief volunteered that when he was younger and working for the Los Angeles Police Department, he ALWAYS operated at the very top of the spectrum. He eventually learned how to dial it down. They laughed about Barry having to learn to be "off the hook" and the Chief having to learn to be more like the "Beachcomer."

Barry liked to recall a conversation he had with his brother. Earl Truman supervised a parole unit in the San Joaquin Valley of California. He would occasionally mention how a couple of his officers were a little too aggressive.

"Remember those two officers that I was worrying about?" Earl asked.

"Yeah - did they beat up a minister?"

"No, but one of them went to a parolee's house in Fresno and found him sick in bed."

"So, he beat him up?" Barry joked.

"The parolee had sheets and a blanket over him and my guy couldn't see his hands. He pulled out his Smith and Wesson, pointed it at the parole's head and screamed for him to slowly pull his hands out and raise them so he could see them. He said the parolee looked terrified but he followed commands."

"Okay," Barry said as if wanting the rest of the story.

"When my guy peeled back the bed coverings, he saw two sawed-off shotguns, one to each side of the parolee's legs. After he carefully extracted them, he found both of them to be chambered."

"Damn."

"Now obviously, he was arrested. But I couldn't help but wonder if the agent that went to that house was not as aggressive, would there have been a totally different and tragic ending."

The supreme skill is being able to correctly evaluate every situation but always erring on the side of safety. Equally as important is having the ability to escalate and deescalate in a fluid manner depending on the threat or other circumstances. This takes experience, training and intelligence, but mostly experience.

Not A Better Man

Barry came home from work at about 7:00 in the evening fully intending to relax with a beer. Michelle met him at the door and was crying. Her makeup was all over her face as if she had been crying for some time. He knew that something must be terribly wrong. He remembered that she had returned that day from a convention having to do with women in law enforcement.

"What's wrong, Sally?" Barry asked. He could not explain why he called Michelle by the name of Sally. It was one of those endearing pet names that somehow come to be in relationships and neither party remembers the origin.

"I feel terrible but I must tell you something that has been weighing on my mind," Michelle said, sobbing all the while. "You are my husband but also my friend and I have to come clean."

Barry, now quite concerned, encouraged her to disclose all. "Tell me everything. I can't stand to see you so miserable."

"I don't want to hurt you but an exercise at the convention made me realize that emotionally and sexually I really prefer women to men."

This took Barry completely by surprise. He was shocked and hurt and perplexed. "You don't love me?"

"Of course, I love you Barry but I ache for female closeness and companionship."

Barry admitted to being stunned. "So how long have you been thinking this way?"

"I guess from the time I was ten or eleven I have been attracted to girls but I buried those feelings. For the past two years, I would have feelings or urges. Sometimes Tricia would brush up against me and it would feel exciting but I would reign in those thoughts. I couldn't put my finger on what all that meant until this last weekend at the convention. Most of the content was about women's empowerment in the industry but one workshop dealt with sexuality and deciphering preferences and the instructor cleared up so many questions and insecurities I had and made me feel like a new person."

"You and Tricia have been lovers?"

"No, that never happened, although I spoke with her today and that is something we intend to explore. I am so sorry Barry - and I really feel that I should move out to truly start anew."

Still stunned, over the next few days, Barry helped Michelle move her things to an apartment in Huntington Beach. He was going through the motions. Michelle and Barry agreed to be civil and, if possible, remain friends.

The fact that Michelle left him for a woman - or women - instead of a man did not really matter. He was devastated. And there was the conflicted feeling of sadness for her in that she had spent so much time with him, wasted time perhaps, while having tendencies contrary to their relationship. It must have been miserable for her and he felt sad and guilty about that.

But mostly, it was the loss of his companion, the person to whom he shared his utmost secrets, the friend that laughed and cried with him, that drove him crazy. A major vacuum existed now and he was unsure how to deal with it. He would miss his Sally.

Verbal Skills and Communication

Verbal skills are so important in the business of law enforcement. Learning how to talk with citizens, criminals, coworkers and fellow professionals makes the work so much easier and safer. Officers are schooled in "Verbal Judo" classes on how to use their verbal skills as a tool to gently persuade citizens and offenders to comply or follow directions. A well-chosen phrase might be the difference between an easy arrest and an officer-involved shooting. Barry was a natural at being able to talk to people probably in part because he wasn't armed at the first part of his career. He had to defend himself and manipulate the situation without the option of deadly force.

Being able to communicate with coworkers is important so that you are on the same page with the same mission, always alerting one another to threats or changes in a fluid incident. Conducting searches and other activities in the community may call for information to be conveyed to other team members such as "ammunition was just located so be aware there may be a weapon in the vicinity." Or there is a giant dog dish at the back of the house so be cognizant that a Great Dane may come around the corner.

Communication needs to be clear to both subordinates and superiors. Tell your workers what you want them to do. You don't need to micromanage but they may need direction. Keep your boss advised of anything he or she may be questioned about by superiors or the media.

Barry was entertained by the fact that one important verbal notification was the same as in the wine and food industry, that of letting someone know that you are coming up behind them. Of course, in law enforcement that is for safety while in the restaurant world, it may be to prevent a catastrophic collision and a loss of both the chateaubriand and the thirty-year old Bordeaux.

And, of course, dispatchers need officers to advise them of the situation and where they are at all times. If you're behind a yellow barn at the northeast corner of a property, that is what you need to convey. If you move to another barn than you need to let them know that as well. If something goes wrong, the time it takes to locate you could impact your safety. As a Big Bear dispatcher once told Barry, "There's no way I can help you honey if I don't know where you are."

Then there are the times where well-chosen words will save your life. Barry, his sergeant and Bruno contacted a resident late at night in Muscoy. Muscoy is a lower socio-economic community technically in north San Bernardino. It can be exciting particularly late at night.

The team was looking for a male that may be cooking methamphetamine. A man of about seventy-five years old, believed to be his relative, opened the front door and immediately pointed a .357 magnum revolver directly at Barry's stomach. There was really no time for anyone to react. The barrel was under a foot from Barry's navel, and the man's hand, with its finger on the trigger, was shaking.

For the next two minutes, which seemed like ten minutes, the sergeant who was standing right beside Barry, tried to talk this guy into lowering the weapon. It became clear he was not upset with the law; he thought the three shabbily clad officers were "dirtbag" friends of his grandson. Fortunately, Sergeant Nady had a silver tongue. He explained every which way that they were cops and not criminal associates of his grandson, who, by the way, was the person under investigation.

All Barry could think of was Bruno standing behind him who five years earlier had been shot by an assailant in the stomach with a shotgun. It was very painful and it took a long time for him to recover. Barry did not want to know what that felt like.

Eventually, the sergeant talked this guy down. He lowered the revolver and the sergeant held on to it until they departed. The man said that his grandson and all his shady friends had stolen everything he had of value. Barry let out a sigh of relief. "Thanks, Sarge."

Friends Forever

A few weeks later, Barry met Michelle at her apartment and they strolled along the walkway close to the Pacific Ocean, sometimes even holding hands. It was obvious that Michelle seemed more relaxed and comfortable since her disclosure. Barry asked her about this and she said it was "like a thorn was pulled from my temple."

Then she quickly followed that comment with, "and no Barry - you were not the thorn."

They briefly discussed divorce paperwork. It was rather anticlimactic and there were no disagreements. Nonetheless, it did seem rather sad for both of them. They agreed to get past it and move forward.

While they walked, they laughed about the good times and marveled at how life can have many surprises. Barry needed to help her set up a new computer and put in a screen door. It seemed clear that they would be able to remain friends to some extent.

A very pretty blonde girl in her mid-twenties skated by in a tiny bikini that was nestled around a toned and sculptured body. Michelle, feeling now that she could comment, exclaimed, "Wow, check her out. Dear, can you imagine what the two of us could do to her?"

It was a surreal moment for Barry and he turned his head towards Michelle, who was still admiring the skater. He collected his thoughts and calmly commented, "Yes, I can."

Bandwagons, Neanderthals, Silliness and The Third Reich

Barry's career spanned so many years that he witnessed bizarre things in the bureaucratic world of government and, more specifically the probation department. This is a cautionary tale as leaders often buy into ways of doing business that are truly of little or no value or that are just plain wrong. Employees are expected to jump on board with the favored program or way of thinking with the penalty for refusing or questioning being a dead-end career, reassignment or, at the very least being accused of being a Neanderthal.

Everyone has dealt with people that are inflexible and fixed in their ways. Often, they are older, but the condition also afflicts the young. These are people that sometimes stand in the way of intelligent change and/or advancements in technology. These are the people that wholeheartedly resisted the transformation of massive report preparation from thousands of reams of paper to a digital process. Barry was the main proponent in this and it is currently the standard way of doing business, but at the time, it was not embraced by many.

Sometimes, officers or other employees just do not want things to change. They just like everything to stay the same. Then there are the employees that believe they are protecting their own turf and/or career so they often support the status quo rather than accept more efficient ways of doing business.

Conversely, it is sometimes good to have a few "Neanderthals" around to keep things in perspective. By virtue of the myriad things they have seen, they can smell a carnival act a mile away. Every change is not good and can even be outright hilarious.

For example, years ago the agency sponsored the concept that colors affected behavior and that the color "pink" would calm a person down. Training was mandatory and carnival workers posing as industry specialists would have volunteers try to lift their arms while looking at different color cards. The "carnies" would try to push down the arms of the volunteer. Of course, when they viewed pink they were helpless to keep their arms up. The science was, at the very least, questionable. Nevertheless, a significant amount of taxpayer money was used for the global training program and for building a "pink room" at the county juvenile hall. Juveniles who were arrested and unruly would be locked in the room with the intent of calming them down. Like Mortsoob said, all the pink room really did was, "piss them off."

Around the same time, "Orthomolecular Medicine" cropped up. This "science" argued that if you took refined sugar away from a criminal, he or she would become a better citizen. Charlatans sold thousands upon thousands of dollars-worth of training to all staff at the direction of administrators.

Participatory Management was another bandwagon sold to the agency. At least this was a widespread affliction that even some private enterprise companies toiled with for a period of time. Barry's agency signed up for a modified version utilizing something called the Probation Leadership Council but the idea was the same thing. Workgroups were made up of management and labor representatives on an "even playing field." Theoretically the groups would be empowered to make decisions. The whole thing wouldn't work if decisions couldn't be made by these groups. And of course, they were never empowered to do anything more than meet or be sent on expensive retreats and additional training sessions. The council was a convenient dumping ground for some problems and when administration would make unpopular decisions, they could point to the "PLC" as the culprit.

Barry questioned one of the main vendors of this process in private and asked how long this bandwagon would last. The trainer and part owner of the company making all the money selling this program told him it was already on the way out and that a type of compassionate dictator concept was already making inroads in government and replacing participatory management. Their company was exploring cashing in on the new way of running agencies and organizations while they were trying to squeeze as much money as possible out of the participatory concept before it all came crashing down. The impression Barry got was that the training providers would train probation officers to yodel if they thought they could convince leadership that yodeling was necessary in corrections and certainly if they could make lots of money.

Barry's friends in private companies reported the concept's failure there as well but, since private companies actually make something to sell to people, they dropped the participatory management scheme early on so they would remain solvent. The probation department dragged it on for years. No widgets made here.

It's difficult to fight major ideas promoted by management. Those that baulk or question are quickly written off as inflexible to new ideas. The reality is that the majority of employees question most obviously flawed concepts but remain silent for fear of reprisal in one way or another. To be fair, there are some employees that would actually believe the moon was made of cheese if the idea was presented in a professional typeset or as part of a power point presentation and if they were sent to Napa to brainstorm.

This is what always bothered Barry. He was convinced if agency heads ordered Jews in the ditch, some employees would actually follow through. No way is this meant to make light of the horrendous acts committed in the name of Adolph Hitler and the Third Reich. Life is generally not in jeopardy for government employees speaking their minds. Instead it is presented to demonstrate how people, employees or soldiers in any organization can act in an effort to please their leaders.

Early in Barry's career, the County of San Bernardino had completed its new government center and a big deal was made about the county's pioneers - not the Earps - but the employees working for all the departments. These were the cherished little people who kept the gears turning. All employees were encouraged to be a part of history and to sign a ceramic tile that would be glazed and cemented on a giant wall in a sacred place near the government center. At first Barry thought it to be silly but then he thought, "Why not?" He signed his name and he would occasionally look at his signature. It was easy to find as it was the last signed tile on the wall. He felt honored.

Employees come and go over the years so only Barry and a few others were amazed at what happened three decades later. With little fanfare, the wall was bulldozed over as part of a drought resistant landscape concept. Those pioneers, the very backbone of San Bernardino County, were dismissed as unvalued personnel from a different era. This is the way of government but never a good way to do business.

Meetings suck the life out of any operation actually trying to accomplish something. Barry recognized that sometimes they were necessary but felt that most often, they were a big waste of time and money. He particularly despised something called "round table." The facilitator or boss would ask each person if they had something to share. Barry felt that as long as each person was brief and the information they were sharing impacted the group, it had a function. Unfortunately, when prompted, many workers feel compelled to take a lot of time sharing material that has no value for anyone else. As soon as an employee commences self-promoting his or her work, the game is on. It seemed to Barry like everyone that followed became competitive and wanted to showcase their own work. As a result, it took FOREVER to complete the "round table." Some people that actually had valuable information never had the chance to present it. More times than not when it was his turn, Barry just said, "Pass."

When Barry conducted his own meetings, "round table" was not on the agenda. Rather, at the close of the session, he would ask if anyone had information that needed to be presented that would impact the entire group. Maybe one or two employees would have something to say and the meeting would be over. Anyone with individual issues could meet with Barry outside of the meeting format.

Sometimes if he had important information that had to be transmitted, he had "stand up" meetings and tried to keep them under seven minutes. While Barry thought this was his innovation, he learned from a fellow supervisor that he had experienced similar meetings in the aerospace industry. Employees just want to get the necessary information and get back to work.

Landeros Case

Jimmy Landeros was a drunk. He was on felony probation having been arrested for his fifth Drunk Driving and for Assault with a Deadly Weapon. But everything he did was related to alcohol. A decade or two later he would not have been afforded so many opportunities to stay out of State Prison. Back in the 1980s Driving While Under the Influence was not viewed as seriously as it would be later in Barry's career. Even then, everyone that worked in Botman's unit knew this guy was dangerous.

Landeros was assigned to Matt Drake. Almost immediately, he received information that Jimmy was drinking and driving again. His probation terms did not allow him to do either, drink or drive. The last time he appeared in court, the judge informed him if there was ANY indication that he was consuming alcohol, he would be sent directly to state prison.

Matt organized a search of Jimmy's residence in San Bernardino. Despite the fact that Jimmy was the biggest lush in the valley, he lived with a relative who was a law-abiding individual that allowed the team entry into the house. Had entry been a problem, officers would undoubtedly have been more vigilant but somehow being allowed to walk in lowered their alertness. Before the residence could be secured, Jimmy shot across the living room between two officers and squirted out the front door.

Matt, Botman and another officer pursued him on foot, running towards "D" Street.

"Foot pursuit west bound on 17th Street - after the primary," Barry radioed in as he and his partner jumped in the Blazer heading in the same direction.

The dispatcher already had the information on the subject and was in the process of declaring a "Code 33." This advisement on the air informs everyone to only transmit in the event of an emergency with the exception of the officers involved in the incident. A foot pursuit is one of the many incidents which can be dangerous and routine traffic on a radio channel or talk group can interfere with officers involved in the incident. Often, dispatchers will order all routine traffic to another talk group or channel.

All of a sudden everyone heard a "crack" which sounded like gunfire. Barry almost radioed that in until he was informed that Landeros had run directly into a vehicle moving southbound on "D" Street. The "crack" was Jimmy's head hitting the windshield frame of a Ford SUV, which was estimated to be traveling at forty-five to fifty miles per hour. Barry didn't see him collide with the metal windshield frame but officers on foot did, and said Landeros flew up in the air about thirty feet. He then landed on his side and rolled down the crown of the street, coming to rest at the curb. The woman who was driving was very upset but there was really no way she could avoid hitting someone running right in front of her vehicle.

Barry moved his vehicle right behind Jimmy so additional vehicles would not run him over. Jimmy was conscious but bleeding from his head. Barry's expertise did not include medical treatment but he knew enough to apply direct pressure to the wound. A crowd of local residents began forming and they were getting rowdy. People were making the assumption that Barry's large four-wheel drive had run this poor lad over and in this neighborhood, law enforcement officers were not real popular anyway. Just about the time things were getting real ugly, the paramedics arrived on scene. This served to calm things a bit and everyone was able to leave the scene.

Injured or not, Landeros was now in custody so Barry and Matt escorted the ambulance and stayed with Jimmy at the emergency room. Amazingly, he was not seriously injured and he escaped with some bruises and a concussion. Such is often the case when a drunk encounters trauma. They seem to be so flexible or pliable that they are resilient to accidents of a physical nature, accidents that would break every bone in a sober person's body.

Jimmy was an ass to the doctors that were trying to tend to him. Jimmy was always an ass when he was drinking, which was pretty much all the time. He refused to communicate with the attending physician, acting catatonic.

Doctors that have been assigned to the county hospital emergency room for any length of time are not "shrinking violets." They deal with all sorts of gunshot and knife wounds and criminals and their families. Arrowhead Medical Center is a level one trauma center so the medical staff at that facility deal with everything. This experienced physician was getting irritated with Landeros so he told his nurse in a routine sort of way, "Prepare his scrotum, we are going to have to remove it and perhaps his penis as well."

"Right away doctor," an equally experienced and callous nurse responded.

Jerking up as far as his restraints would allow, Jimmy yelled, "No way!"

His recovery was remarkable and now with a medical form that cleared him for incarceration, Matt and Barry dropped him off at the West Valley Detention Center. He finally was sent to State Prison.

Lying About Job to Strangers

One of things Barry and his law enforcement friends learned was that, when off-duty, it was often a good choice to lie when asked as to occupation. Particularly in taverns, cops, probation officers, deputies and the like are not really popular with everyone. Even if people weren't angry at you personally, they had stories about abuse or ill treatment at the hands of your brethren. The purported victim didn't even have to be them. It could be an uncle that they thought was illegally searched and arrested by a probation officer or a friend that was disrespected by a deputy. As such, when a stranger inquired as to what Barry "did," he would give them all sorts of answers. Early on in his career he would respond that he was an underwater welder or that he owned a flower shop but, occasionally a patron would know something about welding or flowers so he eventually settled on "working for the assessor's office." Assessors may not be popular but they generally aren't despised and rarely does anyone know much about their occupation other than they assess property.

Meet Gambling Woman

Barry loved to gamble, particularly in Nevada. It just didn't seem the same anywhere else. In Nevada, drinks are free if you are actively wagering although Barry and his friends would joke about those twenty-five dollar beers since that was sometimes what was lost while enjoying that "free" drink. And although one might think it counter to Nevada's colorful casino history, the gambler is somewhat protected by the Nevada Gambling Commission. Probably because gambling is the state's bread and butter, there are rules in Nevada about percentages of payoffs and types of machines and such. If gambling is your main offering, you protect it and make sure it's a quality product.

Barry was appalled that some casinos in California have video poker machines that are not really poker machines at all. They are actually video lottery terminals. It doesn't even matter what cards a player holds. The machine will pay out totally at random. It doesn't mean a person can never win; it's just that the player is being deceived into thinking he or she is playing one thing and it really is something totally different.

Much to Barry's initial dismay, Steve Mortsoob would never hold any cards at these machines because he said it didn't matter. Turns out he was right. It doesn't matter. Fortunately, in Nevada, those machines have to be real video poker devices. They have a random number generator in the machine but the cards are theoretically dealt from a 52-card deck and the gambler is actually interacting to produce the outcome.

Gambling is one of those pursuits that people seem to either love or not be interested in at all. Barry always thought the mindset difference was similar to people who loved nice or perhaps exotic cars and other people who only saw vehicles as something to get them from point A to point B. Barry had close friends in each of those camps.

He always wondered if he liked gambling so much due to his fundamentalist Christian upbringing and the fact that a deck of cards was taboo. Old maid cards were okay but not that fancy real deck of cards in the buffet that was a business gift to the family at some point in the past. Barry's mother grew up in a fundamentalist Christian community and playing cards and gambling were somehow associated with evil. Booze and cigarettes and lipstick and dancing were viewed similarly. There were evangelists in the early twentieth century who preached against these perceived evils and their messages undoubtedly permeated some of these congregations.

Barry was not a compulsive gambler. He had his financial limits and truly became tired of being in gambling cities after about two days. He didn't wager more than he could afford to lose. His preferred games were blackjack, slot machines and video poker.

While "playing the slots" is a solitary type endeavor, some socialization takes place if the player is trying his or her luck at video poker at the bar. But it is also a good place to just "zone out" by pushing buttons and occasionally speaking to the bartender or your buddy. Blackjack, conversely, is generally very social or at least Barry liked it to be. He would talk to the other players and to the dealers and he was genuinely interested in their lives and stories. Everyone has a story to tell. He liked to ask the dealers questions. Barry just wanted to know about everything.

One of the questions he routinely asked his dealers, if they were personable, was what was the most unusual thing they had seen while dealing or "pitching" cards. The most interesting answer came one evening at the Golden Nugget in downtown Vegas. A woman dealer of about thirty-five years of age, who dealt cards in a precise manner at a moderate speed, responded, "An older woman sitting at first base slumped over her cards and chips." She gestured towards first base, the first seat to her left.

"She was dead?" a bookish but attractive looking dark-haired girl sitting to the right of Barry inquired.

"Most assuredly," the dealer emphasized.

"That is a remarkable and sad story," Barry remarked, "but several dealers have told me about players that died at their tables. I guess if you deal long enough, you have a pretty good chance of experiencing something like that."

"You're right," said the dealer, "but what made this so unusual was that the three other players at the table were upset that I stopped dealing cards. They wanted me to continue, presumably bypassing the dead woman!"

After that bit of information, everyone playing at the table looked up in amazement.

The same player then asked, "just curious, but what hand was the lady holding?"

The dealer paused as if deciding whether it was appropriate to answer and then clearly said, "She had a ten and a two." Every player at the table then nodded or gestured subtlety as if they understood why she dropped dead. Twelve is about the worst hand you can get. It wasn't humorous or in bad taste. It was more a group acknowledgement of the plight of the blackjack player.

"My name is Barry," holding his hand out to the librarian. Barry wanted to meet this woman who would ask such a question.

She shook his hand and said "Meghan."

She seemed so pragmatic and very even. She was not warm but not cold. She was more reasoned and calculated. That's probably why she played an excellent game of blackjack. She was at the double deck table not by chance but for the same reason that Barry was at that table. In a crowded casino, a double deck is as good as it gets for counting cards.

The idea in counting cards is to win in the long run by raising your bet when the remaining cards make it more likely that a blackjack could be dealt. But even if the player just utilizes something called "basic strategy," the odds are better than any other game in the casino. Ironically, the casino makes a good deal of money at blackjack because the average player isn't playing in accordance to any recognized playing guidelines.

Unfortunately, in contrast to Meghan's continued excellent play, Barry had lost the count due to his infatuation with her. His Heineken showed up and he tipped the server. Meghan was drinking what appeared to be cranberry and vodka. The guy next to her was moaning and groaning about not being offered a drink.

"Oh, so they get drinks and not me? What the hell?"

That guy was sitting there before Barry arrived but Meghan whispered, "He isn't tipping."

The way it works in Nevada casinos is that cocktail waitresses take orders at the tables or machines and then deliver the free drinks to the players. Some casinos have switched over to taking and transmitting orders on iPads but the concept is still the same. Either way it is common courtesy to give the server at least a dollar a drink. Barry would also give them a dollar for a bottled water and he would tip more if, say, he got a jackpot and a particular server was bringing him his drinks. In most casinos, the tips received by the dealers are "pooled" which just means all the dealers share them. This prevents players from tipping heavily in exchange for great hands or undeserved payoffs. The servers, however, aren't involved in the games of chance so they keep their own tips. Because of this, if they know every time they bring a drink of any kind, they will get at least a buck, they will come back. The dollars add up over an entire shift.

Conversely, if a server brings drinks to a player that never tips, how anxious is she going to be to make sure that player's drink doesn't run dry? Whenever Barry heard someone complaining about not getting served, he suspected they weren't tipping. In this instance, Meghan confirmed that assumption.

The guy kept complaining to the point where it was irritating Meghan and probably interrupting her concentration as well. She asked the dealer to "color me out" which just means she is leaving the table. The dealer consolidates her chips into higher denomination chips so the table doesn't run out of the smaller chips. Also, it makes it clear to the pit boss and the cameras above how much money is leaving the table. Barry noted Meghan received five black chips and a green and some red chips for a total of about $545.

Barry pushed his stack of chips toward the dealer declaring, "I'm out of here too" and then she converted his winnings to four black chips and one green, or a total of $425. He sat down with $200 so that was good.

Meghan had not gone far and Barry walked up to her and commented, "Can you believe that guy?"

"At least you weren't sitting right next to him. You want to find another table?"

"Absolutely," replied Barry, thinking that they would have similar tastes as to rules and number of decks but mainly he just wanted to talk with her.

They walked by several tables but weren't impressed by the offerings. Barry suggested they walk to a place called the Main Street Station, about five minutes away from the Nugget. She had never gambled there and was wanting to try something different.

Meghan found it as Barry had represented. There were two or three double deck games and a single deck that actually paid 3 to 2 on blackjacks. This just means that if you bet say $10 on a hand and get a a blackjack, you will get a full $15 for your winnings. The blackjack player sees these less and less, particularly with single and double decks. The minimum bet was $10 but this wasn't as important to Meghan as it was for Barry as she rarely played the minimum. Meghan felt more comfortable wagering green ($25) and black ($100) chips.

Meghan noted that the dealers were friendly and the place was clean. They again sat at a double deck table that had two seats open beside each other.

If you've never sat at a blackjack table, you may not know that it can be a little cramped with all chairs occupied, especially if some of the players are big. Barry didn't like to be cramped but, in this instance, he was happy that a couple large Samoan fellows were at the table causing him to have to get real close to Meghan.

"Excuse me Meghan. I know we just met about an hour ago." As he said it, he could feel the warmth emanate from her lower body.

"No problem Barry. It feels like longer."

Over the next several hours, the two gambled together. Barry had tired of the focus required to count cards and be social all at the same time. Counting cards is not illegal but it is something best concealed from the casinos. They much prefer to have the average blackjack player take your seat and, once you are labeled a card counter, the casinos, who mostly share such information with other casinos, will do everything in their power to ensure you lose more than you win.

He told Meghan he was going to take a break and play video poker at the bar while sipping on a Heineken. It was very relaxing. In twenty minutes or so, Meghan stopped by the bar and asked Barry how he was doing.

"I need to get one more beer so the price per beer drops to $20." They both laughed knowing that meant he was losing.

"Would you like to get some dinner?" asked Barry.

"Sure, what about right here?" Meghan was referring to the restaurant in the Main Street Station. Barry was all over that as the food was good and not that expensive. As much as he liked Meghan, he didn't really want their first meal together to be too lavish.

Dinner was good and they each shared some basic information about their lives. Barry gave her a brief and sanitized synopsis as to his many assignments over a period of many years. While Barry thought Meghan must be some sort of mathematics instructor, she was actually a seismographic expert for the State of California. Somehow, she had never married and she had no children.

"I've always wanted children," said Barry. "It just has never worked out."

Meghan didn't say one way or another if she wanted children or if she was able to have children. She changed the subject.

"When can you retire?" Asked Meghan.

"Technically I can retire right now but I wouldn't get much money. Plus, I'm having fun most of the time. And then - and this is going to sound corny - I really believe we have value. I'm not talking about dealing with drug dealers or burglars. But when we can make a serious sex offender disappear from the community, it protects SO many lives. If a sexual predator gets arrested for victimizing one kid, the experts say there are 100 more victims that are unknown. But there are NO new victims while these guys are unavailable. Thus, I want to do as much as I can do in this area."

"I apologize. I'm just rambling." Barry laughed.

Dinner was followed by more blackjack, more drinks and more conversation. Now they were brushing each other's arms when they spoke and, almost as a matter of necessity, they were leaning on one another when they walked between casinos. An embrace led to a kiss right out in the middle of Fremont Street. This is a street that runs between the major downtown casinos that is closed to vehicle traffic. Barry accepted an invitation to Meghan's room in the Golden Nugget and they wasted no time in sharing much more than card counting techniques.

A relationship developed and the two would meet to dine, to have cocktails or just to visit in various locations across Southern California, including their residences. Except for that initial passionate meeting in gambling town, Barry rather thought that Meghan was somewhat clinical in her way of making love. Perhaps, more accurately, she was making sex. She seemed to enjoy the physical rewards but there was a lack of spontaneity and, frankly, fun. In the act, her facial expression did not deviate significantly from the way she looked while counting cards. Nevertheless, she was desirable in her own way.

As much as Barry liked spending time with Meghan, he never really shared his inner thoughts. He never demonstrated vulnerability or even mentioned how he wanted to do one thing very impactful before he put down his badge. He probably was responding in kind as Meghan was careful not to expose her inner self to Barry.

Explosive Devices

Barry always felt that not enough training was afforded officers regarding the identification of bombs and bomb-making material. He thought he must be missing something. Even before the rash of recent terrorist acts, extremists were killing people with bombs. Barry still has a T-shirt given to him by the District Attorney's office in Altus, Oklahoma, listing the names of all the dead following the Oklahoma City bombing.[13] Subsequently and through training, he knew the chemicals to search for that caused that mass murder.

In light of terrorist acts and in projecting incidents likely to come to "soft targets," wouldn't it be more prudent to train officers in what to look for related to bomb making, rather than waste their time in obscure training of questionable tangible value?

Barry knew more than most about explosives mainly because of making bombs and rockets as a hobby while growing up in small town Ohio. He had his share of close calls which caused him to respect explosives. Barry could remotely detonate devices and could identify power supplies and transmitters. Early in his career he was fortunate enough to attend bomb classes with other agencies such as the San Bernardino Sheriff's Department where things were actually blown up. Talk to any officer. They love to blow stuff up.

During a search at a residence in Fontana, Barry and Sparky Lewis were searching through a real junky room for methamphetamine or evidence of a laboratory. At some point, Sparky threw a rectangular object towards Barry, advising, "Hey Truman - check out this bomb!"

---

[13]The Oklahoma City bombing was a terrorist truck bombing at a federal building in Oklahoma City in 1995, killing at least 168 people and injuring more than 680 others.

Barry caught what looked like a circuit board with two tubular objects mounted. These objects were the size and shape of sticks of dynamite.

Barry shouted, "What the hell are you doing throwing this around?"

Sparky's viewpoint was that the board was just junk. Barry, conversely, noted large capacitors that could supply power and a bunch of unidentified circuitry. It was not clear if any detonators were present.

Barry's position on finding anything possibly explosive was to err on the side of caution. Always call the bomb squad. If they have to drive all the way across San Bernardino County to the Colorado River to find a legal firework, so be it. They always said they loved the overtime.

Despite being chided by Sparky, Barry carefully laid the device down and radioed dispatch from the front of the property. Sometimes the power generated by a transmitter like a police radio can trigger explosives. Barry realized that there was at least a 50 percent chance that he had found an inoperable device and would be unmercifully kidded by his fellow officers, especially Sparky.

The bomb squad was able to respond within the hour. It seemed like whatever time, day or night, Greg Gordon was on duty. He was dedicated, funny but mostly intense. He looked at the device and directed Barry, Sparky and two other deputies to go out on the street. Barry was being harassed out by the cars for wasting time, particularly right before lunch when, all of a sudden, the ground shuttered and a loud "boom" could be heard. The bomb squad had taken the device way out in the back yard and blown it up. It created a crater about two feet deep and eight feet wide. All Sparky could say was, "I'll be damn!"

Greg is the Bomb

Bomb Squad Expert Greg Gordon deserves additional mention. One evening, Barry and several narcotic team members were enlisted to help with the securing of a large residence in Fontana. It was a federal operation and the local narcs were relegated to watching the back while the federal team made entry through the front door.

There are really two interesting things at play here which are linked by contradiction. First, whomever is putting together an "operation" where entry is made into a residence, will assign officers according to their perceived status. It doesn't matter if the person planning the party is from the FBI, the local police or sheriff, a probation or parole agent or a Franchise Tax Board agent, all involved officers or agencies will be informally assigned by status. The lowest status gets to watch the back of the structure. In this instance, despite narcotics officers having somewhat a special status within their jurisdiction, this was a federal road show so the local agencies assisted but not with anything important like going through the front door.

Second, the back is where everything happens. A team will make entry through the front, often eventually flushing out fleeing suspects. This may take a while depending upon the size and setup of the structure. It's rather like the remaining toothpaste being squeezed out of the tube. That's why Barry always stressed to his people to not abandon their post until they got an "all clear" or in California, a "code 4" from inside the residence.

Barry was one of four officers standing to the rear just outside the fence. They could hear "knock and announce" admonishments and the front door being forcibly compromised. They had been briefed and told to expect lookouts and Barry could see a dark figure in the moonlight standing on a support post for the rear fence close to the house. Then he saw this subject throw an object through the air in his direction. It landed on some asphalt with a "thud" about ten feet in front of Barry. It continued to roll in his direction and was now emanating sparks like from an Independence Day sparkler.

Barry could only back pedal and the object kept rolling, getting closer to him. All of a sudden, about four feet in front of Barry, it made the sound of a rocket launching and it erupted with an extremely bright fan of light. Barry instinctually covered his eyes as he fell back on the ground. Everyone in the residence was arrested and the bomb squad was summoned.

Greg Gordon arrived and he was all excited about confiscating this military illumination grenade. Barry was not really hurt although the white phosphorus burned through his sock and left a mark on his ankle. White phosphorus is nasty stuff that will even keep burning under water. Greg took pictures of all of it including Barry's ankle and sock.

"Barry, if that grenade had been two feet closer to you or if it had been a shrapnel grenade, we could have gotten this guy for murder on a peace officer!"

Barry thought about that briefly then commented, "Yeah but Greg, I would be dead then."

Greg put his head down as if terribly disappointed and remarked, "Oh yeah."

As it worked out, the feds, who are good at preparing witnesses for trial, had Barry ready to testify but it was unnecessary. The guy that threw the grenade pled out to "attempted" murder on a peace officer and was sentenced to the federal penitentiary for a long time.

While Greg Gordon may still have been disappointed, Barry was just fine with the conviction with the designation of "attempted."

Gambling Woman Reprise

Meghan and Barry were spending some weekends together, usually in Vegas or Laughlin, a smaller and more basic Nevada gambling town on the Colorado River. They played a lot of blackjack and they would occasionally retreat to their room to enjoy each other in private. They would visit various casinos but generally finish the evenings where they stayed at the Golden Nugget whether it be in Vegas or on the river.

Particularly at the Nuggets, they were familiar with the employees. Meghan didn't really care about who was dealing cards but Barry always liked a personable dealer for two reasons. It just seemed like a nice dealer wanted the players to win and they occasionally would pay out when they shouldn't, whether by accident or deliberately. Plus, Barry always felt that you could lose with a nice dealer but the experience was not nearly as traumatic as when you lose with an annoying dealer. It's like getting a speeding ticket and a lecture. Just please give me one or the other!

The two found themselves at a table with an unfamiliar dealer at the Vegas Nugget. She was new to the Nugget but had been a dealer for twelve years at two other casinos. She seemed personable so Barry asked his favorite question about the strangest thing she had seen at one of her tables.

In this instance, it was a man who fell off his chair, collapsing onto the floor. It appeared to be some sort of a medical event. Fortunately, an ambulance responded immediately and EMT personnel attended to the man. They decided that he needed to be transported right away to the emergency room. He was barely conscience and was having difficulty answering their questions. A woman seated in a chair at the same blackjack table answered the questions for him making it clear that she was his wife or significant other.

The dealer continued describing the incident. The medical technicians lifted the man on to a gurney, carefully routing his IV. One of the EMTs said to the woman, "Ma'am, you can ride to the hospital in the ambulance with him if you like."

"No, I'm finally turning it around at this table. I'll come by later," the lady said in a determined manner.

The dealer and the EMTs were astounded. The pit boss handed the dealer a new deck of cards and she counted them in preparation for the upcoming hands.

Barry always loved these dealer stories. He guessed that gambling sometimes brought out the devil in people.

Meghan and Barry took a break in the room. It was midday and he drifted off on the bed. When he awoke, Meghan was lying on her back staring at the ceiling or, really, past the ceiling. "This is rather embarrassing but I withdrew my daily limit on my bank card and it's a long way until midnight so-"

Barry interrupted, "Sure - I've had that happen as well. How much do you need?"

"$500 would be great if that's not too much. I can reimburse you tomorrow."

"Done."

They gambled the night away and Barry slept in while Meghan enjoyed some alone time at the spa. When Barry rejoined her, she was back at blackjack.

"You must like this game," Barry kidded. He sat down beside her and threw his player's card and a couple hundred bucks on the table.

The dealer's name plate said, "Ricardo - Mexico." He smiled which is always a good sign. Who wants to sit at a table where the dealer looks like he or she hates life? They played for twenty minutes or so but neither of them seemed to be getting desirable hands. Sometimes that happens and the only solution is to get up, walk away and come back later.

They cashed their remaining chips at the cashier's cage and Meghan gave Barry back his $500.

"Thank you, ma'am. What would you like to do now?"

Meghan wanted to just sip on a beer and do a little people watching on Fremont Street. There is always an assortment of entertainers and entrepreneurs on Fremont Street and some are pretty bizarre. Some are borderline fraud. All are interesting. There's usually some scantily clad men and women dressed in various costumes from Michael Jackson to Taylor Swift who will be happy to pose with you for a donation. There's the eighty-year old guy wearing only a small piece of material over his scrotum who will oblige for a photo as well. Not to cast aspersions on all individuals down on their luck but one guy in a wheel chair looking for donations, claiming to be a disabled veteran, wears gear from the army, navy and marines. According to several blackjack dealers, the one lady (again, there may be legitimate persons as well) has been collecting money for eight years due to her stage four cancer. She proclaims that she only has a few months to live and cries with and hugs nice people from all over the world that not only open their hearts but their wallets. The two nuns that appear to have their breasts exposed are a classic as well. Elvis is ever present. Add on the saxophone player and the artist playing percussion on the Home Depot buckets and you have a well-rounded experience. No wonder young wedding couples fly from the United Kingdom to spend a portion of their honeymoons in downtown Vegas. You can't see this stuff in Covent Garden.

As people do in gambling town, they split up to try their luck at different ventures. Barry played the slots and he wasn't sure where Meghan was playing. Text messaging makes it so easy to keep in touch; it's almost as if it was designed for gamblers. Years before, a group would have to set a time and a location to meet.

The two were back together later in the evening and Meghan was again apologetically asking to borrow money. "I did it again, Barry. I've run out of money and it's not yet midnight!"

"Here's the $500 again. Ya know, you really ought to have your bank raise your daily limit. I think I have mine set at $2000."

"That's probably a good idea. I will do that after this trip. In the meantime, I'm beholden to you."

"You know, there are ways you can pay me back that don't involve money."

"Ha ha - Yes there are," Meghan said in an alluring way. "Why don't we go back to the room and freshen up?"

Barry quickly agreed and they showered and tumbled around on the bed for a while. Meghan was actually a little playful for a change.

Soon they were back on the casino floor going their own ways. They met at the sports book about an hour later.

Barry decided to place a bet for the Packers to win the NFC championship game. He also placed a bet on the longest shot which was for the Cleveland Browns to win the AFC championship. He figured one of these years he would actually win.

The worker behind the sports book betting counter looked up and exclaimed, "Hi Meghan!'

Barry looked at Meghan and she answered back to the guy, "Hi."

The man continued, "No bets today?"

"No not today."

It was clear that Meghan frequented the Golden Nugget sports book at least often enough that this guy knew her name. "I thought you mostly played blackjack," inquired Barry.

"I do but I have to admit I occasionally place a modest bet on college football games and sometimes the ponies."

Meghan hadn't mentioned this before so it got Barry's attention. He let it go as he figured she might have been embarrassed that she bet a little more than what she was letting on.

"Sometimes I get a little carried away. As a matter of fact, keep this money for me." Meghan handed over $1500 in hundreds to Barry.

"What do you want me to do with this?" Barry inquired.

"Just keep it for me and, if I ask for it, don't give it to me. Give it to me when we leave."

"Seriously? That seems a little silly."

Meghan agreed but again said, "Please - If I ask for it, just don't give it to me. I made some money earlier and I have plenty to use for more gambling."

"Okay, but that doesn't make any sense at all."

They walked down to the old Vegas gambling district to play some blackjack at the El Cortez. This establishment is very basic and does not offer much glitch or glamour. What it does offer is single deck blackjack paying 3 to 2 and no strange rules. Often it is a $5 minimum bet. Despite the sometimes-heavy smoke, this place has gotten more and more popular with the young folk.

After a couple hours, both Meghan and Barry were a little ahead. They split up again with Barry "zoning out," playing video poker at the Four Queens while Meghan tried her luck somewhere else. She texted after an hour or so to meet at the main bar at the Nugget.

Barry cheerfully greeted her. "Hey pretty lady! How's your luck?"

"Up and down, but I need that money I had you hold."

"You mean the money you told me not to give you?"

"Yeah, I know it's crazy but I really do need to get it from you." Meghan sounded serious but looked a little sheepish.

Barry was thinking this was a bit odd. Was he to listen to the Meghan of a few hours ago or this Meghan? "I rather think I should continue to hold your money for you because you were so emphatic that I not give it to you."

It was obvious now that Meghan was getting irritated. "Barry! Give me MY money please!"

"Okay - Quiet down. Let's talk about this a little and make some sense of it." Barry, always the investigator, wanted to solve the puzzle.

"It's my fucking money. Give it back to me!"

He was shocked and it occurred to him that he had never heard Meghan curse before. She was loud enough that Barry knew casino security would be stopping by. In Las Vegas, casino security personnel are generally fast at dealing with incidents before they get totally out of hand.

"Here - take it!" Barry put the folded hundreds on the bar in front of her. Just then the security people arrived and asked Meghan, "Are you all right ma'am?" Barry thought, *why are they automatically asking HER?*

"I'm fine. We just had a disagreement but everything is fine now."

They checked further, "Did he touch you at all?"

"Oh God no. Everything is fine." Meghan was now completely composed.

"Maybe I need to get out of your sight for a while Barry. I want you to like me again. I'll play some machines and meet you back at the bar in an hour if that works."

"Sure. I don't hate you. I'm just concerned and a little confused."

"Understandable. I'll see you in an hour."

Before they met, Barry was on the way to the restroom when he spotted Meghan in the high stakes slot machine section. You can make quite a bit of money on those machines if you win but, if you lose, you can dig yourself a big hole. Barry only occasionally delved into these areas and only when he was substantially ahead. Those machines can eat hundred dollar bills, one after another.

Even a $10 machine will cost at least $20 a pull and perhaps $50 when maximum bet is selected. If you don't bet maximum on most any slot machine, there are some payoffs you simply won't get. Maximum bets will not only qualify you for the jackpots calculated for that particular machine but also for the substantial but unlikely progressive jackpots that are available through many networked machines at different locations.

For example, a few weeks earlier, Barry was downtown, listening to a conversation between blackjack dealers. A couple dealers and the pit boss were talking about this lady that won $20,000 playing a slot machine. This would be a wonderful jackpot for Barry but he wondered, in the land of jackpots, why was this such an intriguing topic of conversation?

"Because," said his dealer, "It was her last spin and she didn't add the last dollar to make it a maximum bet. If she had, she would have won 2.6 million dollars."

Barry, who won $200 once instead of $1200 after failing to put in the last dollar, understood. "Oh my God. How she must feel!"

Barry left Meghan alone. Everyone chooses how they want to spend their money and how they want to gamble. When they met back up, Meghan was at least partially forthright about the scope of her gambling. "I do get carried away Barry and sometimes I risk more than I should."

Barry just listened. He had never knowingly encountered a compulsive gambler but he wondered if Meghan might fit the bill. He remembered the case of the premier quarterback from Ohio State years ago, raised in farm country near where Barry was born, who just couldn't stop gambling. He did shameless things and was incarcerated for various schemes many times. If Barry was not mistaken, this guy was STILL in custody for doing scandalous things just because of his gambling addiction. He was confident Meghan was not that doomed.

"My bankroll goes up and down quickly Barry. An hour ago, I was down to $400 but right now I have $5000 in my pocket. I'm on a roll!"

The next morning, they had breakfast and parted ways for their respective residences in California. Meghan and Barry would meet for dinner and drinks on occasion over the next six months or so but things were never the same. It eventually came out that Meghan played about every game of chance available. She played the horses, college and professional football and basketball, craps, slots and, of course, blackjack. She bought lottery tickets almost every day. She bet on practically anything she could online with her smart phone. She had borrowed against her house and her government 401K to keep afloat. Barry, who had gradually loaned her a little over $3000, figured that was the price of the experience.

"Barry - I think you now understand my plight and why I am alone but I really will pay you back at some point."

"I know you will Meghan. You take care of yourself."

Who Would Have Guessed

Many times, when a subject is contacted, barring the unexpected, officers know they are going to place him or her under arrest. This happens more with probationers and parolees than when a new crime is being investigated and, of course, there are times when information needs to be obtained and delaying arrest furthers that pursuit. But often there is no benefit in delaying arrest. In fact, if an officer knows he is going to arrest a subject, and there is no reason to put it off, a delay can get downright ugly.

A felon with time to think and plot an escape route or who is just allowed the forum to express his displeasure in being taken into custody, can make an easy arrest turn into the necessity to use force and the preparation of the reports that follow. Also, scrutiny by superiors and outsiders is commonplace. Attorneys of the civil variety see dollars signs and love to question the use of force after the fact.

Barry believed in quick efficient arrests that were accomplished without incident. You contact the offender, clearly direct him or her to put their hands behind their back and you install handcuffs. Any conversation regarding anything else can come after the subject is secured.

Much to the chagrin of the troops, there are officers that have a reputation for taking forever to take someone in custody. If the subject is considered a high risk to run or fight, and personnel are available, one strategy is for officers to linger about in plain sight until the subject is in custody. If the felon tries to escape, resists or attacks the arresting officer, then several other officers are available to subdue him or her without incident. Often just the obvious presence of other officers, particularly big ones like Steve Mortsoob, will cause the subject to comply, thereby preventing a problem before it occurs. One has to remember that males in particular tend to evaluate the situation as it pertains to their physical capabilities. Experienced felons have come out on the losing side enough to not take a chance if the physical odds are not in their favor.

That brings us to Probation Officer Tim Cline. Tim was a really nice guy that supervised juveniles who had mental health problems. He was slender in build, short and about ten years older than Barry. His manner was soft and easy-going and he was viewed as an officer that enjoyed the therapeutic side of supervising these kids.

Tim needed to arrest one of his probationers, a seventeen-year old male who had recently assaulted a teacher and was originally placed on probation for blowing his fingers off when a pipe bomb that he placed in a school locker, went off prematurely. Barry did not work with Tim or, for that matter, in juvenile division but he was summoned by an administrator to help Tim accomplish the arrest. Apparently, some other important case or activity had tied up all his usual sidekicks.

Barry rode with Tim to the house of the probationer. He assured Barry they did not need further backup. As much as he liked Tim, Barry was concerned that everything would go to hell as Tim would want to talk to the kid and not arrest him right away. The kid would get upset and Barry would have to step in and clean things up. Injuries could occur as well as a trip to the hospital and reports would have to written. As it was a Tuesday, this simple arrest might blossom into something that might prevent Barry from attending his weekly Judicial Review Board meeting.

Tim told Barry that he had been looking for this kid and that the mother telephoned and explained that he had finally returned home the night before. Tim said the mother was cooperative and wanted her son locked up. Barry knew not to count on this as parents often change their minds and she may very well be screaming at them as they attempt to subdue him. Sometimes when an officer is just trying to restrain an individual, it looks to an outsider like a beating is taking place. Things were not looking favorable for an uneventful arrest.

Tim knocked softly at the front door of the residence and the mother allowed the twosome entry, nodding to Tim and pointing upstairs. Barry and Tim quietly crept up the steps to the second floor.

A rather large juvenile could be seen sleeping on his back on a twin bed. Barry prepared himself to step in as he knew Tim would wake him up and start talking with him, getting him all riled up in the process.

To Barry's surprise, Tim lunged quickly and grabbed the kid, flipped him over and cuffed him before he awoke. The kid was literally still asleep when he was handcuffed. When he awoke, he was quite surprised.

"Jesus Tim," Barry exclaimed, "That was the damnedest arrest I have ever seen."

"Over the years, I've learned that this is the preferred way to arrest these mentally challenged young men," Tim remarked in the even tone of a professor.

"I've never seen anything like that before. I'm impressed."

As they drove the kid to juvenile hall, Barry was pondering how you sometimes learn new things at the most unexpected times and places. Arrest them before they wake up, "Damn," he murmured softly.

And he was not late for JRB.

Barry's Glass Runneth Over

By now, Mortsoob was divorced just like Barry. He was lucky in that within a year of that dissolution he bumped into an old neighbor by the name of Barbara and they hit it off. It's funny how fast things can progress when all of the "getting to know you" stuff is out of the way and there are no worries about the prospective partner being a serial killer.

Barry was on his own and he would sometimes impose and be the "third wheel" with Steve and Barbara. On just such an occasion, Barry met them for a day of wine tasting in Mendocino County. They picnicked at a nice winery by the name of Campovida in the vicinity of the town of Hopland and then proceeded to visit another nearby tasting room belonging to Haven Cellars. The woman serving wine behind the counter was very attractive. It always seemed to Barry that wineries would hire servers that were either retired persons or pretty young women. Barry was always taken back by how knowledgeable the young servers were. It seemed the females had particularly good palettes. Barry had spent most of his life drinking and analyzing wines and these twenty-two year olds were far more perceptive.

The woman serving the threesome was not twenty-two but she surely was in her thirties. A "spook"[14] told Barry years before that analyzing a person's hands is the best way to determine age. Barry thought she looked to be thirty-two but her hands suggested she may be in her early forties. Regardless of age, she was fit looking. Barry generally liked long hair on a woman but this girl's short blonde cut

[14] Slang for an espionage officer or agent employed by the Central Intelligence Agency.

was appealing and complimented her personality, which was both subdued and bubbly all at once, if that's possible.

Barry, Barbara and Steve were the only customers. That's the great thing about tasting wine during the week, especially in places like Mendocino, Lodi or Paso Robles. It just isn't very busy and the servers have more time to talk to their customers, sometimes offering a special wine not on the tasting list. Since Steve and Barbara were quietly conversing, Barry introduced himself to the server, who revealed her name was Sarah.

Sarah and Barry talked about the various offerings, how the Malbec had a subtle nose and how the Zinfandel was powerful but balanced. Sarah asked Barry where he was from and they exchanged pleasantries. Barry couldn't believe how informed Sarah was about wine and how she did not present her knowledge in such a way as to be boastful or belittling. She was a good listener and responded accordingly to Barry's comments. There didn't seem to be anything cold or calculating about this woman.

Sarah was the only representative of the winery in the tasting room and she talked with Barry for probably thirty minutes. At some point Barry asked about how the wine club worked. He didn't really want to join another wine club but was just extending their comfortable conversation. Sarah softly and clearly said, "If you want to join the wine club, you know you'll have to give me your address and phone number, right?"

She was looking squarely into Barry eyes and even he could tell she was talking about more than the wine club. She was so calm and quiet that Steve and Barbara didn't seem to be paying any attention. She would keep pouring wine in their glasses as well and Mortsoob would turn and comment on a wine from time to time. When they had exhausted the list on the counter, Sarah would bring something else out to share and she also encouraged them to revisit any wines that had already been poured.

Barry didn't want the opportunity to get away. "Would you ever be interested in sharing a glass of wine somewhere else or a cup of coffee for that matter? I've really enjoyed talking with you."

"The feeling is mutual. I would love to meet for either."

They exchanged information in such a way that Barbara and Steve did not seem to notice. Sarah's last name was Evans. Barry told her he was returning to Southern California the following day but that he would call.

Sarah then said to the group, "This is not on the list but since it's not busy, I will open a bottle. It's a limited production Petite Sirah that is our first bottling and I think you will appreciate the peppery finish. This whole area used to be planted with this varietal but the populace wanted Cabernet and the low yield per acre of Petite Sirah made ripping most of it out a matter of economics. Now, some of us that love the grape are bringing it back."

Sarah had been in the industry since her twenties and had been at this particular winery for over ten years but she was not part of ownership. Right before the group left, a tanned and fit-looking gray-haired man came in the tasting room from the back and Sarah elevated her voice to say, "and this is our owner, Robert Haven."

Everyone shook his hand and complimented him on his winemaking and Barbara, Steve and Barry left. Barry was wrong in that Barbara didn't notice anything beyond wine being sloshed around in the tasting room. Fortunately, she didn't harass him too much.

"WHAT was going on down at your end of the counter Barry?"

"Oh nothing - We just seemed to hit it off."

"Apparently."

Don't Fork Me

Barry was assisting in the search of a sex offender in Rialto. He fought to keep the thought of Sarah out of his mind while working. He was the supervisor on site but he was assisting one of his officers search a bedroom. The case agent, Carlos Garcia, had secured Randy Potsdam in the living room and he was as docile as most sex offenders. Unfortunately, his father was present and was a real pain in the neck. He was eating some macaroni and cheese and was allowed to continue. Some family members like to play the role of household defense attorney, saying things like "you can't do that!" and "what is your name?" But Carlos seemed to have control of the situation so everybody just put up with the guy bitching. Sometimes that's just part of the job.

At some point, however, Barry heard the sound of people abruptly moving about and Carlos yelling at the father to sit down.

"Sir, you need to sit down!" Carlos loudly exclaimed.

Carlos continued, yelling this time, "I said sit down!"

Barry left the bedroom and headed towards the living room to assist. He could hear what sounded like someone running on the carpet, getting closer. Barry pulled out his Glock just in case and, all of a sudden, the father raced around the corner from the living room to the kitchen area running in a collision course with Barry. The guy had a shiny object that appeared to be a knife in his right hand over his head, holding it as if he was going to stab someone.

Barry, concerned that he might be that someone, pointed his gun directly at the guy, yelling, "Drop the knife!"

As soon as the words left his mouth, he realized it was not a knife but it was a metal dinner fork.

In training sessions, officers are always cautioned as to how quickly they can get stabbed. Barry knew that a perpetrator could cover the distance of twenty-one feet and stab you before your gun cleared the holster. He participated in training scenarios where he would be the officer trying to draw his gun and shoot before he got stabbed and then he would try his hand at stabbing the officer. It was a real dose of reality. Barry knew in an instant that a fork was no different. He could be stabbed just the same and seriously injured. This subject was only ten feet away but, fortunately, Barry's gun was already out and pointed.

So now he again gave a command, this time, "Drop the fork!"

Potsdam's father stopped abruptly and froze, looking at the business side of the Glock barrel but still holding the fork. Barry again screamed at him, "Put down the fork!"

Fortunately, he dropped the fork on the carpet. As directed, he got on his stomach at which time he was handcuffed. He then followed every subsequent command. Ultimately, dispatch advised of a bookable outstanding warrant and he was arrested. Nothing could be located which would jeopardize Potsdam's probation grant so he was left at the residence.

Barry was always thankful that he didn't have to shoot the dad. While totally justified, it wouldn't sound good to anyone not in law enforcement. And, of course, he would be the recipient of plenty of playful ribbing from his brethren due to the fact he shot a guy for wielding a dinner fork.

Sarah - The Return Trip

Barry did not wait long to call Sarah. He was not of the opinion that intentionally not calling a woman right away was a proper move. He actually reached her later that day and she agreed to meet for coffee the next morning before his trip back to Southern California.

Even with no glasses filled with wine, it was very comfortable talking with Sarah. She was the furthest thing from a "Type A" personality and she was thoughtful in her remarks. Sarah had not been in any regular relationship for three years, which seemed rather amazing. Barry told her more than he would normally share in a first - time meeting with a woman. Talking with her was just so easy.

Barry told her that he didn't visit Mendocino that often but he would like to see her, perhaps for dinner or drinks and he could return in a couple weeks if that would be something she would be interested in. "That would be something I would look forward to," Sarah remarked.

Two weeks passed and Barry and Sarah met at an informal pizza place in Hopland. Some of the servers and waiters knew Sarah, not unusual in a small community. You could tell that she was well-liked.

They shared a local inexpensive Sangiovese that was recommended by Sarah. It was quite good and uncommonly intense for a Sangiovese. They emptied the bottle long before they finished their tasty pepperoni pizza. They had two glasses of an unremarkable Cabernet and then departed. There were other places to drink wine or talk in Hopland but Sarah seemed to want to get out of town. They drove to nearby Ukiah and spent the next hour or so sipping wine on the patio of one of her favorite taverns. The weather was perfect, 77 degrees with a slight breeze. It was October, Barry's favorite month wherever he happened to be.

They took turns giving background information. Their pasts were so different as to occupation and community but it seemed that their morals and feelings towards people and life were very similar. The streets of San Bernardino were in direct contrast with a farm by the Russian River. Barry always said that it would be difficult for a person raised in a large city to settle later on in a small community. People might seem in your business when they actually were being friendly and perhaps trying to help. There seems to be more tolerance in a small town or community because everyone really has to get along. A person used to "burning bridges" in a metropolitan area can't get away with that in a close-knit community. So even though Barry worked the majority of his life in the San Bernardino Valley, he was from small town Ohio and he never completely removed his feet from that soil. He felt comfortable in the small Mendocino communities and he felt very comfortable in the company of one Sarah Evans.

Sarah talked about how she felt guilty sometimes because she enjoyed life so much and she knew that many others did not fare as well. Barry agreed and shared his goal of doing at least one major tangible thing during the course of his career to make things better for people.

They ended the evening with a warm embrace at Sarah's car. She seemed slightly impacted by the wine but she assured Barry she was fine. Her house was one quarter mile down a side road. She proposed that, if he wanted to come back up to see her, that she would cook him dinner at her house. Barry chuckled, "If I want to come back to see you? You set the date and I will be here."

He did follow that up with a qualification that his team was working on a big case that could interfere at a moment's notice. Sarah suggested, "Let's talk on the phone this week and pick the best date for both of us."

"Agreed"

"Oh, and Sarah added, "I have an extra bedroom so if you like you can stay the night."

"Good to know - Thanks Sarah."

Roll Jordan Roll or The Never-Ending Case

Barry had an informant by the name of Cindy that used to have a brother who cooked methamphetamine so she knew the obvious indicators when someone was in the business. She did not use drugs and her information was ALWAYS good. She didn't require any monetary compensation but always appreciated a fresh pack of cigarettes.

Cindy told Barry that a man from the middle east by the name of Sam Hatter, ran an Arco Station in San Bernardino. His main business was selling large amounts of pseudoephedrine, a precursor to the manufacture of methamphetamine. Barry did some preliminary checks and discovered that Sam was short for Samir and he was originally from Jordan. He dabbled in expired batteries and cartons of cigarettes that had been stolen in quantity and he had some minor negative contact with law enforcement but nothing earth-shattering.

Cindy emphasized, "Barry, Sam is into EVERYTHING." And boy was she right.

Eventually, through an intermediary, a meeting was set up to purchase fifty large boxes of pills primarily containing pseudoephedrine for several thousand dollars. A moving surveillance that involved five different cars eventually ended up at Sam's business, essentially implicating him in the transaction. The business was closed down and Samir and one employee were detained until Barry could write a search warrant and have it signed by a judge. It specified his business and his residence.

After the judge signed the warrant, the business was searched, although a convenience store and gas station have so many places to hide stuff, it is all but impossible. Another team searched his house with negative results. It was later discovered that he had a hidden room in his residence but this was not known at the time.

The warrant also specified all vehicles registered to Mr. Hattar and Barry found a key to a safe deposit box on the driver's side floorboard of his SUV. Mr. Hatter denied any knowledge of that key. A denial such as that is always a good indicator that you have stumbled upon something of value. It took a couple telephone calls to locate the bank where the box was secured. A Bank of America branch in San Bernardino confirmed that Samir Hatter was assigned the box number that was stamped on the key.

As the warrant narrative already detailed the reason Barry felt that a felony was being committed, he contacted the judge by telephone and had the warrant modified to include Mr. Hatter's safe deposit box.

Barry and Bruno contacted bank officials and informed them of the warrant. When they arrived, bank personnel advised that the defendant's wife was attempting to coerce bank officials to allow her to gain access to the box and thwart execution of the warrant. Barry thought it felt like a race to the finish, but they were successful in serving the warrant and opening and searching the safe deposit box.

The process of itemizing everything located in the box took about two hours. The branch was closed by then. Items included credit cards, about twenty pounds of gold jewelry, ingots and trinkets and $423,000 in cash. The cash was counted three times by Bruno and Barry and documented.

The gold and items other than the credit cards were eventually returned as they could not be tied to the manufacture or sales of controlled substances. Under California's asset forfeiture law, the cash was never returned and was distributed according to statute to combat drug sales and manufacture.

Mr. Hattar did some time in custody but his ultimate punishment was being deported for "moral turpitude" which is a phrase used to describe anything from shoplifting to murder.

This investigation took a while and Barry was worried he would spend his entire career on this guy. Samir Hatter was involved in everything. The more Barry investigated, leads would take off in various directions like a spider web. Most of the credit cards that were taken from the safe deposit box were in the name of aliases or various unknown persons. Sam was involved in tax evasion with the IRS and was being investigated by the California Franchise Tax Board. The State Department was working something on him they would not share and the FBI was snooping around as well. It probably was terrorist group related.

Sam had a few insurance fraud cases including workman's compensation fraud pending and was under surveillance by one insurance carrier while he was out on bail. Barry personally released the gold to him while one insurance company took video of the exchange, as Hattar was getting paid a couple grand a month for not being able to pick up anything heavier than five pounds. Prior to having his passport confiscated, he and members of his family would move cash through the Netherlands between the USA and Jordan. There came a time when Barry had to close this guy's local case as it was overwhelming and he was being booted out of the country anyway. Samir would certainly not be morally opposed to helping terrorists but someone would have to make it worth his while financially. That's how he rolled.

Back to Sarah

Barry didn't waste time getting back to Mendocino County - and it wasn't for the wine. He located Sarah's house easily as it sat by itself surrounded by large lush trees of some variety. She met him outside with a hug that was more than cordial. It was late afternoon but the weather was perfect in the shade underneath those trees. Barry always wished he knew something about trees but he didn't. You can't be an expert in everything he thought.

Sarah had a few simple appetizers displayed on her picnic table by two soon-to-be-filled wine glasses. A slight breeze tossed Sarah's hair a bit. She covered the glasses with cardboard drink coasters to prevent leaves and debris from entering. Here was an experienced wine host. She was dressed very casually but, nonetheless, the whole package was alluring.

"I have a lot of possibilities," Sarah remarked. Barry knew she was speaking of options as to types of wine.

"You are the expert. I like a complex red but you take charge and bring me what you think I might like."

Sarah retrieved a bottle from the house and Barry could see that it was a white wine.

"I know you prefer reds, but I would like to share this very special Chardonnay with you. We need to drink this first to truly appreciate it. Next up will be a Barbera."

"Whatever you say. I am but a student in your class."

Barry was happy to share any wine with her and the experience of sitting outside alone with her in this beautiful country was so relaxing but, at the same time, truly electric. They toasted to their meeting. He sampled the wine. It was slightly chilled.

"Wow. This is delicious." Barry continued, "It is crisp but buttery and it is not overwhelmed with oak. Good choice!"

"When I sip it, I feel like I could chew it," noted Sarah. "I was hoping you would enjoy it."

The two of them spent the next hour or so catching up on their activities while apart and upcoming challenges. Sarah knew she would be busy at the winery soon as it was time to send out wine shipments and plan pickup parties. Barry had a number of cases scheduled to go to court. Their lots in life were so different that the other's stories and endeavors were like fresh air.

Sarah and Barry moved on to the Barbera, a light Italian varietal with a distinctive taste. Barbera's can be a little tart and fruity. Barry was a fan of this varietal and this one was excellent. There was a hint of vanilla in the nose.

Neither of them really got into past relationships and baggage. There was another time for that. This was an afternoon for bliss and enjoyment. The time flew by, it got a little cooler and they retreated indoors. Barry hadn't yet been inside her house except to use a small bathroom with access from the outside.

The house was probably built in the 1930s. It was well maintained and tastefully furnished. Barry noticed that despite the antique decor, the windows had been replaced with double-pane units.

Sarah directed Barry to the couch, a well-used and very comfortable place to sit. She brought their next wine, a Mendocino Syrah, and poured it into fresh glasses on the coffee table. She sat down about a foot from Barry and they toasted again.

"To a wonderful day" said Barry. Sarah added, "and evening."

Again, Sarah had picked a fine wine, a good example of a Russian River Syrah.

"Are you going to be able to stay? This is not a proposition. It just makes sense, it's more about being responsible and I have plenty of room."

"Only if you can convince me it is not inconveniencing you in any way," said Barry.

Sarah exclaimed, "I will make my case while we savor this wine!"

"Agreed!" Barry said as he raised his glass. By now, they were both feeling the effects of the wonderful elixirs they had been sharing. Sarah lit a couple candles and turned off one light. She looked even more beautiful in candlelight. When she returned, she sat a little closer to Barry. He noticed it but, thinking like a man, he wasn't sure if was intentional or not.

They were talking to each other in soft tones, playfully discussing how wine feels in your mouth and how a person just feels warm and relaxed all over when drinking it. "Oh, I'm sorry Barry. I need to get your bedding for the spare bedroom. Did you decide to stay?"

"I guess that would be the prudent thing to do. Also, if I'm not driving anywhere, we could share another glass of wine." Sarah and Barry had consumed a good deal of wine but it was over several hours.

"Absolutely you may. Let me be a good host and when I return we can make one last toast." Sarah jogged up the staircase.

Barry remained seated, sipping in a rather blissful state as if all the worries in the world had dissipated. Five minutes went by and Sarah returned but only with a toothbrush, something Barry had actually brought along. She carried no bedding and had changed her clothes. While her Mendocino County Crab, Wine and Beer Festival shirt looked great on her, she now wore a white cotton nightgown that caused Barry to stammer when he spoke.

Her cute little face smiled at Barry through her hair, which, although short, had a windblown look. She was a little giddy, a little anxious. The bottom of her covering barely concealed an area of high interest.

Barry was having trouble breathing as she held his hand and led him up the stairs. His chest was tight and his breathing was shallow. It was as if the air was being sucked from his lungs. He was light-headed from a combination of the wine and all of his exploding senses.

Sarah's room was tastefully decorated in a style consistent with her country home. Dark woods and cotton fabrics were prominent even in the soft light seeping through a window. Barry didn't know any more about plants than he did about trees, but the aroma emanating from them was very floral and feminine.

Sarah was fussing with things, moving pillows and candles about, acting like a host. She started some soft music on her iPhone and then, as if everything was exactly as she wanted it, she abruptly stopped, looked at Barry and stood by her bed. The dwindling light from the window clearly showcased the shape of her nipples rubbing inside that nightgown. There was something terribly erotic about being with her but also about being in HER bedroom. This was her secret chamber.

Sarah reached out and held Barry's hand again, this time very gently pulling him closer to her. Dusk had given way to night leaving only candlelight for illumination. They were both standing up facing one another when they kissed. Sarah unbuttoned Barry's shirt and he removed the rest of his clothes. Again, they caressed. Barry was not sure he could get any more excited, but over the next few hours he realized he was wrong.

Everything just worked. It was all so exciting and they quickly became comfortable with each other's entire bodies. Barry rather felt that Sarah's body was like an amusement park with lots of fun rides from which to choose. Later on, they held each other, Sarah's head on Barry's chest. They were a little sweaty. Barry was in heaven.

"Sarah, could I ask you a question?"

She hesitated and then said, "Sure!"

"Did we ever eat dinner?"

Knowing they hadn't, they both laughed out loud.

Sarah got up to make coffee. She slipped her gown back down over her head and kissed Barry ever so softly before leaving the room. Barry knew he needed to get up and head home but he really wanted to stay, forever.

Courtroom High Jinks

Low Tech

Arrest warrants become problematic if the subject of the warrant hides inside a structure. Very basically, if you can't see your subject through a window or if you haven't followed him or her inside of a residence, you can't kick down the door and invade people's privacy. You need a search warrant to have authority to invade the premises.

Barry devised a technique that always worked to accomplish an arrest in such a case. He did not want to reveal his method (and still does not want to) but he wanted the sentencing judge to know Brian McCarthy did not surrender and he had to be tricked into making himself available for arrest.

As such, the judge was informed that Brian's arrest could only be accomplished through the use of "subterfuge."

In court, Brian was sitting with about ten other inmates in the jury box, all dressed in orange dungarees, as is the practice in San Bernardino.

The judge made all the advisements in McCarthy's case and then scolded him, saying that Mr. Truman had to use subterfuge in order to arrest him. He repeated and emphasized the word "subterfuge" with a loud and deep tone.

Always paying attention to anything new that could jeopardize their criminal careers, the other inmates were displaying perplexed expressions and some of them were talking to each other in low tones. Barry watched and listened and knew they were all trying to guess what this new technology was that allowed this guy to be arrested. Was it a new kind of Taser, electronic net, silicon bullets or special chemical spray?

They talked more and a little bit louder until the bailiff sternly told them, "Quiet!"

Two Eskimo Pies Please

It was a sad week for Barry. It was his last week working for the street level narcotics team. There would be fun stuff ahead but not at this moment. Barry would help search several more houses before he was through but he was trying not to collect evidence or be a case agent or get involved in a use of force incident. That way, he wouldn't be spending time away from his new assignment to come back and testify.

At a residential search in Colton, Barry did not make entry with the rest of the team. He stayed out front to deal with "walkups" with one other officer. "Walkups" is a term used for people that show up during a search. They could reside there or they could be strangers or associates. Barry could elect to send them away if they weren't wanted, especially if there were quite a few of them. He might do consent searches on suspected associates which could end in their arrest or he could send them away as well. Everything is a judgement call. For family members, unless they were interfering, it was just a matter of keeping them out of the house until the search was completed.

While the man of the house was present inside, his wife returned during the search with her two girls, age seven and ten. Since she needed to watch the kids and not get involved in the search, she was told she could stay in the front yard if she liked.

As is often the case in a Hispanic community, the ice cream vendor came down the street. It was a hot day and the ice-cold offerings looked good to Barry. But eating a frozen Zero bar while the search was still going on was not particularly professional.

The kids were nagging their mother about getting some ice cream and she told them she couldn't afford it and to be quiet. Barry diplomatically asked, "Would it be okay ma'am if I bought ice cream for your kids?" He wanted to do it and, also, it would occupy the kids for a while.

"Sure! Thanks." The kids picked out what they wanted and Barry paid the man.

A few weeks later the matter was in court for a preliminary hearing as a quantity of methamphetamine had been located. Barry was on the stand. It took a while to figure out what defense counsel was trying to establish. They had Barry draw a picture of his Glock 17 on a board. It was mildly comical as drawing freehand was not something Barry did very well. It was stupid anyway as, except for one officer that carried a shotgun, everyone on the team carried a Glock.

The attorney was trying to get the whole case thrown out on a technicality. It was being alleged that one of the officers broke the plane of the residence by putting his Glock inside a window before the officers at the front door "knocked and announced" for the execution of the search warrant.

Frankly, Barry wasn't sure if any of the team jumped the gun, so to speak, in that manner, but it certainly wasn't him. But the mother testified that it was Barry, one of two officers who never drew their weapons. She remembered Barry because he bought ice cream for her kids.

When Barry was finally asked directly about his involvement, he denied every pulling his gun but confessed, "But she's right. I did buy her kids ice cream." The courtroom officers and audience chuckled.

The wife may or may not have witnessed anything with anyone's gun; she was trying to help her husband and make her statements sound plausible. Barry somehow felt betrayed for doing a good deed. But he decided that if similar circumstances arose, he would do exactly the same thing. It was still something to keep in mind.

Purina Power

One of Barry's golden informants gave him information about a meth dealer in Colton who was on probation. It was easy. Barry and a couple officers visited the home of Bobby Perez, searched it and located a quarter gram of methamphetamine hidden in the garage. Bobby was taken to jail and Barry was subpoenaed to his probation revocation hearing. Bobby had a couple other minor drug convictions so a guilty finding for this small quantity would probably land him in jail for six months to a year. He was maintaining that he didn't know about the methamphetamine and that his friend may have left it in the garage a few days earlier.

Following Barry's testimony, the Judge started asking the defendant direct questions. This was rather unusual but perfectly legal in this type of hearing.

"What kind of dog do you have?" asked the judge in a very friendly manner.

"Not really sure. I think he has some German Shepherd."

The Judge continued, "Oh that's nice. Do you treat him well?"

"Yeah, I treat it fine," Bobby emphasized.

Barry, the defense attorney and the district attorney just listened and occasionally glanced at one another.

"How often do you feed and water him?"

"Everyday."

All of a sudden, Barry realized what the judge was doing. Since the district attorney wasn't thinking on his feet and the meth was found inside a dog food bag right on top of the food, the judge was directly questioning Bobby, setting him up big time.

The judge spoke from the bench to everyone. "Okay - I've heard enough. I'm going to make the finding that probation is revoked and we can move on to sentencing."

Arguments were heard for and against time in custody. The judge, obviously irritated that Bobby was lying to him, gave him one year in custody.

Busy Sarah

Barry called Sarah at the winery to make arrangements to meet again. It was clear the tasting room was busy as she responded very business-like.

"Thank you for calling." Then she said in a lower tone, "Call me later on my cell."

Barry was anxious but he called her several hours later, anticipating that she would be off work. The call went immediately to her voice mail. Barry then received a text that she would call him in a few minutes. It was almost 9:00 p.m. so Barry surmised that Sarah must be inundated at the winery. He knew that this was shipping customer week, the time when wine shipments for club members are put together and payment issues and shipping address problems converge.

Barry answered his phone and heard an exhausted Sarah speak softly, "I'm sorry Barry. It was hell today. How can I make it up to you?"

Barry noted that she also sounded like she may have been sampling some of the quarterly offerings as she prepared the shipments.

"Not necessary. We both have jobs and they sometimes get in the way of fun. I must say this is the first time I have heard your work voice. Are you okay?"

Sarah didn't answer the question but remarked, "Let's get together, not this week but the following week if that works with your schedule. Things will slow down here and that will give me time to sort a few things out."

Barry was curious. "Is it anything I can help with?"

"Thank you but no. I've just been contemplating going to work for another winery. The stress level here can be off the hook and the dysfunction is toxic at times like these. Don't worry about me. I'll be fine and we will see each other and we will thoroughly enjoy each other and all will be right with the world."

Sarah sounded more upbeat at the end of their conversation and Barry felt better about things. He theorized that when emotions become intertwined with someone you care about, you feel bad when they feel bad, and good when they feel good.

His own thoughts betrayed him. He was falling in love with Sarah.

Sex Offender Unit

Barry approached the new Chief Probation Officer about forming a unit designed specifically to supervise those individuals that were sex offenders. There had been sex offender units in the past but they focused on treatment which, as anybody knows that deals with genuine predators or pedophiles, is a total waste of time. As a matter of fact, according to the California Department of Justice, changing a predator from say, liking six-year old girls would be similar to changing the sexual preferences of anyone else. For example, it would be like Barry, who was attracted to women, being sent to treatment to cure him of liking women. It's just not going to happen. The best you could do was to keep track of these people and arrest them when they violated their terms of probation.

Barry not only wanted a unit to be put together, but he wanted to supervise it. He explained to the Chief that he wanted to incorporate a great deal of surveillance, technology and any other modality that would detect behavior that could threaten people, mostly children in the community. An arrest and conviction was viewed as a success as the public would absolutely be protected as long as the perpetrator remained in custody. Sex crimes generally carry hefty sentences.

The Chief was eventually convinced and Barry assembled a very talented bunch of officers to work in the unit. They received as much training as possible to understand the methods employed by sex offenders. Barry received extensive training to conduct forensic computer exams and was qualified to testify in court as an expert.

As a group, sex offenders are very compliant felons. They rarely miss appointments with a probation officer and don't miss treatment. It is not common for them to commit violations that a peace officer can plainly see. Rather, they are very secretive about their activities and careful about any detection of violations of their probation or commission of new crimes.

Herein lies the problem. A sex offender will appear to be a model citizen. A probation officer that is untrained with neither the tools nor the time to monitor the activities of this unique type of probationer, will never detect behavior that may very well threaten public safety. Since they are so skilled at hiding activities that compromise the safety of community members, particularly children, the tool of greatest value is surveillance. Barry parlayed his knowledge of surveillance from working drug cases into clever ways to catch sex offenders.

Barry's unit had special equipment including a surveillance vehicle that could be parked anywhere unnoticed. Many sex offenders report phony addresses so that they can be involved in nefarious activity without detection. An investigation may be as basic as following an offender to a suspected true residence and then setting up on it to establish that address as the correct one. Often, victims or potential victims are located at the real address.

Many sex offenders, hopefully the most dangerous, have to register their addresses to the local authorities. Their information may be available online to the public. Barry estimated that twenty percent of those addresses were not correct. That was what was problematic with law enforcement agencies conducting sex offender sweeps. In California, these are called 290 sweeps after the penal code section regarding sex registration. Teams of officers are given addresses to visit to confirm residency. But there really isn't time to do much more than contact whomever is at the house. Barry's unit participated in these.

"He's at work now but he stays here."

"Okay, have him call upon his return," says the officer with the paperwork. A form is filled out and returned with all the others to the command center.

Sometimes information of value will come up during these sweeps but mostly they are political operations to demonstrate something is being done with sex offenders.

Barry's unit had the ability to concentrate on a far lesser number of persons that were on probation or parole, allowing officers more latitude, information, flexibility and authority.

The sex offender unit also conducted special programs for this population. For example, prior to Halloween, all subjects convicted of crimes against children were ordered to stay in their homes and not host any trick or treaters by opening their doors or passing out candy. Several teams checked those residences to ensure that they were in compliance. Officers also drove by the homes of sex offenders who were not under supervision or who had not received the admonishment to ensure that these predators were not interacting with trick-or-treaters. Sex offenders love Halloween even more than Barry, but for entirely different reasons.

Barry was very committed to these Halloween checks. Not that the teams could be everywhere at the same time, but the fact they checked and sometimes surprised perpetrators, undoubtedly made their offender brethren hesitate in taking advantage of the plentiful prospects ringing the doorbells and wandering the neighborhoods. And, of course, Barry always thought fondly of those innocent days in Norwalk, Ohio and, as such, he was devoted to keeping the kids safe on Halloween wherever they may be.

On occasion, if it appeared that candy was being handed out by a perpetrator, a costumed officer would be sent to the front door to gather information. For such a serious task, it couldn't help but be humorous at times. On one such instance, a volunteer for Halloween patrol from another unit, Mo Campbell, was sent to the front door of a perpetrator who was not allowed to have any contact with kids. Barry wanted Mo to wear the Spiderman costume, his favorite, but Mo insisted on wearing some sort of a monster outfit with a bulky mask, which was made out of rubber with clear plastic eye bubbles.

Barry and another officer watched from afar as Mo joined Wonder Woman, a couple ghosts and a witch at the front door. It looked like he was standing there for the longest time. Finally, he returned to the street.

"Okay Mo, was that our guy handing out candy?"

"I don't know," was all he said.

"You don't know?" asked Barry. "You were standing there for a good two minutes!"

Mo answered in a helpless tone, "My eyes fogged up."

There was one other tangible thing that was of emphasis in Barry's unit. While holding offenders accountable and putting them away where they could not victimize kids, the team also worked on the other side of the equation and provided Internet Safety classes to any requesting group or agency. The idea was to prevent the victimization of children from the start. A program was developed to educate parents about the dangers of the Internet with suggestions to protect their children.

With the help of the National Center for Missing and Exploited Children (NCMEC), Barry and his team made presentations to schools and churches and girl scout troops and seminars. Most of the contact and grooming of victims occurs online and parents and kids need the information to become aware.

It was not all serious. Specialty units enjoy more latitude as far as what is considered appropriate on the job site. This has been upheld in court cases with the commonsense reason that a sorted type of material just naturally begets a sorted type of comedy. If you're dealing with the bottom of the drug culture every day and the officers in the unit adorn the Christmas tree with quarter grams of simulated methamphetamine and small electronic scales, that is okay and can be funny. People have to vent in some manner.

If the members of a sex unit are often looking at despicable images with children and animals or listening to a predator describe how he seeks out his prepubescent victims, these officers need to be allowed to share topical jokes that would be inappropriate anywhere else.

In Barry's sex offender unit, not unlike any other unit as far as arrests go, there were always those arrests that were rock solid and represented the locking up of a subject that truly needed to be taken out of circulation to protect society. At the other end of the spectrum were arrests that just as well could have been out of custody citations. This will always be the case. It's just a matter of contrast.

To recognize the officer with the "weakest" or "cheesiest" arrest in the unit, a symbol of that arrest, a sort of trophy, was bestowed. Every month one officer would earn that distinction and display the can of Cheeze Whiz [15] prominently in their office.

[15] Cheez Whiz is a processed cheese sauce or spread sold by Kraft Foods.

He Never Goes Away

Although excited about being on the ground floor of a unit he could design to take sex offenders out of the community, Barry's enthusiasm was quelled by a phone call from Mortsoob. A nine-year old boy disappeared from a campground on 3N14, a forestry road in the Big Bear area.

Steve reported, "Search and Rescue is out there but the word from the station deputies is that it looks real suspicious. Have any suspects in mind? I know you have lots going on right now but I knew you would want to know."

"Christ. When will it ever stop? Keep me advised please. I'll talk to you tomorrow. Give my regards to Barbara."

Barry knew there was no way to say for sure that Drisco was responsible, but when you have a boy in the right age range disappear from a campground in his community, it's a distinct possibility.

Barry called the station detectives to make sure they knew about Drisco. They did not and were not interested. "Our investigation is proceeding. We think we have our subject."

"You need to at least check Drisco out," Barry urged.

"Like I said, we know what we're doing and will close this investigation soon."

This is a common problem with some investigators. They get focused on their careers and what they feel the outcome of their investigation should be and proceed in that direction even if incoming information suggests a different course. And there is quite a bit of ego involved.

Barry always remembered how it took months for the LAPD to pick up a .22-caliber revolver used in the Tate Murders committed by the Manson Family in 1969.[16] An eleven-year old boy found the gun while working in the yard and his father was totally frustrated trying to convince the police to pick it up. An officer eventually did retrieve it but couldn't have thought it was of any evidentiary value as he left his fingerprints all over the gun and the two loaded rounds.

Barry also had a very close friend that was a probation officer who was informed by a felon the name of the person responsible for starting a major fire in the San Bernardino Mountains. Everything matched including the subject's vehicle. The investigator with the sheriff's office was convinced someone else was responsible and never even questioned this guy. He wasn't interested. The probation officer finally gave up. About two years later, she received a call from a deputy district attorney asking, "Did you have some information about the person who started the Waterman Canyon fire?" Apparently, the information she received was accurate. Unfortunately, her notes were no longer available.

In the case of Drisco, no one was still in local law enforcement that knew this case as well as Barry. It wasn't anyone's fault. It's just that most of Barry's contemporaries from the sheriff's office were now running the agency or retired, due to their excellent retirement system.

He made a final attempt at getting someone's attention. Calling the Undersheriff, who used to visit houses with Barry when he was a station detective in Lake Arrowhead, he made his plea.

"I remember that perp. He was extremely bad news. He isn't in custody somewhere?"

"Nope," said Barry.

"That's not good. That guy was as bad as they get. Let me make a call and educate some people."

"Excellent! Thanks. I am getting totally frustrated."

"No shit. Thanks Barry. By the way, come to my retirement."

"I wouldn't miss it. I know you're a big shot now but I have stories to tell."

"Boy - don't I know it."

They both laughed and Barry was happy he called.

---

[16] Helter Skelter by Vincent Bugliosi (Bantam Books 1974), pages 265-266.

Global Positioning System

Due to running the Sex Offender Unit, Barry was put in charge of the GPS monitoring program. This system gathers information from a group of satellites and transmits that information to the officer and/or vendor by way of cellular transmissions. Ideally, the offender's movements can be followed on a map. This is the same system used by the military to acquire targets but it is detuned for civilian purposes which just means it is not as accurate.

Politicians and government administrators talked up (and still do) the use of this technology to monitor the location of felons, particularly sex offenders. This was the surefire solution. After Barry experienced the subject who defeated the electronic monitoring technology to go to another location undetected and commit a murder, he wanted to test the GPS equipment up front. He did not want this technology to be used as an alibi as well.

There are different GPS reception and reporting systems but all of them have their weaknesses. The equipment Barry was examining used a cell phone to receive the satellite signals and to report locations. In order that the cellular phone stayed with the subject, an electronic bracelet was secured to an ankle. The cell phone and the anklet communicate with each other via short range signal so if they are not near each other, an alert will register.

As he had eventually checked out the electronic monitoring equipment, Barry spent a good deal of time with the actual tech department for the vendor that sold the GPS systems. Like before, he wore the gear around for a couple of days all the time being monitored by the vendor's software. Without sharing specifics, he was able to spoof his location for hours, particularly when he was at a location with a weak GPS or cellular signal such as the lower floor in a shopping mall or the basement of a brick or concrete building. Specifically, he could leave the mall or basement and go somewhere else for an hour or two while the monitoring software would show him still in the mall or basement. Barry's concern was that an offender could be raping little kids in Redlands while the software reported to the probation officer that he was shopping miles away at the other end of the valley. That's not protecting the community. That's called creating an alibi.

Barry submitted his findings but the report was quickly dismissed by his own agency. Somehow word got out and the manuscript was requested by other jurisdictions from across the country.

Barry never recommended against this technology. He merely wanted every professional that used it to understand its limitations.

There are also inherent problems with this tool that have nothing to do with technology. For instance, you need the personnel to actually watch monitors back in the office to determine the location of the device and the attached subject; alerts alone cannot be relied on. This requires personnel.

If something doesn't look right on the viewing monitors, officers have to be available to physically check on a subject's location.

Barry also studied the accuracy of locations generated from the signals received from the satellites. The government commissioned a study by the Volpe Center that examines this. The locations generated by civilian signals and sometimes military ones are not always right. Sunspots, FM and VHF signals as well as ordinary earthly terrain and city buildings interfere with the signals. Barry compared actual positions with GPS reported positions and discovered that, while usually very close, they could also be quite different, perhaps as much as a half a mile apart.

Barry summarized in his report that GPS monitoring is a valuable tool when adequate personnel resources are incorporated and ALL users have a thorough understanding of its limitations.

Computer Forensics or You Can Delete but You Cannot Hide

When Barry started his career, sex offenders who were interested in children would hide child pornography somewhere in their residence. Pictures were often kept in a shoebox or cigar box so the mission of the searching officer was to find that cache of photos. These offenders would use these containers to transport their favorite pictures to share with other like-minded individuals.

Nothing much has changed as far as the perpetrator's desires or behavior but the content now is of a digital nature. Child porn fans can now network online and meet other people who have their distinct interests. If Joe likes five-year old girls with blonde hair, he can now find other subjects who have the same preference. When you interview these guys, they say that meeting other groups of people online that have the same perverted preferences seems to normalize their behavior. *They are not alone.* They share, view and download this type of content over the Internet. These people still can be involved with sharing with other offenders in person but they are bringing a USB drive instead of a box of photos.

It became clear that in order to properly monitor sex offenders on probation, there would need to be an in-house examiner, someone trained to be able to examine digital media in a forensically sound manner and be able to testify as an expert in court. Computer forensic investigators are available at various agencies but there are not enough of them, so there tends to be a backlog.

Barry supervised the unit but he was really the only one with an inclination for this type of work. He took all the highly specialized training, networked with other computer examiners and, eventually, became skilled enough to convey his findings as an expert in court. This work paralleled his last seven years of employment.

Barry examined hard drives, removable media, smart phones and tablets for a variety of crimes mostly for his own agency but also for other law enforcement entities.

Many serious cases, including capital crimes, go to trial in some jurisdictions with a lack of digital evidence. If a person stalks a victim before committing a murder, there will likely be some digital footprint left by the stalker, whether it be browser history regarding research on a person or maps or metadata from a phone, which includes locations. Barry was always amazed at the lack of emphasis on digital evidence in court or rather, the lack of resources to allow for computer evidence in many cases.

Mostly what Barry searched for was child pornography. Computers, smart phones and other computer media are where illicit material including erotica and child pornography are stored and/or accessed. Sex offenders tend to spend a great deal of time on computers. Many engage in computer usage as a hobby. They seem to like the detached communication and the organized way computers work. They like to operate devoid of real human interaction. Organization is paramount. Look at a sex offender's sock drawer. Rarely will a sock be out of place.

Computers and mobile devices are also used to communicate with minors. This could be by texting, in chat rooms or on video. The predator's forte is "grooming" the kids or essentially earning their trust and gradually making them their victims. Sometimes they will blackmail a child by getting them to do something silly online like a boy taking his shirt off. They will coax him to remove something more with the threat of getting him in trouble with his parents. Ultimately, perpetrators will want to meet him.

When Barry would find evidence of communication with a minor, particularly a young girl, he would also find a lot of browser activity with sites that detail the insecurities a girl may experience. Or they may be sites that are of general interest to a girl of that age. The perpetrator then uses all this information to earn trust and exploit weaknesses. True pedophiles would tell Barry that they do this ALL-DAY LONG. They are always working on potential targets.

Unfortunately, many police agencies and most probation departments and parole agencies do not invest in the technology to investigate this kind of crime. This creates a situation where there are many more computers and mobile devices that should be checked than qualified personnel to check them.

Barry was always behind on his computer cases. Everything has to be undertaken very methodically so it will stand up in court. There are so many different places to hide things on computer media and, of course, the media itself can be hidden. One can imagine, during the search an entire residence how difficult it is to find the smallest flash media that can be put in a digital camera.

There are hidden drives, both virtually and physically, encryption, steganography, locked drives and a host of other ways to hide stuff. But there are tricks of the trade that many of the offenders don't know about unless they can somehow get specialized law enforcement training. Just deleting or hiding items is insufficient to prevent an investigator from making a find.

Offenders like to have their alluring images available and, as such, they can be their own worst enemies. They might have a regular routine for cleansing their system at least to protect them from a preliminary exam, perhaps at each restart or on a key command, but they may have a USB drive in their pocket with a thousand images of child pornography. More than once Barry came upon offenders who had taken numerous software precautions but forgot and left an optical disc loaded with illegal images in the CD tray. That's really an easy case on a disc.

One of the most entertaining capers started off with a routine check of a sex offender at his residence. He was a little slow in answering the door but when he opened it he was friendly and welcoming. Sex offenders usually are. Barry introduced himself and proceeded to the computer area. Since there was no waiver of any fourth amendment rights in this case, everyone was on the lookout for incriminating material that would support the issuance of a search warrant.

This visit would probably have been short if not for the AOL (American Online) dialogue box open on the subject's computer screen. It read, "Warning - Are you sure you want to shut down and stop downloading the file, "Little girl with dick in mouth?" Barry wasn't sure of the final disposition of this case, but the search warrant was issued and served by another agency.

Forensic computer examiners spend a lot of time checking with other forensic computer examiners. There is just so much information to learn and keep up with. It is so specialized. Some large operations such as ones operated by the FBI have people in every area. You really need someone for each operating system, eg., Apple, Microsoft, Linux, and for Android and Apple mobile devices and for automotive units and gaming units. It's really hard to be an expert on everything digital. As such, there is quite a bit of consulting going on.

There are really two types of examiners: true computer "geeks" that are often civilians that have specialized training in forensics, and law enforcement officers that have also been trained in computer forensics. There are a few examiners that are really on the top of the game in both arenas but most are not. The civilians tend to understand every nuance of an operating system but aren't great investigators so they don't always know what to look for, and the cops are great investigators but they are not complete "geeks." Preferably, these two types work together and most good labs have it set up that way.

Barry was much stronger on the investigation side and he had a great advantage. Most digital media items are examined in a vacuum at a lab for an officer or agency. On the locally generated sex cases, Barry could also investigate the crime surrounding the digital evidence. He would conduct interviews with the subject of the investigation as well as other people with knowledge or that may have access to the same digital media. Establishing a time and date is great for a browsing history or a download session or other action but if you can't put your perpetrator in the chair at the right time, you may have problems proving he or she was the one who was interacting with the operating system at that time. It could have been Uncle Louie.

With this in mind, Barry would interview all parties with questions that would establish their interaction with their devices. As for the perpetrators, it is amazing what some of them will tell you even after being advised of their Miranda rights.[17]

One very soft spoken and diminutive subject with lots of child pornography on his computer told Barry the exact abbreviations he would use to search for preteen female pornography on the Internet. This was all under Miranda. Barry was having trouble keeping up so he asked this person if he minded writing this down. The subject was more than happy to oblige and he was detailed and organized and even "proud" about the information he printed on the yellow legal pad. Barry asked him if he would sign it and he did so. Barry almost felt bad that this perpetrator "cooked" his own "goose." Almost.

NCMEC

The National Center for Missing and Exploited Children does much more than the name implies. They never give up on a missing child. They even circulate age progression pictures as time passes by. They assist families and law enforcement when kids come up missing and also maintain the Cyber Tipline. This provides a way for the public and electronic service providers to report online (and via toll-free telephone) instances of online enticement of children for sexual acts, child sexual molestation, child pornography, child sex trafficking, unsolicited obscene materials sent to a child, misleading domain names, and misleading words or digital images on the Internet.

NCMEC provides specialized assistance to law enforcement to consolidate investigations and link up with special task force members who work on child victimization cases. They maintain a database of varied digital information which assists law enforcement. Sometimes just one call to the Cyber Tipline by a citizen might provide that final bit of information to make it possible to obtain a search warrant for a particular investigation somewhere in the world.

NCMEC was of great assistance to Barry as their database includes digital fingerprints for all known images of child pornography. They

---

[17] Miranda was the California case decision that required a subject to be admonished of certain rights including the right to remain silent and to have legal representation.

would analyze images seized to determine if they were part of any known collection. Barry always kept in mind the fact that even though an image may make its rounds on the Internet, at some point in the past, whether it be a month or ten years ago, an actual child was sexually exploited.

NCMEC also provides support in the form of advice and materials for Internet Safety education programs. Barry was a true believer in this organization.

Well-Groomed

Early on, Barry was made aware of a deviant by the name of David Finman. Mr. Finman was on probation most recently for sending and receiving child pornography on the Internet. Finman was a real sicko but not like Drisco, who was Lucifer in the flesh, in Barry's opinion.

Finman's case file was tragically locked away in an administrator's desk. Officers were ordered not to do anything with that particular subject. Keep in mind that the perpetrator was a dangerous individual that had molested many children and who, while on probation, was found with an incredible amount of child pornography. Child pornography, unlike child erotica, depicts children being victimized in a sexual manner in any number of ways. These pictures are bought and sold primarily over the Internet. Of course, at the onset, there is an actual child that was raped or victimized to generate the picture or video. The viewers of this material have an absolute obsession.

Barry inquired about this case to try to understand why this criminal was allowed to roam around the community without any supervision. Apparently, there were past allegations of pictures being planted on his computer by a sheriff's office examiner and, a lawsuit was filed against the government. The perpetrator did not prevail. Barry learned later that there was absolutely no basis for the allegations. Someone at a much higher pay-grade than Barry decided to ignore the case for fear there would be another lawsuit. Barry felt differently as he was getting information that the offender was back doing the same old things.

As new Chief Hancock seemed to actually understand law enforcement and protecting the community, he agreed with Barry that this guy needed to be monitored and he essentially didn't give a damn about possible lawsuits. Barry loved the fact that his head boss was confident, supportive and unafraid. With exception, he had suffered through too many tentative and ineffective chiefs. The administrator who had been holding the file, was ordered to deliver it to Barry's sex offender unit for investigation and supervision. He was not happy.

The conventional manner of supervising adults is to call them into the office and structure them as to what is expected of them and what is required of them by the court.

In this particular case, there was no need to alert the perpetrator that his case was back on the San Bernardino County probation officers' radar. Besides, sex offenders tend to be very sneaky and it was to the department's advantage to use a little subterfuge.

While this case was technically under the supervision of the court and probation office in San Bernardino, Finman was actually reporting to a probation officer in Los Angeles County. This was due to the fact he was allegedly residing in a house in the city of Pomona in that county. This was not unlike games other probationers play with jurisdictional lines to avoid being supervised by anybody.

Barry assigned the case to his very capable Senior Probation Officer, Kate Ruley. Her office was close to the Los Angeles County border and she was as sneaky as they come. One of the first things she did was to check with the Los Angeles County probation officer to see how Finman was doing so that she could document the information in the agency offender database. She really wanted to assess the officer more than get a report on Finman. She spoke with a probation officer in the Pomona office about Finman and right away determined that this woman was charmed by Finman.

"Oh, David is doing so well. He is doing everything he is supposed to and is such a pleasure to have drop by."

"Drop by" turned out to be the operative expression as Kate determined that Finman showed up at the Pomona office whenever he chose rather than when his probation officer ordered him to come in. And anyone that knows anything about sex offenders knows that they are virtually all cooperative and often charming. They do everything asked of them.

Barry and Kate discussed the case and decided this LA County officer might very well compromise any investigation they may undertake. As such, the conversations between Kate and the LA officer were pretty superficial and information was only going one way and that was incoming.

At an early stage, Kate had a feeling that Finman's LA County address might be a phony. After all, San Bernardino County officers were the ones that tried to lock him up. Also, offenders often prefer supervision in larger counties. That's not because the officers are incompetent but because the jurisdictions and agencies are so large and underfunded that it is easier for bad guys to get away with illegal behavior. Also, sex offenders often report bad addresses to keep officers away from anything or anybody that could incriminate them.

Both Kate and Barry commenced searching every database that might provide a clue as to possible residences. Real estate records and material from his gigantic case file were examined closely. Their old buddy Tim Aguilar from the Department of Justice assisted with online record searches as well. Finman was close to his parents and they owned several properties so many different locations would have to be checked out.

One of the tendencies in modern police work is to rely too heavily on all the information that is derived from computer databases. Online information is often wrong and does not replace the intelligence gathered by surveillance and actually talking to human beings. Some officers have actually forced entry into residences solely based on information derived from databases. That's not a good idea. Barry knew that online information was only the start; traditional investigative techniques must follow.

The possible addresses where Finman resided were narrowed down to six. Including the address in Pomona he provided the LA County probation officer, that made seven properties to check out. All eight officers in the sex offender unit were utilized at some point in order to gather information on houses in the valley and in the San Bernardino mountains. Places were watched, license plates were run and, eventually the possible addresses were reduced to three, all in the San Bernardino Mountains. Kate continued to check the Pomona address and believed this property to be occupied by a woman that was later determined to be Finman's aunt. It was also later determined that Finman would sometimes stay there for one night before or after visiting with his LA Probation Officer. While not impossible, it is very difficult to follow someone with one car, especially in Southern California traffic and mountain roads. Kate never knew he was there until the last minute, so she wasn't able to gather a team fast enough. On the infrequent occasions he was at his aunt's house, his car was situated way around the back, making the attachment of a tracking device problematic.

While someone might question the technique of Kate taking her young children with her for a quick look at the residence on the way to work, it was actually a good use of resources and was totally convincing. Who would ever suspect a mother of conducting a surveillance while changing a diaper in the back seat of her vehicle?

Barry and Kate were convinced he was not staying in Pomona but they hit a stone wall in trying to find his real address. The three remaining houses were down mountain fire roads making surveillance difficult even with a specialized vehicle.

While continuing to check on mountain properties, they spotted a delivery truck in the Crestline area. Kate commented, "I wonder if Finman orders things to be delivered to his residence?"

Like many other offenders who love downloading, viewing & sharing kid porn, Finman had a love of computers. Barry, himself a computer enthusiast, responded, "Of course he does! He is always going to be getting hard drives and circuit boards and dongles and such!"

They stopped a delivery truck driver and showed him a picture of Finman. The driver didn't recognize him but he suggested they show it to all the mountain drivers at a central location when they were loading their trucks with packages for the day. It was hard to tell who was more excited - Kate or Barry. Barry decided to go to the departure point the next morning at 6:00. He only slept three hours. After all, they had been trying to locate Finman's real address for months.

Barry found the driver who made the suggestion. This driver called over six or seven drivers that mainly worked the "front side" of the mountain. Barry explained that they were looking for this sex offender and that he would likely receive packages from computer device companies. He learned long ago in similar situations that it doesn't hurt to make sure private citizens know the person on the run is wanted for something other than traffic offenses or smoking marijuana. People generally want to help catch sexual perpetrators.

"I know exactly where that guy lives!" said a curly haired driver. "I delivered a package to him just last week." He continued, "He is always getting packages and he's kind of creepy."

Barry couldn't wait to call Kate. He wouldn't get the exact address until later that evening but now they could make plans for corroborating the information.

"Awesome!" was Kate's response to the phone call. Barry and Kate began plotting as to the next logical moves. They decided to discuss the case further the following day. The driver called Barry that night with the exact address. Finman lived in Lake Arrowhead.

This address was close to but not one of the places the team had been checking out. That's undoubtedly why they were at a standstill trying to put him with those properties. It was agreed that Kate would start running the address through several databases and Barry would do a "drive by" of the Lake Arrowhead home.

Kate called Barry while he was headed to the home to tell him that the residence was listed under the name of another family member. Some of the other homes were under the names of Finman's parents but this one was under the name of an unknown uncle.

Barry drove by the house and thought he saw Finman standing in the driveway. Since Barry was "dressed down" and Finman had never met him, he took advantage of the fortuitous situation and stopped in front of the house to ask for directions. After all, mountain roads can be confusing.

"Excuse me sir," said Barry in an upbeat manner. After looking at Finman's picture for months, Barry knew this was him in the flesh. "I'm having trouble locating Pine Cone Lane - would you have any idea where that might be?"

"I believe it circles around down there," motioning past some pine trees.

"Oh - I thought I came from there but I'll try again. These roads are kind of confusing. By the way, you have a very nice house."

Finman looked back at the residence and said, "Thank you - I'm always trying to make improvements."

Barry thanked him and drove away, satisfied that he knew where Finman really lived. When he was able to get a cell signal, he called Kate and filled her in.

"You're not going to believe who I was just shooting the shit with!"

When Barry told her, Kate became ecstatic and wanted every detail. Now they were in business. They had a house owned by an uncle where a delivery driver had personally delivered packages to nephew Finman on multiple occasions. Barry actually contacted the sex offender in his driveway and he admitted that he lived there. What remained was to establish if he used more than one residence. The only way to do that was to watch the Lake Arrowhead property and the place in Pomona. Neither Barry or Kate believed that Finman stayed at the Pomona address for more than a night every month or so but they had to be sure. The Pomona address on file with LA Probation could be very compelling information for a judge or jury. Theoretically the LA PO could actually be subpoenaed by Finman's defense counsel to testify that he lived there. She had been to the house to see Finman, but, of course, it was by appointment.

Now was the time to coordinate the search and arrest of David Finman. Providing a fraudulent address was sufficient to cause his arrest but Barry and Kate wanted to really see what he was doing and send him a way for a while.

At this juncture, Barry and his team not only needed to do a little more surveillance on the Lake Arrowhead residence; they needed to watch the Pomona house during the night time hours so that it could be documented that Finman WASN'T living there.

Team members took turns at the Pomona house on different nights. Barry had to admit he fell asleep on his front seat at about 4:00 one morning for twenty minutes or so. Finman was never seen staying there during the night time.

What sometimes helps with organizing a convoluted search or searches, is to brainstorm on a chalkboard or story board so everyone can stand back and analyze the different pieces of information. Then it can be determined what has been done and, perhaps what needs to be done. In viewing the houses and information on the board it was decided that six officers would be needed to search the Lake Arrowhead residence but only three at the Pomona house. Both searches would take place at the same time. The two locations were a good fifty miles apart. Tim Aguilar from the Department of Justice was at the briefing and he agreed to go with the Lake Arrowhead team. Any computer media would be confiscated by him as Finman would claim bias if anyone from San Bernardino County did the forensic examination, and that included Barry. Tim would deliver all of those items to another government agency if not his own.

Surveillance and all the other information had confirmed that Finman was living at the Lake Arrowhead house. The downside of doing such a good job with surveillance on the Pomona house was that, since it was determined that he rarely showed up there, it would be difficult to show he had control of that residence or an area in that residence. While he could have possessions there including illicit and/or incriminating material, a search based on his terms of probation would be weak. An attempt could be made but if the woman that Kate believed was Finman's aunt said he didn't live there or that he did in the past but did not anymore, officers would not have legal access.

As such, Barry decided to deploy his secret weapon, Patrick McGee, to the Pomona house. This officer was one of the toughest officers in the sex offender unit, but if you didn't know him, you would assume he was a philosophy professor and the last person in the world to put handcuffs on a subject. He was very soft-spoken and polite with a tepid and non-threatening demeanor. He was also likable. These characteristics, along with his intellect and a silver-tongue, made him the perfect officer to handle assignments that involved finesse. This task required Patrick to conduct a "knock and talk." He would contact whomever was at the Pomona house and either establish that Finman had enough control over the residence or part of the residence to enforce the probation search term or attempt to get consent to search any areas that Finman may or may not control. It was a delicate maneuver that required excellent verbal skills and on the spot decision-making based on observations and interviewing. Many officers, whether they work for the local police department, the FBI, parole or probation have difficulties with these cerebral and legal adventures. For Patrick - it was a piece of cake.

At 7:00 a.m. on a Friday, searches were initiated simultaneously in Pomona and in Lake Arrowhead. Officer McGee worked his magic by contacting the aunt and establishing that Finman rarely came by. He kept props there in a bedroom such as a razor and some clothes, undoubtedly to fool his LA probation officer.

There was some delay at the door of the Lake Arrowhead property as other family members were there and they took exception to the officers' presence. Forced entry was not necessary, however, as Kate Ruley persuaded the occupants to cooperate. Realizing the lawsuit from before, the team had four separate audio recorders activated.

Finman was cooperative and was not yet handcuffed in the hopes of him spontaneously revealing information. He was diminutive and docile and never a physical threat to an adult.

Most of the computer gear was in Finman's bedroom. Barry tagged and inventoried it and, to maintain the integrity of the chain of evidence, released it to Tim, the officer representing the Department of Justice.

By virtue of a warrant for his arrest and a violation for reporting an incorrect address, Finman was arrested. He made a request to Barry before being handcuffed.

"May I comb my hair?"

Only because this guy couldn't punch a hole in a paper bag, Barry relented, "Go ahead."

Finman looked in the mirror, examined his reflection, combed his hair very carefully and then placed his hands behind his back.

"Go figure," remarked Tim.

A few weeks later, Finman's problems were exacerbated exponentially after one of his hard drives was examined. Hundreds of images of full blown child pornography were located. As such, a new case was filed. David Finman was sent to state prison.

Illumination

Barry was exhausted, having spent a good deal of time conducting surveillance on the Finman case. As such, he was off for a few days to remove some compensatory time from the books. Sarah wasn't as lucky but she could meet locally after work so again they met at the pizza place in Hopland. She was as pretty as ever but seemed a little uneasy.

"Sarah. As you know, we don't usually offer the McNab Primitivo by the glass but we opened a bottle suspecting the case was heat damaged. Turns out it is more than fine. I can offer you a couple glasses. It's the 2012 Reserve."

"What a wonderful surprise! Thank you, Maria." Sarah was happy but not as animated as usual. Barry tried to analyze her demeanor.

"You need to wind down a little. I have a feeling you have been working too much and not putting any time aside for Sarah."

"It has been somewhat hectic at the tasting room but I need to talk to you about something Barry."

The serious tone of her voice was concerning. The seriousness would continue but any curiosity on Barry's part would diminish very soon.

The heavy metal door to the street swung open at the hands of a nicely dressed fifty-year old woman. She was attractive but her auburn hair was disheveled and she sported an intense expression.

"There you are you little slut!"

At first, Barry thought she was yelling at Maria, the bartender, but then he realized that she was speaking directly to Sarah.

"At least you are with someone other than my husband! Are you spreading your legs for this guy too?" She was of course referring to a stunned Barry.

Barry felt he needed to protect Sarah but as angry as this woman was, he didn't really think she would do anything physical. He also wanted to completely understand the situation so he just stared in amazement, taking everything in.

She then reversed field and held the outer door open while continuing with her tirade," …and if you think you're going to get a penny from MY winery, you've got another thing coming, sweetheart!" She slammed the door behind her.

Instinct took over and Barry looked out the window to make sure she wasn't retrieving any firepower from her vehicle. She just drove away, spinning her tires on the decomposed granite surface, shooting debris all over the street.

Sarah hadn't moved since the lady arrived. She still had this hurt look on her face. Barry didn't question her. He just waited for her to address it. The few employees had scurried to the back room.

"I'm so sorry that you had to hear that Barry. Let's go somewhere else, anywhere else so that I can explain this to you."

Barry suspected that he knew the summary but said, "Okay - where do you want to go?" He hastily threw $40 on the table knowing that amount would easily cover the two glasses of wine that they didn't finish and a tip. He did not want to wait for a bill.

"Might as well go to my place. At least everyone won't be in my business."

"Are you okay to drive?" Barry asked as Sarah was shaking.

They had met at the pizza place but Sarah got into Barry's passenger seat to leave. "Not really. You can drop me off at my car later."

They were both quiet during the very short drive to her house. It was getting dark so they adjourned to her living room.

"I have an open bottle of "People's Red," which was the Havens Cellars everyday drinking wine.

Barry declined, "First, just let me know what the hell is going on. I don't think I can relax with a glass right now."

"That's fair," Sarah said in a resigned sounding tone.

"That was Christy Haven and I have been having an affair with her husband, Robert."

"That explains a lot," Barry responded in monotone.

"But you need to know Barry that it is over. The day you called was the day we ended it. I think somehow with all the turmoil and tension at the winery that Christy picked up on it. She confronted Robert and he spilled his guts."

"So how long has it been going on?"

"About two years off and on. We were just working so closely together and it just happened."

"Do you love him?"

"I have feelings for him but I don't know that it is love. I'm not really sure. I guess I'm confused and tired and distraught."

"Can I have that glass of wine now?"

Sarah poured them both a glass and they sat on the couch without saying a word for a full minute.

Barry carefully chose his words saying, "It sounds like you need some time to sort things out. I would imagine I just complicate the whole mess. Maybe it would be best to give you some space until you can parse through all the emotions and the situation."

Up until that point, Sarah had not cried but now tears were streaming down her cheeks. "I just don't know what to do."

"That's the point," Barry quickly responded. "Come here. Let me give you a hug so when I take you back to your car, everyone in town won't catch it on video." She called up a pathetic smile.

They embraced and kissed each other very softly. Barry dropped her off by her car with the agreement that they would talk in a couple weeks.

"Sarah, just know that you can call me at any time regardless of the situation, okay?"

"Thanks Barry." She started tearing up again as she drove away.

Disturbing the Peace in Muscoy

Back at work, Barry was just starting a swing shift in San Bernardino when he heard a call for service in the Muscoy area. Most service calls are transmitted by way of MDCs (Mobile Data Computers) in police vehicles but many like this one were broadcasted by voice. Deputies were being dispatched to a "415" between a man and woman. This is essentially a report of Disturbing the Peace and generally not the crime of the century. Perhaps a man and woman living together were yelling at each other and maybe throwing things. This type of call can be, however, dangerous for responding officers.

Barry didn't pay much attention until the dispatcher refined the circumstances calling it a "415 with chainsaws." This immediately caused every officer on the same talk group to listen closely. After all, this was not routine and might be entertaining.

Barry never did hear the disposition on the call as he had his own cases to work. He did later confirm that it was a man and wife who had a disagreement and each was holding a running chainsaw as if reenacting the light saber contest between Darth Vader and Obi Wan Kenobi. The situation was apparently resolved in a matter of minutes due to the verbal skills of the responding deputy sheriff.

Teflon Drisco

Investigators were eventually motivated to put their egos aside and they questioned Drisco about the missing boy in the mountains. They still didn't have a body but they did have a North Shore Inn bar patron that heard a very drunken Drisco boast about dealing with things so "the kid wouldn't tell." With a few more tidbits of evidence, they were able to pick him up. That was the good news.

Then, at the preliminary hearing, the bar patron recanted his statement. It was unknown if he was afraid or he just didn't want to get involved. His earlier statement was very clear. The other pieces of evidence were not enough by themselves and the charges were dismissed. Drisco then relocated to San Bernardino probably to get out of the jurisdiction of the Big Bear Sheriff's office. Barry had not been sleeping and it looked like tonight was not going to remedy the deprivation.

No Wet T-Shirt Contest Here

Barry needed to interview a sex offender at the West Valley Detention Center. While on probation, his computer was seized and it was determined that he was video chatting with fourteen and fifteen years old girls, having them show their private parts. The victims in these scenarios get trapped as they are duped slowly in increments to where they are extorted into exposing more.

For instance, a perpetrator will coax a girl to wear a revealing blouse or perhaps only a bra. Eventually, he will want to see more. So, he asks the girl what her mother or father would think if they knew she was being videoed in a bra. And the victims are not only females. A boy might show his bare chest. What you have is a blackmail situation.

In this instance, the perpetrator was deaf and he sought out victims who would communicate via sign language. Barry had done a forensic examination of his computer and located many video chat recordings and transcripts of the conversations. Communication was mostly done by video and by keyboard so remnants of these conversations were all over his hard drive. Mike Salazar, who actually supervised this guy's case, accompanied Barry and an official government sign language translator to the jail.

Barry knew Heather Johnston, having worked with her in the past and they also had common friends. She was a very good translator. She presented as very pretty but also very proper. She was always impeccably dressed. Barry always thought she was attractive but he was never available when she was plus she was a little too good looking. In Barry's opinion, she was out of his league.

To set the stage, Mike and Barry were standing on either side of Heather and a bullet proof glass separated them all from the perpetrator. Heather began signing, asking questions provided by Barry and Mike. A transcript was being reviewed by Mike that Barry had printed out from his forensic report where the perpetrator was telling the victim to show her "tits." Heather was doing a lot of signing and Mike asked her what was happening.

"I keep on asking him about breasts and he keeps on saying he doesn't know what I am talking about."

Heather continued signing, speaking as she signed, using all the slang terms. She quietly said, "Breasts, tits, ta tas, boobs, jugs" as she spelled them out with her hands. The perpetrator looked puzzled even though he knew exactly what she was talking about. Everyone was getting irritated. This guy just didn't want to give up any information.

Finally, after the perpetrator shrugged like he had never encountered a breast in his life, Barry looked towards Mike, who held the transcript which spelled out "tits" very clearly, and said, "Just show him!"

Barry was startled when Heather turned and looked directly at him in disgust and exclaimed, "No!"

Barry & Mike laughed and so did Heather once she understood it was the transcript they wanted to display, not Heather's breasts.

The Truth about Sarah

Ten days went by and Barry had not heard from Sarah. They agreed on two weeks but frankly, he expected her to contact him before that. Should he call? He finally decided he was being too "nice." He might finally have located his true love and he needed to not be so damn considerate.

While Barry would usually just leave a missed call when he got no response, he left a message. "Sarah - I want to make sure you are okay. Please call me as soon as you are able to. I've been thinking a lot about you."

Two excruciating days passed before Barry saw her incoming call while in a meeting. He excused himself from the conference room and quickly answered.

"Hi Barry. Sorry it took so long to get back to you."

"I'm so glad you did. I was worried. You were very upset the last time I saw you."

"I'm much better now. Things have settled down somewhat. I'm not such a hot mess." Sarah seemed reluctant to say much more.

She eventually continued, "Barry, Robert left his wife and he wants to marry me. I don't want to hurt you but I think it is the best thing for me."

Barry stammered, "I guess I thought you felt the same about me that I feel for you. You know I love you."

"Yes, I know and frankly, I love you as well. But Robert will be good to me and be able to take care of me."

"I don't understand that at all. You would rather be comfortable than in love?" Barry asked.

"I've struggled my entire life and this would be an opportunity to finally get a handle on things." She was really pushing the words out almost as if she was trying to convince herself.

Barry just naturally became more assertive as he was witnessing everything going south. "Let's go away for a weekend just so you can evaluate everything before you make a final decision. I will take you anywhere you want to go and we can lounge around and talk and-"

Sarah interrupted in a loud voice, "Barry! You don't seem to be getting it! Sure, Robert is a little older and we do not share the same passion as the two of us, but he owns a winery! And he has millions Barry! Millions!"

Barry didn't intend to sound mean but it came out that way. "Are you telling me his wife was right?"

"About me being a slut?"

"No! I meant-"

She interrupted again, "Well you're making this a whole lot easier for this slut!"

They terminated the call at about the same time. There was no going back for either of them. Barry couldn't believe that the person he thought he knew, the woman who made him feel wonderful, the partner he imagined being with going forward, would turn out to be a gold digger. Barry was upset he never picked up on that at all. Everything he experienced was a mirage. As usual, he was a good investigator except when it came to love.

When Barry got back to the Inland Empire he met Steve for a cocktail. He explained everything the best he could and Mortsoob, as always, was very supportive, even when he was just sitting there listening, sipping on his beer. Steve was concerned about Barry because he had never witnessed him be so inconsolable. All the emotions had drained Barry of his energy and Steve had to teach an academy class early in the morning so they called it an early evening agreeing to meet the following day.

This time they met at the Tartan Cocktail Lounge in Redlands. "How ya hanging in there Barry?"

"I haven't been sleeping much, doing stupid careless stuff. I almost had an AD[18] in the weapon cleaning room. Any suggestions?"

"Sleep more."

Barry responded, "I'm glad I'm not paying for this advice."

"Okay - I know you are really being affected by this whole thing but it sounds like you have no control over it. You guys had a great time and it's over. I'm just disappointed it ended this way."

"Excuse me if your disappointment doesn't make me cry but I really think, in her heart, she wants to be with me. I'm thinking about calling her again."

"Mistake. She has tried to convey to you that love is secondary and her affluence is more important. Calling her will merely upset you more and extend your grief even longer."

Barry let out a breath and thought about that with a resigned expression.

"Look at it Barry. I will make this very clear based on what you have shared with me. I wouldn't put it this way if we weren't best friends. Sarah presented herself to you as a soft, engaging, and passionate woman. It was easy for you to fall in love with her. Unfortunately, her true identity is defined in the words of the wine guy's wife. She's a slut going for the gold, specifically the Haven Cellars double gold medal. I'm truly sorry."

Barry didn't change his expression much. He got up and said, "I gotta go." Steve wasn't one to worry but he had to admit to himself that he was concerned.

---

[18] Accidental discharge of a firearm.

Ethical/Judgement Errors and/or Screw-ups

There were so many cases and capers undertaken and people contacted by Barry over the years, that he made his share of mistakes. A few notable ones not already mentioned are:

Whoops

Barry requested and was granted a bench warrant due to a Big Bear probationer moving. Barry had confirmed that he wasn't living at the reported address. Except that it was the wrong street. It was the correct number, just the wrong street. The probationer complained after he was arrested and Barry realized the error but the mistake was mitigated somewhat in that it was discovered he was selling drugs out of the correct address.

Homeless Housing

A probationer was trying to avoid Barry by saying that he was homeless with no address, making it impossible for him to be monitored. Homeless people sleep somewhere at night, whether it be in a car or under an overpass, and this guy refused to provide any information as to his location. Irritated at the scam, Barry told this subject that if he didn't provide a good address within twenty-four hours, one would be provided for him, the address of the West Valley Detention Center. The guy came up with an address but then wrote a long letter to the judge complaining about Barry's mean behavior in threatening him in such a way. Fortunately, the judge disregarded it and forwarded the letter to Barry for entertainment purposes.

It All Looks the Same

Frank Ramos was a heroin dealer in Loma Linda. During a search of his residence, a hypodermic kit was located in a clothes hamper but no heroin. Later, suspected tar heroin, that sometimes looks like "rat turds," was located in the attic and Frank was arrested. He admitted to the violation of parole and was swiftly sent back to prison. Frank was resigned to the fact that his stash was located and he cooperated, even making the false statement that he only used and did not sell the substance. Three months later, the laboratory report on the analysis of the suspected tar heroin made its way through inter-office mail. It was negative. Apparently, the real heroin was not located and the confiscated material was probably real rat excrement. Technically, since he was on parole, the hype kit was enough to arrest and sentence him but, if the facts were corrected, he may not have gotten as much time in custody.

A Loaded Trunk

Law enforcement trunks are like a general store. They contain practically everything. Guns, ammunition, holsters, raid and ballistic vests, cold and wet weather gear, refills for everything, ice chests and pry bars are just some of the items that fill every cavity. Barry's partner, Bruno, once found a Styrofoam container with two-week old chicken remnants on top of the spare tire. He only found it after Barry was sure there was a dead body under Bruno's rear seat. Without a doubt, the odoriferous chicken was the result of a prank but it demonstrates what is possible to get lost in a super crowded trunk area.

Barry thought it was time to organize and condense the gear in his own trunk. In the process, he located a nice stainless, Ruger .22 bull barrel pistol. Where did this come from? It was possible he confiscated it months before but there was no evidence tag attached. It was also possible one of his teammates casually dropped it in his trunk as a gag. Not smelling like rotten chicken, it could have been hidden for an extended period of time. Keep in mind that guns were confiscated all the time and it's easy for officers to get behind with their cases. The sergeant was always badgering his team to get the evidence off the floor and out from underneath desks and in trunks and officially log it into the appropriate place.

After waiting a couple days to see if anyone claimed the behavior or the weapon, Barry ran the serial number to see if it was stolen and/or to locate the owner. As was often the case in returns from the firearms system, the result was, "not on file." Also, there was no entry for the gun having been confiscated by any police agency.

Barry now had possession of a pistol with unknown origin that was not registered as stolen and was not logged into evidence. If he submitted a report documenting a found firearm and neglected to say where it was found, he would be submitting a false report. If he admitted to finding it in his trunk after who knows how long, he would undoubtedly be subject to some sort of discipline. Also, there would probably be an investigation within the unit for prankster suspects with interrogations and then eventually some draconian new evidence procedures. Everyone would be punished.

With all these poor available options, Barry chose to deal with it later. He threw it back in his trunk and time passed. He forgot about it. Evidence from other cases came and went. After so many years passed, he made the decision that he would always keep it secured somewhere at work. That way, he could never be accused of stealing it and, right before he retired, he would put it with many other pieces of misdirected and mislabeled evidence. The end result would be that it would be destroyed down the road rather than now. Barry felt guilty about this but, again, the options available were poor.

Water Witching

Toby Squire was on probation for diversion of construction funds. Quite simply, this crime occurs when a citizen pays a contractor or worker to do a job but the money is used to pay a past debt or for anything else accept its intended purpose. There is no money available to actually start or finish the job for which the money has been collected.

Most of these guys later claim to just be bad businessmen and there is some truth in that it would be easy for them to just keep getting behind and only completing a job here and there to avoid trouble.

While diverting money from one job to the next is definitely illegal, there are differences as to severity and Toby's behavior was scandalous.

His business was locating and drilling water wells and he made promises to lots of different people to get their money. He guaranteed that he could find water in areas where wells had never been. Toby did not appear to have any real knowledge of this industry and Barry was never able to find a case where Toby actually located water and then drilled and completed a well. Toby was a conman.

Even with being on probation and having cases ongoing in both Riverside and San Bernardino counties, Mr. Squire covertly continued to extract money out of thirsty landowners convinced his divining rod would find the next big aquifer.

Eventually, things came to a head and he was ordered to serve jail time for a year in both counties. Barry couldn't recall why State Prison was only suspended. White collar criminals always seem get a little more sympathy and the judge in this matter just couldn't seem to pull the trigger. He was a nice old man but he always was a sucker for a sob story. That's what he got every week in court from Toby's attorney as he came up with excuse after excuse.

Several times defense counsel argued that Mr. Squire would kill himself if he went to jail. Barry kept firing back memos to court, labeling this as more nonsense and a ploy to convince the court for leniency. This was not a new tactic and one used often on sympathetic judges by attorneys on behalf of their clients.

Finally, the Riverside judge had enough and gave Toby twenty-four hours to get his affairs in order before surrendering to authorities. He walked outside the Riverside Superior Court, retrieved a handgun from his Chevy truck and shot himself in the head. He died immediately.

Good Doggy

Sometimes a person does things because of instinct or fear. Both of these were in play when Barry made a split-second decision and jumped back out and slammed the front door of a residence when a large Rottweiler headed right for him, jumping over a couch in the process. He didn't have time to pull his spray or his gun. He then immediately realized that his partner, Matt Acevedo, was still in the house. Fortunately, the dog tolerated Matt so all was well.

The dog was secured by the owner and Matt looked at Barry with amazement and with a sprinkling of humor he exclaimed, “What the…?”

“Sorry Matt.”

The Issue of Privacy

Partially due to his age but also because of his knowledge of the digital frontier, Barry cherished the privacy of citizens. He wasn't old enough to remember how information was used as power when Hitler was a menace but he did remember the firsthand stories of individuals who suffered at the hands of the Russian KGB. In today's age, governments do need information for the security of their nations but they have an insatiable appetite for every possible tidbit. Obviously, the need to combat terrorism has skewed the balance somewhat between security and privacy but this is always something that needs to be reviewed from time to time. Also, while people currently with access to the information MAY be acting responsible, who will have the information in the future?

Barry was a benefactor of the Patriot Act. Part of that measure allows for more information to be accessed faster by law enforcement. No one knew how much information until the bombshell revelations concerning the National Security Agency (NSA).

Barry's team was working with the Feds, trying to locate a narcotics dealer in Ontario. The investigation led to several houses and information was collected. It was learned that a second cousin of the subject was a registered nurse somewhere in the Inland Empire. It was also determined that she had no criminal history - not even a speeding ticket. There was a home address listed with the Department of Motor Vehicles but she could not be located there at that time.

"No problem, stand by," said the officer from the Drug Enforcement Administration.

He placed a phone call and in five minutes he had her current location.

"Wow," said Barry. "Great source! How did you do that?"

"Patriot Act," the officer responded. Her smartphone location was determined by GPS. If she had her location services turned off like most bad guys do, her position would have simply been triangulated, but that wasn't necessary. Also, the GPS module on her car confirms that location. But the smartphone is always best as everyone takes their phone with them. She is at work a few miles away.

At the time, Barry thought this was pretty neat. As officers, they had good intentions and the information aided the investigation. Everyone had sources, whether they be utility people, real estate employees, records clerks, etc. There were also special secret numbers that Barry would call that generated quite a bit of information on criminals.

But this was different. This officer was calling a number where everything was already consolidated and no one was vetting the names being submitted and there was no requirement that persons actually be under investigation. The information was immediately available but the reality was that private information about a law-abiding citizen was gathered with no warrant or court order. Keep in mind that no terrorist was being investigated in this scenario and even if there was, there would not have been legal cause to intrude on this lady's life except with exceptional or exigent circumstances. By the way, this lady was interviewed at work and there was no indication that she had even seen the drug dealer in a couple years. Multiple raw private sources were accessed immediately which means that information was, and still is, in a database just waiting for a search command to sort through it for a myriad of scary reasons.

This is what is called "mission creep." It is a constant problem for surveillance technologies. An entity may give one reason for acquiring a technology such as for fighting terrorism. But once the capability exists, there is pressure to use it for other circumstances. And again, as with the history of Germany or Russia, "Information is power." In Barry's opinion, that is why the current German government does a much better job of protecting their citizen's privacy than the United States. They remember. As for Russia, Barry wasn't sure the government there ever got entirely away from snooping on their people.

Governments like to explain that they only have immediate access to "metadata" of the citizenry as if this is insignificant information. Metadata regarding communications really could be described as the container or the envelope rather than the contents of an email. The reality in all of this is that they may not know your medical testing results but they know a piece of mail came from the company, "HIV Testing, Inc." From phone logs and website information they can determine your ovulation cycle, alcohol intact and tobacco usage.

All smart phones are capable of collecting all sorts of information. Other than email, Internet and texting information, a very important piece of data chronicled by metadata is location information, generated by the GPS chip. While the fact you are being treated for AIDS is protected by HIPAA[19], the fact you were parked in front of the AIDS clinic for two hours every week is not. Many vehicles today, some as early as the 1990s, have electronics on board that cannot only collect information about the operation of the vehicle but also, the location of your vehicle. Some manufacturers are much better than others about protecting this information from private entities such as insurance companies and, of course, the government.

Add other forms of data into the mix such as your ATM card linked to your grocery store loyalty program and you have the makings of a very robust personal dossier. The original intent in collecting some of this information is for marketing but there is potential for major abuse. The bigger picture having to do with civil liberties, especially in the future, concerned Barry.

Barry always remembered that saying in the cyber world, "If it's free, then you aren't the customer." Think of Facebook. Think of other social networking. Your information is sold to various entities and taken for free by the government. Despite what one thinks of Edward Snowden, patriot or traitor, the information he disclosed started an important dialogue that still goes on today. The NSA has access to practically everything and the Foreign Intelligence Surveillance Court (FISA) has apparently not held them in check. Various pieces of legislation have been proposed to quell this theft of personal data.

---

[19] Health Insurance Portability and Accountability Act of 1996.

As far as Barry was concerned, the loss of rights in matters such as this comes in degrees. Gradually, the state has control over everyone by virtue of the information they possess. He fought the apathetic and ignorant notion he heard all the time, "I don't care what they collect. I have nothing to hide."

In no way was Barry in support of the viscous and senseless acts committed by terrorists. But there has to be a balance. Checks and balances need to be in place that will not impede law enforcement agencies from hunting down the bad guys while, at the same time, protecting the general public's personal information.

The Final Act

Barry was bothered more than he wanted to admit about the way things ended with Sarah. He seemed to be fine and then would slip into a cloud of depression, something no one had ever seen him do. An aching vacuum existed now and he was unsure how to deal with it. Every time he opened up a bottle of wine, he thought of her expertise, in wines and other things. To his credit, he was trying to muster the energy to get past it all. It was difficult in that he was at a point in his life where everything of a disappointing nature was seeming to converge. "No luck in love" sounded like a country song and it summed it up. Barry always hoped he would have his soulmate and a couple beautiful children by now. He thought at least he had his career - and he was good at it. And, despite all the personal distractions, he still believed he could make a real tangible difference in his line of work.

He agreed to go out for a beer or two with Steve. It was early afternoon so it was quiet at Morgan's.

"I think I'm going to buy a truck," he told Mortsoob.

"That sounds like a good idea. Have you seen that aluminum body Ford F-150?"

"I really like that whole idea. Ford got rid of about 800 pounds of weight by switching from traditional steel. But no, I need a project. Perhaps, a 60s, 70s vintage truck, something I can fix up and drive around town."

Steve thought a project was just what the doctor ordered and he applauded the idea. "That would be fun, something easy to work on, no electronics other than maybe a radio. You don't need GPS and navigation to get to the dump."

They both chuckled and ordered another beer. They were happy Patricia was waiting on them. She didn't usually come in until later. Patricia was super-efficient and a classic professional bartender. She could see problems before they occurred. She kept many secrets that would never be disclosed. Barry knew she had to have a few years on her as she was working at Morgan's when Reagan was president. Despite the chronological facts, she still had her figure and she was very easy to look at. And she was loyal and nice. What else could you ask for?

"You're getting a truck?" asked Patricia. "I thought you were more into high tech coupes."

"I'm trying to expand my horizons, or I'm going back in time. I'm not really sure which." Barry chuckled.

"One more?"

"Thanks, but we need to take off. We'll see you on Tuesday!"

The next day, Barry called Mortsoob. "I need to get out. Do you want to look at a few trucks today?"

Steve was surprised how fast Barry was on top of this. "That was quick. Sure, I'll pick you up just in case you buy something."

Barry had called four different owners listed on Auto Trader and Craig's List and set appointments. It was Saturday so there might be competition for the nicer vehicles. Barry decided to start with the best possibilities. First up, he wanted to look at the mid-60s Fords.

At a Colton residence, they could see the problem before they even got out of the car. Rust. Barry grew up around rust and he could practically smell it. He didn't need to, however, as you could see it from a distance around the fender wells and lower body panels. The owner was in the driveway and Barry got out, commenting, "All that rust didn't show up on your pictures."

"Not sure why that is but this vehicle has been in California since new."

Barry quietly said to Steve, "Yeah, apparently parked in the surf."

Barry thanked the man and they proceeded on to stop number two. Just as the first truck was eliminated by initial visuals, this one looked like a winner.

A woman was selling it for her dad, who had driven it since 1969. It was a 1966 Ford "F" Series with a 360 cubic inch V-8. The gray paint was all faded but all the metal was straight. It had 126,000 original miles and was obviously a California ride. There was no sign of corrosion under the fenders, but evidence of good old desert sand-blasting.

"My dad doesn't drive anymore. Frankly, I would keep it if the gas mileage was a little better."

Anyone can be fooled but Barry had a sense that this lady wasn't hiding anything significant about the truck. The engine sounded good and, other than needing an alignment and a couple tires, it drove fine. As nice as this woman was, she wasn't stupid and had set the price high at $11,000.

She was a tough negotiator and she knew what she had, so she only came down to $10250. Barry knew someone else would come along and scoop it up so he pulled out the cash and drove it away. On the way back home, he thought of basic mechanical things to check and other things to get it up to par. He hadn't decided yet if he wanted to paint it. It looked pretty neat as is. And as he told Steve later on, "The only thing "high-tech" on this truck is the AM radio, and it actually works!"

Stunned

The next day, Barry was at home working on his truck when five or six officers, four of them uniformed, walked up the driveway. "Hey, what's up?" said Barry.

"We have a search warrant for your premises," the team leader announced. Barry didn't know any of these guys so he asked for identification.

"You must have the wrong address. I'm a probation supervisor for San Bernardino County."

"Yes, we know sir. Here's the warrant."

Barry checked the warrant for the correct address, correct description and for items to be searched for. "Child pornography? You gotta be kidding. I'm also the forensic computer examiner for the agency. I investigate these kinds of crimes!"

"We know that too."

Undoubtedly befuddled, Barry knew the paperwork was correct. As far as he knew, he had nothing incriminating in the house or on his computer media. "I guess you better execute your warrant then."

There was really nothing he could do. They had a legal search warrant. He must have felt helpless as they tagged his computer gear with evidence tags. Hopefully, he could sort this out later. What the hell happened?

The officers did not trash the place and seemed to be focused on the computer equipment. They did not arrest Barry, apparently not having the immediate information to prove any child pornography charges.

Barry didn't seem to have any idea where the information came from or what it consisted of. He met up with Mortsoob.

"Steve - this is perplexing. I never mix work material with personal material. I have on occasion opened up a PDF file of a case report on my home iMac to prepare before early morning court but that would be obvious work material and it would be clear that those individual images were not downloaded or copied by me."

Steve said, "I'm not much on conspiracy theories, but this stinks to holy heaven."

"It's driving me crazy because when we serve a warrant, I have the affidavit and I know the reasons that the warrant was issued but, being on the other side, I have no idea what was presented to the judge."

Barry continued, "Well, they shouldn't find anything but that doesn't make me feel any better. I suppose they will put me on administrative leave."

"They already have," Steve revealed. He had heard from the Captain.

"Oh great! How embarrassing! And if that happened so quick, that means that our agency had their fingers in this several days ago."

"Yeah," said Steve, "and you know it had to be Pecker Becker that handled it."

"Without a doubt. That dick. He never bothered checking his facts. Rather, he probably just said, "goodie, goodie" and forwarded it to Internal Affairs. He probably made a call or two outside the agency as well to propel it along."

"Typical Carl Becker affair. Everyone knows I'm on administrative leave and I haven't even received notice."

"Let me know if you hear anything more," said Barry.

"Copy."

Barry decided he better secure representation. He belonged to the sheriff's association but if they decided he committed a crime intentionally related to his employment, they might be reluctant to assign an attorney. As such, he secured the services of a Santa Monica firm that he knew was good. It would cost a great deal but Barry wanted to make sure he got the talented motivated attorney rather than the disinterested "lop." The stakes were just too high.

Turns out it was none too soon. Barry's computer media was being examined by an Orange County agency because of Barry working with San Bernardino and Riverside personnel. Barry's attorney, Steve Goldman, called Barry in just a few days. A report had already been submitted to the Riverside District Attorney's office alleging four counts of possession of child pornography. The complete forensic exam had not yet been completed but there was enough information to file a few counts and get a bench warrant signed for Barry's arrest.

In a telephone call to Goldman, Barry emphasized, "We need to get our own forensic expert. I can give you a few names. And I cannot be locked up. I've put a lot of those guys in there."

"I'll get back to you." Barry could tell that Goldman was totally on the ball."

In less than a week, Goldman called and informed Barry that, according to the court clerk's office, a warrant was signed for issuance. "We had some informal discussions and due your law enforcement background, considering public trust and such, the judge is not inclined to release you on your own recognizance."

"Oh great. Could you do some checking and see if they could keep me out of custody pending the preliminary hearing maybe on electronic monitoring or GPS?"

"I don't think they would entertain hooking you up on EMP but, if you paid the maximum fee per day, it's possible the judge would go for GPS. It looks good to be able to say that you are being tracked all the time. I know they are short on participants, particularly participants that are willing to pay the maximum fee rather than on a sliding scale."

"I'm not real crazy about being hooked up, but considering the options, please give it a try."

The warrant was issued and the judge told Goldman he was okay with GPS. Barry surrendered in court. He had to be booked into jail and then released on the GPS program. This entire process was humiliating. Despite the fact he was innocent, he couldn't help but feel ashamed.

Barry was receiving a lot of calls on his home phone. His iPhone had been confiscated along with his computer gear. The search team did not get his MacBook Pro laptop as he had left it at Mortsoob's house. Barry certainly wasn't volunteering that information.

Some people offered their support. One of his supporters was Kate Ruley who told Barry, "This has GOT to be David Finman. You remember when that little pervert hired that private investigator to follow the previous forensic investigator around?"

"Yeah, the thought had occurred to me. We should know more soon and see if anything points to him. I'm being set up for sure!" He thanked Kate for having his back.

Some people didn't know what to say. Barry knew people were reinventing history out of earshot as they tend to do, eg., "I knew he was up to something" or "You can't investigate those kinds of crimes without being pulled over to the dark side."

Barry felt confident that he would be exonerated at some point and, as such, all his property would have to be returned, so he picked up a cheap cellular phone that wasn't smart at all. It had no Internet capability and not even a GPS chip. Not that he would ever be lost however, not with a court tracking program GPS phone on his belt.

Just for a little more irony and travesty, prosecutions for child pornography that Barry was actively involved with, had come to a standstill due to this inexplicable witch hunt into his activities. Barry had some excellent cases in process and he hated to see them go down the tubes. Some of these people were very dangerous.

After some initial demonstrations of support, people tend to shy away from anyone in trouble unless they are family or very close friends. In Barry's case, it was pretty much his family and friends, Steve Mortsoob and Big John that knew for sure that he was not a pervert.

Barry had quite a bit of free time on his hands so he continued to work on his truck and one day he grabbed his camera and took his jeep into the mountains. Steve joined him. It was October, his favorite time of the year and, if not for the situation, all would be right with the world. Barry glanced at the rear of his jeep and, seeing Julie Joseph's super afghan, he thought of how long ago that was.

Trying to be optimistic, the two of them planned a trip to Laughlin for the first part of November. Nevada gambling was always an excuse to unwind or to celebrate and both were confident that this nightmare would be resolved by then. The next court hearing was actually on November 1st. They hoisted their beers saying almost in unison, "To Laughlin!"

Barry had trouble sleeping. Undoubtedly, he was racking his brain trying to figure out how in the world his life got derailed. How could anyone sleep with all the brain activity being used to solve this distortion of justice? And then you add on the depression caused by the recent loss of and betrayal by Sarah.

"Good News!" Goldman said on the phone at 4:53 AM. Barry was a wake anyway.

"What? What?"

"I haven't prepared the paperwork yet but that forensic guy we retained says it is quite clear that those images and a bunch more were downloaded to your iMac remotely. You need to talk to the guy cause he's speaking in another language. Something to do with spoofed addresses, encrypted files and your home Wi Fi. Please sort it out for me and I think we can get this thing thrown out."

"Fantastic!" Barry exclaimed. Barry contacted the examiner and confirmed it was a clear case of someone high-jacking his Wi Fi connection, probably sitting in front of his house. That got the attention of authorities as illegal images that were downloaded show Barry's IP address as the address that was engaged in the downloading. Those actual images didn't go to Barry's hard drive but a separate action over the Internet was taken to essentially force an encrypted self-extracting file onto his media. This action placed a folder with child pornography files on his computer's hard drive. It was too much a coincidence for both of these actions to take place. It was pretty clear that all this was done intentionally to discredit Barry Truman.

Barry called Steve Goldman and explained the forensic expert's findings in layman's terms. Goldman's only advice was to "lay low" until the hearing.

"Just chill out at home or strictly with adults until the hearing. People understandably get a little crazy about these kinds of crimes and we don't need any false allegations, however unfounded, to put a judge in a political - or - a - bad spot."

It was probably with that in mind that Barry decided to stay entirely away from home on Halloween. It wasn't like he would be missing out on any frivolity. After all, the last several Halloweens he had been making sure sex offenders weren't handing out candy or worse.

Barry knew that an exhibition on the history of winemaking was taking place in the San Bernardino County Museum at 6:30 p.m. He always marveled at this familiar but massive concrete building that kept the interior cool even in the dead of summer. But forget using a cell phone downstairs or in the basement.

Exhibits and the movie were free but, following the program, the tasting could be enjoyed for a tax deductible $25 donation. Barry knew the wine offerings would be dismal but it really was just passing the time until he regained his freedom - or so he hoped.

Steve came over to Barry's house to have a beer. It was early Halloween and Barry said he really didn't want to go anywhere until the museum show and tasting. They sipped on their beers while examining the truck, a rather male thing to do.

"How's it looking?" Steve asked.

"I can't imagine that they would proceed with this but you just never know. The District Attorney's office never wants to look like they are soft on sex crimes. I'm just hoping that the evidence will be viewed with an open mind. Goldman thinks if they proceed with the information they have, the government will be writing me a big check down the road. That's great but what about the interim? I just want to get this behind me."

"Yeah - no shit. We are going to Laughlin either way, right?"

"I see where your concerns are." They both laughed. "Yes, Steve, we will tear it up in Laughlin either way!"

"We also have to celebrate your promotion." Steve was now a sergeant assigned to central patrol. There had been a sheriff's department get together but it was right in the middle of the worst days of Barry's life.

As planned, Barry went to the museum on Halloween evening. The movie on wine history was being shown in the basement where the giant screen was installed. At an hour in length, participants were undoubtedly looking forward to climbing the stairs afterwards to actually consume wine.

Barry was accurate in that the wine offerings were mediocre, but that was okay. It relaxed him all the same. He didn't sleep well that night with his brain processing everything that had happened and everything that could happen. Court was the following day.

He was very nervous the day of court. Turns out, no one presented open court arguments and no one took the stand. Everything happened in chambers. Barry was used to being involved in these types of conversations so he felt helpless just sitting out in the courtroom. After about twenty minutes, everyone came out of chambers and court was called into session.

Goldman stood beside Barry and patted his shoulder as if to say everything was okay. The judge went on the record, announced the case, and asked the deputy district attorney if he had anything to say.

The deputy district attorney stood up and announced, "After considering all the factors in this matter, amounting to insufficient evidence to prosecute, we have decided to dismiss all charges related to Mr. Truman."

The judge spoke next, "Before I close out this matter, I would like to make a comment for the record. After a conversation in chambers with all parties, it became clear that this matter should have never gotten to this stage. The search warrant was flawed and the forensic exam was rushed for whatever reason. Frankly, the entire case smells. The move to dismiss is granted."

He then looked directly at Barry and said, "And I would like to apologize to Mr. Truman on the record. With your exemplary record in law enforcement, it must have been much more than disheartening to deal with all of this."

Barry was a little choked up. "Thank you, your honor."

Goldman said it all started with Pecker Becker inappropriately referring an anonymous complaint about Barry to Internal Affairs. IA did their part by referring the case to the sheriff's office without ever verifying anything. Pretty predictable really. The sheriff's department punted due to jurisdictional problems and the fact that they had been working with Barry for years.

Riverside County authorities received the information and discovered that not only was there a "We Tip"[20] report on Barry possessing child pornography, but there was a report logged with NCMEC that came in through the Cyber Tipline.

An over ambitious but inexperienced detective with no computer background utilized information from NCMEC to determine that child pornography was downloaded to Barry's "IP" address, the address of his home computer or modem. He was able to get a judge to sign his warrant to search Barry's house based on information that seemed three-pronged in its origin. But, in fact, all of information may have easily come from one unknown person. IP addresses are high-jacked all the time over Wi Fi.

Barry's private forensic expert made the forensic guy for the prosecution look like he should be examining Commodore 64s.[21] He quickly pieced everything together and explained it in such a way as to convince the average person or judge that the prosecution's case was totally without merit. The only unknown was the source of all this fraud. Barry had to wonder if Kate was right about it being Finman.

For the time being that didn't matter as Barry was able to rid himself of the ankle bracelet and GPS phone within the hour. He could pick up all the confiscated items later that day.

Goldman presented the transcript and court order of dismissal to the probation department. He was met with resistance from Internal Affairs about Barry being reinstated. Goldman told them to notify him when they figured out Barry's status within the next week.

"They don't know what to do with it," said Goldman on the phone.

"I would imagine. If they deal with it like many of their investigations, they will begin a fishing exhibition. They will probably look at my email if they haven't already done so in search of some

---

[20] WeTip is a hotline system that allows for anonymous citizens crime reporting.

[21] An 8 bit home computer introduced in January 1982.

malfeasance. Once an investigation commences in that unit, it's hard for them to admit they don't have a case."

"That works for us,' said Goldman. "We are going to litigate this matter and that type of ill-advised, unprofessional behavior will just hurt their position."

"Am I still on admin leave? If I'm not, I need to request time off; we are going gambling in Nevada."

"Their problem is not yours. You are on administrative leave until they advise us you are not. I'll talk to you when you get back - and win big!"

Barry called Steve immediately.

"That's fantastic! Talk about a weight being lifted off of you. Let's get out of here tomorrow morning. I bet your brother Earl will join us. I think Big John is back east."

"I'll check. I always figured since it wasn't too hot, I could get away with wearing jeans so the casino employees wouldn't see my ankle bracelet. Now I can wear shorts!"

Jesus

Steve, Barry and Earl sat down at a blackjack table at the Laughlin Golden Nugget when a gentleman approached the table and announced to the dealer and all the players, "I am Jesus."

The dealer responded, "You'll have to wait until I finish this deck." This is a common tactic to keep players from jumping in to play when "the count" is right.

This person, who did in fact look similar to traditional pictures of Jesus Christ, repeated his introduction after the fresh deck was shuffled. "How is everyone? I am Jesus."

Barry answered, "I'm doing great. The name is Barry. This is Steve and Earl and these fine people are Diane and Richard from Des Moines."

"Nice to meet you," Jesus responded as he placed four hundred dollar bills on the table. "Just blacks please," and the dealer gave him four sole black chips.

Mortsoob responded, "How you doing?" Diane and Richard just stared.

Jesus placed two black chips in his betting circle and the dealer pitched the cards. This guy got two aces so he split the aces and put his remaining two black chips on the table for the second ace. Whether it be by divine intervention or pure luck, the dealer dealt him two face cards, giving him two blackjacks. She paid his winnings of $600 and he walked away from the table with $1000 total.

"God Bless you," was all he said. He disappeared somewhere on the casino floor never to be seen again, at least not by Steve, Earl or Barry.

The Sand Bar

Barry, Steve and Earl were still in the Nugget, relaxing and playing video poker at the Sand Bar. This bar was small as casino bars go but had an intimate feel and the best bartenders. "So, who do you think set you up?" asked Earl.

"Hard to tell. Could have been this sex offender by the name of Finman. I'm not sure. The person would have to have a good deal of computer knowledge. At this juncture, I'm not thinking it matters. It would be hard to prove anyway."

Barry had an incoming call which made him think how nice it was to get his iPhone back. The first words out of Barry's mouth were, "You're kidding." Steve and Earl could tell that he was listening to something rather astounding.

"Thanks for letting me know, Kate. I'll talk to you more when we get back. Wow!"

Barry relayed the news. "I know Steve that you know Arthur Drisco."

"Yeah, that sick son of a bitch."

Earl remarked, "I've heard you guys talk about him over the years."

"Well, he's deader than a doornail." Barry emphasized. "Someone walked right up to his front door on Halloween and shot him in the head and chest with a .22 pistol." Drisco was so evil, Barry couldn't help but smile slightly.

Barry continued, "I would say even Drisco didn't deserve that but I would be lying."

Steve added his opinion in a very serious tone. "Barry, this really was a community service. The person who put an end to this guy's life saved a whole bunch of little boys."

Barry's phone rang again. It was Tim from DOJ. "Yeah, I just heard," said Barry.

"Oh wow. Thanks! We are in Laughlin so I'll get back to you in a couple days. Thanks again Tim."

Tim knew that Drisco was someone always on Barry's radar and he would want to know. He also congratulated Barry on being exonerated.

"That was Tim Aguilar. He said it was actually two shots center mass and one to the head. Drisco died instantly."

"Suspects?" asked Earl. "Two shots center mass and a head shot almost sounds like a cop!"

"If anyone had enemies, it was Drisco. Sounds like identifying this trick or treater may be difficult, however, as he had a Spider Man Halloween costume on. The entire event was caught on Drisco's high definition video doorbell. The pistol was a .22 caliber stainless and looked like it had a bull barrel or a silencer. Probably didn't need a silencer though as he was living in San Bernardino."

Mortsoob spit out his beer and chuckled. "I'm sorry. It's just the visual of seeing Spider Man take down Drisco."

Earl had to use the restroom and he left Barry and Steve at the bar. They stared at the back bar, sipping on their drinks. Steve, who was smoking again, lit up a Marlboro Red and assessed the current state of affairs.

"The way I see it, this has been a good day. We're gambling, you've been cleared and Arthur Drisco is dust."

"What are you going to do now? They will have to eventually reinstate you but do you really want to return? You don't need to, right?"

"No - In fact, Goldman believes I will be a very wealthy man within a year or two. I might just retire."

Steve said deliberately, "I can't believe you haven't retired already. Why on earth did you stay so long?"

Barry said, also deliberately, "Well Steve, I had one last thing to do."

Steve, who was staring straight ahead, slowly turned his Darth Vader head towards Barry.

THE END

Addendum

Barry's Fifteen Commandments or Comments

Don't kick in trailer doors (Spoiler: They open to the outside. The trailer will fall on its side before the door kicks in).

Don't sleep with informants, probationers or parolees.

Don't lie in court.

The fact that a suspect is lying does not mean that the lie is to conceal what you are investigating. It may be something totally different.

Surveillance is always fruitful whether you find what you're looking for or not. Remember, the absence of data IS data.

Trust your instincts. Sometimes your subconscious picks up on something that your conscious mind ignores. If you just have a feeling that you saw or noted something, even a shadow, or if something just doesn't seem right, investigate further. It may save your life.

When in doubt, get backup.

When in doubt, call the bomb squad.

Never totally trust handcuffs.

Utilize but don't rely too heavily on technology.

Don't freely share information with informants.

Assume you are being recorded on video.

Always make sure your dispatcher knows your EXACT location.

When it has been determined that a search has run its course, whether or not illegal items were discovered or not, stop for five minutes and visually evaluate the search area. Scan the room or area with your eyes from top to bottom. *What did we miss?*

When you are assigned to watch the back of a house or structure, do not abandon your post until the house is clear of people.

Regrets

Barry was generally satisfied with the way his career had transpired but he still had regrets. One of these was that he never got to repel from a helicopter like his buddy did when they were working in narcotics. His friend would drop down from helicopters when tasked with eradicating giant marijuana grows, mainly in northern California. Barry's team was rarely included in that particular kind of fun stuff.

In an old movie, John Wayne, a very famous actor who starred in numerous western movies over several decades, once admonished a bad guy who was getting up from his chair to undoubtedly do bad things. Barry always wanted to find the occasion to mimic John Wayne and say, "Mister - Unless you're growing - sit down!" Plenty of subjects got up against the wishes of officers but a more immediate methodology or dialogue was usually more appropriate.

Of all the toilet tanks that Barry searched over the years, he never was successful in finding a gun taped to the inside of the porcelain lid. He must have seen this on television and it looked like a clever location but apparently none of the bad guys he encountered thought so - or maybe they just couldn't get the duct tape to stick. Who knows.

As a radio trainer, Barry would often distribute the complete "ten-code" to class members. This code is just a way to convey a status or activity without using a great deal of radio time. There are particular codes that are used all the time like "10-8" meaning "in service" or "10-15" which tells the dispatcher you have someone in custody. But there are obscure codes that are rarely used and Barry was hoping that sometime before he retired, he could call in a "10-89," which was a request for an armor-plated gunship. Of course, in light of escalating terrorist activity, maybe it was good he never had to make that call.

Thanks for The Memories, The Entertainment and The Education

Barry encountered many individuals during the course of his career, whether they were other officers, probationers, suspects or victims that made an impression. Here are the stories of a few of those unique people.

Probationer Reggie

As a felon, Reggie was not allowed to own firearms pursuant to federal law. Barry never knew he possessed nine assault rifles, a shotgun and three handguns until Reggie's Big Bear home was burglarized and all the guns were taken. Reggie supplied a comprehensive list, which included fully automatic weapons, to sheriff's detectives as part of items stolen. Reggie was arrested. What was he thinking?

Squeaky clean

Without mincing words, many felons smell like they spent the night with a wet dog in a giant ashtray. Squeaky Clean, who was also young and attractive, was the exception to the rule. She got her name because it was obvious she just stepped out of the shower or a bubble bath before coming to the office.

Ironically, she was in the shower when officers forced entry into her apartment. Her boyfriend was selling drugs. She was later able to get her charge reduced. Squeaky was a rare success story, eventually becoming a fire fighter. Barry attended her graduation from the fire academy.

Dr. Vince

Vince worked for Kaiser Permanente as a physician. He was on probation for being a little free with the dispensing of narcotic prescriptions. The state agents posed as patients and nailed him. Despite his bad judgement, he was a great source of information into medical factories, the difference between the medical model and the business model and such.

Probationer Asumi

This was an older Japanese American woman who resided in Redlands, California and was known by most businesses as she had a propensity to steal things. A true kleptomaniac, she would steal anything that wasn't nailed down and she could hide. She often stole steaks or chops. She had plenty of money but she just couldn't help herself. She was a nice old lady that no one really wanted to lock up.

Girlfriend Tammy

Tammy was a nice-looking girlfriend of the subject of a search warrant. She was not a criminal but during the course of the search of her residence, eleven intriguing looking vibrators were discovered plugged in to several power strips in the corner of her bedroom. All the lights created a soft glow in that corner of the room. Some of the devices were rather gnarly looking with spikes and forks and other adornments. Everyone, male officers and female officers alike, took turns checking them out. Tammy knew what everyone was doing but was entertained by the activity. "Yes, officer, they are all mine!"

Officer Ronnie

When Barry was cleaning out his portion of the evidence locker, he produced a dusty five-year-old six pack of Budweiser beer for disposal. Being facetious, he offered one to co-worker Ronnie who was walking through the unit. Ronnie proceeded to blow off the dust, pop the top and chug the warm stale beer in one gulp. Not breaking stride, he said, "Thank you sir" as he threw the empty in the trash and exited the unit.

Officer Rich

Rich was a probation officer assigned to the adult division in Ontario, California, He was with another officer visiting and searching homes, calling in his locations as was the routine.

"Don't hang your hat on the mike"[22] is an ancient tip that was preached to police officers in early "radio" cars. The problem was that the officer would sometimes remove his hat and put it on the dash-mounted microphone. On occasion this would key the microphone so that the dispatcher and anyone else on the channel or talk group could hear everything said in the vehicle. This had the potential of being very embarrassing.

Rich didn't have a hat or a dash-mounted mike but he had a Chevrolet Lumina which had a tendency to trap the microphone between the seats and keep it keyed. In this instance, the dispatchers listened for several minutes as Rich proceeded to say every possible negative thing he could say to his partner about the current Chief Probation Officer. The dispatcher didn't transmit "open mike" until everyone (except the chief) was thoroughly engulfed in tears of laughter.

Supervisor Bill

Temporarily located at a desk in the midst of some of the biggest prankster officers in the agency, Bill suffered through disconnected mouses, switched keys on his keyboard, stolen items and many more juvenile tricks.

Barry was coming from lunch when he noted a glossy card on the ground that was an advertisement for some sort of upcoming male dance review. Barry picked it up and examined the picture, which showed four male dancers in various poses with their shirts off.

---

[22] Patrol Procedure by George T. Payton, page 93

Talking to one of the pranksters when he returned to the office, Barry wondered out loud if that picture would be something of value in harassing Bill. After all, it was all in fun.

Apparently for Bill, who was having trouble concentrating on his work, this picture being posted in his office was the "last straw" as it was later learned that he complained to the Chief Probation Officer about the "pornography" that was posted in his office.

The next thing Barry knew was that a Deputy Chief paid him a visit seeking information on this "pornography" placed in Bill's office. Probably because Barry supervised the Sex Offender Unit and possessed plenty of real pornography, he was a suspect. Barry explained that it was just some guys with their shirts off and it was undoubtedly posted in Bill's office as a joke. He conceded everyone was unmercifully harassing Bill.

The Deputy Chief had Barry accompany him to Bill's office to view this poster. Bill was sitting at his desk and the Deputy Chief asked him, "Bill, can you show me that poster of the nudes?"

Bill stammered with his words and the Deputy Chief said, "Bill, I just need to see the poster."

Then Bill confessed, "Well, I, a, I took it home."

Case closed.

Jabba the Hutt

A search warrant for drugs was conducted at an apartment in Highland. Upon entry, officers noted only one individual sitting on the floor with her back against the wall facing the front door. Barry and the other team members had never seen anyone so large. This lady was maybe thirty-five years old and weighed no less than 650 pounds. She was sprawled all over the floor almost covering one entire wall.

The apartment was searched for drugs with negative results and then everyone's attention was drawn to the person that forever after would be nicknamed Jabba the Hutt[23] after the fictional character depicted in a Star Wars saga. The furnishings in the apartment were sparse and the only place left to search was under the folds of skin

[23] Return of the Jedi (1983) created by George Lucas

around Jubba's midsection. A female officer had her raise her folds one by one and, sure enough, an eight ball of methamphetamine was located. Due to her size, it was obvious Jabba wasn't using speed, so it was probably just a business venture to make money to buy ding dongs.

Normally an eight ball would land you in jail unless a deal was made for information, but in this instance the issues really dealt with her health and the reality of getting her to jail. After consulting with the jail medical staff and alternately looking at Jabba and the front door dimensions and also the size and suspensions of everyone's vehicles, it was decided to submit what is known as a "long form" where the information is submitted to the District Attorney for review but the person is not immediately taken to jail. If the case was later filed and a warrant issued, then whomever encountered Jabba during the course of their work would have to deal with her unique issues.

Detective Hanna

When Barry heard about Carson Hanna's arrest of a robbery subject on his first day as a newly promoted detective, Barry called him to verify he heard the story correctly. Carson confirmed that he was driving his new white undercover vehicle in the city of Redlands. Hearing the dispatcher advise of a robbery in progress at a sporting goods store on Orange Street, Detective Hanna was unable to pull up short of the business as he was already right there. His vehicle was stopped right by the front door.

The dispatcher continued calling out details and Carson could hear "40 King," the Sheriff's helicopter, hovering overhead. He called in his location but was interrupted by the passenger door opening and a white male in his twenties getting in. He was holding a large pile of sporting goods, partially blocking his vision. Now a detective, Carson was able to ascertain that this was one of the sporting goods store robbers. It was later determined that the getaway car was also white but the driver got cold feet and took off. Detective Hanna placed cuffs on the lad and reported to dispatch that he had captured one of the perpetrators.

Carson told Barry, "I never realized that this detective work would be so easy."

Sunday School

It was Christmas time and Barry was a rookie, writing reports in juvenile division. Sometime after lunch, his supervisor, Bob Anderson, called to him from his office.

"Have you seen the Lord?"

Standing alone in the middle of the unit, Barry just looked at him. Bob had delivered the message with emphasis with elongated tones, much like the expressive rhetoric Barry had heard from the pulpit as a youth.

Again, Anderson asked, "Have you seen the Lord?" This time he motioned for Barry to come in his office.

Barry obliged and Bob shut the door. It was then Bob opened his side desk drawer and pulled out two glasses and a bottle of Lord Calvert Canadian Whisky.

As a subordinate, Barry had no choice but to join in Bob's toast. "Merry Christmas Barry!"

Made in the
USA
Monee, IL

13832618R00184